TOUJOURS AMIS

Always Friends

SAMUEL JAMES FREAS

SAI Publications
Vero Beach, Florida

FIRST EDITION printed April 2010

Book design by Delaney-Designs
Cover design by Samuel James Freas and Pamela Trush
Cover information available at http://www.toujoursamis.net/
Editing by Barbara Ryan and Darlene Redfoot

Library of Congress Control Number: 2010903658

ISBN 978-0-578-05261-8

Toujours Amis
is dedicated to my loving family—
my wife, Rosemary Steadman Freas,
and my wonderful children,
Samuel, Sarah, Stephen and Sydney.

Contents

New York

Exodus

About the Author

There are times when you meet someone who makes an indelible impact on you. Samuel James Freas is one of those individuals. He has touched, challenged, entertained, and changed many searching souls along his way.

Sam is what we in Ireland call a "colourful character." He has always been full of mischief and nonstop fun, and he insists on getting the most out of each day. You get the impression that he was actually awake before he woke up.

Despite all of the antics of his youth, Sam achieved career success and managed to marry and hang on to his beautiful wife, Rosemary, and produce four great kids. These days, you want to hang out with him to recall and relive the unpredictable, unbelievable and unparalleled experiences of his incredible journey through life.

Sam is a people magnet; he is charismatic, and his spirit and good humour are infectious and contagious. He is a complicated concoction of characters: confident, cosmopolitan and articulate while being impulsive, gregarious and mischievous. He is spiritual, selfless and humorous as well as loyal, lucid and legendary.

All these characteristics combine to give us a storyteller extraordinaire and a man who sows hope, love and excitement in all our lives. He is without doubt the most unusual and unique character that I have had the privilege and the pleasure to call my friend. I found this story so compelling that I dedicated my efforts to see the film version Baton on the big screen.

—Mike Fitzgerald
Dublin, Ireland

The Genesis

City of Brotherly Love

Decades had gone by in the blink of an eye. Here was the same hometown gang, almost as it had been in 1965, more than forty years earlier. Only this time they were unaware that the only one missing was really watching them from above, searching his heart as he sought a glimpse of them...and remembering. The day was just as it had been back then—late spring in Philadelphia—great running weather, in the 60s without a cloud in the sky. Things hadn't changed all that much either; it was the same grand stadium, same capacity crowd bursting with excitement, the same pent-up anxiety for some as if they themselves were at the starting line, and pretty much the same racial makeup of the teams. It had bothered Big Sam Easley when Sean was running in the 60s and probably still did when he noticed that the teams were either all colored or all white. Sean wondered from afar if this was the case, and as he caught sight of his dad, he sensed his disappointment. His team had been the anomaly—two coloreds and two whites united in spirit.

If he hadn't known better, he would have thought the announcer was the same, too, with that booming voice, somehow stylish yet full of excitement and anticipation. While the span of years had passed through war and peace, loneliness and joy, birth, death and rebirth, it suddenly seemed like only yesterday as Sean's mind drifted back to that day he heard, "Ladies and gentlemen, this is the seventieth running of the Penn Relays, and 1965 looks to be one of the best." Over 50,000 spectators cheered wildly as they blurred into a sea of muted colors and noise.

Sean had a vivid memory of the bull horn pressed to the mouth of the clerk of course from his six-foot-high podium overlooking the teams gathered for that championship final where he first heard, "High School Mile Relay Championship of America: Brooklyn Prep, hole one; Kingston, Jamaica, hole two; Morgan State Prep, hole three; Abington, hole four." The sixteen fastest qualifying teams were readying in the famous Penn Relays' paddock, having performed best out of nearly 600 high school quartets from the morning's qualifying heats. One team in particular was poised to make history.

Abington's peculiarity was its white anchor, Sean Easley. For many, and not the least of which were Cassandra and the Easleys, the appeal was that Abington was America's dream team. Even though integration had supposedly happened in the North, folks still referred to the Abington High team as "salt and pepper"; the other fifteen teams were either all colored or all white. The suburban Philly team qualified by winning their morning heat and besting their personal time by over a second. This was still two full seconds behind returning champion, Cal Poly Long Beach, and placed them eighth fastest to qualify for the championship final.

Cassandra was anxiously standing with the Easleys and the rest of the Abington contingent near the finish line, scanning the paddock in search of Sean as the sun bounced off her russet skin. Waving anxiously, she hoped to catch the eye of her six-foot-plus, angular-faced beau whose sandy hair was unfashionably long. Even the way he wore a T-shirt under his Abington jersey seemed to place him in another era and revealed his humility.

With him was tall, dark, and handsome Sonny Goldman, tough and Jewish with a Star of David around his neck. Front of the quartet was Leander Davis—tall, lean, and the perfect running machine, clutching his Saint Christopher medal and prancing in place like an anxious thoroughbred that is being reigned back. Lined up closest to Sean stood the regal-looking, ripped, six-foot-four Louie Jackson.

The Abington gang in the stands, as diverse as the relay, stood, leaned, craned their necks and jostled to get a glimpse of their boys. Cassandra stood between Margaret and Big Sam. Louise Jackson insisted that Dewey, Louie's twelve-year-old brother, switch places with her so the brim of her hat would somehow help shield him from the glare of the sun, even though it obstructed his view of the paddock. Abe Goldman stood behind Big Sam and repeatedly slapped his back when the relay foursome finally looked up and waved.

The runners, fueled by the near-frenzied crowd, performed their individual warm-up rituals in the clerk of course paddock area. Some stretched while others flew out of the start to an imaginary gun only to run a few yards and then return and repeat the drill all over again. Jumping in place and swinging arms were routine as was the occasional sign of the cross. Sean took a knee to lace his grandmother's Celtic cross in his spikes and then stood to speak to the huddled Abington relay.

"They're g-getting t-too excited to r-run their best," said Sean who was very shy but still shared his thoughts with a peacefulness that only a young Quaker might have despite his stuttering. The others nodded.

"Run within yourselves and be confident. Remember, let's have fun and close hard!" Louie added with a smile as he extended his hand first and each one followed in unity.

Continuing to hold their clutch, Sean began praying, as he often did before a race, "God, give us the strength and courage to be agents of your love. *Toujours a-amis.*"

"*Toujours Amis,*" they returned in unison.

Leander was rearing to go and was alternately shaking his legs and stretching when Sonny lightened the air with, "Yo, Louie, we're agents of love. How 'bout that?"

Returning a smile Louie asked, "What's that make Cassandra?"

They all chuckled as Leander made his way to the starting line. With a heavy southern accent, a colored runner from Morgan Prep in Baltimore asked Louie, "What's that *toojays* thing you was sayin?"

"*Toujours Amis* means 'always friends.' It's French."

"He your friend, that boy who stutters?"

"Yep, the best."

"Where I come from, you can't even drink from the same water fountain as white folks." The Morgan Prep runner checked out Sean some more and asked, "He fast?"

"Closest thing to lightning I've ever seen."

Leander made his way to 2d position from the pole on the inside track. After 200 meters, the eight runners on the outside track would merge into the inside lanes with the other eight runners.

Lined up in order along the stadium wall, runners waited to enter for their leg. Sonny was closest to Leander and yelled over the crowd noise, "Do it, Leander! Do it!"

Leander flashed a wide grin and semi-saluted with his baton while readying for the start. The critical leadoff leg was always a dogfight for early positioning. Leander fit the bill; he had great up-front speed and didn't mind mixing it up.

"Quiet for the start!" echoed throughout the stadium.

The starter raised his pistol, as his words hushed and stilled the enormous crowd, "Take your marks." With all eyes on the top sixteen teams, he called out, "Set!" and then his pistol blasted as the runners exploded from their marks.

After juggling for position, Leander settled in behind the lead runner on the inside track and found himself in the middle of the pack, as the two groups converged.

In horse-racing fashion the announcer began, "It's Saint Christopher's from the Bahamas, followed by Stuyvesant of New York, Long Beach Poly from California, Kingston of Jamaica, Arlington of Virginia, and Morgan Prep of Baltimore followed closely by Abington."

Sonny and the other runners made their way from the sideline to take their positions to receive the baton from their incoming, spent teammates.

Moving along the stadium wall with the other third-leg athletes, an excited Louie cheered, "Yo, Sonny! Yo, Sonny!" as Sonny seamlessly accepted the baton in 5th place from Leander's outstretched arm.

"Way to run, Lee!" Louie cheered, as they herded an exhausted Leander and the other runners off the track.

Several runners were overtaking Sonny as the announcer's voice resounded, "The Abington team has three all-state football players in these three legs. Running now is quarterback Sonny Goldman who led his team to their first Pennsylvania State High School Football Championship last fall."

Whether because of the announcer's comments, the excitement of the crowd, the group's prayer, Sonny's determination, or a combination of these, Sonny began to regain lost ground and passed the baton to Louie in 7th place. Fueled by emotion and with the tightness of a precision engine, Louie made an early move on the lead pack, his glide-like gait belying his real speed. Sean just watched with quiet confidence as Louie pulled to within five yards of the leader.

"It's Cal Poly, Stuyvesant, Saint Christopher's, Austin Lakes of Texas, Kingston of Jamaica in 5th, Morgan Prep, and moving up for Abington is Louie Jackson, the all-state running back and all-American basketball player," blared like surround-sound to the cheering, near-frenzied crowd.

The lead teams began distancing themselves from the pack, and Louie was keeping an easy pace with them. As they hit the final turn, four runners had clearly pulled ahead for the final 100-yard sprint. The Abington fans were cheering wildly. Cassandra clung to Big Sam and Margaret, as Louie passed the baton to Sean about five yards out of the lead in 4th place.

In awe, Cassandra watched Sean pass as she whispered to herself, "You beautiful, beautiful thing."

Sean immediately tucked in behind the 3d place runner until after the first turn. Catching the attention of the spectators was this sole white anchor among the leaders, the one with atypically long, wind-blown hair, running with a distinctive and impressive stride that signaled victory might be attainable. His unique grasp of the baton, tucking it alongside his forearm from palm to elbow, was obviously different from the other runners.

"Ladies and gentlemen, running the anchor leg for Abington is the Galloping Ghost's wide receiver, Sean Easley, and he's closing the gap!" yelled the now excited announcer.

It was now obvious that the announcer wanted Abington to win, possibly because of the team's racial makeup or because no Pennsylvanian team had won before.

Sean made his move and slid in behind leader Cal Poly just before the last turn. In unison, the spectators erupted in an expectant chorus that seemed to spur on both runners. Sean broke off the final turn to draw next to the Cal Poly runner. Shoulder to shoulder, each contender pushed himself to the limit in front of an admiring and awe-struck crowd.

As the runners neared the finish line, the announcer's voice rose with an air of hope that filled the stadium, "It's Cal Poly then Abington…Abington, Cal Poly…and yes!…at the tape it's Abington!"

In front of the excited crowd, Sean turned and embraced the colored anchor from Cal Poly. The crowd reignited to near hysteria with his obvious colorblind, heartfelt display of sportsmanship rarely witnessed then between coloreds and whites. The press flooded the track and cameras frantically clicked the clenched duo. At race's end, Sonny, Louie, and Leander spontaneously rushed to join Sean near the finish where they huddled, heads bent and raising their hands in appreciation and triumph.

To the attentive crowd, the announcer added, "Ladies and gentlemen, let's give a hearty Penn Relays' congratulations to the runners from Abington High—the first team from the state of Pennsylvania to win this coveted title."

With that, Sean reverently gazed skyward. The four bowed in each direction and then locked hands as they ran around the track to acknowledge the fans. Flooded by reporters, Leander, Louie, and Sonny entertained questions as they gradually make their way to the stands. Sean hurriedly slipped past and arrived first to the hugs and pats of their personal cheering section. "Way to go, boys! Way to go!" Abe shouted as he stood clapping his hands.

"What was the press asking?" Margaret Easley inquired.

"How we coloreds and whites got together," Louie responded with a shrug and then smiled.

"All they asked me is why you're so ugly, Louie," Sonny said, amused. The group roared with laughter at the obvious absurdity due to Louie's stunning looks.

The group made their way out of the stadium to head to Goldman's Deli-Land for a victory party. Reporters continued to jockey for position to hear from Sean.

"Sean, can I talk to you?" a reporter from *Sports Illustrated* asked.

"Sonny and Louie usually d-do the talking," he managed, exposing his speech impediment but with a calmness and serenity that surprised the reporter.

"We've got you covered," Louie answered, as he and Sonny stepped in so Sean could ease past. Sean reached for Cassandra's hand and they quietly left the hullabaloo of captivated onlookers.

"He just ran one of the fastest quarter miles by a high school boy ever and he won't even talk about it?" the flabbergasted reporter asked. "Forty-five plus is just amazing. He's sure to win the state championships."

"He doesn't run individual events—only relays," answered Sonny.

"What on earth are you saying?" the aghast reporter asked.

"It's a long story. Any other questions about the race?" Louie asked in an effort to change the subject.

"How did your families become friends? Is that Sean's girlfriend that he left with and how did...that happen?" the reporter hastily asked.

Louie began telling how their friendship started and how they had made a pact early on. It was clear from how he spoke that they supported one another.

A reporter from *The Philadelphia Inquirer* spoke up postulating, "You kids have figured out something that America is still struggling with."

Louie and Sonny just looked at each other and smiled. No one could have guessed that their story, as told by *Sports Illustrated* and *The Inquirer*, would have captivated the fascination and hearts of Americans. It had to be providence.

It had really begun more than a decade earlier in Abington Township where Sonny's and Sean's paths crossed in elementary school.

The Goldmans owned the restaurant and delicatessen across the street from Sean's home in a nearby shopping center.

Good looking and bright, Sonny took after his mother Susan who came from a long line of Jewish leaders, including Louis D. Brandeis, the primary force in the American Zionist movement who later became a United States Supreme Court Judge. Sonny had a traditional Hebrew education at Beth Shalom Synagogue and was always the best or near best in everything he did.

The Goldmans lived in a new split-level home a few miles from Deli-Land. School was less than a mile from the family business, and on most days Sonny worked there after school. A major difference between Sonny and the rest of the Jewish kids at school was that Sonny was tough—real tough. He was the first one to step in and dissuade neighborhood bullies from picking on classmates who were easy marks—vulnerable targets nervously awaiting a tap on the shoulder or a verbal taunt. Usually, his presence was all that was needed, but an occasional word or fist was necessary to discourage the loitering ruffians and give the underdogs a reprieve until they gained the courage to return. He was legend at school: an honor student, the best musician, popular without even trying. His physicality and athleticism set him apart from the other students. He was the fastest runner, could throw a ball the farthest, and, of course, was the quarterback of the Cedar Road School flag football team. Sonny's world changed when he met Sean Easley.

Despite living near one another, Sean and Sonny came from different worlds. Sean's parents taught and coached in the Philadelphia school system. His dad, affectionately known to most as Big Sam, was a converted Quaker with Irish-Catholic roots and had moved to the suburbs of Philly from the inner city to attend Abington Friends Meeting. Theirs was a humble home in the poorest section of a mostly wealthy township. Customary for Quakers, Sean dressed simply, mostly in dark colors, and had unusually long hair when crew cuts and flat tops were the rage. His mother Margaret was warm and friendly while Big Sam was a true intellectual who read incessantly. Brigitte was a beautiful, young French Quaker woman from Paris, placed by Abington Meeting in the Easley's home to help care for Sean, their youngest. She became an influential force in the development of Sean and his friends.

Sonny and Sean's first meeting was, by no coincidence, on a football field. It was there that their different cultures collided. Sonny, the undisputed leader and star football player at Cedar Road Primary School, found himself in an untried, prickly circumstance when the new boy with blistering speed walked on the field for the first time. The obvious contrast between Sean, who lacked any fashion sense or need for it, and the stylish, well-groomed Sonny profoundly masked what they had in common.

As the new kid on the block, Sean understood the exclusion he felt as he waited alone on the sideline of the football field. He was new to the school and was used to kids making fun of the way he spoke. He was reserved with characteristic aplomb, but his approach toward the coach appeared impulsive and signaled to Sonny a need to maintain status-quo. Completely out of character and unprovoked, Sonny found himself suggesting fists to discourage the imaginary impertinence from the new kid. Sean attempted to explain to Sonny that he was a Quaker and could not fight. Sonny's response was atypical and bigoted; he not only made fun of him for being a Quaker but also further made disparaging remarks about the neighborhood where Sean lived and the way he stuttered. Sean simply turned and walked away.

Abe and Susan Goldman could tell something was bothering Sonny when he returned home that day. He knew the pain of being called a kike, Jew boy, and other derogatory slangs, and now he experienced the stabbing realization that he was no better than his peers. Sean's passive reaction added to Sonny's shame and somewhat perplexed him. He had been wrong and was too quick to judge the new boy at school. He felt justified the other times, but this was different. The dilemma brought about by this new Quaker kid challenged Sonny's identity and value system and he found that he was not looking forward to going back to school. Conjuring up thoughts of his family's courage and history were not giving him the confidence to deal with the situation as they once had.

Sonny had no idea just how unlike the other kids Sean really was. Having been under the care and direction of Brigitte, Sean spoke French well and was familiar with other cultures and aspects of life unknown to most kids his age. At times, it seemed he thought and acted more French than American and definitely like someone more senior in years. These qualities and his blindness to skin color did indeed distinguish him from his schoolmates. Sonny's comments bothered Sean more than he let on. Even though he did live in the poorest of the township's neighborhoods, he was still surprised when judged so severely without even having a chance. Neither one had any idea what a tremendous influence they would have on each other for the rest of their lives.

The Goldmans of Huntington Valley

Early on Sonny discovered that he could draw strength from recounting his family's Jewish heritage and from their success as a result of hard work and determination. He often reminded himself of this when he was in tight situations, but his attempt to rationalize his actions on the day he met Sean failed; no family history or pride in his heritage could assuage the nagging guilt he felt about his behavior toward Sean.

Abraham Goldman was born in 1915 in the Mt. Airey section of Philadelphia. His mother and father were reformed Jews but diligently maintained the high Jewish holidays. Brother Milton declared his intentions to become a rabbi at a young age, and eventually, he became a great orator with a wonderful voice for singing the Torah.

During the Great Depression, Abe watched his father, a successful clothier, lose everything. He declared that this would never happen to him. In his teens he committed to being debt-free—to owe no one, no credit, not even for education. He would pay in cash, always. Abe entered Yeshiva University after attending Central High School in Philadelphia and graduated number one in his class.

In high school and college Abe became a skilled boxer and his six-foot, chiseled frame made him quite a spectacle in the ring. The administrators at Yeshiva attempted to discourage him from boxing, but he continued by training with some of New York's finest and was good enough to turn professional. He declined several offers from promoters and remained at Yeshiva where he was a classmate of Susan Urbach, a bright and beautiful girl from a fine New York City family. Susan first noticed Abe while he was boxing in a match at Madison Square Garden. Her girlfriends told her he was smart but shy. They marveled at his boxing ability and appealing physique. Susan wasn't impressed by Abe, however, until they had a class together the following semester and she found herself attracted as much to his mind as to his physical appearance. His flirting skills were quite obviously nonexistent; however, his humility captivated her.

The USA team invited Abe to box as a light heavyweight at the Maccabiah Games in Israel in the summer of 1935. Susan was visiting Israel with her family and was sitting in the stands when Abe won the gold medal for the USA. He enjoyed the comfort and company of touring Israel after the Games with a classmate from Yeshiva, and while there they became more than friends. Abe's parents and relatives back home were all so proud of their boy. When Abe told his mother he had found a wonderful girl in Susan, she was quite pleased.

During the fall of Abe's senior year, though nearly first in his class, he suddenly dropped out to join the 101st Airborne Division of the United States Army. Everyone was in shock. He headed for Camp Campbell, Kentucky, for basic training. In the spring of 1941, Abe proposed to Susan and she declined. She was not interested in marrying a man who could be killed in the war. He was heartbroken and humiliated; it was perhaps the boldest move he had ever made asking Susan's hand in marriage only to be rejected. Soon after, his unit received orders for action in the European Campaign. When Susan found out about his orders she reconsidered, and they were married in Philadelphia that May. By the first of June, Abe was on a ship bound for England.

Not until the final stages of World War II was Abe ever afraid. He had been a highly decorated warrior in the 101st with two Purple Hearts and two Bronze Stars and had taken down several of the enemy in hand-to-hand combat, but on the day that Abe learned from the American Red Cross that a car accident had taken the lives of both his parents, he found himself in a state of fear. Now a captain and having received a field commission, he was mentally disoriented in his grief-stricken state when a mine detonated near him in the Black Forest. With an injured hip, they sent Abe home just before V-E Day. He returned to the family home but nothing seemed the same. He was different and so was life in Philadelphia.

Nine months later Sonny was born. At first, especially given Abe's penchant for thriftiness, things were not easy for the Goldmans. His hip was healing, but it left him with a slight limp. Susan's relatives were actively recruiting the return of Jews to Israel and Abe and Susan were great candidates. His military background made him ideal for helping Israel and its army to establish the sovereignty and independence of Israel. Convinced that it was the right thing to do, the Goldmans, with Sonny in tow, arrived in Israel in 1946.

After almost four years in Israel, Colonel Abe Goldman resigned his commission in the Israeli Army to return to Philadelphia. He had demonstrated his bravery and leadership during Israel's fight for independence, but the dangers of living there while trying to raise a son and wanting another child, found the Goldmans back in Philadelphia at their Mt. Airey home. With insurance money from the death of his parents and with the sale of the family home, Abe was able to buy a home in Huntington Valley, open Deli-Land, and have some money left over for Susan to open a women's apparel shop. Soon to follow was Sarah, the Goldman's only daughter.

Sonny's quick mind and the advanced early schooling he received in Israel put him ahead of others in educational development. He possessed keen language skills. His athletic ability set him apart, due in part to the personal trainer Abe had hired. Much to Susan's dismay, Sonny's proud father would also handle the boxing lessons.

Their Huntington Valley home followed the new 1950's trend and was a split-level twice the size of their Mt. Airey home. It was just a few miles from the Beth Shalom Synagogue where Susan insisted the family attend services regularly. She even wanted Sonny to attend an all-Hebrew elementary school, but Abe fought her and eventually won the battle.

"The goyim are always a problem," said an exasperated Susan who had been educated in the finest and strictest of Hebrew schools in New York.

"Nuts! My best education was at Philadelphia Central High or in the 101st Airborne; if it weren't for those experiences and those goyim who you think are such a problem I wouldn't be here. That's all there is to it," Abe said from his heart.

Susan relented, yet demanded that Sonny attend Hebrew summer camp and the Philadelphia Conservatory for violin lessons. Secretly, and on regular occasions when Susan was not at home, Abe would hustle Sonny into the den to teach him boxing. Although many thought Susan was the driving force in Sonny's intellectual development, it was Abe who subtly preached the holistic approach to life that made Sonny special.

At summer camp he was far ahead of the other kids in both Hebrew and sports. He swam like a fish; the counselors often told him that swimming was his greatest talent. From camp in the New York Catskills they transported him to a special music group where his talent on the violin was polished and perfected.

When Sonny reached the age of ten, Abe no longer agreed to Hebrew camp, insisting instead that he spend that time with Sonny. Unbeknownst to Susan, father and son often took the subway to the North Philadelphia gym where Abe had honed his own boxing skills. There Sonny worked with several other young boxers making ready to enter the Golden Gloves. To his surprise he found himself to be better than any opposition in the Philadelphia area. It seemed to him that a lot of colored boys boxed, and one of his favorite opponents and sparring partners was none other than the well-known Buddy Nelson.

Susan was under the impression that they were working with Uncle Milton on advanced readings of the Torah and on football plays, but Sonny was actually perfecting his overhand right and left. It was sometime later that Susan discovered from reading *The Philadelphia Inquirer* that young Sonny Goldman won the Golden Gloves by defeating Buddy Nelson.

She was livid. "That's it! I went along with your decision to keep Sonny out of summer camp, but I did not agree for you to live your life through him. No more boxing. It's over!" Susan raged.

"No way! The Goldmans are fighters and you know it!"

Abe insisted.

Sonny increasingly realized that their different rearing styles were a source of great conflict for his parents. Susan liked swimming and found it to be beneficial for her boy. The heat was off of Abe in the summers when Sonny swam for Rydal Country Club, emerging as their champion in all his events in spite of having had little training.

According to the maternal Susan, "At least he won't end up with a broken nose and swollen eyes."

Beth Shalom Synagogue served many purposes for the Goldmans. Abe and Susan were heroes in the local Jewish community because of their dedication to Israel. Visiting dignitaries from Israel always requested an audience with the revered Colonel and Mrs. Goldman. Invariably, Abe would invite them to Deli-Land to eat in the special attached room off the small restaurant. It seemed like the whole synagogue would show up on those occasions, which helped Deli-Land become the success that enabled Abe to attain a degree of financial success.

The Goldmans weren't extravagant with their newfound prosperity, and the lessons Abe learned in World War II and in Israel were deeply ingrained in his character. At the deli it seemed like he always fussed over non-Jews more than Susan who preferred to serve the people from the synagogue. Whenever any of Abe's 101st Airborne buddies showed up, it was a special time for recollecting with true friends.

Secretly, Sonny never wanted to be in a business like his parents or a rabbi like his uncle or the violinist his mother wished for; he dreamt of being a warrior just as his father had been. He was anxious to read the Hebrew newspapers to find out what was happening to the Israeli military and their quest to keep Israel safe. He dreamed of victoriously leading troops in battle to recover other holy lands. He had a natural leadership style in school and was comfortable with the half-Jewish, half-Protestant population.

The Easleys of Hollywood

Sean's background and heritage were very different from Sonny's. Sam, having lost his mother and father at a very early age, was brought up in Catholic foster care. He was a bright, hard-working, huge man—six feet, five inches and over 250 pounds with a Phi Beta Kappa intellect and an unusual personality. He first saw Margaret in the early thirties while delivering ice from an ice wagon in Wildwood, New Jersey—a beach town that swelled with tourists during the summer months. His daily route took him past the tennis courts where his ice melted as he watched this beautiful, athletic female dominate the court. One particular day he summoned up the courage to ask her if she would like a ride home. She declined, but he followed her just long enough to find out where she lived while losing his entire load of ice to the heat of the day. "It was worth the investment," he used to say.

Sam repeatedly went to the tennis courts until his tenacity paid off and Margaret accepted an invitation for a ride home. They were married three months later. Because Marge was Episcopalian and Sam was Catholic, the differences created a void where they attempted to never venture.

Sam was big enough to play college football and enrolled at the University of Alabama after graduating from Wildwood

High to play with Bear Bryant, Don Hudson and the famous Alabama teams of the thirties. He was a better student than a football player. At first Margaret attended the Philadelphia Normal School while Sam was at Alabama, but they decided that separation was not healthy for a marriage. She and three of her brothers headed for Alabama to join Sam at college. Sam, the poor intellectual, was able to do well enough in school to maintain his academic scholarships and continued for a time as one of the Crimson Tide's finest benchwarmers.

After graduation, Margaret began teaching school in the Philadelphia School System while Sam became a social worker in the Pennsylvania Prison System and worked nights as a burlesque comedian in a downtown theater. He was extremely witty and quite the ham but Margaret soon forced a decision, the family or the theater. Sam chose family and never looked back. During this time, the aggressions of Hitler and Japan placed the United States into World War II and Sam was one of the first to enlist in the United States Navy.

After a few months passed, Sam received a letter from Margaret saying that she was expecting. Shortly thereafter, while alone at watch on the bow of his ship, Sam felt the call of God very clearly for the first time. It was a happening that he acknowledged but did not take the time to pursue. Later, while on maneuvers in rough seas, several pieces of munitions fell on him before he ever got the chance to see action. He found himself evacuated to the Philadelphia Naval Hospital with an injured hip and knee. There the Navy promoted him to an officer because of his educational background. In a matter of three months he was an ensign aboard the U.S.S. Schley, which was active in the Pacific Campaign. At sea Sam received notification that Margie Easley, an eight pound-four-ounce girl was born. Once again, this time while in the Pacific, Sam felt he had received another revelation from God telling him to do everything he could to save lives, not take them.

His quandary was how could a naval gunnery officer save lives and still perform his duties? He knew that kamikazes and the Japanese Air Force were going to attack the fleet. Because the Schley was a destroyer escort, Sam created the method of throwing fire in a cross pattern well before the manuals dictated that any fire should be rendered. Strangely enough, aided by Sam's innovative, effective, and early pattern of fire, God had his hand in the protection of the Schley and the fleet. Sam knew for sure that something was happening spiritually but did not have the time or energy to follow this thing that was taking place in his heart and mind. Berlin fell, Japan surrendered, and the Easleys were back in Philadelphia with their little daughter Margie.

Soon after, Sean was born. While settling down in a Philadelphia row house, Sam read the teachings of George Fox, founding father of the Society of Friends who recognized what was later to be called "the inner light." He began to attend the Cherry Street Meeting in Philadelphia. Most of the men at Meeting had been conscientious objectors during the War and found Sam to be quite unique yet very spiritual when he explained his calling for peace while on active duty in the service. Few members of Meeting verbalized any concern with his World War II participation, and he and his young family were welcomed into the Society of Friends with open arms. Sam asked to officially become a Quaker in 1949.

When the North Philadelphia section where the Easleys

were living became unsafe for rearing a family, Sam called on the G.I. Bill to get a slice of heaven by buying a humble home in a section called Hollywood in Abington Township, close to Abington Friends Meeting. Sam and Margaret adopted Nicky, a young orphaned boy who had been attending the elementary school where Margaret taught. His parents had died of accidental arsenic poisoning. Taken by the tragedy, Margaret offered to keep him until they found permanent housing. Still with the Easleys ten years later, they officially adopted him.

With only one bathroom in the Easley home, morning time proved interesting. The ability to "hold it in" became imperative, and there was definitely a pecking order that often went according to one's tolerance for certain offensive odors. Each visit to the toilet required speed of execution before Big Sam terrorized the room.

The Society of Friends, known as the Quaker church, became the highlight of the week. The entire family attended Abington Friends' First Day School, Meeting, and a meal, after which the adults stayed to talk about the issues of the day. During this time the young Quakers would set out to demonstrate God's love through service. They helped the needy by raking leaves, shoveling snow and doing various other chores. This was, of course, until football season rolled around, and the Easleys would cut short their Meeting stay to enjoy the Philadelphia Eagles' games. Heading for Wildwood to inject themselves into the culture of "the Shore" each summer further interrupted Meeting attendance and participation."

One summer in June, the Society of Friends held their annual conference in Cape May, New Jersey. Abington Meeting selected Sean to be the youth representative because no one else was able to attend the weeklong affair. He was taller than others his age and most thought him older. No one suspected just how scared, quiet, and intimidated he was as he found himself dropped off with a fifty-dollar bill and a small suitcase at the famous Admiral Hotel. One would have expected that a parent would accompany a child of this age to such an event, but Nicky dropped Sean off at the hotel to conquer the seemingly endless set of marble stairs leading to the registration area alone.

Walking up to sign in, Sean announced like the scared young boy he was, "I'm Sean Easley from A-Abington Meeting."

He found great comfort in hearing the wonderfully passive voice almost whisper, "We have been waiting for you. You are the youngest member of this year's conference, and you have been asked to join the roundtable discussion that is set to begin very soon."

"Where d-do I go?"

"It's a mile away at the Congress Hotel Conference Center. Here's the key to your room so you can drop off your bags and we'll give you a lift over there."

It was the first time he had ever been in an elevator with an operator dressed in a snazzy uniform. Dropping the bags in the room and quickly checking out its stateliness, he hurried downstairs to catch his ride.

"I don't know why they want you at this discussion. You seem too young," said the driver with an underlying tone of displeasure.

Sean just shrugged his shoulders. When he arrived at the conference, he opened the door to find several hundred people, seven seated on the stage and the remainder in the audience. He gravitated toward the one person he recognized, the moderator, Mrs. Colby. She had been nervously awaiting Sean's arrival and proceeded to lead him to the only empty seat on the stage.

Mrs. Colby began, "We're here today to discuss integration and how the Friends can help. With us today, ladies and gentlemen, is Miss Brigitte Hebert from Paris, a member of the La Rive Gauche Meeting."

As Mrs. Colby introduced other members on the stage, Sean's eyes were riveted on Brigitte. He thought how pretty she looked in her tight red sweater and long black skirt. He had never seen a Quaker look like that at Meeting before. After several introductions, Mrs. Colby introduced a colored man, the Reverend Dr. Martin Luther King, pastor of Peachtree Baptist Church in Atlanta, Georgia. Sean knew there was something very special about this man when the entire room stood in his honor and applauded. He had heard of Dr. King when his father and others at Meeting talked about his goals of equality for all. Margaret and Sam were particularly interested in the work of this great preacher and statesman after their experience witnessing injustices in Alabama while attending school there.

Finally, Mrs. Colby introduced Sean as the youngest member of the conference. As he stood, he caught Brigitte's smiling eyes that gave away her inner self, a radiating love, and an obvious understanding of the inner light. Sean concentrated on Mrs. Colby's words, "Before we begin the conference we will use the panel as a facing bench to prepare our hearts and minds in silence to allow God to work through us as we proceed with a plan to help integrate our society."

Sean closed his eyes and began to pray when within a few moments a blind man rose to speak from the front row. "God is love." Somehow this one comment touched Sean as he began to listen to God speak to him. Even though he had only spoken one other time in Meeting, he suddenly felt the need to speak. Inexplicably, Sean never stuttered when he prayed or spoke in Meeting, "How could God love one kind of man more than another, or love a flower more than a tree or say one star is better than another? Just as God made the earth and found a way for all living things to be together, we should find a way for people of different colors to live together."

Sean sat and silently began to question himself for several minutes before Mrs. Colby thanked everyone and the conference began. Audience members asked the panel insightful questions, spurring a dialogue with hopes of finding answers to eliminate segregation. They directed several questions to Sean regarding a youth's analysis of prejudice. By the end of the discussion, Sean found Dr. Martin Luther King to be more than just a Baptist preacher—he was extraordinary. The Quakers loved him and pledged to do all they could to help the cause. Later in the conference they voted to donate a great deal of time and money from the Friends Service Committee to help fund Dr. King's mission to abolish racial inequality.

They announced at the conference that young Quakers from overseas were looking for families in the Philadelphia area with whom to live and work. Who would have imagined that when word got back to the Easleys, they would jump at the opportunity and it would be Brigitte who would eventually move into their home? Sam and Margaret decided that it would be a good idea to have live-in help so Sean could attend the elementary school less than a quarter mile from home. With Brigitte looking after Sean, Margaret could coach after school and

Sam could work part time at a nearby factory on an assembly line for extra money.

The Easleys were comfortable with their new home and new "church," but had no idea of the negative light in which the rest of Abington Township viewed both the Hollywood section and the Quakers. As Sean entered Cedar Road School, he not only found this out on his own, but he became well acquainted with the universal intolerance of youth toward the likes of a stutterer.

Summers brought them to a stilted cottage strutting out over the water where they enjoyed rooms half the size of the ones in Hollywood. It was understood that while Sam was working days as a policeman on a beat at Wildwood's famous boardwalk, Margaret would be crabbing while Sean clammed and Nicky fished for their meals. Brigitte was contributing with a part-time job, as was Margie, who was in charge of helping her mother sell any abundance of seafood to the local restaurants.

Sleeping arrangements became even more complicated in the three-bedroom bungalow when Brigitte's friend from Paris came for a lengthy visit. Usually two or more Easley cousins made the Easley quarters their home base on weekends, and including visitors, there were often eight to ten people using one toilet and an outside shower located on the dock. There was no privacy and certainly no room for modesty; everyone knew everything about everybody. Thus were the summers in Wildwood, New Jersey. Everyone thought it was just fine and considered themselves lucky to be on the water at the Jersey Shore. One thing never changed no matter who visited them— Margaret and Sam always had their own bed.

Sean had it the best of all the Easleys. Because Sam and

Margaret both worked after their teaching jobs, he got to go to the local YMCA for a few hours each day after school. It was at the Y that he became an exceptional athlete, competing in gymnastics, swimming and track. He could do a giant swing on the horizontal bar at an early age and became a real dare devil who mastered several stunts in gymnastics that few his age could perform. In the summers he spent most of his time in the bay swimming, clamming and rowing or at the beach running, surfing, and swimming. At the Philadelphia YMCA championships in track and field, Sean won every event he entered while colored children won most of the other events.

Living in Hollywood—the lowlife of Abington Township—subscribing to the Quaker faith, and growing up in the Easley household with Brigitte all contributed to the molding of a most unusual young man. He was also about to get an education in social dynamics from the Abington Township schools.

Cultures Unite

Sean and Sonny's next encounter did not happen until sometime later during orchestra practice. Sonny was the first seat, first row violinist, and Sean occupied the seat next to him. The orchestra teacher introduced Sean as someone who could play the violin, cello, and viola. He announced that Sean would be playing the violin, and because of his versatility, he would play other instruments as well. During down time the two boys found themselves talking together for the first time since the football encounter.

"I didn't know you played, Sean," Sonny said in an inquisitive manner. Sean did not respond.

"Why be like that?" Sonny quipped. Sean only smiled.

As destiny would have it, music brought these two kids together. Knowing that they both had talent, the orchestra teacher had them play a duet at the annual school holiday pageant with Sonny on violin and Sean on viola. Everyone present recognized their talent. After the concert Sam and Abe were introduced to each other.

"I think our sons are pretty competitive," Abe began.

"I know they are. I think it might prove good for both of them. What sports does Sonny play?" Sam asked.

"Football, boxing and swimming," Abe responded.

"Why don't you join the Abington Y? They have terrific developmental programs," Sam offered.

"Do they box?" Abe immediately asked.

"No, you're going to have to handle that one outside the Y. Swimming, gymnastics, and track and field; you can do no better. If the boys will be taking violin lessons together, maybe we can carpool for both music and the Y," Sam suggested.

"Sounds good to me. I think that's something we can work out," said a welcoming Abe.

Susan and Margaret were making small talk while their husbands figured out the children's schedules. On the way home Abe told Susan about the carpool arrangements. Susan would take the boys to violin lessons and the Easleys would be responsible for the YMCA part.

"I want Sonny to start at the Y in their gym/swim program right after the holidays," Abe instructed Susan.

"Who are you kidding Abe? Listen to yourself; first it's public school and now the YMCA. Why not the YMHA?"

"Susan, it's important for Sonny to develop in the best programs available regardless of who runs them. If they'll take him, he's going."

"Do you realize where the Easleys live? Hollywood, of all places!"

"Susan, I love you dearly but you're a Jewish snob and that's the last thing that I want my children to be. Please allow them to be part of Abington Township and let's not bring this up again."

At first Big Sam picked up the kids because Brigitte hadn't yet learned to drive. She was busy studying for the test and would eventually become the boys' shuttle for all their outings together, spending hours together with them and often having the unintended benefit of helping mold these special young boys.

On day one, Sam got the boys to the Y fifteen minutes before the activities began and while referring to Sonny, the desk clerk directed his question to Sam, "Who's paying for him?"

"I am," Sam answered.

"You'll need to fill this out," the clerk said as he slid a paper across the counter.

"Sonny, help me fill this form out. What's your middle name? Date of birth…your address…how about your religion?"

When Sonny responded to the last question with "Jewish," the registration clerk sneered. Both Big Sam and Sonny noticed.

"That's all Sonny, have a good time. I'll pick you boys up at seven. You're gonna have to shoot some pool and play ping pong until I get here."

When Sonny disappeared out of hearing range, Sam lectured the clerk about being kind to everyone because kindness exemplified the mission of the YMCA.

Everything went well for the boys at the Y until some jerk, who was getting off the horizontal bar, called Sonny a kike. To be sure, it was the last time that he ever made an anti-Semitic remark. Sonny hit him in the chest so hard that it knocked him almost twenty feet and took his breath away.

Looking down at him he finished with one word—"Don't."

Sean just smiled and you could tell that Coach Allen approved. The class continued as if nothing ever happened.

"Sean, show everyone how to do a back uprise, hip circle, half giant," instructed Coach Allen.

When Sean got off the bar he could see that Sonny was amazed. When Sonny got his turn he didn't do a back uprise. He had too little of a swing and did a muscle up, rolled around the bar and fell from the bar when he pushed off to do a half giant. It was kind of a special moment when the jerk that had just called Sonny a kike did a great job spotting and caught him well before he hit the ground.

Sonny thanked him and Coach Allen smiled and said, "There's a lot more to be learned in sport than most people understand."

Soon the gym period was over and they were off to the pool. The twelve boys in the class went to the locker room. It was always an interesting phenomenon when they had to undress. Some boys seemed particularly shy like Sean and especially wanted to hide their private parts. After showering, they entered the footbath, went up the stairs and into the pool. They could always tell where the pool was—all you had to do was follow your nose. The smell of chlorine was pungent, but the water was clear and inviting.

Coach Allen had all the boys line up against the wall and instructed them to count off by fours. Each number represented a heat for the twenty-yard swim. Sean swam in heat two and Sonny, following, looked great in the water. Coach Allen was surprised.

"You have a great future in swimming, Sonny. Where did you learn to swim?"

"Israel."

"Uh-huh," Coach Allen responded. "Have you ever raced before?"

"Yes, Coach, summer league at Rydal Country Club."

After swimming Sean and Sonny had about an hour to play ping-pong, shoot pool and eat stick pretzels. And so it was violin on Tuesday and Thursday, and the Y on Monday, Wednesday, Friday, and Saturday.

Brigitte finally got her driver's license and sang French songs as she chauffeured the boys back and forth to their activities. She drove a black 50's Studebaker that Mr. Lafoussier, a Canadian Quaker, had donated to her. It used to annoy Sonny and Sean that Brigitte would insist on teaching them French in the car, but they were soon to become conversant and would someday be grateful for her persistence.

Summer came and Sonny went to work on his pugilism in Philly while Sean had three months of fun in Wildwood. In the fall, they were leaving Cedar Road School for Huntington Junior High, a school of 2,000 students. They were both about to enter a new and different world.

Philadelphia

Huntington Junior High

On the first day of school Sean boarded bus number seventeen at Cedar Road School parking lot to take the five-mile ride to Huntington Junior High and sat alone. Sure enough, Sonny was at the second stop, and as he boarded the bus everyone was excited to see him. It seemed that Sean would continue to be the mystery boy he had been at primary school.

Sonny plopped down next to Sean, "Hey, Sean, how was Wildwood?"

"Great."

"What did you do?"

"Clammed, surfed, and w-worked a little too," he said quietly.

"Surfed?"

"Yep, I taught myself how to surf this s-summer. My mom let me buy a surfboard out of the Sears' catalog. It's really fun; you'll have to t-try it."

"We never go to the beach," Sonny complained.

"That's okay; I'll t-take you sometime."

"You sure did get bigger this summer, Sean. How much did you grow?"

"I don't know for sure."

"Why did you work?" Sonny asked.

"We can't afford to be in Wildwood unless w-we all work. Clamming was where I earned money. After work I ran a lot in the sand so I feel like I got a lot f-faster."

"Are you going out for football?" Sonny wondered.

"Yeah, what did you do this s-summer?

"I learned Beethoven's 21st Symphony. Did you play at all?"

"No," Sean said with a smile. "Did you b-box, Sean asked?"

"I won the Junior Olympics," Sonny answered. "Knocked out a kid in the second round in the final bout."

They were laughing by the time the bus rolled up to Huntington Junior High. Exiting together, they both began to notice how much bigger they were than their classmates.

"Sean, what homeroom are you in?" Sonny asked.

"114."

"No kidding! That's mine too," Sonny said excitedly.

They walked down the hall to find a smiling Mr. Butler greeting the protégés he would be mentoring for the school year.

"Well, I've heard a lot about you two from Coach Allen at the Y. Are you still going there?" Mr. Butler asked in a tone as if he got the pick of the litter in his homeroom.

"Y-yes," Sean stammered to a surprised Mr. Butler.

"I'm hooked; I go there now too," Sonny added.

"Three of the best athletes we've ever seen in Abington Township history are in my homeroom. Do you guys know Louie Jackson? You'll probably recognize him from some of the programs you've been in," Butler bragged.

When Louie walked into homeroom, Sean and Sonny immediately knew who he was—tall, good looking and always smiling.

"Hey, did you get one of those physicals?" Sonny said in a way as if to ask if they had to cough while the doctor felt their privates.

Sean and Louie both affirmed by shaking their heads and frowning.

"Did you know that there are three teams and then the varsity team?" Louie asked.

"Coach Weber thinks there will be 500 of us out for football," Sonny said and looked at Sean because they had already planned on being on the varsity.

Louie continued, "They only take about forty players on varsity."

School was exciting as first days usually are. For some unknown reason, Sean was able to sing without stuttering and impressed everyone in French class with his rendition of *La Marseillaise*. Then the real highlight of the day came for Sean and Sonny—football. Louie was right; there were hundreds of kids out for the team. They placed the boys in heats of ten to fifteen and line them up on the goal line to run a fifty-yard dash. Sean had become faster over the summer and caught Coach Weber's eye as he won his heat by five yards.

"What's your name, son?" the coach asked.

"S-Sean Easley."

Sonny handily won the next heat. It seemed like Coach Weber already knew Sonny, and after every boy ran—many of them twice—Coach Weber chose some for a race-off to determine the fastest. Included in the final group with Louie were Sean and Sonny. Sean easily won with Louie two steps behind, and Sonny, too, had a notable finish. To Coach Weber's amazement, all but one of the kids in the final heat was in the seventh grade. Sonny won the day when it came to the throwing. He could throw a ball fifty yards, and the coaches had never seen anything like it before at Huntington.

After more running and calisthenics, Coach called everyone together and said, "We'll continue to practice in our shorts and t-shirts and work on some plays. We don't have enough equipment for everyone, so after today if you don't think you want to play let us know so we don't have to scrounge around for the extra gear. But, my philosophy is that anyone who wants to play will. I was never fast or impressive but I was able to play pro ball mostly because I worked harder than anyone else did. Let's be a hard-working team. Now huddle up for a team cheer."

As Sonny and Sean walked to the mobbed locker room, the coaches talked. "What's going on here?" Weber asked in amazement. "All of a sudden we have some athletes."

Coach Metzger chimed in with his theory, "It's simple, Coach, these kids are all post-war babies. Their dads are a different breed because of the war, and they obviously have spent a lot of time developing their kids. Plus, with all the new housing developments in Abington Township, we'll be tough to beat in the future."

The sports bus dropped Sonny off at Deli-Land. Abe was slicing roast beef. "How'd it go Sonny?"

"Great."

Abe could tell that Sonny was proud. "Come and help me fill some orders and tell me about it."

"I can't believe hundreds of kids are out for football, Dad."

"Well, how'd you do?" the anxious dad asked.

"Good," Sonny said as he prepared an order.

"Sonny, my dear, we need six Kaiser rolls too," a customer hollered over the counter.

Sensing that his dad wanted more detail, Sonny continued as he began bagging the rolls, "Sean and I did really good, and so did Louie Jackson, a boy from Cresmont. He can flat out play."

"Does Sean still have a stutter and what was so impressive about him?" Abe asked his son.

"He got faster over the summer, Dad. He's also easily the fastest kid out for football and yeah, he stills stutters."

"Are they gonna let seventh graders play?" Abe asked while slicing some kosher salami.

"They better or they're gonna lose!" Sonny said emphatically.

Sean arrived at home to Brigitte who was anxious to get a full report about his first day. She was more interested in hearing about French class while Sean was reeling with the excitement of his success at football practice. Brigitte always made him feel comfortable, and he rarely stuttered when they spoke. The rest of the family didn't get home until Sean was already in bed.

That year the football season for Huntington Junior High, grades seven, eight and nine, was unique. Of the starting eleven, seven were seventh graders. Of the seven varsity games played that year, they only had one touchdown scored against them. They averaged over thirty points in the first half for the entire season. Coach Weber played everyone else in the second half. Sonny had a seventy percent completion record, Sean had ten touchdowns, and Louie had fourteen on the ground and receiving.

Abington High varsity played on Saturdays, usually in front of 2,000 to 3,000 people, and the junior high school played on Friday nights. Both teams used the junior high field. Huntington Junior High was located in the old high school buildings, and when the high school moved to a new, modern campus, they kept the old football field to share with Huntington. As word of the boys' success and talent spread, the junior high team began drawing nearly as many spectators as the high school team.

The year progressed with continued success for the three boys who had grown very close. Louie lived in Cresmont, a poor Hollywood-like section for coloreds, which was located at the opposite corner of Abington Township. The three boys sometimes talked about the racial problems in the South, and Sean made it clear how the Quakers were trying to assist Dr. King. Louie often visited the Easley household and especially liked Brigitte. The Easley home was surprisingly comfortable to him, and he felt very much a part of it.

During one visit Louie told Sean, "It's almost like your family doesn't even know I'm colored."

"The Quakers are supposed t-to look at the inner person, not on the outside," Sean responded.

Susan Goldman was working on the invitation list for Sonny's bar mitzvah when he peered over her shoulder and said,

"Mom, be sure to invite the Easleys, Brigitte, and Louie."

"Why?" Susan asked.

"Because they're my friends, that's why," he answered without reservation.

"Sonny, my entire family will be here from New York."

"It's not your bar mitzvah, Mom, it's mine."

Some weeks later, Louie and the Easley gang arrived at Beth Shalom Synagogue for the start of the bar mitzvah ceremony and accompanying festivities. They donned loaned yarmulkes and were amazed by Sonny's beautiful baritone voice, as if Hebrew was his native tongue.

At the post-ceremony gala, people were surprised to see that the Easleys, being Quakers, danced so much. It seemed like they danced every dance, and Abe was quick to join them in their celebration. After the fifth rendition of *Hava Nagila*, Abe and Sam sat down at the Easley table.

"I think our boys are good for each other, Sam," Abe said sounding grateful.

"I'm really happy that Louie is included in their group too. What a great kid. By the way, do me a favor and don't mention to Marge that Sean's playing football." Sam confided.

"You have the same problem I have. I've almost convinced Susan of how beneficial sports are and I think the Y was the answer."

"We need to keep them swimming, Abe. I'm convinced that it helps develop them and will compliment their other sports. Besides, it'll keep Susan and Marge happy," Big Sam said as he watched their daughters twisting on the dance floor.

"These kids sure aren't as bashful as we were, are they Sam?"

"That's for sure. Lots of things have changed since the war," Sam said in a pensive tone.

"Did you serve?" Abe asked.

"In the Navy—Atlantic and Pacific. How 'bout you?"

"Army, 101st Airborne."

Both men stood up and just hugged each other, saying nothing. Nothing needed said.

Bonding Agents

There were several reasons for the bond between Sonny, Sean, and Louie. First, of course, was the success of the Huntington football team. Despite their differing personalities, they truly enjoyed each other's company. Sonny was a natural leader. Louie was confident and smooth. Sean, who was more laid back, laughed more than the other two. Sonny had strong features and kept his hair short while blue-eyed Sean still had hair that was longer than the style of the day. Louie was a light-skinned colored who kept his hair cropped short. All three were over six-feet tall and looked older than their peers looked.

Perhaps their most distinguishing mark was their difference in dress. Louie's style was conservative ivy-league or preppie. His mother was a single parent and demanded that Louie always look his best. Sonny always wore the latest fashions, with Susan trying to make him a trendsetter. Sean's style was no style at all. He dressed in hand-me-downs, which were always clean and usually wore a sweater or sweatshirt over his characteristic white-collared shirt.

Their success in football made them the topic of conversation among their classmates and the town folk. Since they were in the same homeroom, it seemed like they were together all the time, and the Friday night dances in the school gym strengthened their bond. During the dances the coloreds stayed to themselves, the Jews stayed to themselves, the country clubbers stayed together and then there were the rest. Sean was, by far, the best dancer in the school and was strangely uninhibited, partially because of his natural ability and partially because he danced with Brigitte every day after school while watching *American Bandstand*.

Ten minutes into the first dance, Sean, looking at Louie and Sonny said, "This is the st-stupidest thing I've ever seen. No one's havin' a good time. They should have just stayed home."

"I can't ask a white girl to dance," Louie said with hope in his voice.

"You gotta be kidding me. You're not marrying her, you're just dancing with her," Sonny fired back.

"I want to dance with Cresmont g-girls. They're much better dancers," Sean added.

"I don't care if I dance at all, I just want to hang out with you guys," Sonny joined in as they all laughed.

Soon, most of the kids were dancing to almost every song but it still seemed too segregated for Sean. On slow dances, Louie, Sonny, and Sean would change partners. Sean, who knew the latest steps, was quick to teach others dances like the slop, the Bristol stomp, the hop, and the classic jitterbug.

Amazed, Sonny asked, "Where'd you learn all that stuff? Isn't it weird that a Quaker would be such a good dancer?"

"No question. The Easleys aren't like most Quaker families. I dance because Brigitte watches *Bandstand* and then p-practices on me every day. We all dance. My dad's probably the b-best dancer in my family."

Brigitte recognized how special the trio was and liked that they enjoyed spending time with her. They could talk to her about things they couldn't talk about with their parents. Not only was she optimistic and fun to be around, she was nice to look at. She liked hearing the scoop on the way home from the dances and often gave advice to satiate their inquisitive young minds.

On one occasion, Sonny came out with, "Brigitte, I have to ask you something. What do you do if you get a boner when you're slow dancing with a girl?"

Sean and Louie started giggling.

"Mon cheri, do not be afraid of anything that is natural. Most women are proud when they arouse a man. There's only one way for her to know and that's for you to hold her tightly. If she rejects, you just smile and say, 'I am sorry, I guess I should not slow dance with you,' and then say something very nice about her. Men should create love with words. What you say to a women and how you say it are very important."

Brigitte felt the need to change the discussion to loftier matters. "I was thinking you two should go to Meeting with Sean and me."

Louie immediately jumped in with, "I'll go, but I should ask my mother first."

"My mom might not let me go, but I'd like to see what it is like," added Sonny.

Brigitte was a great recruiter for Abington Meeting. She wanted everyone she met to feel the love that she had discovered, and Abington Meeting was pleased when she brought guests.

Sonny told Susan that he was going to go to church with the Easleys. She flipped out and screamed at Abe, "That's it! This is where I have to put my foot down. First the Y and now the Quakers. Absolutely not!"

"Susan, simmer down. Sonny knows who he is, and he's going to do this if he wants," Abe calmly replied.

Louie and Sonny enjoyed their visit to Quaker Meeting. They liked the basic and simplistic way of worship. The Meeting House was on a beautiful, tree-covered piece of expansive acreage, built entirely of natural stone with wood shutters. Inside there were plain wooden benches with cushioned seats. A few Quakers sat on the facing bench toward the rest of the Meeting. Everyone sat in total silence until someone felt moved by God to share with others.

After his first time at Meeting, Sonny said to Brigitte on the way home, "I think I get it, everyone is a minister or rabbi."

"Exactly, God loves everyone and it's our job to get close to him and tell others what he says through us," Brigitte explained.

Sonny wanted dropped off first because Sundays at Deli-Land were a very busy time for breakfast and brunch. He could tell Susan was mad, but Abe was curious to find out how he liked it and half whispered to Sonny, "How was Meeting?"

"I'm glad I'm Jewish," Sonny said for his mother's sake. Secretly, the warmth and love he felt at Meeting moved him deeply.

As Brigitte, Sean and Louie drove to Cresmont, Louie asked, "Do you mind if we stop off at Howard Johnson's? I'd like you to meet my ma."

Louie's mom was a chambermaid on the weekends and cleaned private homes during the week. She was committed to Louie and his brother, working seven days a week to give them the things she hoped would help make them successful. Louie went to the front desk and asked if they knew where he could find her. The front desk clerk called housekeeping to request that Louise come to the front. Louie instinctively knew, however unfair, that if he met his mom in the lobby, the management would not be happy, so he waited to greet her in the hallway. Minutes later a large, dark woman with a muscular frame entered the hall. As Louie hugged her, his love and pride were obvious.

"Mother, I'd like you to meet Brigitte," Louie said.

As Brigitte hugged Louise, Sean could tell that Mrs. Jackson was taken by Brigitte's natural beauty. "Louie has told me so much about you, Mrs. Jackson. I hope you will be able to go with us to Meeting on First Day," Brigitte said.

"I can't because I work here every Sunday."

"Maybe it would be possible to work something out so that I could pick you up just for Meeting and then drop you off as soon as it is over," Brigitte offered.

Somehow Brigitte's charming yet sincere appeal worked during her conversation with the hotel manager, and Mrs. Jackson and her sons began attending Abington Meeting regularly. Brigitte never failed to invite Sonny who would occasionally attend. Through this time together, the Jacksons and the Easleys became close friends and eventually the Jacksons became an integral part of Abington Meeting.

Football and Meeting brought the families together for

sure, but it was probably the sport of swimming that created the greatest bond between the Goldman, Easley, and Jackson families. Susan and Margaret preferred swimming for their sons and daughters, and just about every weekend there was a swim meet against another YMCA. They usually lasted two hours, and the Abington Y team won nearly every one. Sonny was the best at longer events and Sean in the sprints. It worked out great; they didn't often compete against each other and they were always together on relays. When Sonny swam, Susan went berserk by cheering loudly and jumping up and down in a way that always embarrassed Abe. Once she realized that there were other families from Beth Shalom Synagogue who enrolled their children in the Y programs, she became comfortable with the whole idea.

The swim coach had a large home and usually hosted post-meet gatherings. Families brought covered dishes and the adults played charades while the kids ran around outside having fun. Of course, Brigitte was always eager to include everyone and would invite the Jacksons and other friends to the meets and after parties. Many of the social barriers that separated families were erased here. Abe and Sam were the life and soul of the parties. Their frivolity and dancing were contagious to the rest of the group.

It was at an Abington Y swim team party that Louie first admitted that he couldn't swim. "Don't worry, Louie, we'll go to free swim and teach you," said a compassionate Sonny. Within a month, Louie was no longer afraid of the water and could jump off the diving board and swim to the end of the pool.

In the locker room after one of the swimming sessions, Sonny said, "I'm invited to a party tonight but I don't wanna to go.

It's at Barbara Brownstein's house. Ever since Brigitte told me what to do when my pants start to breath it seems like all they do is play slow songs and all the girls want to take turns dancing with me. I know it would be more fun if you guys were there."

Smiling and chuckling with Louie, Sean came back with, "That's a great idea, and we s-should make a deal, if someone has a party, we all go."

"Even at Cresmont, Sean?" Louie asked as the tone became more serious.

"Even in Hollywood, Louie. Let me call Brigitte and see if she can pick us up f-for Barbara's party." Brigitte kindly obliged and gave the boys a ride to the party.

"This is gonna be interesting," said Sonny as he jumped in the car.

"Just remember to be yourselves, and remember that God loves you. Never fear, he makes a way," Brigitte said confidently.

With noise and music coming from the den, Sonny rang the doorbell of the Brownstein estate. Mrs. Brownstein opened the door as Mr. Brownstein appeared behind her. "These are my friends, Sean and Louie, Mr. and Mrs. Brownstein," Sonny said hopefully. It was immediately apparent that Louie would be welcome, but Sean received a sneer from Mrs. Brownstein. She obviously had a preconceived opinion about him. "These are my best friends. I told them what a wonderful family you are and that you wouldn't mind if they came along," Sonny added to lighten the air. Mr. Brownstein, interested more in football, intervened immediately with questions about the season.

On the way down the stairs to the den Louie chuckled as he sarcastically said, "The Brownsteins sure were excited to see me at the door." The party was a great success and Sean danced for three hours straight, equalizing his time with each girl even though some of them weren't much to look at. Sean just liked to dance.

When they got in the car to be shuttled home, Sean said, "That worked p-pretty well."

Sonny added, "What happens if we're invited to two parties on the same day?"

Brigitte responded, "Why you should go to both."

And so it was, the threesome sometimes dropped in on as many as three parties on a Saturday night. Brigitte was content to read scripture or a book while she waited for them in the car. Louie was only invited to Cresmont parties; Sonny was invited to all the parties except for Cresmont; and Sean was invited to very few Jewish parties, some Cresmont parties, and a real mixture of others. They liked the Cresmont parties the most and would stay there the longest. Kids of different ages were there and the boys got a chance to dance with older girls. It was apparent that some of the older colored guys didn't like Louie spending so much time with Sonny and Sean. It was at the Cresmont parties that Brigitte joined in rather than wait in the car. Somehow she fit in and was comfortable dancing and laughing with the group. Sean was glad that she did not have to sit in the car and wait and liked the fact that she was having some fun, even if it was at one of his school parties.

Few could understand or appreciate the unique bond and special friendships that were being formed between Sonny, Louie, and Sean.

The Coalition

By ninth grade, the trio had become so well liked at Huntington that Louie decided to capitalize on their popularity. "Everyone in the school knows us. If we team up, I'm sure we can get elected to any position we want and then we can have a real say."

"What p-positions are you talking about, Louie?" Sean asked.

"Student body president, secretary, or whatever…how about class president? Elections are coming up soon. What do ya think?"

"What position would you like to hold, Louie?" Sonny asked.

"None, I just wanna be the juice behind the scenes. What do you want, Sonny?" Louie asked.

"President has a nice ring to it, unless Sean wants to be president."

"No, Sean said, I just want to c-count the money and be in charge of the d-dances."

Louie said, "Okay, we're officially forming a political party that has the Jewish kids, the colored kids, and everyone else who doesn't think they're neat or special. We'll figure out a name that fits."

Sonny said, "I got it, SDS. No one will really know that it

stands for Sonny, the dimwit who thought of the thing, and Sean."

It worked like magic. They overthrew the incumbent group by a landslide and so formed another building block in inter-racial communication. Sonny became president and Sean trea-surer.

The part Sean liked was that the treasurer did get to be in charge of the dances. He thought up the themes for each dance and organized them. It was two dollars to get in and it wasn't unusual for 1,000 students to attend on a Friday night. They rocked to the tunes of Jerry Blavat, the Geator with the Heator and the Record Machine. He was a disc jockey from WIBG, the most popular radio station in Philadelphia. Sean had danced a couple of times on *American Bandstand* and on the Geator's show because both shows would visit Wildwood in the sum-mer. Sean was able to use this connection to make a few of the dances special.

The first dance under the new SDS command was a mystery dance using Sadie Hawkins rules. Girls were supposed to invite someone they didn't know to the dance. Once they arrived and the dancing began, the couples were supposed to mix it up and only dance with each other a few times. If a guy wasn't asked to the dance, he was allowed to ask a girl as long as they really didn't know each other.

The week of the dance, Cassandra Washington called Sean to formalize their plans for the big night. She was a colored girl whose mom and dad were both teachers, just like Sam and Marge Easley. Her dad was also a big wheel with the NAACP. She had never been near a white boy socially before, but she liked Sean because he was always nice to everyone. He was both happy and proud to go to the dance with Cassandra. They could sense there was something between them that they wanted to explore. When she called Sean about the dance, she reminded him of the day he just held her hand and told her how beautiful she was. The colored girls liked Sean because he went to a lot of the Cresmont parties, loved to dance, and was always friend-ly to them in the hallways. They knew he was a Quaker and somehow knew that it meant he didn't judge people by their color. Some of them also knew that the Jacksons had become Quakers and that Louie, Sonny, and Sean were best friends. White and colored boys being friends was one thing, but society definitely looked down upon a mixed couple.

Sonny's date for the dance almost caused his mother to have a heart attack. Elisha Johnson, maybe the wildest colored girl in the school, called and asked him to take her to the mys-tery dance. Sonny bragged to Louie and Sean that Elisha had invited him and he had accepted. She was probably the fastest girl at Huntington, not only on the track but also with the boys. When Mrs. Goldman accidentally found out, she was livid with Sonny and with his dad for allowing him to go to Abington.

Louie's mother was on the phone almost every evening so Louie missed calls from girls wanting to ask him out. But one day, and to everyone's surprise, Cheryl Topkins, the richest, quietest girl in the township, asked Louie to the dance.

Brigitte was pleased with Sean's mystery dance concept and told him she was certain God would bless him for continuing to work to remove the racial and social barriers that plagued Abington.

"How did you get Jerry Blavat to be the disc jockey?" asked Brigitte.

"Easy," said Sean. "I just t-told him what I was trying to do. I asked him to help me g-get the colored, white, Jew, Quaker, Catholic, P-Protestant, rich, and poor together. He's doing it for free. He said he c-can't understand why people treat each other the w-way they do and that his TV station wouldn't even allow c-colored kids to be on his dance show. He w-wants to see what happens tonight and how everything w-works out."

When Brigitte blew the horn for Sonny, Mrs. Goldman came out to the car to lecture Sean, "You know what you are doing is very dangerous."

As Sonny was getting in the car, Sean got out, hugged Mrs. Goldman, and said, "Everything will be all right, Mrs. Goldman." He could see the concern on her face as the car pulled away leaving her standing alone in the driveway.

The conversation that Sean had when he picked up Cassandra revealed the apprehension and tension Cassandra's parents had.

Mr. Washington asked Sean, "What are your plans with Cassandra?"

"I'm p-planning on dancing her sh-shoes off," Sean answered.

"Make sure that's all that comes off, Sean."

Sean smiled and said, "M-Mr. Washington, Cassandra is the nicest g-girl at Huntington. You will n-never have to worry about things like that."

Mr. Washington looked at his wife as if to say, 'How could Cassandra possibly be attracted to this boy—a stuttering honky.'

Leaving the house, Cassandra squeezed Sean's hand and whispered, "Thank you."

When Sonny went into Elisha's house to pick her up, Cassandra surprised Sean by throwing her arms around him and kissing his neck. She whispered, "I've always had a thing for you because you are the nicest boy in the school. Isn't it funny that you told my parents I was the nicest girl? I know they'll never allow us to get to know each other, and we both know it's a no-go in Abington anyway. Too bad, because I think we really could be best of friends."

"So d-do I." Sean smiled and hugged her.

Louie was nervous when he arrived at the Tompkins's house. The guard at the front gate treated Brigitte rudely. She drove as close to the front door as possible and let Louie out. When he approached the door, a man in white gloves met him. A short while later he and Cheryl emerged from the house and hopped in the back seat, necessitating a move up front for Sean and Cassandra.

"Now please, have a good time and conduct yourselves in a manner that will be pleasing to *Dieu*," Brigitte said when they got to the dance.

"*Merci beaucoup*," Sean said as he smiled at Brigitte and closed the car door.

That's when it all began. At first, all the cool kids and the rich kids rejected the idea and said that they were going to blow off the dance. Louie figured they were probably the twenty percent that didn't vote for the coalition. In no time, though, something unique and unheard of was happening; colored and white, Jew and Gentile, and rich and poor began interacting. What Louie, Sonny, and Sean naturally experienced began happening to the rest of the students at the school.

With the encouragement and sense of permission from Jerry Blavat, students were dancing with each other and the social barriers and human hang-ups seemed to disappear for a time. By mid-dance, there was a bunny hop chain that was hundreds strong. It continued for a good ten minutes. Jerry Blavat did his job, and Huntington Junior High changed that night.

The girls who usually weren't asked to dance were thrilled and had more fun than ever before at the unforgettable event. Classmates in a spirit of true friendship taught guys to dance who didn't know how. This transformation was remarkable considering the trend of the day was to either mock or ignore one another.

By the end of the dance, the three couples were back together again in what appeared to be more of a grinding session than dancing. As the lights went on after the last dance everyone cheered, and Sean convinced Sonny to take the stage, "Let's hear it for the Geator with the Heator, Mr. Jerry Blavat." A deafening applause filled the gymnasium as Jerry waved to the youngsters and Sonny continued, "Wasn't that fun? Just think, you met people you see every day, but now you know them in a different way. Imagine what this school would be like, or for that matter our whole society, if we treated each other like this all the time. Be good and bless you. Stay safe and good night," Sonny said with the smoothness of a professional entertainer.

The ride home was a continuation of the last dance. Brigitte was beside herself, wondering how to handle the petting she perceived was going on. Cassandra and Sean couldn't keep their hands off each other.

After Brigitte dropped off the girls, she blasted the boys in a tearful decree, *"Mes cheris,* you have not done what men of

God should do. I will never drive you again if you act like that in front of me. A relationship with a woman is private, between you, her, and God. Anytime it is shared with others—well, *c'est tres mal.* When Brigitte dropped off Louie, she reiterated, *"Jamais, jamais, jamais."*

Louie responded, "Brigitte, I'm very sorry and it won't happen again."

Back at school the following Monday, Sean asked Cassandra to help him count the money from the dance. They were to deposit the record amount of $1,956 with Mr. Turner, the vice principal. By the end of the school year, they had earned over $14,000 from dances. Sean stood proudly at the last student council meeting to make the financial report and speak to the class about deciding what to purchase for the school as a class gift.

The faculty advisor present at the meeting interrupted, "Sean, there is less than $4,000 in the account."

"No w-way! It c-can't be. I've been giving Mr. Turner all the money after each d-dance, and it's more than $14,000."

A cloud of suspicion hovered over the room, and eyes darted between Sean and the advisor.

"Do you have the deposit receipts?" she asked.

"No, I-I just gave the cash to Mr. T-Turner," Sean said.

Sean knew for the first time what it felt like to be a criminal. Some of his friends wouldn't speak to him, thinking he had stolen money. Sonny and Louie were, of course, supportive, but it was Cassandra who knew for sure that Sean did exactly what he said. Defending Sean, she vociferously attacked Mr. Turner verbally in his office and became a legend at Huntington because of it. Cassandra announced over the school intercom that she was with Sean every time he made a deposit, and she demanded that Mr. Turner make things right and return the money.

It wasn't until Big Sam Easley made a visit to Huntington that the money miraculously appeared, supposedly deposited into the wrong account. The Easleys made an Abington Township educator look unethical, and little did anyone know how that would eventually affect Sean at Abington.

Huntington's graduating class gift included books for the library, new track and field equipment, new football gear, and new art supplies. They gave the balance to the athletic department.

The bond enjoyed by Sonny, Louie, and Sean would officially become a pact that would last for the rest of their lives. Their battle cry became *"Toujours Amis!"* (Always Friends). They pledged to remain the best of friends during good times and bad and to encourage each other to be the best at school and sports and at just being people. They knew without saying that their commitment to each other would help them overcome any barriers placed before them at Abington and elsewhere.

Cassandra also wanted to be in on the pact, and from the trio's perspective, she always would be. They grew very close, and knew each other from many perspectives. For Sean and Cassandra, it was more than just first love; they were soul mates and shared parts of their inner selves that some never explored. The *Toujours Amis* quartet looked forward with great anticipation to what was to come at Abington Senior High, one of the newest high schools in suburban Philadelphia.

The Summer of Change

As school ended, Sean, Louie, and Brigitte headed to Cape May, New Jersey, for the annual Society of Friends Cape May Conference. Sean and Louie were now actively engaged in the Young Friends Society and Brigitte was active in several Society of Friends' movements. The Admiral Hotel appeared to have made a mistake in accommodations when they checked in. Louie had a roommate from New York and Sean and Brigitte were to have adjoining rooms. What really happened was that Marge and Sam were worried about Sean's advanced social behavior and they wanted Brigitte to monitor him. Louie's assigned room was on a different floor, away from Sean and Brigitte.

For another year the main topic of the conference was harmony between the races, and again, Dr. Martin Luther King attended. Brigitte's friend, Mr. Lafoussier, a Frenchman from Montreal who was very close to Dr. King, was also attending the conference. Louie and Sean were with Dr. King on several occasions throughout the week because Brigitte always included them as her family in nearly everything she did.

One night at 2:00 A.M. and midway through the week's activities, the door opened between Sean and Brigitte's room. She was crying as she entered and slid into his bed, pulling the covers over herself and nestling face-to-face into Sean. He lay quietly, taken by how magnificent she felt at that moment in just her slip and by how delicious she smelled. He tried to pretend that he was not fascinated but his breathing and excitement gave him away. She turned around into him and placed his arms around her.

"Just hold me, Sean," she whispered as she quietly wept.

"What's the m-matter? Sean asked. "What happened?"

"It's what I did."

"Did what?" Sean asked.

"Non, it is not just what I did; it is also why I did it. I was with a man purely to get what I wanted," she confessed now sobbing harder.

"Well, how c-can I help?"

"Just hold me."

Sean did not mind accommodating her. Embracing her, he could not control becoming aroused. She knew what was happening and for a moment liked his natural response.

"Don't feel b-bad Brigitte. You're just confused. Tomorrow morning you'll feel b-better."

"Sean, I used to sleep with men all the time, and then God pulled me towards Him. I just did what I said I would never ever do again—sell myself, but this time not for the *l'argent*—for opportunities."

"What do you mean?"

"Cars, opportunities, travel—it doesn't matter. It is a terrible feeling when you know you have sold your body. It's especially difficult when you know God forgave you for your past and then to repeat it," she confessed.

"No one is p-perfect, Brigitte," Sean assured.

She drifted off to sleep while Sean lay mesmerized.

Brigitte rose early that morning. "You're going to make some woman very happy one day, Sean. Your sensitivity and caring are most appealing. *A bientot*," whispered Brigitte, sliding through the partially open door.

Brigitte had violated two promises in one night: using sex with another man for material gain and using Sean, her charge, for self-comfort. Even though they continued through a very enlightening conference, somehow Brigitte and Sean's relationship had changed. On the way home, Sean was the first one dropped off in Wildwood, just twenty miles from Cape May, so he could start clamming and earning some money for the family. Driving Louie on to Philadelphia, Brigitte had somewhat of an unsettling issue to deal with when he dropped this bomb: "I'm going to marry you someday, Brigitte, just watch," he proudly confessed in an innocent tone.

She smiled and said, "Louie, things just do not happen that way. I take it as a wonderful compliment, though."

"Well, it seems like you're the happiest when Sean's around and maybe even a little jealous when he's around other girls," Louie observed.

"Louie, you are a bright, wonderful, talented boy, but you are confusing my maternal feelings as a caregiver with something else all together. When you have cared for someone since childhood, you have motherly love for him—that is all, nothing else. Now you forget all about this and go and have a great summer and come visit us in Wildwood."

On the way back to the Shore, Brigitte again became emotional. She couldn't believe that she had crawled in bed with Sean, slept with someone inappropriately, and now had Louie all confused. She pulled into the cottage driveway just as Sean steered his clamming boat into the slip and was tying up. She got out of the car and walked toward the dock. She watched as he hoisted bushels of clams from the boat.

"I must speak with you Sean. Please come up here and sit down. Do you know anything about my past?" Brigitte said as Sean climbed the short ladder and took a seat on the dock bench.

"Just that you're a w-wonderful person and that you've been a real b-blessing to me and my family."

"No, I mean do you know what I did before I came to America?"

"Why does it m-matter?" Sean asked.

"I was a teenager who worked the streets of Paris. The Quakers were the only people who were there for me. Mr. Lafoussier took me to church one day at La Rive Gauche Meeting, and a woman was there who ministered to prostitutes. She helped me understand God's love and in a few months got me off the street. Within a year, the World Peace Organization placed me in a home in America. Your home, Sean," Brigitte confessed.

"Do my parents know?"

"*Oui, mon cheri.*"

Obviously surprised by her news, Sean was able to offer, "You're s-special to us, Brigitte. That's all that m-matters.

"Merci, Sean. *Je t'aime.*"

For several nights Sean heard Brigitte crying. It was early

in the season, and they had been alone in the cottage for almost a week. Brigitte decided that she could no longer continue under the current living arrangements and announced that she would make other provisions.

"Why?" Sean asked, knowing the reason.

"Because I know I'm corrupting you and your friends, and I'm not doing what *Dieu* wants me to do."

"No, I disagree," Sean responded.

"I must. I'm going to call Marge and Sam and talk to them about it."

Margaret and Sam tried to talk Brigitte out of moving but she was determined. They contacted the Meeting to have her placed in another home after Labor Day and made temporary arrangements for her to stay at a large home on the water, just a block from the Easley's cottage.

Most days after clamming, Sean worked at a trampoline center on the boardwalk. Opportunities abounded for him to have interludes with teenage girls who got a charge out of watching him in a full sweat, performing what they considered amazing and daring feats on the trampoline—double backs and triple twisters. It was his athletic prowess that lured them to him—like a dancer, always graceful but powerful. He liked working there because he didn't have to talk very much and found it easier to communicate nonverbally through his facial expressions and gestures. Sean's long hair and tanned, muscular body, coupled with his raw innocence, was attracting attention from passersby, most of them women.

Surreptitiously, Brigitte often walked along the boardwalk after work to catch a glimpse of Sean. She loved to watch him perform and was careful never to allow him to spot her. She was proud of her special creation but didn't want anyone to misunderstand the way she cared for him.

Fortunately, in early August, Louie and Sonny arrived in Wildwood to start preparations for the football season. Louie had worked at Willow Grove Amusement Park during summer break while Sonny worked at Deli-Land. Sonny's summer was especially noteworthy, having won the National AAU Boxing Championships for the first time.

American Bandstand also came to Wildwood in August, giving the trio a chance to perfect their dance steps and to be on television. Sonny and Louie kept busy while in Wildwood with two grueling football workouts by day and a great social life by night. Their arrival helped rein Sean in from further spinning out of control with the young women and straying further and further from being a good Quaker boy.

The early morning beach workouts had begun to attract a group of fans. At seven thirty, they would hit the soft sand near the boardwalk. Sean had convinced Sonny and Louie that running in soft sand provided a great foundation for speed. The tourists on the boardwalk were always entertained as they watched their exhaustive workouts of distance running, sprints, and various drills. But it was jumping and somersaulting off the boardwalk railings that gave fans the greatest thrill. Sean would often do a double-back somersault, followed by Sonny's somersaults with half twists. After two hours of that, the boys snoozed or went to the beach. Later in the afternoon, they were back on the beach but this time on the hard sand for sprints, hopping, skipping, then throwing and catching. Sonny's arm not only caught the attention of the boardwalk folks but some other footballers passing by. On one occasion, a man dressed unlike a summer tourist, came to watch one of their evening beach pickup games. Sean, Sonny, and Louie had just finished whipping some college guys in touch football. He introduced himself as a coach from West Point, Mr. Schroeder.

"Do you know who you just whipped up on?" he asked.

"No," the boys replied in unison.

"That was the starting quarterback from Syracuse and their best wide receiver and someone I don't know. You ran right by them. Where do you fellas play?"

"We'll play for Abington High this fall," Louie answered.

"You mean you're still in high school?"

"Just st-starting; this will be our f-first year," Sean added.

"Wow! You guys are somethin' else. What are your names?"

"Louie Jackson, Sonny Goldman, and Sean Easley," Louie proudly announced.

"Do me a favor and keep West Point in mind when it comes time for college. We have a great football tradition you know."

"Thanks Mr. Schroeder, we'll do that, but Sean and I are Quakers, so West Point would be a tough choice," Louie answered.

"That's okay; just think of us when the time comes. I sure won't forget you guys."

While Sean was committed to working out and loved honing his football skills on the beach, he was usually eager to have an evening activity planned that involved Sonny and Louie and a choice of girls he had met at the trampoline center. Once they chose the lucky girls, Sean would arrange for the group to get into the dance at the Starlight Ballroom. Many of the male ballroom regulars were effeminate and this made the trio even more popular with the girls. Louie's favorite dance was the strand; Sonny's was the stroll, which he was particularly good at, especially when it was his turn to do the interpretive dancing down the center; and Sean liked it all. All-American boys and good dancers added up to romantic opportunities at the end of each evening. When it was time to go, the boys often found that they wanted to be with the same girl, which had the makings of a potential problem. Many times they would walk the girls home, have some romantic fun and head on out to the Easley's cottage in West Wildwood, a mile from the beach.

During a walk home one evening Sonny said, "Maybe we shouldn't be doing this."

"Doing what?" asked Louie.

"Dating every night and going to the Starlight. Seems like competition over the senoritas might change things between us. When it comes to girls, I don't want it to mess up our thing."

"*Toujours Amis*," Sean reminded them. "You're right Sonny. When it comes to sports, we're really t-tight, but when it comes to g-girls, something changes. Let's cool it, even at Abington."

"By the way, how is Brigitte doing?" Louie asked in an effort to change the flow.

Sean answered, "I d-don't really know."

"Did anything happen between you two?" Sonny asked.

"No, nothing compared to Louie t-telling her he was going to m-marry her," Sean laughed.

"I'm still planning on it," Louie said.

Sean countered, "She had to leave because she felt b-bad about corrupting us."

"That's pretty lame," Sonny said.

"Yeah," Louie said. We'd all be better off praying more instead of hustling the ladies."

It's agreed then," said Sean. "*Toujours Amis*, f-forever. I need to break away from all this s-stuff anyway. It's habit forming."

"Fess up, Sean. How many times did you get some this summer?" asked Louie.

Sean just smiled.

"Oh, you stud. Or should I say you st-st-stud?" Louie mocked, even though he knew Sonny was going to pound him for making fun of Sean's stutter. "What's Cassandra going to say when you get back to sc-sc-school?" he yelled as he ran ahead with Sonny on his heels.

Sean thought it was funny. "C-come on, you guys."

As they continued their walk home, the smells of the Back Bay became more pungent.

"I love that smell," Louie said as he inhaled deeply.

"I prefer the smell of our bakery at Deli-Land," Sonny said, waving a hand in front of his scrunched up nose.

They walked by Dot's Spot, one of West Wildwood's finest nightclubs. From the street, you heard the sounds of the band and people laughing.

"We could end up like that," Sonny said.

"Like what?" Louie asked.

"Like them in there, the regulars, lost in the same old routine—going nowhere." Sonny motioned with his head to Dot's Spot.

Knowing that they had settled some important issue on the way home, they knew they would get a good night's rest at the Easley's cottage and then be off to football camp in a few days.

That summer Sean changed forever. He was maturing quickly, and even though he had deviated from what he knew in his heart was right, his "forever friends" were there to help keep him on track.

Abington High

The first week of school had not ended when a six-foot five, colored basketball player challenged Sean to a fight over Cassandra. Apparently, she had professed her love for Sean. When the basketball player asked her why, she wouldn't give him the time of day. He didn't cotton to whites in the first place and couldn't stand seeing the nicest looking colored girl at Abington having a thing for Sean. The confrontation happened in the locker room right before football practice and preseason basketball practice. Sean who was putting on his football gear was shocked when Leon pulled a knife on him in front everyone.

Sonny and Louie tried to jump in, but Sean calmly raised his hands and said, "I d-don't fight. Do what you w-want, but I will not raise a hand against y-you."

"Big pussy retard!" yelled Leon as he lunged and stuck the knife in Sean's leg.

Coach Carter heard the altercation and came running to find Louie and Sonny dragging Leon away from Sean.

"What's up, men?" asked Coach Carter.

He was the youngest coach on the basketball staff and immediately assessed the situation to Leon's benefit. The knife was on the floor in front of Sean and blood had saturated the right leg of his football pants.

"Whose knife is that?" Coach Carter asked a silent Sean. "You know you can't bring a knife to school. I'm sorry, but I'm going to have to tell Dr. Hiram, Sean," Carter retorted.

Dr. Hiram was the disciplinarian at Abington High. Unfortunately for Sean, he was best friends with Mr. Turner, the vice principal at Huntington Junior High, who Sean had the run-in with over the dance funds. This was a chance for the Abington administrators to get back at Sean and the Easley family. Sean entered Dr. Hiram's office about the time practice was beginning in only football pants, a T-shirt, and socks.

"Why a switchblade, Sean? How can a Quaker carry a knife?" asked Dr. Hiram.

"I d-don't carry a switchblade, Dr. Hiram."

"You know knives are not allowed in school."

"I d-didn't have one in school D-Dr. Hiram."

"That's just too bad, Sean. You're suspended for tomorrow's game, and by the morning, I'll have decided about suspension from school. And don't think you can ride the bus home either."

Sean was devastated. The rumors spreading around the football field crushed Sonny and Louie.

"That ding dong," Sonny said. "Why wouldn't he just turn Leon in?"

"I sure don't know," Louie said. "Sean is just different. You should know that by now."

Sean wouldn't be able to reach his parents. The only person he could call was Brigitte who was now living with another family from Abington Meeting.

"Brigitte, this is Sean. *Je ne vais pas bien.*"

"What's wrong?" she asked.

"Can you pick me up at sk-school."

"*Pour quoi?*"

"Please, just d-do it. I'll explain later."

In ten minutes Brigitte drove up and Sean jumped in.

"What's wrong?"

"I got s-suspended."

"For what?"

"Carrying a switchblade."

"That's impossible. You'd never carry a knife."

"I didn't."

"Then why are you suspended?"

"Some dummy w-wanted to fight me and then knifed me 'cause I wouldn't fight. It was over Cassandra."

"This is serious, Sean. Think of the paradox, a Quaker who will not fight but carries a switchblade. This must be corrected," Brigitte demanded.

During a break in practice, Sonny and Louie had already gone to Coach Weber and told him the true story.

"There are some people who are really out to get Sean, but I'll see what I can do," Coach replied.

Cassandra was at cheerleading practice when she heard the news and immediately called her father. Mr. Washington hated the fact that Cassandra had feelings for Sean but also wanted Sean treated fairly. He called Dr. Hiram on Sean's behalf. Because of his position with the NAACP, it appeared that most of the administration of Abington listened to Mr. Washington.

Little was said during the ride from school to Sean's house in Hollywood. Pulling in front of the house Sean said, "I miss you, Brigitte."

"I miss you too, Sean," she told him. "I was looking forward to watching you play tomorrow night."

"Sometimes things d-don't work out as planned. I was really psyched for the game, but I guess I'll be l-listening to it on the radio."

"*A bientot*, Sean."

Sean turned and kissed Brigitte on the cheek before he hurried from the car. "Thanks for the lift, good-bye."

The chemistry between Sean and Brigitte was still there but remained confusing for both of them. As Sean shut the car door, he smiled and winked at Brigitte, but then began welling up with tears as he headed upstairs to his room to wait for Sam and Marge, his hopes of playing in the first game apparently down the tubes.

Shortly after he arrived home, Dr. Hiram called Sean. "I understand there might be some extenuating circumstances in your case, Sean. Come to school tomorrow and report directly to my office so we can figure this out."

When Sam and Marge got home, Sean explained the situation.

Margaret was irate. "Sean, how could you lie to protect someone who attacked you?"

"I m-made a mistake, Mom, but I'm going to st-stick with it."

"Sleep on it son," Sam said. "God will show you the way."

As Sean entered Dr. Hiram's office the next morning, he was wearing what he wore most days: dark pants, a white collared shirt, and a dark sweater. He still had the longest hair in the school, over the ears and collar. His long hair was a silent protest against people being judgmental when it came to appearance. He wanted them to look at the inner person. For him, his hair length was a barometer of just how judgmental some people were.

Sean found Leon sitting in one of the two chairs in front of Dr. Hiram's desk.

"What are you going to tell Dr. Hiram?" Leon asked.

"The s-same thing as yesterday," answered Sean.

"It doesn't matter because I'm still going to mess you up bad," threatened Leon.

"Do what you gotta d-do, Leon," Sean responded, looking him right in the eyes.

Dr. Hiram treated Sean differently from the day before. He started with, "I need to know whose knife it is."

Sean just looked at him.

"Is it yours, Leon?"

"Yes," Leon admitted.

"Then you're suspended, Leon," Hiram said, in his futile attempt to be fair.

Leon quickly defended his position. "Dr. Hiram, you don't understand. I don't live in the district. I live in North Philly. Unless I carry a switchblade, I won't make it on the subway, and I have to make two bus transfers just to get to and from school every day!"

"Well, Leon, that does change things somewhat, but you

both have ten detentions for fighting,"

"That's impossible, Dr. Hiram," Sean said. "I get a detention for f-fighting? You know I wouldn't f-fight."

"Well, *you* created the conflict," Hiram forced.

"How?" Sean countered.

"I think you'd be better off not being so close to Cassandra," said Dr. Hiram. Leon shook his head yes.

"I c-can't accept the detentions," Sean said emphatically.

"Oh really, Sean? Not only do you have ten detentions but also because of your arrogance, you're not playing in the first half of the game tonight. I'll give Coach my disciplinary orders."

Sean stood to leave and said with uncharacteristic sarcasm, "Thank you f-for your understanding."

Hiram was irate as Sean left his office. Cassandra was waiting. She quickly grabbed his hand in an effort to console him. "I'm so sorry, Sean."

"You're w-worth it, Cassandra," Sean smiled at her, squeezing her hand.

Beaming, she desperately wanted to hug him.

Cassandra was startled to find Leon and Dr. Hiram coming out of the office door, shaking hands and laughing.

Glaring at the two of them, Cassandra commanded Leon through pursed lips, "Don't *ever* talk to me again!"

The first football game was to be Louie's and Sonny's real coming out party. Sean was okay with not starting, but Sonny and Louie were both upset by it.

"Don't w-worry about it. This is y-your day. *Toujours Amis.* I don't know when I'll get in the g-game, but I'll make sure everyone knows I'm there."

The Jacksons, Easleys, and Goldmans sat together at the first game, as they would at all the games. Susan and Margaret passed the time talking about their families and missed most of the nuances on the field that made their sons special. Brigitte made sure to make it to all the games and sat with Mrs. Jackson, as they intently watched every play.

On the opening kickoff, Louie ran the ball ninety-seven yards for a touchdown and left the entire stadium spellbound by his speed, open-field running, quickness and confidence. When he scored, he simply placed the ball on the ground and ran to the sideline. Four plays later he was back on the field to return a punt. He fielded it on the fifty-yard line and running full speed, he was in the end zone in less than six seconds for the second score.

On the ensuing kickoff, Central Bucks fumbled. The next play, Sonny threw Louie a swing pass in the right flat, and he scampered thirty-seven yards untouched for a third touchdown in less than four minutes. The crowd went wild. At the end of the first half, Louie had scored four touchdowns.

At thirty-five to zero, it appeared that Sean would never get in the game, but surprisingly, Coach Weber called him at the beginning of the second half saying, "Do a buttonhook!"

Sean did a 'buttonhook and go,' leaving the defender on the ground and scoring an eighty-eight-yard touchdown. The crowd went ballistic!

"We don't want to run up the score, Sean. It was just supposed to be a buttonhook. Why did you do that?" questioned Weber.

"The d-defender cut in front of me on the buttonhook, so the g-go was open and Sonny knows that I'll go if the defender breaks on the hook. It's n-natural," Sean responded.

"You should have moved back towards Sonny, not the goal line. Sit down, Sean," Coach adamantly instructed.

Sean got one more play in the second half but Sonny was not the quarterback. He caught the ball over the middle and ran seventy-seven yards untouched for another touchdown. His speed visibly astounded the spectators. Oohs! and aahs! swept through the stands. At the conclusion of the game, Louie had five touchdowns, Sonny had five touchdown passes, and Sean had two catches, both for touchdowns and over 160 yards in receiving. The final score of the game was 58-17.

Unlike most of the other boys on the team, who leave their parents in the stands after the games and do their own thing, Louie, Sonny, and Sean, along with their families, go to Deli-Land to eat and celebrate their friendship. Cassandra was always on Sean's arm, and everyone treated her like family. Abe, during these affairs, was always at his best—dancing around the restaurant with someone. Business was terrific after games, mostly due to the draw Abe had. He would introduce the gang to the other patrons, which established a spirit of camaraderie and a real following for the boys.

The day after the opening game, *The Philadelphia Inquirer* headlines read, "Jackson and Goldman Dominate Central Bucks." The first week at Abington was a foreshadowing of much that was in store for the trio. Sonny and Louie were living their dreams, and the Abington High administration was committed to complicating Sean's life.

A Time of Testing

With the trio and Cassandra becoming the talk of the town, the rest of their years in Abington flew by. They were "all–something or other" in whatever sport they did, including Cassandra. Academically, Louie and Sonny were doing great, making high honors without fail. Sean found school extremely easy but did not get the grades he deserved, and Cassandra was continually one of the brightest students at Abington. The four friends continued to become closer and closer. Sean and Cassandra were always together, no doubt, in some part due to the abhorrent racism they faced on a daily basis. Cassandra always defended Sean against those who poked fun at his speech, and she absolutely flipped out over those making light of his religion. Maybe it was because of the constant realization that society had yet to fully accept their respective heritages that brought them closer together, or maybe it was just fate.

Sean soon found out that he had bigger problems in school than football. He had taken the SATs in October and scored a combined 1410 with a perfect score of 800 on the SAT French achievement test. Dr. Hiram, upon finding out about his sterling SAT performance, officially made a request to the Scholastic Aptitude Testing Board to determine if Sean could have cheated. When Mrs. Chandelor, Sean's guidance counselor, called Sean in and began questioning him about where and when he took the SAT, he realized she was assuming that he had done something wrong.

Sean immediately called his dad, "Something is r-really wrong, D-Dad. They don't b-believe I took the SAT. They're questioning me like I c-cheated."

"I'll be right there, Son," Sam assured.

When Big Sam entered Mrs. Chandelor's office, about forty-five minutes later, he asked, "What's wrong with Sean's SAT?"

"We find it very difficult for a person with an IQ of less than 100, who is matriculating in general studies, and has a serious speech impediment to have achieved such a high SAT. Dr. Hiram has ordered an official investigation," Mrs. Chandelor said.

Sam blew up. Sean had never seen his father so angry. "Sean's IQ is 143 and he speaks French fluently and stuttering has nothing to do with intelligence!" Sam yelled, losing his usual subdued demeanor.

"That's impossible! And don't raise your voice at me," said Mrs. Chandelor.

"I apologize," Sam said, storming out and heading directly for Dr. Hiram's office suite.

After a frustrating visit with Dr. Hiram, he went directly to the superintendent's office where he surmised that Mr. Turner must have changed Sean's official records in a vengeful move over the missing money incident in junior high. To complicate matters even more and much to Sean's and his father's vexation, the superintendent defended his administrators, and the incident accelerated Dr. Hiram's resolve to get Sean.

"You know, Sean, although it's exceedingly unfair, Abington is not going to give you a fair chance," surmised Sam.

"What should we d-do?" asked Sean.

"We'll figure something out. You just do the best you can. I'm very upset about what's going on. For now, be careful about what you say and do. It's only going to get worse until we get this sorted out," Sam advised.

Football season ended with Abington going undefeated. When all-conference, all-city and all-state honors came out, Louie made first team on them all. Sonny was second team across the board and Sean wasn't even listed in all-district but was named first team on the all-Philly team and all-state honorable mention. How was it that someone leading the district in receptions, yards gained as a receiver, and touchdowns could not make all-district? It was easy to figure out—coaches voted for all-district and the media voted at the all-city and all-state slots.

Sonny and Sean had a great swimming season. Louie blew people away in hoops and on the track. Their accomplishments, including Cassandra's, did not go unnoticed. She had become a champion in the quarter mile, partially as a result of her desire to run and workout in the same events as Sean.

Sean, although accomplishing a lot in sport, was different from his peers. This was never more apparent than at social gatherings where he wasn't afraid to tell any girl how nice she looked. He often did more with smiles and hand gestures than with words, minimizing his speech malady. Brigitte had fostered a young man with few hang-ups and who enjoyed complimenting women. Even though he did not like exposing his speech problem, Sean was regularly surrounded in the lunchroom by an eclectic group of girls—white, colored, rich, poor—laughing and making them feel comfortable, putting to ease their fears of not being accepted and boosting their self-confidence. Some thought they rallied around because they felt sorry for him, but to the astute observer it was because he was the kindest boy in school and they wanted to be the recipient of his gentleness and compassion. Amazingly, Cassandra never got jealous because she knew that Sean had a unique capacity for loyalty that was truly remarkable compared to his peers.

Some of the country club boys thought he was queer and often told him so. They were usually rich white kids who weren't involved in sports and didn't like to dance, thinking it was for sissies. They took pride in the fact that their fathers were members of Manufacturers' or Huntington Valley Country Clubs. These kids made fun of everyone. It was hard for Sean to like most of these types.

Some of Sean's friends thought that Dr. Hiram was fueling the continual negativity coming from some of the teachers. One teacher, Mr. Ryan, substantiated that theory when Sean asked why he received a C with a ninety-five average instead of an A on his report card.

Mr. Ryan apologetically offered, "Sean, I'm sorry, but I can't discuss this with you other than to say that your grade stands." Ryan knew he would jeopardize his future tenure and might even lose his job if he ratted Hiram out. Ryan continued, "I can say that you are a familiar subject in faculty meetings, and some feel you just don't belong at Abington. I'm sorry, Sean."

After this blatant admission from Mr. Ryan, something happened to Sean—he stopped caring.

Even Cassandra knew for sure what was going on and called

apprehensively to confirm his impending doom at Abington. "I know for sure, Sean, that you're being screwed by Abington. My dad asked Dr. Hiram why Sean Easley isn't in the Abington Hall of Fame like every other person who has made all-state. He told my dad that a bastard like you would never graduate from Abington. I don't want you to leave, but the way things are stacking up, I'm afraid I won't ever see you again."

Sean said sadly, "Cassandra, m-my folks don't have enough money to help me go anywhere else. Besides, how could I ever leave the finest B-Bristol Stomper in Philly? I'll hang in there."

Cassandra laughed because she hated the Bristol Stomp and thought it was the biggest honky dance of all time.

Despite the downward turn of events, the highlight of their time at Abington had to be a few days around the Penn Relays. They were in the finals of the High School Mile Relay Championship of America, competing against several Caribbean and southern high schools. They got in the finals by posting one of the sixteen fastest times in the morning preliminaries out of the 500 other schools competing for the coveted title.

The finals were something to behold. The late April afternoon was sunny—the temperature in the seventies with no wind. Sixty thousand track and field enthusiasts filled the stadium. There was something that set Abington's relay team apart from the others—they had two colored boys and two white boys. The other teams were either all colored or all white. Even though integration had occurred in the North much earlier, there were still too few totally integrated schools.

The boys pulled off one of the most stunning upsets in the Penn Relays' history. They had been lucky to even make the finals, winning their heat because of Sean's come-from-behind performance and doing their best time by some three seconds. If several of the top 500 teams entered in the event had run their best times, Abington would not have qualified. Sean never wanted to run individual events—no one knew why or how fast he really was, but he demonstrated remarkable ability on relays. He never cared about time; he just raced.

It could have been the media that created such an unusual reaction to Abington's success, or it could have been that an unknown white boy ran down the nation's elite runners. Most likely, it was the hope that stirred in the hearts of Americans for racial equality and unity portrayed by the achievements of two white and two colored boys. The pictures in *The Inquirer* and *Sports Illustrated* were everywhere—in schools, businesses, and in every Abington home.

On the surface it seemed to be a sort of healing between the races, but as soon as they left Franklin Field, Cassandra and Sean were reminded that society had a long way to go. They had left the stands shortly after the press started pursuing Sean. Hand-in-hand they were smiling as they passed a group of colored men sitting on a wall outside, people watching. They began shaking their heads and loudly grumbling to make sure they were heard.

"What a waste of an African queen," one protested with a disapproving nod.

Sean and Cassandra kept walking and just squeezed each other's hand a little tighter. Within in a few moments they passed a white man with a lunch box coming from his shift at work. He spit in disgust. Again, they ignored his actions and kept walking. Each such encounter seemed to make them closer and more committed to overcome the obstacles their relationship presented.

Abe had summoned everyone to the back room at Deli-Land for a victory celebration. He and Susan were there with Sonny and his new girlfriend, Bunny Herrman, and were pouring drinks and putting food on the table for a feast. Big Sam, Margaret, and Brigitte were sitting next to each other. Louise, Louie, and his rotund brother Dewey were also there with Leander and his grandparents. Sean and Cassandra entered the festivities to clapping and cheers. They took seats at the table across from his family and close to the dance floor. Brigitte smiled at Sean. Cassandra curiously took note.

Big Sam stood and gained the attention of everyone by repeatedly tapping his knife against his glass. Lifting his glass for a toast—or prayer—he said, "To God's love and may He bless this food."

All followed with a chorus of "Amen!"

Abe stood, commanded everyone's attention, and began, "I remember when Sonny met Sean. I never thought our families would become friends and now here we are celebrating together—the best of friends. Louie, Leander, it has been terrific getting to know your families. Now, here's to the High School Mile Relay Champions of America!"

Everyone stood in honor of the winning relay team. The toasts and speeches continued with Brigitte standing to be recognized. *"Mes chere amis*, I am so proud of my boys."

Big Sam interrupted with, "And we're so grateful to you, Brigitte, for all you have done for them."

Brigitte smiled and continued, "I do not know if I can get

through this." Taking a deep breath she continued, "It was ten years ago when I came here, just your age," she said as she looked at the boys. "I had no home and no future, but Sam and Margaret, you made me part of your home. You entrusted me with the care of your son."

Again Big Sam interrupted with, "A finer caregiver there never was," as everyone nodded in agreement.

"And Sean, you were always a challenge. *Mon Dieu*, always running, running..."

This time Louise interrupted with, "Fastest white boy I ever did see!" creating excitement.

Big Sam added, "His mother is faster than he is on and off the track!" Everyone laughed as Margaret blushed with slight embarrassment.

Again, Sean and Brigitte looked at each other in a way that made Cassandra very uncomfortable.

Brigitte continued, "Yes, Margaret may have caught Sean but I never could. For all of this I am eternally grateful." Pausing to drink some water, she then continued, "As you can tell I am very emotional tonight—not just because of the boys' success, but because...I have decided to go to Montreal and work with the World Peace Organization."

Noticing the stunned look on Sean, Margaret stood to offer her hand in support and hugged Brigitte to break the clear awkwardness. Brigitte held her hand tightly, and many followed suit to congratulate her. Sean sat completely stunned and crushed.

"I have one final request—to see Abe and Sam dance together one more time."

"Boogie Woogie Bugle Boy" abruptly blared from the juke-box, signaling Abe to grab Sam's hand for the jitterbug to ev-eryone's delight. Big Sam always played the role of the woman. Everyone found amusement in their antics except Sean. He was in shock over Brigitte's announcement.

Finishing big and to everyone's applause, Dewey, Louie's younger brother, approached Big Sam and stuck out his finger, "Hey, Mr. Easley, give it a pull."

Sam complied with a yank that triggered Dewey to rip a very impressive fart. Both started laughing hilariously and Sam rewarded the sonic boom enthusiastically with more than the ordinary congratulatory hug.

Not pleased, Louise pled, "Please Sam, don't encourage him."

Hava Nagila played next on the jukebox, and everyone be-gan dancing, except for Sean. As the celebrating continued into the night, Sean's despondency over Brigitte's announcement lessened somewhat.

The next day, Sunday, Sean, Louie, Sonny, and Cassandra sat in a row near the back of Abington Meeting for worship service. Except for the faint tick-tock of the old clock, the silence was al-most overwhelming. Brigitte was on the facing bench with her Montreal friend Guy Lafoussier and a few others. While Sean sat holding Cassandra's hand, he and Brigitte made eye contact several times during the service. The exchange was telling of their complex relationship.

Big Sam stood to speak and broke the twenty-minute si-lence. "As I sit here in the presence of God in this Meeting House, my thoughts are with our forefathers—what they had to endure and the challenges they faced every day. Rather than driving a car to Meeting, which some us today take for granted, they drove a horse and buggy or walked. Rather than warring with the local Indians, they consistently showed God's love to them. Rather than fighting in the Revolutionary and Civil Wars, they advocated peace and worked in the Underground Railroad. Rather than just working to free the slaves, they embraced them and invited them to worship. I am very grateful that the doors of this Meeting are wide enough to allow someone like me because as many of you know, I served as a commander in the U.S. Navy during the War. I appreciate the tolerance that you have shown me. I truly appreciate that word tolerance—it seems to be what we, the Society of Friends, are about. Recently, Dr. King spoke to us and requested help in his movement. Yes, we will help him lift the oppression that continues in the South and elsewhere in our country. I know we will, just like our forefathers have in the past, but let us walk the extra mile and not take the easy way, but the right way, just like our forefathers."

Sam sat down. Louie and Sean looked at each other. Cassandra squeezed Sean's hand. There wasn't another speaker until minutes before the end of the hour-long worship when a woman on the facing bench rose to speak.

"Everyone is invited to a celebration in the John Barnes Room to say *au revoir* to Brigitte. She is leaving us to be married to our frequent visitor, Mr. Guy Lafoussier, from Montreal Meeting and the World Peace Organization." She turned to Brigitte and said, "Brigitte, we will miss you. May God keep you and continue to bless your life. You certainly have blessed ours. I see the boys you helped raise, sitting in the back of Meeting—

our own Sean and Louie with Sonny Goldman. The picture of them on the cover of this morning's *Bulletin* and *Inquirer* transcends more than words can say. Brotherly love is a wonderful thing. This Meeting and our entire community are very proud of your amazing win, and we're proud and thankful for you, Brigitte, and we wish you and Mr. Lafoussier God's very best. Let us all go out of our way to be kind to a stranger this week. God Bless."

This news blew Sean away and Cassandra could sense it. The announcement affected all the boys, but it was a dagger in Sean's heart. He was not himself the rest of the day.

It was obvious that the Abington High administrators particularly hated the picture of Sean and the relay team that was on the cover of *The Philadelphia Inquirer* and the *Bulletin*. *Sports Illustrated* put a picture of the boys' finish-line celebration on their cover later in the week and called them "America's Dream." This seemed to renew Hiram's resolve to "do in" Sean. The school year closed with Sean coming to terms with the fact that he was never going to get a fair shake at Abington. Putting the bad parts of the year behind him, Sean anticipated another great summer in Wildwood. Little did anyone know that it was going to be life changing for him.

Wildwood Beach Patrol

It was this summer that Sean would join the Wildwood Beach Patrol. Because of his swimming accomplishments and the fact that an old classmate from his dad's Wildwood High School days was the captain of the famed beach patrol, his dad arranged for a special lifeguard tryout. Dutch Huffman was genuinely excited to see Big Sam and his son enter the beach headquarters on Lincoln Avenue.

"He's a good looking boy, Sam," Dutch said. "I saw his picture in *The Inquirer* after the Penn Relays. It's hard to believe he's *your* son."

"Thank God his mother's side of the family has good genes," said Sam and they both grinned.

Dutch lectured Sean as to what was going to happen that crisp day in May. "The water temperature is fifty-eight degrees, which means your balls are going to become peanuts as soon as you enter the water. This is a timed test of running through the surf, swimming out 200 yards, circling a boat, and returning back as fast as you can."

Sam, Sean, Dutch, and a few of the beach patrol crew walked down to the water's edge. The crew launched a surfboat to escort Sean during his test. They went out 200 yards and waved to Dutch.

"You ready, Sean?" Dutch asked.

Sean nodded. His body, for a teenager, was very well developed at six feet, two inches tall, and 180 pounds. Dutch was impressed when he saw Sean in his suit getting ready for the start. On "go," Sean ran and hurdled over the waves with ease and was out to the turnaround boat in less than two minutes. When he got to the running depth of the water on his return Dutch told Sam, "He's a real talent, isn't he? No one has ever finished this test in less than five minutes, and he's going to finish a tad over four and a half."

Sean became a member of the Wildwood Beach Patrol that day. In Dutch's office, filling out paperwork and determining when Sean would start, Dutch said, "You know, Sean, you have to be eighteen to be a lifeguard, so I'm sure all of your paper work will reflect that."

The summer challenged and changed Sean's values for the worse. Maybe it was because he had to lie about his age to be a lifeguard and was working on the beach everyday with older, less principled young men. The change was obvious to all who really knew him.

His physical talents set him apart, both as a lifeguard and with the ladies. The days were given to Lifesaving 101 and learning emergency procedures to handle the half million people that would pack the Wildwood beach.

On Sean's first day of work, Dutch announced to all the other guards, "We have a new guy who took the test in May and broke our long-standing record by thirty seconds." The guards stood in uniform with their equipment during muster as Dutch took roll call, made some announcements, and gave out the daily lifeguard stand assignments. This ritual occurred at nine thirty every morning.

When most of the other lifeguards left the beach patrol headquarters, Dutch summoned Sean to his office. "Please shut the door, Sean. So where do you go to college?"

"I'm g-going to be a freshman at Dartmouth."

"Good. What are you going to say if someone says they saw you running in the Penn Relays this year representing a high school?"

"I'd have to say that they had m-mistaken me for someone else."

"Good. I've decided to put you with Jack Downs together as stand partners. He's a Philly firefighter in the winter, and I know he'll take good care of you. He's about to get married—drinks infrequently and doesn't screw around a lot."

"Great, Captain."

"Let's get in the Jeep and I'll drive you down to meet him."

Wildwood extended north from the Lincoln Avenue beach headquarters for almost a mile. Sean's lifeguard stand assignment ended up being on the street where he had bathed as a young boy, and he knew the waters of Pine Avenue like the back of his hand. On the way to Pine, driving along the beach in the Jeep, Dutch must have stopped ten times to say hi to folks he knew, introducing Sean each time. Arriving at Pine Avenue, Dutch told Jack to take care of Sean.

Sean climbed up on the stand and Jack showed him how to hang his rescue buoy and gave him instructions on how to watch the water. After thirty minutes, Jack asked Sean, "Are you fifteen or sixteen?"

"I'm eighteen."

"Cut the shit. We've watched you play football on the beach with your buddies since you were a little kid. In fact, we're real proud of how things turned out for you. I was at the Penn Relays when you ran down those brothers from the Bahamas to give Abington the win—pretty exciting stuff. Remember, Sean, I've been sitting on Pine Avenue for ten years, so let's get one thing straight—you don't feed me any crap and I won't feed you any."

"That's a d-deal," Sean said. "I'm eighteen."

"One thing for sure, Sean, you'll need to take it easy on the partying. The girls are different when they come to the beach. It's like they don't have to worry about their reputations and they really let it all hang out—know what I mean? If you're not careful, they can ruin you! They're easy, fast, and aggressive, and if you don't put them in perspective, they'll cause a big problem for you," Downs lectured.

"Sounds like an interesting p-problem," Sean joked.

"You'll find out."

And he quickly did. Sean talked to lots of people on the beach each day but usually in a manner that was different from the other Wildwood guards. He complimented the girls on their bathing suits, hair, smiles or anything that led into a conversation. It took them a while to overcome his speech pattern, but he had learned that if he disarmed them by being honest and open about his speech malady, they quickly looked past this flaw. He discovered what Brigitte had taught him was true—*how* you say things to a woman is the key. He also discovered that by being nice he could say or ask just about anything to a young woman. Brigitte had always said to "love a woman with your lips" but until now it only had a sexual connotation. Talking to fifty or sixty people a day gave him an advanced course in human relations. He talked to females of all ages, not just the ones he found physically attractive. They talked about their backgrounds and all kinds of stuff, and he intuitively developed abilities to discern what was important to each new acquaintance.

Clearly, Sean was the best swimmer on the beach patrol, and his foot speed found no equal. Consequently, he was first to several rescues, virtually unheard of for a rookie. Somehow, he managed to do more than his share of socializing while constantly scanning the water.

Sean's claim to fame on the beach was introducing a new concept to the lifeguards: mouth-to-mouth resuscitation. The American Red Cross would not teach this controversial technique until years later. Fortunately, one of the instructors at the Abington YMCA had confidence in mouth-to-mouth and taught it to those participating in Y water activities.

One day in August, Jack ran up to the stand and yelled, "Get ready!"

"W-what's happening?" Sean asked.

"Two people are caught in a wash off Oak. It's going to be a long one."

Because Sean sat on the right side of the stand and nearest Oak, he was the first to cover Wildwood Avenue when the Wildwood Avenue guards entered the rescue. His job upon arrival at their stand was twofold. He had to find out if he was needed in the rescue and make sure the bathers at Wildwood Avenue were safe. Sean quickly assessed that it was a multiple victim drowning. Bypassing the Wildwood Avenue stand, he waved Jack into the action and proceeded to sprint toward the two victims who were now well out at sea. Sean took the waves like hurdles and swam past one victim that the lifeguards were towing to shore. He headed further out to sea searching for the other victim. The waves continually interrupted his vision, and the frantic bather disappeared in the waves. Sean dove under water, finding the lifeless body of a middle-aged woman by sheer luck. She had been trying to help her son when the riptide sucked her out.

By the time other guards reached the area, Sean called them to form a human chain to help get her to shore. While still in the water, he worked on her to bring her back to life. He continued to place pressure on her chest by hugging her rhythmically, with interspersed breathing into her mouth while balancing her on his lifesaving buoy. She wasn't responding. After four rotations, still a long way from shore, she vomited. He turned her, using seawater to wash her off and went back to work. Again, she vomited, but this time it seemed as though she was breathing on her own. When the chain got chest deep, he locked her arms around his neck and with her on his back, he ran to shore. He continued to work with her on the beach as she lapsed again into unconsciousness and was not breathing.

With the arrival of the emergency Jeep, the guards told Sean to put her in the back of the vehicle. He refused saying, "Not until she's all r-right." After a few more rounds of mouth-to-mouth, she came to. Looking up at Sean, she tried to smile in between sobs.

"Thank you…thank you," she sputtered as the other guards placed her in the beach ambulance. A huge crowd assembled and began to cheer. Sean and the other guards returned to their own stands.

Jack was already at the stand when Sean arrived. He was grinning ear to ear and said, "Great job, punk. How does it feel to save a life?"

"Pretty dang g-good!" Sean responded in appreciation.

"There is no better feeling in the world. That's why I'm a lifeguard and a firefighter. Just think, Sean, if you weren't here, that woman probably would have drowned. You have preserved a life today, you Quaker ding-dong. By the way, what was that stuff you were doing to her while we were busting our chops trying to pull you in? It looked a little kinky—poor lady," Downs joked.

"It was mouth-to-mouth resuscitation, and c-considering we were 200 yards offshore when I g-got to her, I thought she'd be dead for sure by the time we got her in, unless I started w-working on her right away in the surf," Sean explained.

"I'm a fireman and we don't do that," Downs admitted.

"Yeah, I guess it's pretty controversial. A guy at the Abington Y used to s-show everyone. He believes it's the best method. I g-guess it's as old as the Bible. Elijah or someone s-s-supposedly started people thinking about it. Just blowing air in the mouth isn't g-good enough; you have to p-push on the chest too," Sean continued.

"What were you thinking when we were training you on back pressure arm lift and back pressure leg lift?" Downs asked.

"Not much," Sean smiled.

"Seriously, Sean, I'd like you to teach me."

"No p-problem, but I'm not going to put my lips around yours, if you d-don't mind!"

Just then a Jeep pulled up, and the driver told Sean to jump in. When he arrived at the building that housed the guard headquarters and the beach hospital, they were transferring the woman to an ambulance. Captain Dutch told Sean to change his uniform and ride to Burdett Tomlin Hospital with her.

"Why am I g-going, Cap?" Sean asked.

"Because Mrs. Whittaker's family asked for you to be with her," Captain Dutch yelled back.

While in the back of the ambulance, Sean observed that attendants didn't seem to know much. He wondered if they were part-timers because they didn't appear to have training in any emergency procedures. Mrs. Whittaker began having a panic attack when she heard the siren blaring, so Sean took her hand and calmed her with reassuring words.

"Hopefully, you'll be back on the b-beach tomorrow."

Fifteen minutes after leaving the beach, they arrived at the emergency room. There the ambulance driver completed a report that indicated that Mrs. Whittaker had drowned. Mrs. Whittaker's daughter who had met them at the hospital turned to Sean and asked, "If she drowned, wouldn't she be dead?"

"Give m-me a minute to speak with the doctor. I'll be right back," Sean assured her. Entering the trauma center, an orderly stopped him. "The only way you'll know what happened is to allow me in here. I was the g-guard who pulled her in and resuscitated her. They *may* just want to see me," Sean declared.

The obnoxious orderly held his ground and wanted Sean to leave until Mrs. Whittaker lifted up her head and forcefully told him, "He saved my life, Sir, and he's staying with me."

Shortly thereafter, the doctor entered the examining room.

"For a drowning victim you look pretty good," he smiled. "Tell me what happened."

Mrs. Whittaker, nodding toward Sean said, "He will."

"And who are you?" he asked.

"I'm the guy who p-pulled her out. She must have been underwater for at least thirty seconds and no t-telling how long before that she took in water. I was lucky to find her at all. She was more than 200 yards off shore and five feet under when I found her, and she wasn't breathing," Sean reported.

"Okay then, did she just wake up?" the doctor asked.

"No, I gave her mouth-to-mouth resuscitation. I just kept compressing her ch-chest and blowing air into her mouth," Sean continued.

"Where did you learn that? We don't even use the technique in the hospital because it hasn't been approved yet," he said, both surprised by the technique Sean used and by his speech.

"I d-don't think I had an option. It was just a natural thing to do. I started w-working on her in the water when she vomited almost right away, Then I started b-breathing into her again. On shore the same thing happened, in and out of b-breathing on her own, and then finally she seemed to have all her faculties back," Sean further explained.

"He was my angel," whispered Mrs. Whittaker.

Sean realized he needed to get to work at the trampoline center. The doctor finished asking some questions and confirmed that Mrs. Whittaker would be fine. Shaking Sean's hand, the doctor thanked him for his hard work. Mrs. Whittaker smiled and gave Sean a long and silent hug.

The ambulance driver and attendant gave Sean a lift back

to the beach. While sitting in the back of the emergency vehicle, Sean reflected on the events of the day and realized that neither cheering fans in a stadium or the caress and adoration of a woman could ever compare to the feeling of saving a life. Sean knew that God had given him some special abilities and he needed to use them to help mankind. He remembered his dad saying how he felt when he invented how to do things in the war that saved lives and how he felt when God used him, but he never could quite understand exactly what he meant until now.

While lifeguarding was giving Sean a new purpose and conviction, the rest of the summer was going the wrong way. He was caught up in partying and carousing until Cassandra caught wind of it. With her bikini-clad knockout body, she surprised Sean one day by showing up at the lifeguard stand. He was glad to see her.

They were a good fit in every way except color, but that didn't bother either one of them. It did, however, bother a bunch of other folks. Sean never experienced racial bigotry as he did in Wildwood, and each time they encountered prejudice against their relationship or Sean's speech difficulties, they became closer and more determined to fight such stupidity.

Louie and Sonny headed to the beach for football pre-camp. Cassandra and Sean said their good-byes as she headed home for summer cheerleading. Their time together in Wildwood made them more than just young lovers. Sonny and Louie could sense that something about Sean had changed, but with autumn breezes in the air, football consumed their minds.

Enemies at Abington

Leaving Wildwood after their preseason workouts, Sonny and Louie were in great shape both physically and scholastically. They were looking forward to a great school year all-around, especially after learning that a program for gifted students had accepted them for the following summer and that they both had the potential promise of athletic scholarships to Duke.

Sean wasn't so lucky. During the football physical, the Easley's physician, Dr. Santo, suspected that Sean had contracted hepatitis.

"What does that mean?" Big Sam asked Dr. Santo. "How do you get it?"

"It's very contagious, usually contracting it by coming into close contact with someone who has it," Santo told Big Sam. Sean's white blood cell count is off the chart. It could be many things, but I am pretty sure from his liver analysis that it is hepatitis.

Overhearing the conversation, Sean asked, "What d-do you mean?"

Dr. Santo continued speaking directly to Mr. Easley, "I recommend hospitalizing him because his liver enzymes indicate he is very ill. The whole family needs to get gamma globulin shots and so does anyone else with whom he has come in contact in the last month. I'm recommending he be quarantined."

"How 'bout f-football?" Sean asked with a degree of despair.

"Not this year. It will take about eight weeks just for you to get better and then months until you get your strength back," Dr. Santo said adamantly.

"How do my family and friends not get it if it's infectious?"

"Like I said, they need to get shots. So, Sam, if you would call all those who were in close contact with Sean in Wildwood and have them go to Jeanne's Hospital, I'll make arrangements for them to have shots and further testing. Your son is a sick boy, Sam. Notice the yellowing in his skin and the discoloration in the whites of his eyes. He is very jaundiced."

Sam drove Sean to the hospital. They admitted him and took him to a stark room with no television. All those entering the quarantined room were required to wear a mask, gown, and gloves.

The Washingtons needed to be informed. Mr. Washington answered Sam's call unaware of its nature, with concerns of his own. "I'm glad you called, Sam. I've been worried about our kids. Cassandra has totally flipped over Sean. Her entire room is plastered with his pictures. You know I have no problem with their relationship, but we both know that it's going to take them nowhere."

"Well, let me tell you why I called. They quarantined Sean in Jeanne's hospital with infectious hepatitis. We're all getting the necessary shots, and since Cassandra stayed with us in Wildwood, she will probably need them as well."

"Oh my, I'm so sorry. Is Cassandra in serious danger?"

"I think we're all in some danger of contracting it, so please take her to Jeanne's Hospital as soon as possible. Dr. Santo has arranged everything. Sean's temperature has spiked to 105, so please keep him in your prayers. He's in isolation."

"We'll take her right over, but let's make sure we continue our conversation very soon to discuss the kids and where they're headed," Mr. Washington pleaded, concerned about Cassandra.

"Will do. You know, times are changing. I'm not sure we can do anything to stop them. I know they have strong feelings for each other," Sam acknowledged.

"Another time, Sam. Thanks for calling."

Sam called the Goldmans and Jacksons to make sure Sonny and Louie had been checked out and had received their shots.

After a two-week stint, Sean was well enough to leave the hospital. His weight had dropped below 185 pounds. Louie and Sonny, along with their mothers, felt badly for Sean, knowing what football meant to him and that he was in no shape to play.

Susan and Louise convinced Margaret to have Sean recuperate at the Shore for three weeks while waiting for the okay to return to school. Neither Sam nor Marge could take time away from their teaching, so they contacted Brigitte in Montreal to solicit her help in Sean's recovery. Brigitte was truly eager to help.

Sean was glad to go back to the beach, even though Wildwood was nearly void of any activity by the end of September. Cassandra was the only one who totally disapproved of the arrangement. She knew that Sean being alone with a beautiful, twenty-something was not in her best interest, but she knew in the back of her mind that he needed help. She rationalized that since he *was* so sick, she would not have anything about which to be concerned.

Many for her involvement with Sean had already admonished Cassandra. Her parents were at a complete loss as to what to do with this go-nowhere, benefit-no-one, salt-and-pepper affair, and now, this new challenge.

Sam picked Brigitte up at the Philadelphia Airport and then gave her the car to take Sean to the beach. The plan was for them to return to Philadelphia every few days for Sean's checkups at Jeanne's Hospital. The Easleys would be spending the weekends with them at the Shore.

For the first week, Sean was a vegetable, barely getting out of bed, hardly eating and not exercising at all. By the third week, things began to change—he was hungry, going for short jogs, and sunbathing in sixty-degree-plus weather.

Brigitte, overcome with guilt each time she found herself gazing at him soaking up the sun, knew she couldn't go there.

After a few weeks, Dr. Santo gave Sean the go ahead to go back to school. Brigitte was on a plane back to Montreal. Sean was on the phone with Cassandra.

"I have to see you right away," Cassandra whispered into the receiver. Arriving at the Easleys, the first thing out of her mouth was, "I'm afraid for you when you go back to Abington. I think my dad has rallied the colored folks in Cresmont against you to scare you away from me."

"What would you do if I was pregnant, a hypothetical question of course?"

"Well, Cassandra, it looks like we'd only have one option. We'd be getting m-married, no matter what folks would think. Since we both know what it takes to get p-pregnant and we haven't gone there, we're okay," he announced boldly and with a smile.

The next day, Big Sam took Sean directly to the guidance counselor's office where Sean had made arrangements to talk to Mrs. Rudnick about classes. Mrs. Rudnick really liked Sean or at least he could always count on her being honest with him.

"Good to see you, Sean. Abington football is not the same without you," Mrs. Rudnick said as she entered her office.

"Thanks, Mrs. Rudnick. I didn't know you liked football."

"I don't, I'm just a *big* fan of *yours!* Somehow you've challenged a lot of us to rethink our hang-ups. You know, we used to have lots of Quaker boys at Abington, but none who attracted attention quite like you! Let's have a great year, even if there is a six-week delay. I've worked out a schedule for you. Most of your teachers are fans and should be willing to work with you, but keep an eye out for a few of the teachers. You didn't hear it from me, but they may just be in Dr. Hiram's pocket," she said as she directed her attention to Big Sam. Moving her gaze back to Sean she added, "You know, everyone's been talking about you and Cassandra. The topic is certainly stirring up some emotions, so I'd be *real* careful if I were you two," she warned as she led them out of her office, prepared to escort Sean to class.

Louie and Sonny were waiting outside the office door and both jumped on him with hugs.

"You look better than ever!" Sonny said.

"Thanks, g-guys. I wish I could say I missed you bozos!" They all laughed.

"You're a schmuck. *Toujours Amis* my butt!" Louie grumbled.

"You're right. I'll make it up to you. I'll be your p-personal cheerleader," Sean promised and they all grinned.

"E-easy for you to say," Louie mocked. "From what we hear, you've been practicing on a particular cheerleader and know *all* the m-moves," Louie jabbed.

"This is not a locker room, boys, and I need to get Sean to class," interrupted Mrs. Rudnick.

"Later," said Louie and Sonny in unison.

"T. A.," replied Sean, as Sonny and Louie chuckled down the hallway.

After school Sean went home and fell asleep the couch. He woke up to Cassandra's caress.

"I think I made a big mistake last night by telling my mom that I'm pregnant. I wanted to get her reaction. I thought she'd be cool about it, but she blew her top and told my dad. I wasn't even given a chance to explain. I'm sorry I put her and my dad through such a stupid test. I just wanted her to know you'd marry me, and that we've talked about it. She flipped in such a bad way. I heard her bawling in the bathroom half the night; then she and my dad stayed up talking real loud."

"Maybe not the best idea, but what's the worst that c-could happen? We'll be together forever. Some day society will catch up with us—someday," Sean answered unalarmed and not the least bit perturbed by Cassandra's shenanigans.

His words were comforting to Cassandra. They sat in silence and embraced each other.

The Washingtons and Easleys arrived at the Easley home at the same time. Mrs. Washington did not acknowledge Sam or Marge as she barged in their front door and yelled, "Cassandra! Sean! Come here—right this minute!"

Sean tucked in his shirt and straightened his hair with his fingers, sweeping it back from his face. Cassandra straightened her clothes the best she could and fussed with her hair, before they ran up the basement stairs to the kitchen.

Mr. Washington confronted them with, "Why, Sean?"

"Why w-what?"

"Why dishonor my daughter like this?"

"I haven't dishonored her and I never will."

"Do you want to marry Cassandra?" Mr. Washington asked.

"When the time is right, s-sure!"

"If she weren't pregnant, would you want to marry her?" Mr. Washington asked.

"You're making some a-assumptions that are incorrect," Sean calmly stated.

Mrs. Washington's emotions exploded as she blurted out, "You stuttering honky piece of shit!"

Big Sam calmly interrupted, "Let's hold on a minute. Just what's happening here?"

Mrs. Washington lost control as she blasted, "He knocked her up—that's what's happening here!"

Marge tried to console Mrs. Washington, but she pushed her

away. "Quakers? I don't think so. You're a bunch of hypocrites!"

By this time Mr. Washington was fuming. Just as he was about to explode, Cassandra confessed through tears, "I'm so sorry. I made the whole thing up. I got my period a week before Sean came back to school. I love him so much, and I needed to prove to you that he loved me enough to be with me forever." Glaring at her father she loudly accused him, "You told me he'd never want me. And see, he *does* love me!"

"That's it!" "We're out of here and you're out of Abington. Glaring at Sean, Mr. Washington ended with, "I forbid you to ever see Cassandra again! Do you hear me?" The stunned and confused Easleys watched as Mrs. Washington stepped forward and slapped Sean's face.

Sobbing, Cassandra headed toward Sean but was intercepted by her father and dragged to the front door, kicking and screaming. "I love you, Sean! I will always love you!" she cried.

Mr. Washington, Cassandra in tow, headed directly for the still-open car door. Mrs. Washington looked as though she wanted to spit on something or someone. Getting in their Mercedes, the neighbors heard Mr. Washington yelling to his wife, "I think she's brainwashed! I've heard of people capable of doing this. Those Quakers—maybe it's something they just do naturally."

The rest of the ride home was a frenzy of emotions and name-calling. Cassandra cried herself to sleep that night, with thoughts of life without Sean while Mr. and Mrs. Washington conspired against Sean well into the night.

Meanwhile, the Easleys were doing some soul searching.

"Where have we gone wrong? Margaret whined loudly, being overly dramatic as always.

"It's simple, Margaret. You cannot take a vacation from God. Every summer we allow ourselves to skip Meeting and allow the world to be our greatest influence. Those are ingredients for failure and unhappiness," preached Sam. "And Wildwood isn't like it used to be—it's Sin City now. What can we expect? We know what we need to do—talk and listen to God. Would you like to say anything before we pray?"

Just then, Sean's younger sister Margie returned from art school and joined in, "What's going on?"

"Cassandra told her parents that she's p-pregnant, and they flipped," said Sean.

"Is she?" asked Margie.

"Fortunately, not!" Margaret whined loudly.

Sean interjected, "Cassandra is a beautiful and c-caring person. I know she loves me. Because of the color thing—well, we became c-closer, and it's difficult to explain just how it all happened."

"Don't even try. Let's not go there. Let's pray together," Sam said. Sam closed the prayer with, "Let's continue to pray for the Washingtons and for us to get on track serving God."

Margaret cornered Sean and asked him in her hysterical voice just how far he went with Cassandra and how many times and where? Sean refused to answer. She sent him to his room for the rest of the evening.

At school the next day, Dr. Hiram summoned Sean to his office over the PA system. Sean had heard the same announcement before, usually indicating trouble. As he entered Dr.

Hiram's suite, he found Mr. Washington, the police, and some other officials.

"Sean, you're under arrest," said Dr. Hiram.

"W-what? F-for what?" You could hear a slight laugh of unbelief in Sean's voice.

"For sexually abusing Cassandra. You committed a school board violation," Hiram proudly announced. "You're finally out of here!" He waved his hands as to say go! Get out of here!

"Where's C-Cassandra?" Sean asked.

"She's in Abington Hospital," Hiram said in an accusatory tone.

Sean bolted out of Dr. Hiram's office and headed for the woods near the north end of the high school, where he thought he could get away and eventually get to a house to call Big Sam. The cops were good-old boys, and Sean knew both of them well. They did exactly what Sean thought they would do—pretend to chase him but then go in the opposite direction.

Sean was composed when he talked to his dad. Big Sam agreed to pick him up and then find Cassandra. It was about twenty miles from Big Sam's work to Abington, which could take over an hour during the morning rush hour, but Sam got there quickly.

They proceeded to Abington Hospital, where they found Cassandra with her mother. When Mrs. Washington saw them coming, she became loud and obnoxious. Cassandra ran to Sean. Just then the entourage from the high school arrived. They were all supporting the Washington's contention and proceeded in attempting to throw the book at Sean. The police were trying to take Sean into custody.

"I would not be doing that, Sergeant. He's not going anywhere. Give him the courtesy to hear him out," commanded Sam.

Mrs. Washington continued to stew. Cassandra pleaded with Sean, "What's going on, Sean?

"They w-want to charge m-me with r-raping you."

"What?" her mouth fell open.

Looking at Dr Hiram, Cassandra blurted out, "Sean never raped me, nor did anything else wrong to me! My mother and father are making things up that they want to believe." Mrs. Washington slapped Cassandra with such a wallop that even the police were stunned. Cassandra turned to Sean, took his arms and wrapped them around her as she backed into him.

Big Sam took control. Looking at Hiram he said, "Here is the deal. We will not file charges against the school board or the Washingtons or even you for knowingly trumping up false charges. Sean leaves Abington with an excellent record with no asterisks, and if we ever hear of or suspect any undermining of this covenant, we will file with the appropriate authorities immediately. Yes or No?"

"All right, I'll agree," Hiram conceded, after a moment of consideration.

Sean hugged Cassandra. Mrs. Washington wanted to spit in Sean's direction but Cassandra restrained her. The Easleys nodded good-bye. Sean looked straight at Dr. Hiram and smiled, which further infuriated him. So it was, Sean was officially withdrawn from Abington "because of sickness," and the Easleys headed back to Hollywood, totally wiped out emotionally.

"You have had an interesting couple of days. Are you okay?" Big Sam asked Sean.

"I d-don't think it's sunk in yet. I'm not sure what's g-going to happen now," Sean replied hesitantly.

Sam continued thoughtfully, "You know, Sean, problems and the fear of the unknown are sometimes what God uses to get our attention. If we listen to Him, we will get the right answer. Pray, Sean—you will find the right answer through prayer. You will always encounter people who are mean or unfair to you, so be prepared. God also can use others to get you going in the right direction."

Sean was proud of his Dad because he was the only dad he knew who openly spoke of spiritual things. He knew that Meeting House was always better when he spoke. This whole affair was like a bad dream to Sean. It had affected him more than he let on or indeed realized. He was looking forward to getting home to sort things out and petition the heavenlies for needed assistance.

People Who Love People

Sean knew his dismissal from Abington might just give him an opportunity to change for the better. He took a nap in his basement when he got home. When he awoke it was evening, and he could hear voices upstairs. Louie and his mother, Mrs. Jackson, and Sonny and his parents were all in the living room with Sam and Marge. It sounded like a party, as Sean ascended the stairs, with Deli-Land aroma wafting in the air. The Goldmans had brought a spread that could feed the whole football team, and they were going to enjoy it.

Louie greeted Sean by saying, "It's going to be nice not having you around anymore to steal all the headlines. Now, Sonny has to use *me* as his favorite receiver," he laughed. Clearing his throat for serious talk, he said, "All kidding aside, you know that I really love you, man, and I'm gonna miss you, you ding-dong. Just let the "inner light" show you the way, and trust in Him—just like you have often reminded me," he finished with teary eyes.

Sonny countered Louie's farewell remarks with, "You're a schmuck, Sean—anything to make me work harder. Throwing to Louie is no fun. He's got hands like a brick, and if the ball doesn't hit him in the numbers, he complains. But you, if it was in the air, you got it!"

In Susan Goldman's commanding tone she ordered, "Everyone come and eat! We brought some really good stuff, and I even have your favorite drink, Sean—cream soda."

Afterward, they adjourned to the living room, where Mrs. Jackson took the lead. "I know that what happened to you, Sean, was unfair," she began, "but it was also inevitable. Abington Township still cannot handle salt and pepper. I feel God has impressed me with a solution to your problem. I waited until now so I could see you face-to-face to explain what the "light" is telling me to share with you. I think you should go to high school in Montreal. You are fluent in French and the Montreal Friends are a solid group. Brigitte and Mr. Lafoussier can help with all the arrangements and maybe you can even live with them. Things will have a chance to cool down here and maybe, just maybe, Sonny, Louie, and you can be together again."

Margaret wanted to talk about where she went wrong. Sam just wanted to continue to eat. Sonny wanted to play table tennis in the basement, hopeful of defeating Sean before he left for greener pastures. Susan wanted to console Margaret while Louise Jackson was on a mission calling Brigitte in Montreal.

"Hi, Brigitte, this is Louise Jackson."

"*Ma cherie, comment vas-tu?* Is everything okay?" Brigitte asked.

"Not really. Sean needs your help once again, Brigitte. Dr. Hiram has run him out of Abington, and as you know, the Easleys cannot afford to have him live anywhere else or to pay for any schooling. I think you and Guy can play an important role in helping Sean get through high school," Louise continued as Brigitte cut in.

"You know I absolutely adore Sam and Margaret, and Sean and I have always had a special relationship," testified Brigitte. "Put Sam on the phone, *s'il te plait. Merci beaucoup*, Louise. Tell Louie I miss him."

"Hey, Brigitte," greeted Sam.

"Hi, Sam. I sure do miss you, and I miss Abington Meeting very much. Louise asked if Guy and I could help Sean. Perhaps we could assist by keeping him while he attends high school here. I think it is a great idea, but I just have to talk with Guy first. There is a great high school here, St. Jean-de-Brebeuf. It is French, but I know he will fit in quite well."

Before going to the airport, Sean asked his mom to stop by the Meeting House. He spent time petitioning God, praying for a positive experience in Canada. Sean surrendered himself to God. He wanted God to change him, so He could use him more fully. He really hadn't had time to think about everything that was happening, as he hurriedly packed his belongings, and Marge took him to Meeting and finally to the airport.

She noticed that Sean was not stuttering during the ride to the airport. "Sean, I don't notice your speech impediment anymore. Seems like it's gone all of a sudden." Marge was thinking it was because the stress of Abington had been lifted," Sean had a good idea where it came from and just smiled in recognition of His answer.

Before he knew it and after many good-bye hugs, he was aboard a Canadian Air flight to Montreal with a chance to start a new life.

Departing the plane in Montreal, he noticed how markedly colder it was. He was surprised that Mr. Lafoussier greeted him at the gate instead of Brigitte. He had always found Mr. Lafoussier a little creepy, and this time it looked to Sean like he was more than three times older than Brigitte, half bald, and always wearing a hat and dark clothing.

Guy Lafoussier had an angular face and sported a skinny little mustache that Sean considered ugly and scary. He just couldn't understand what Brigitte saw in this man. He was also perplexed as to why Guy and not Brigitte met him.

"*Bienvenue*, Sean. Welcome to Montreal," greeted Guy. "If you don't mind, we will speak in French."

"Manifique," welcomed Sean.

Continuing in French Guy asked, "How many bags do you have?"

"Just two."

"Since the baggage takes such a long time, let's have a coke," suggested Guy. "We were very fortunate to get you in the best school in Montreal. Of course, there won't be any speaking English. I know you can handle that. I think you'll enjoy our home, and you should like the room we've prepared for you."

After Guy ordered two cokes he continued, "I think you will be very comfortable in Montreal and especially with Montreal Meeting. The members are genuine and truly good people. I should tell you, though, that most of them think Brigitte and I are married; we are not, and for the time being we are content to let them think that we are, so please keep that to yourself. Brigitte uses my surname. They believe we were married in Philadelphia. Now let's get your bags and get you to your new home. We can continue talking in the car. I have something I'd like you to consider doing for both Brigitte and me."

Sean and Guy walked to baggage claim where an Oriental-looking man met them and spoke to Guy in French. Guy introduced him to Sean, but Sean failed to catch his name. Sean and his new acquaintance each grabbed a bag. They were heading toward a large black car, the likes of which Sean had never seen before, parked, and guarded immediately in front of the airport. Mr. Lafoussier and Sean situated themselves in the roomy backseat, separated from the Oriental man and the driver by a soundproof glass partition.

As the window went down, Mr. Lafoussier suggested, "Let's take a ride along Riverside Drive, so Sean can see some of Montreal. I'll let you know when to head home."

Pushing the control to close the partition, Mr. Lafoussier continued privately with Sean, "As I told you earlier, I'm really worried about Brigitte, and I could use your help. She is a lovely, wonderful young woman. We're not officially married, and our relationship is platonic by choice. Yet, I would like to provide for her happiness."

Sean could see Guy's eyes begin to water as he continued, "Sean, please look at me and believe me when I say this to you—I want you to know that I need you to be with her when I travel. She gets terribly lonely when I'm gone and she needs comforted and protected."

Although Sean had dreamed of comforting her before, he couldn't believe what he was hearing. He had been in "la-la land" for months back at Abington, but this one was way out there. Is he asking what I think he's asking? Sean pondered.

I had been praying about the situation when Louise called and asked if you could finish high school in Montreal, so I believe your being here is an answer to prayer. I've asked you to protect Brigitte in my absence, but please do not bring dishonor to the Lafoussier name and home. You and Brigitte have a very unusual relationship that most people will never understand. I just want her protected and cared for always.

Sean was in shock, as he sat looking more out the window than at Guy.

Guy started back into his orientation of Montreal, without skipping a beat, "You will find here in Canada that unlike the English, the French are not racists. A complicated comment for a French Canadian Quaker," continued Guy. "Even in historic Penn's Woods, bigotry prevailed. Sometimes, you have to pay a price for what is right, and your situation back in Abington was very complicated from what Brigitte told me."

Sean thought to himself, "You've got to be kidding me. This man just asked me to be with his lady, and he is talking to me about doing what's right." Sean stared through the window at the St. Lawrence while thinking how many nights he had dreamed about having an opportunity with Brigitte. But now this seemed perverse and wonderful at the same time.

"Sean…," Guy raised his voice to get Sean's attention, "Sean, that's Nuns Island, *a droite*. I grew up on that island as a boy. It used to be farms and estates, but now look at it."

Lowering the window, Guy said to the driver, "Henri, let's go home."

"Oui, monsieur," the driver responded in the strangest French accent Sean had ever heard.

"Where is he from?" asked Sean.

"Vietnam," answered Guy. "He is one of my projects, Sean."

This man is starting to really scare me, Sean thought to

himself. Project? What's that mean?

Guy Lafoussier lived in Upper Outrement, where the upper crust of the Montreal French Canadian society lived. Typical for a Quaker, he lived on an estate bestowed with natural beauty and devoid of any gaudiness or pretense. The three-story house was on a side street of Avenue du Parc, and adjacent to a beautiful tree-filled park. It was made of natural cut stone and adorned with beautiful lawns and gardens.

Arriving at the front, the driver's and Guy's oriental friend grabbed Sean's bags, as Guy took Sean to meet the rest of the "family."

There were several people on hand to meet. He quickly observed that everyone was from the French-speaking world: Angola, French Guyana, Vietnam, Algeria, and some others he could not understand. Guy showed him around the house. It was magnificent, yet without any ostentation—mainly antiques, but wonderfully functional. Guy was particularly proud of the dining room. The windows were large and beautiful, exposing the exquisite outdoor gardens. The dining table was a big, inviting square, conducive for large gatherings, yet comfortable. The whole first floor was big enough to be a Meeting House. The second floor, he learned, was exclusively for Guy and Brigitte, and now him. He wasn't shown the third floor or the basement where he was told the others lived.

"How many others are there?" Sean asked.

"About ten," said Guy, "but they travel often, so there are never more than a few around at one time. Your dad knows how involved I am with the World Peace Organization, and these people are studying to be field workers for the WPO. You'll understand more when we all go to Meeting on Premier

Jour. Montreal Meeting is a wonderful group of people, very alive, very active."

Guy took Sean to his room. He pretended to be tired from the trip and asked if he could retire for the evening. As he unpacked, he could not stop thinking about Guy's proposition regarding Brigitte. "How weird," Sean said out loud.

He slipped into bed, noticing that it felt like Grandma's—soft, warm and comfy. He liked his new room. It had high ceilings, and it was much cooler than the small house in Hollywood where he lived. He always slept naked because he liked the feeling that came from the warmth his body generated between the sheets. He nodded off and awakened from a dead sleep by a knock on his door.

"*Reveille-toi mon cheri,*" Brigitte said to Sean, who was hearing her voice for the first time since his arrival. He looked toward the window to see if it was morning. It was still dark. Looking at the clock near his bed, he saw that it was just after 10:30 P.M., and he had only been asleep for a while.

As Sean looked up, Guy and Brigitte, hand-in-hand, were walking toward his bedside. Brigitte hugged Sean and quickly returned to holding Guy's hand.

"We've made every arrangement," she said. "Tomorrow, Claude will wake you up in time to have about fifteen minutes to shower and dress. You'll need to wear a white shirt and tie for your first day of school. We'll have breakfast and then head for the school. It's twenty minutes away—near the University. I'll be in the city all day, so I'll have Henri pick you up after school."

Sean thanked them both for taking care of everything and

soon dropped off after Mr. Lafoussier turned out the lights.

At *seis heures et demie* an African man entered Sean's room, turned on the lights, and with a deep ancient said, *"Je m'appelle Claude. Reveille-toi*, Sean, *s'il te plait. Immediatement. Allons! Allons! Le petit dejeuner en quinze minutes. Vite! Vite!"*

Sean waited until Claude departed before getting up. After he had showered and shaved, he turned to see that Brigitte's bathroom was directly in view from his bathroom window. She was leaning over her sink in her slip and applying her make-up. As he walked toward the window to pull down the shade, Brigitte saw him and waved. Sean hurriedly got dressed and rushed downstairs with everything he thought he would need for his first day at school. After some quiche and juice, he was off to the College de St. Jean-de-Brebeuf. Brigitte kissed Guy good-bye and Sean eased into a Mercedes-Benz with the same goofy window between the driver and the back seat.

As the estate faded behind them, Brigitte rolled down the divider and directed the driver in French, "Please take us by my flat in the city." Feeling a need to explain herself, she added, "I want to show Sean where it is, in case he cannot get in touch with Guy or may need something."

With the window again providing privacy, Brigitte directed her comments to Sean, "I heard about you and Cassandra and your difficulties at Abington. Sometimes problems create wonderful opportunities. Make your stay in Montreal an opportunity. I know you will. How did your speech difficulties get better?"

He didn't answer her question but only smiled as they drove by her flat. She handed him the telephone number of the flat, in case he needed anything during the school day. Brigitte explained that she preferred to stay in town when Guy was traveling and that Sean might find it easier and more convenient to do the same. She had told Guy that some of his houseguests were scary to her, and without Guy at the house, she would rather stay at her flat in town. She continued to brief Sean about Jean-de-Brebeuf. They arrived fifteen minutes before school started. Sean was about to begin a new chapter of his life.

"*Bonne chance, mon cheri,*" were Brigitte's parting words.

Brother Aubert met Sean at the school entrance. He was a rotund Franciscan brother with a warm and bubbly personality. As they walked together, Sean noticed that Aubert walked on his toes, clapping his fingers together excited by the prospects of this new student.

"Welcome to Brebeuf, Sean. I think you will like it here very much. We have heard great things about you. We're excited to have you join us. I know Brigitte very well, and she told me of your past problems. Here, at Jean-de-Brebeuf, we do not normally take new admissions without first thoroughly scrutinizing them, but because Brigitte works with the homeless and other social concerns in the Diocese, we could not say no to her. I have grown quite found of the Quakers and their selfless missions."

Sean liked Brother Aubert immediately. He was a real piece of work. He made Sean smile just being near him.

"She raised me and is like one of our family," Sean said. "And by the way, young Quakers are required to study other religions, and during my brief study, I discovered that St. Francis is called by many 'the Quaker Saint.'"

"Indeed, St. Francis, what a guy," Aubert said as he skipped down the hallway in excitement. "You know, this school is run by Jesuits, but there is another Franciscan here, Sister Mary Elizabeth, who teaches religion."

He continued his orientation. "We have Mass twice a week with everyone in *ecole secondaire*, and we would ask you not to take communion unless you convert to Catholicism."

They arrived in front of a huge wooded door and entered the office of the headmaster, Father Nicolas.

"*Bienvenue*, Sean. It's good to meet you." Brigitte told us all about you and we are pleased to welcome you." Sean could tell he was going to like this man as well; he was as big as a house, had a great smile, a firm handshake, and was a man's man.

"Sean, I wanted to have a word with you before Brother Aubert accompanies you to your classes. I'm here to help you in any way I can. My office door is always open. We have a policy here at Brebeuf—if you have a question, just ask. We have very few rules—live in God's love and treat each other accordingly. And at the College, we expect you in uniform. It's a Jesuit thing," he said, smiling at Aubert. "Brother Aubert will fill you in on other pertinent things, as he shows you around. *A bientot*, Sean."

Brother Aubert and Sean proceeded to French V, advanced French grammar and French Classics, where Father Jean Paul was instructing. There were about twenty students—more girls than boys. Aubert introduced Sean to the class, and they both took seats in the back row of the classroom.

The class was studying *Les Miserables* and Hugo's unusual use of the plus que parfait tense. Sean began his participation in the discussion when Jean Paul asked Sean if he was from Paris because of his accent.

"Non, Monsieur, I was taught le Francais by a Parisian," Sean responded in French.

"*Tres bien*, Sean."

Sean loved French and soon realized that he would be very comfortable living, studying, speaking, and thinking in French. He was quite surprised with the Canadian accent, having thought it would sound sort of "hickish."

The day flew by, meeting new people and realizing he would have a lot of work to do to be successful, but he was determined to make the best of his time at Brebeuf. The last bell rang, and Brother Aubert said that he would be happy to accompany Sean another day if needed.

"Non, Brother Aubert, but thank you for all your help. I want to try to make it on my own tomorrow, if that's okay?" Sean requested.

"Extraordinaire, Sean, I will be your mentor while you're here at Brebeuf. You'll do great! Have a good evening and study hard," Aubert said then waved good-bye to Sean.

Brother Aubert went immediately to the office and gave Father Nicholas a full report of the day. "He is special, Father, very bright, a physical and mental whiz kid, but unfortunately the girls are very much attracted to him. The boys wanted to know whether he was English, and the girls thought he was Parisian. The boys want to create a conflict, and the girls want to be his friend. You should see the way he compliments the girls and he is positive and engaging. He appears to have no hang-ups at all, I mean *zero*. We should get him involved in sports right away. He is superior in P.E., and it's the only way the boys are going to accept him quickly."

"Thank you for that report, Aubert. Let's watch him carefully to protect him from himself and the stupidity of others. Brigitte was right; he is very unique. Let's keep him in our prayers—he's going to need them," Nicholas proposed, as Aubert left his office.

Canada

Montreal—an Impressive City

The education at Brebeuf was excellent and kept Sean's head in the books. Doing everything in French kept him on his toes, better preparing him for daily classes than he ever was at Abington. Teachers truly appreciated his diligence. He was soon to become one of their favorites.

Brother Aubert and Sean became instant friends, as was the case with many students and Aubert. He petitioned Sean to play football, hockey and lacrosse—the three sports for which Brebeuf was famous. They were midway through the football season, and Sean knew he wasn't ready to take a good hit because of his recent bout with hepatitis and the resultant condition of his liver. Hockey was out; he could hardly skate, but lacrosse was a possibility. To get things rolling, Brother Aubert arranged a one-day tryout with the varsity soccer team the day before their fifth game. They arrived on the field as practice was beginning.

"Have you ever played soccer?" Coach Bertin asked Sean.

"Non," was his quick reply. "Just for fun." Coach Bertin frowned at Brother Aubert.

"All right, I promised Brother Aubert a tryout, so let's see what you have."

Brother Aubert was thrilled to see Sean immediately have

an impact. His soccer skills were nominal, but they had never seen foot speed like his at Brebeuf.

"How 'bout fullback?" Coach Bertin asked.

"I'm a speed guy, Coach. Could you put me up front?"

"Okay," Coach Bertin said in disbelief that Sean asked.

Within minutes, a fullback on Sean's team cleared a ball over the heads of all the defenders. Sean got to the ball a good three meters before anyone else, and he dribbled, shot on goal and it hit the goal post.

"*Peut etre, peut etre,*" Bertin whispered to Brother Aubert.

Sean knew positioning and the basics like gives and goes. This allowed him to mix it up as an outside right in a four-man front. The next time he had an opportunity to touch the ball, he threw a hip fake, which left the defending fullback on the ground as he dribbled alone toward the goal. He faked a kick with his right as he ticked the ball with his left over to his teammate, who one-timed it into the net.

"He's in, Aubert," said an amazed Bertin. "I'll carry him for the rest of the year. Of course, he has a lot to learn and I can't promise him anything, but I'll do the best I can." The players congratulated Sean.

"You have a lot to do, but I trust Brother Aubert will help you," Bertin said. "You need to get a uniform because we play Stanstead in Magog tomorrow at four. In order to travel, you'll have to get a physical, permission from your parents, and soccer boots that won't give you blisters. I can't guarantee that you'll play, but from what I've seen today, I should take you along."

The roly-poly Franciscan skipped along, patting Sean on

the back, as the two of them left the field.

"Stanstead is a bunch of wealthy English boys who beat us last year five to three," he eagerly told Sean. "They are our rival and the best English school in Quebec, and of course, we are the best French-speaking school."

Sean was appreciating Brother Aubert more and more. He swooped him into the infirmary for the physical. With his papers signed and uniform in hand, Sean called Brigitte to request a pickup from Henri at six by the field house. When Henri arrived, Brigitte was in the back seat.

Sean proudly announced to Brigitte, "I'm playing soccer tomorrow for Brebeuf at four against Stanstead in Magog."

"Fantastique, Sean! You know I love soccer, and it is Guy's most favorite sport of all. Can we go?"

"Of course! But you might travel all the way down there just to watch me sit on the bench, but I think they *are* impressed with my speed."

When Sean told Guy about the next day's game at dinner, there were nine others around the table. Guy was excited and asked the whole gang to travel to Magog for the game. The entire table began chattering about soccer and football, World Cup, whose country was the best, and more. Sean felt like a valuable commodity in his new home.

"I don't know if you have enough room, but I sure would like Brother Aubert to go," Sean implored Guy. "Without him, I would not have this opportunity, and one of you has to sign this parent permission slip."

"No problem," answered Guy with a smile.

There was excitement in the air the next morning at breakfast, with everyone giving Sean tips on what to do if he got in the game. The school day flew by, and he reported to the field house to board a very nice small bus to Stanstead. The trip down near the U.S. border took almost an hour. Sean sat next to the goalkeeper, Marque, who totally consumed with soccer. After forty-five minutes of listening to him talk about soccer, five minutes discussing where Sean was from, and ten minutes of silence they arrived at Stanstead. It was quite a place with hundreds of acres and neatly groomed soccer fields and other impressive buildings and facilities. The whole Lafoussier household was at Stanstead with both Brother Aubert and Father Nicholas in tow when the bus arrived.

Eyeing the Lafoussier clan as if they were somehow weird, Marque asked, "Who are *those* folks—who are *they*?"

"They're my Canadian family," Sean proudly said with a new sense of belonging.

"Can I have a date with your sister?" asked Marque, having spotted Brigitte.

"You'll have to ask her husband," Sean said smiling.

"Who are those other people?" Marque continued.

"Mr. Lafoussier runs an international organization and those are some of his friends. Brother Aubert and Father Nicholas, I think you know."

"Duh," Marque responded, jumping off the bus.

Brother Aubert was by far the most excited. He looked liked a dancing bear, watching Sean and the team get off the bus. He felt like an agent who had negotiated some big fantastic sports deal. He could not hold back his enthusiasm nor did he even try.

"I'm so excited, Sean! We are going to win because of you!" muttered Aubert. Sean was the last to get off the bus, and fortunately, the other boys could not hear Aubert's comments.

"I might not even play, but thank you all for coming," Sean said, seeing Guy and Brigitte smiling at him.

"It has already been a nice outing for all of us," Guy responded.

Sean went to the locker room to get changed. The rest of the folks enjoyed the last of the Indian summer and continued to visit with one another. The temperature was in the 60s, with blue skies and a slight wind. The sun was warm on Sean's face and comforting, somehow reminding him of Philly. The day before, during his tryout, it had to be fifteen degrees colder, which negatively affected his speed.

In the locker room, Coach Bertin said to Sean, "Those aren't soccer boots. Soccer boots are brown or black, not white and silver."

"They're track flats with no spikes, and they match our uniforms." Sean could tell Bertin was into soccer boots and said, "I'm sorry, Coach. By the time I got everything done for the trip the stores were closed." Sean was not about to put on a heavier soccer boot and compromise his speed. His football coaches were not happy that he did not wear cleats, but they were glad when Sean outran the opponents.

As the Brebeuf team jogged onto the field, there were about twenty more Brebeuf well-wishers that had arrived. The field was firm with freshly cut grass, and it made Sean feel like his old self, back on the playing fields of Abington. As he warmed up he could not help but notice Brigitte watching him. He was happy that his once-upon-a-time nanny was there. What Brigitte was watching, though, was not a boy anymore but a man. His white shoes set him apart from the other players, and it was obvious to Father Nicholas that he had special talent.

"You were right, Aubert. He is not only the biggest player on the field but by far the fastest," Father Nicholas observed.

"I told you. I told you!" Brother Aubert exclaimed while he made his emotions known by jumping up and down.

The game started with Sean on the bench. Stanstead was 1-0 within the first 10 minutes on a great shot that just beat Marque. Interestingly enough, Sean observed that Brebeuf held, pushed, and played the opposing team far dirtier than Stanstead. Then Stanstead was up 2-0 on a header from a good cross to an unmarked midfielder, who was running full speed toward the goal when he finished the play to score. Marque did not have a chance to make a play to stop it.

Three things were happening on the sideline. The Lafoussier gang was really enjoying the game and were all giving each other a running play-by-play. Brother Aubert was going nuts talking and whispering to Bertin almost all the time to the point of annoyance, probably petitioning him for Sean to play. Brigitte's attention was not on the game but on Sean, who would often reciprocate with a smile.

Then it happened. Brebeuf got a breakaway and the fullback sliced the outside of the Brebeuf player's leg right out from underneath him outside the penalty area. A bench-clearing brawl broke out, with Brother Aubert right in the middle of the action. The only people that weren't on the field were the Lafoussier gang, Father Nicholas and, of course, Sean. It took several minutes to unwind what was going to happen, but it

resulted in the ejection of one Stanstead and two Brebeuf players, with a direct kick awarded to Brebeuf.

Sean thought he was about to enter the game as Bertin approached and said, "Sean, I expect you to mix it up on behalf
of your teammates. Do not stay on the sidelines next time."
Sean was in shock. Meanwhile, Nicholas reprimanded Brother
Aubert for getting involved in the fracas, but Aubert quickly
turned him around, "I just could not help myself!"

A few minutes later the Brebeuf star attacker turned his
ankle, and Sean was put into the game, getting his first opportunity to help the team soon thereafter with a corner kick for
Brebeuf from the opposite side of the field than he played. With
everyone stuffed in or near the goal, the ball scooted towards
the Stanstead goal with a Stanstead attacker bearing down for
the kill and an easy score. From at least ten meters back, Sean
took off and by midfield had the Englishman well within his
range and neatly stepped in front of the attacker to pass the
ball calmly to Marque. The Brebeuf sideline went nuts. Everyone was cheering in different languages, and of course, Aubert
was riding on Nicholas' back in excitement. The half ended—
Brebeuf still two down.

During halftime, Coach Bertin, impressed by Sean's speed,
told his defense and midfielders to clear their kicks over the
top of the Stanstead defenders and to let the Brebeuf attackers
run underneath for a scoring opportunity. Sean was grateful
that everyone was having such a good time, but he continued to
sense something different about Brigitte's attentiveness.

Bertin's plan worked perfectly. Sean ran down the clears
twice within the penalty area, and he passed to a trailing teammate. At a 2-2 draw, Stanstead had to double-team Sean so

it wouldn't happen again. The Lafoussier gang cheered with abandon when Sean used a head or hip fake to leave the two of them ineffective and often on the ground. Regulation ended 2-2, and sudden death overtime was soon to start when Bertin called Sean aside out of hearing range.

"I don't know who you are or why you're at Brebeuf, but right now I'm real glad. Listen and listen closely. You're going to have to do this yourself. They are a better team but no one can keep up with you, so when you get your chance, do not shoot. Do one of those fakes you do and then just run the ball into the goal."

"Okay," a grinning Sean agreed.

Within minutes into overtime, the two defenders marking him were left in dust. The ball was rolling towards the goal just over the midfield line when Sean demonstrated his real speed for the first time. He got to the ball extremely fast, through a head and hip fake and pretended to shoot, which left the goalie on the ground as he dribbled the ball into the goal.

He could see and hear Aubert running towards him. His teammates wrestled him to the ground in celebration. Aubert pulled them off to get to Sean.

"Manifique! Extraordinaire! I told everyone about you and no one believed me. I'm so happy for you and I'm happy for me!" he exclaimed, running on his toes towards Father Nicholas. "I told you, I told you!"

"Yes, Brother, you were right," Father Nicholas said. "Great job, Sean. You looked like a man playing against boys. Terrific, just terrific," he added calmly.

Sean had been part of amazing victories before at the Abington Y, Huntington, and indeed at Abington. However, there was a crucial difference between Sean and his teammates—he *expected* to win, while other guys were only *hoping* to. It felt great to help the team win, but igniting the spirit of his new home and housemates felt even better.

"Great game, Sean! I'm so proud of you. Not just because you played great but also because you demonstrated real restraint—those English could not get you mad. Did you hear them making frog sounds at you?" asked Guy, smiling.

"Yeah, what was that all about?" Sean responded.

"The English have always called the French "frogs" in derogatory sense. We were laughing so hard because the two players marking you kept trying to get you mad with their frog noises, but you were completely oblivious to what was happening. We had to restrain Aubert, but other than that, it was a riot!" Guy laughed.

Sean noticed something different about Guy after the game. He was the only Brebeuf well-wisher that spent as much time congratulating Stanstead as he did Sean's team.

Sean was not allowed to travel back with the Lafoussier gang, but the ride was fun nonetheless.

The French love to sing. They must have sung *"Alouettre Chantez Alouettre"* fifty times.

Marque analyzed everything Sean did ad nauseam. He told Sean that the word around school was that Sean was at Brebeuf because he got a girl pregnant in Philly.

"Close, but no cigar," Sean laughed.

"It's weird because the last new boy who came from Vancouver with the same "rep" got his ass kicked several times and had to leave school. The guys wanted to destroy him and the girls wanted to test him. He only lasted a week. Heck, I'd like you to stay until at least the end of soccer season," Marque lectured.

"Thanks for caring, Marque," Sean replied sarcastically.

Aubert was at school to meet the bus, excitingly patting everyone on the back as they got off the bus.

"Is he always like this?" Sean asked Marque.

"No, he probably has a bet with Father Nicholas that you will make it longer than a week."

"Thanks, Marque," Sean laughed.

"Just watch out for the hockey boys. They think they're something special, but they're not," Marque advised Sean as they both got off the bus.

"Wow! That was exciting. I'll meet you tomorrow at school, Sean. We have a lot to do tomorrow," said Aubert.

Marque whispered to Sean, "He thinks you're going to get your butt whipped tomorrow. He bet on you, for sure. You should stay home from school tomorrow, so it will throw those hockey boys for a loop."

"Okay, good-bye, Aubert," Sean said, smiling at Marque.

It was a festive occasion at the Lafoussiers—a great meal, wine, and much talk about soccer. It was gratifying to Sean to know that he was the catalyst that warmed an otherwise cold environment. With the soccer gang still there, Sean excused himself after the meal and went to his room to study. He noticed Brigitte undressing in her room. She had just her slip on, and as she leaned over the sink on her toes, her derriere was exposed. She was watching Sean's reaction in the mirror.

Sean quickly left the desk to pretend he was reading on his bed to discourage Brigitte from going further, and fortunately, it worked. After a few minutes Sean started thinking that maybe he just imagined that her actions were intentional. He studied for three hours, said his prayers, and fell asleep thinking about Sonny, Louie, and Cassandra, realizing how much he cherished their friendship.

Miracles Happen

Marque was right. The next day at school the hockey boys greeted Sean at the front door. This day was to be one of those turning-point experiences for Sean. Patrick, a thug of infinite stupidity, grabbed Sean and pulled him into a classroom while the other hockey boys blocked the door. Patrick started throwing punches. Sean blocked them, like when he sparred with Sonny. He couldn't stop smiling, thinking how proud Sonny would be, since it was really aggravating Patrick. Aubert was on the scene in no time to find that Patrick had injured himself because of his own aggression and was, consequently, badly bruised. Sean never threw a punch.

"Patrick! Go to Father Nicholas' office," Aubert commanded.

"I think I should go to the clinic first; I might have broken my arm," Patrick responded, as he entered the hallway to cheers of the boys.

Sean was snickering with Aubert over the ordeal when they left the scene. He told Aubert about his friend Sonny, a golden-gloves champ, who sparred with him and taught him a lot.

As they walked together in the hallway, Sean asked, "Did you really bet on whether I'd make it at Brebeuf?"

Aubert's face turned scarlet. "Of course not. I'd never bet

on a Quaker over a Catholic, that is, if they didn't come from Philadelphia! Let's just say I'm going to be your guardian angel for a while." Aubert was the hockey advisor because no one else would take it. "They're good guys; they just think their testosterone levels will get them through life, as I did growing up. I knew this was going to happen sooner or later. It will continue to shadow you for a while, but then they will ease up. The last boy that went through this was knocked out in the first round. They also think that the world is a big hockey rink, meaning aggressiveness equals success. Pretty stupid, eh? Besides, I'm protecting my investment," Aubert rambled.

Aubert and Sean walked to Sean's English class (as a second language). "This class must be a cake walk for you, Sean," Aubert said.

"Absolute hardest—it's all grammar, which I'm lousy at." They entered the classroom and sat in the back.

Aubert remained after class to talk to Sister Theresa while Sean ventured on to his next class. The girls were quick to talk to Sean in the hallways. He always had something kind to say or to communicate through his body language. Thus, he had many female friends.

On Sean's way up to the third floor, he heard screams and ran ahead. It was Mother Superior. She had passed out and Sean quickly checked her out. No pulse—not breathing. Sean instructed the onlookers to get back. He pulled off the part of her habit that covered her head, loosening the area around her neck and chest. Sean started mouth-to-mouth and chest compression as the on-looking students stood screaming. She was not responding. Aubert was the first faculty member on the scene and did not know what Sean was doing, but he instinctively commanded, "He knows what he is doing. Everyone get back. You!" he picked out a screaming student, "go the office and tell them to call the hospital. She is in her late sixties. She collapsed last week in the convent," Aubert informed Sean.

Sean kept working on her and then she regurgitated. All the onlookers gasped when Sean cleared the airway and kept working. She started responding as he worked on her and threw up again. He cleared her mouth, and held her head with his hands as he talked to her. "You're going to be all right," he said softly to her. Everyone clapped.

Brother Aubert was on his toes again with a huge smile, sort of jumping and clapping at the same time, when Father Nicholas arrived and immediately knelt at her side and prayed. Brother Aubert knelt and held her hand. Sean continued to hold her head off the ground. After the prayer, Sean asked Aubert to elevate her feet. Aubert put her legs on top of his, as he sat talking to her. It was several minutes until the ambulance arrived.

Sister Bernadette tugged on Sean's hand. "God Bless you, Sean. You must be from Galway. Thank you," she said in English, with the heaviest Irish brogue he had ever heard.

"Get better fast," Sean said to her in French. The ambulance crew arrived and carried her off.

Brother Aubert beamed with pride as Sean and he entered Father Nicholas' office. Father Nicholas wanted to know how Sean had learned that resuscitative technique and why he had felt confident enough to start working on her right away. Sean explained that a Korean War medic taught the kids this at his Y and that he was able to use it a couple of times last summer as a lifeguard.

"God bless you, Sean. You did a great thing today," said Father Nicholas. Aubert nodded with an "I-told-you" smile.

Sean explained that saving a life was the most gratifying experience he had ever had and told them about the incident last summer on the beach. Aubert started jumping up and down in his seat, wanting to say something when Nicholas said, "God gave you running ability like I have never seen before and certainly a gift of discernment to know what to do in an emergency. Think about this—there are only a few people in all of Canada that probably know of, or for that matter, would even attempt to administer mouth resuscitation."

"It's called mouth-to-mouth, Father," Sean said. "Soon, everyone will be doing it because it works."

"Truly, a miracle has taken place at Jean-de-Brebeuf College. Thank you again, Sean," Father Nicholas said, shaking his hand. Turning to Aubert, Father Nicholas said lightheartedly, "Stop standing there smiling like a Cheshire cat and take Sean to class."

Sean turned to Father Nicholas and asked, "Bernadette said something I didn't understand when she thanked me. Do you know what 'you must be from Galway' means?"

"Don't have a clue—she's Irish—ask an Irishman."

Leaving the office, Aubert was anxious to tell Sean about his Franciscan friend, Francois, from Point Claire Parish. Francois loved swimming, and according to Aubert, his parish had the best swim club in all of Canada.

"Someday, before soccer season is over, you should drive to Pointe Claire to visit Francois. I can't wait to call him," he said, walking on his toes and clapping in excitement again.

Sean thought to himself how wonderful it was to be around a person, even if he was a Brother, who really got into the little things in life and was happy all the time. As Brother Aubert was talking and walking about, Sean continued to admire how Father Nicholas let Aubert be Aubert, not trying to change him but allowing him his eccentricities and what a difference that was from Abington.

Turning down a different hallway, there was Patrick with the hockey boys, standing in the middle of the hallway. "Get to class boys, or you will be ineligible for hockey season!" Aubert proclaimed.

The instruction went unheeded. Patrick looked past Aubert and addressed Sean with his head down, "We've been thinking, Sean, and…uh, well, you're okay, considering you helped Mother Superior and everything."

"Thanks, Patrick," Sean said and smiled at them. He thought that hockey players must be connected by their collective brains or collectively have one brain. Aubert started clapping his hands really fast again, which meant he was happy and started skipping as he and Sean headed to their next class.

After practice that day, Nuy, a Vietnamese WPO employee, picked up Sean. "Everyone has heard about you saving Mother Superior, Sean. Brigitte is very proud of you, as we all are. You have given us some great gifts of which you probably are not even aware. First of all, Guy is happier than he has been in a long time, and that makes us all happy. You have also brought life into our workplace—we talk about soccer, and in particular, Brebeuf soccer, all the time now. But most importantly, it's wonderful to see a young Quaker show God's love by example."

They continued to talk about Montreal, his native country

of Vietnam, and why he was working with the World Peace Organization. Sean learned of the complexities that were going on in Nuy's country and around the world.

"What do you do up on the third floor all day?" Sean asked.

"We learn invaluable methods to help us in the field to bring peace and tranquility to each one of our regions of the world. Guy has traveled all over the world and knows how to get things done. All French-speaking or French-influenced countries train in the Outrement House and are partially sponsored by Montreal Meeting," Nuy said.

"Are you folks Quakers?

"No, but some of us have either converted or have come to identify with the World Peace Organization's mission. By the way, Guy wants to see you as soon as you get home."

The aroma of a roast from the kitchen made the house really feel like home. Guy was waiting to congratulate Sean for saving Bernadette's life and ask Sean to join him in his study. The study was an exceptional place—a high ceiling, cherry woodwork, burgundy leather couches and chairs. There was a special chair that Guy particularly liked with a reading light and ottoman, pillows, and afghan. He had organized his reading material neatly on the end table by the lamp.

Guy sat down and asked Sean to have a seat and tell him how things were going for him in Montreal. He also wanted details of how Sean saved Mother Superior's life and how he learned this new method. They discussed world events and the World Peace Organization. Sean began to realize that Guy was a very good man, even though he sported that sleazy, skinny mustache. They talked for about thirty minutes when they heard the supper chime. Before Guy got up he said, "By the way, next week I must go overseas for two weeks. I hope you will stay with Brigitte at the flat, and please give Nuy the results of all your soccer matches in detail. I'll look forward to those reports while overseas." Then he and Sean went into the dining room.

After a lengthy dinner conversation followed by dessert, Sean was summoned to the phone.

"Sean, this is Sonny."

"Yo, Sonny."

"Yo, Scan," Sonny answered in his Philly accent. "I'm at your house, getting my Easley fix and just yearned to hear your 'pussy-ass' voice. What's been happening with you, man? No more stuttering, I heard? I won't be able to understand you anymore. Hey, are you coming home for Thanksgiving or what? And what's it like going to a 'mackerel-snapper' school?"

Sean laughed and said, "You will always be a stone bigot— mackerel snappers. Actually, it's absolutely fantastic." He went on to tell him that he was now playing soccer, and Sonny started howling when Sean told him about Aubert. They always made each other laugh. Thanksgiving was out because it fell at a different time in Canada.

They continued to talk for another ten minutes when Sean asked about Louie. There was silence before Sonny answered. "Louie...Louie—he pisses me off. You have to get Brigitte to call him. He's really changing. I swear he dropped two touchdown passes last game on purpose, just because he had scored twice and didn't want me to get mine. And I think it's all over Cassandra," Sonny confessed.

"Cassandra? What do you mean Cassandra?"

"We are both trying to adjust to your being gone, man, Cassandra and I, but Louie—he keeps trying to hit on Cassandra. She keeps telling him no way—that she's yours forever. Then Louie gets real freaky." Sonny reported.

They talked a little longer, ending with the mutual *"Toujours Amis,"* and Sean added, "You're the man."

Sean talked to his mom and dad then asked his dad about what Bernadette meant by the Galway thing because his father knew much about Ireland lure. There was a long pause after Sean's question before his father responded. "You know our roots are in western Ireland, and the Irish call that area Galway. My mother, your grand mom, grew up in a village called Cleggan, near the sea as far west you can go in Ireland. Our people always felt God watched over them by sending other kin from Galway to protect them."

"You're kidding, Dad."

"No, Son, that's for real. My mom always taught me that God often used us to save one of our own. I know it's uncanny, but there are many examples I could site in my own life," Big Sam replied.

After the phone call, Sean went to his room to study. He fell asleep that night reviewing the day's activities and thinking of home and the ever-present rivalry between him and Louie over girls, whether it was Brigitte, Cassandra, or any girl they danced with at Abington or Wildwood. He wished that the opposite sex would not get in the way of friendships. He took comfort in knowing that Brigitte could help Louie, but the Galway thing was really blowing his mind, making it difficult to fall asleep.

Sean did not have a chance to speak to Brigitte until on the way to school the next day. He explained to Brigitte why she needed to talk to Louie, relaying all that Sonny told him.

"Are you asking this for Louie's sake or to stop him from trying to take Cassandra?" Brigitte asked.

"To tell you I don't care for Cassandra would be a lie. Sometimes you have to do things that could make you look selfish or self-serving—things that people could misinterpret, but if it's the best for everyone, you still do it anyway, regardless of how it's perceived. I love them both. Louie has to stop being competitive with me, and Cassandra, well Cassandra—I don't know what to do in that case. I know we were out of control, and being here with you has allowed me to look at things from a much different perspective," Sean said.

"What do you want me to do for Louie?" asked Brigitte.

"Tell Louie not to be jealous because it does not allow him to be the best he can be—that he is a beautiful person. Heck, Brigitte, you know better that I. If he has real feelings for Cassandra, then he should pursue them, but if he doesn't, he needs to let it go. It's that simple."

"What are your intentions with Cassandra, Sean? I'm sure he'll ask," Brigitte questioned.

"We haven't talked for a while. Maybe she feels differently now, but I'll always have a special place for her. You can put that in the bank," Sean confessed.

"What did you mean by its different now since you're with me?"

"I cannot answer that on the grounds it could incriminate me," Sean answered, making eye contact as they both smiled.

Later that evening, Sean went to his room to study. Brigitte went to her bathroom and lit a candle. She undressed slowly and sensually. Sitting on the side of the bathtub in Sean's full view, she bathed. Sean turned off his light and moved far away from the window, so she could not tell that he was watching. After the show, Sean crawled in bed to read but could not concentrate. Who could? He considered his lack of self-control in having to watch. He finally fell asleep, debating whether she wanted him or simply enjoyed teasing him, knowing that he would need to make a decision real soon.

The next morning when she got into the car she looked unbelievable, "You look great," Sean said. "What's up?"

"Many meetings—very important—wish me luck," smiled Brigitte.

"You won't need it, not the way you look," he gushed.

"Would you, Sean, give me what I want?" she asked.

"Absolutement!" Sean said emphatically and they both grinned.

Brigitte went on to line out the weekend events, "Soccer game at 1600. Dance at 1900. Guy and I will go to dinner then pick you up at the dance at 2130. Guy flies to Europe *a midi* on Saturday, then we will move to the city, go to a cinema or something, attend Meeting at noon on *Dimanche*, and then we can do anything we want for the remainder of the weekend."

"Great schedule. How long is Guy going to be gone?" Sean asked.

"*Je pense deux ou trois semaines*," Brigitte looked at Sean.

"I'm going to miss him. I've grown really fond of him." Sean confessed.

They continued to look at each other without saying a word. Sean was grinning and thinking, "You have no idea whether I saw you last night, and you will never know for sure, but gosh, you are one fine, fine lady." Brigitte knew she could make him forget Cassandra and want her. "Watch, just you watch," she thought, as they continued smiling at each other.

The day flew by, and Sean thought of Brigitte every free moment until the soccer game. Sean had his best game to date. Sean could tell that Guy was very pleased and so was the Lafoussier gang. All of them were excited to be part of this newfound excitement, especially in light of the tips they all gave Sean to improve his game. Brigitte looked incredibly magnificent. She wore a long fur coat and a red ear warmer that amplified her natural beauty. The chill in the air made her breasts stand out when her coat blew open—her red blouse, clinging to her contours. Even her below-the-knee black skirt silhouetted her remarkable figure. But something else was happening at the soccer game that also caught his attention.

Les jeune filles de hockey were out in force at the soccer game, and they were all cheering for Sean. Many of the hockey girls did not wear underwear, as a sign of defiance for school rules. It also came across loud and clear that they were always "ready." They were definitely trying to get Sean's attention when he was put on the bench with Brebeuf leading 4 to nil. Marque, the goalkeeper, was taken out of the game and sat next to Sean on the bench and said, "Stay away from them, dude. And don't think you're special just because they are 'shooting beavers' at you." Looking across the field he added, "They are nothing but trouble."

"No problem," Sean responded.

"Be careful at the dance tonight. There's a lot of stupid stuff that can happen. We used to be able to dress how we wanted, but now we have to be in school uniform. Fortunately, lots of girls go to the dances with no underwear—in protest—not just the hockey groupies. That's why I look forward to each dance with eager anticipation—to see what they do. Only at Brebeuf," Marque shared with Sean.

When the game ended, Aubert, accompanied by Guy and Brigitte, introduced his friend Francois to Sean. "This is my friend, Francois, who is connected with Pointe Claire Swim Club and the parish priest in Point Claire," he said, on his toes and clapping his hands again.

"He's here to chaperone the dance with me and talk to you about swimming. I've worked it out. Brigitte can you drive down on Sunday afternoon after Meeting to try out for Quebec's best swim team," he said enthusiastically.

"It's good to finally meet you, Sean. Aubert has been bragging about you. He is right; you're quite an athlete, and if you can swim the way you can run, Point Claire is going to be quite lucky. I've already spoken with Guy, and he said it's up to you."

Francois was a man of considerable girth—even more so than Aubert. He was also a little balder and a little older, but he was cut from the same cloth as Aubert—big smile, big heart.

"It's been a long time since I've been in a pool, so tell the coach to not expect much. Right now I could not last twenty minutes in a swim workout," Sean said.

"I'll invite Aubert to our parish after his early Mass, and we will meet you at, let's say, 1300 at PCSC. Practice is over at 1330, so you can tryout and then we will have tea together after," Francois suggested.

"Okay by me if it's okay with Guy and Brigitte," Sean answered.

"That will work out well. I leave tomorrow for Europe, so Brigitte will have to take you, as long as you save your legs for the rest of soccer season, *s'il te plait*," laughed Guy.

"It is no problem," said Brigitte, smiling at Sean.

"All right then, let's dance!" said Aubert, and he started to jitterbug with Brigitte.

A Bite of the Apple

The dance was a sight to behold for a Philly boy. All the lights were at full blast in the gym like a basketball game. It was filled to capacity with "penguins" and priests; two fat, happy Franciscans; a couple of parents, and over 400 dancers in school uniforms. Aubert was the disc jockey and danced every song by himself on stage behind the record player.

It was obvious that Montreal kids liked to dance but not like Philly kids. They didn't know any of the new dances like the stomp, mashed potato, slop, strand, etc. The twist was big at Brebeuf, as well as the stroll and jitterbug, which they called "the Lindy." To get couples to adhere to the meter rule, a distance of one meter between bodies, the Sisters would patrol the auditorium and tap the dancers on the shoulders.

Sean stuck to his normal tactics: dance with the more rotund girls to start out with, which usually gets the other girls' attention. As it was, Sean liked the biggest girl in the school. They laughed their way through both math and religion class, mainly at the hockey boys, who they thought were just insane. Claire had to be just less than 1.8 meters tall and almost 100 kilos and, like Sean, was very uninhibited when she danced.

"Let's do it," Sean grinned, grabbing Claire's hand and easing into a jitterbug. She was standing in a group of about ten girls.

"You want top or bottom? Right here or where?" she quipped back, and all who heard laughed. She was popular—a great dancer and a totally free spirit. Sean did all the American Bandstand dance moves. Many just stood and watched. When the record ended, the onlookers clapped and cheered. Claire and Sean were having a ball.

"You were great, Claire," Sean told her.

"Enjoyed it, I just had two orgasms!" Claire said, and they both started howling. Claire's dad was a professional football player, who attended Notre Dame and played football for the Montreal Allouettes as a defensive lineman for over fifteen years. He met a French gal and Claire was their first child. Claire was an absolute riot.

Sean went up to Aubert, who was dancing in a trance-like state, and asked, "Do you have the bunny hop?"

"What's that?" responded Aubert.

"It's a group dance—lots of fun," Sean said.

"I'll send Francois to the record store down the street," Aubert replied.

Sean spent much of the dance talking with the hockey boys, including Patrick. The hockey girl groupies were there as well. Aubert played a Calypso number, but no one was dancing, except Aubert—by himself. Sean led Claire onto the floor again for the cha-cha-cha. She followed Sean very well and, of course, everyone was watching. Someone else tapped Claire on the shoulder and started dancing with Sean. It was Martine, a gorgeous Haitian girl. As soon as she started dancing, it was obvious that she was in a completely different league than anyone else, including Sean. She got into a trance-like state as she danced, and her moves were very sensual, rhythmic, and exotic. Sean caught on in a matter of seconds and was mirroring her moves. Martine started sweating profusely, causing her blouse to cling to her, which was extremely sexy. She knew it as well.

Everyone stopped everything to see this exhibition. Aubert bumped the record player so that the music stopped suddenly. Sister Mary Francis was making a beeline to the couple, when Aubert shouted, "Let's "twist!" turning up the volume to help deflect what was about to happen to Sean and Martine.

"You're too much, Martine," Sean said, absorbed in rapture as the record stopped. "I'm going to check in with Aubert," he said turning to divert attention from the obvious, unaware that the Sister Mary Francis was approaching.

"That was way too suggestive for my blood," Sister Mary Francis reprimanded. "We'll have no more of that! No more!" Sean threw his sweater at Martine, so she wouldn't get in trouble for not wearing a bra.

"What a disgusting display of vulgarity!" she fumed.

Sean needed to pull out a trump card for this one. "It's not what it appears, Sister. It's kind of like when I had to pull off Sister Bernadette's habit to work on her the other day. The kids thought I was being disrespectful, but they didn't understand. That dance is from her island; it's a traditional thing," Sean averred.

Mary Francis left them with a smirk, acknowledging by the look in her eye that Sean was full of shit.

"Wow! That was interesting," Sean said to Martine, referring to the dance.

"I heard you prefer your women colored, so I wanted to make myself available," she smiled, catching Sean off guard.

Sean grinned with a nod, wondering what in the heck was going on.

Somehow Aubert managed to get his hands on a recording of the bunny hop, so Sean and Claire once again took the floor and proceeded to teach the crowd. Aubert abandoned his DJ position to help get the "hop line" started. After a few slow songs, Aubert played the bunny hop again because it had everyone dancing, even his colleagues of the cloth. Sure enough the hop got everyone involved. Claire positioned herself in front of Sean in the bunny line. Time flew and soon they were saying good-bye. As he was leaving the dance, his eye caught Martine blowing him a kiss. Later that night after Sean was nearly asleep when one of the house staff asked him to pick up the phone. It was Martine, calling at 2345.

"Sean, I still have your sweater. I did not want you to think you lost it. I also want you to know I want you, and I will pursue you until we are together."

"I'm honored, Martine. You certainly are one great dancer," Sean responded, trying to deflect her thought.

"You *will* be with me; just wait and see. You will not be able to sleep tonight, thinking of how we danced together. I'm sleeping with your sweater; it will help you think of me." Sean heard a click but Martine was still on the line. Was it Brigitte listening or was it Martine's family? Either way, Sean loses.

"*Au revoir, ma belle Creole, dormes bien,*" said Sean, and he hung up.

Oddly enough, Sean fell asleep immediately but dreamed

through the night of being on a beach in Haiti with Martine dancing in front of him. He woke up smiling but shaken over his bizarre dreams. He realized he had not prayed before falling asleep, so he got up and prayed. When he looked at the clock, he was surprised to see it was after noon. He also realized he had missed saying good-bye to Guy before he departed for his trip. Sean packed two bags for the week and went downstairs to see Brigitte, who was waiting.

"Are you ready, Sean? Guy said to say good-bye and wanted me to remind you to give Nuy the results of the soccer games," Brigitte said.

In less than ten minutes they were at Brigitte's flat. It was very cozy and nice with a bathroom, a large bedroom, another large room that served as a study and living area with a large fireplace. The flat had an extra bedroom, and also a combined kitchen/dining area. She instructed Sean to take the large bedroom because she stayed up so late at night.

After they finished supper, they talked for a little while, and then Sean said he was tired and kissed her on the cheek and went into his bedroom. As he lay in bed his mind kept reviewing the bizarre events that were unfolding and questioned why they were happening. An hour later, his life got more complicated—the door opened.

"I hate sleeping alone, Sean, would you mind?" Brigitte purred, standing in the doorway in a black silk slip. At first they just held each other and then came the stored-up passion that had been consuming them both for years. As daylight broke they embraced. Brigitte nestled snugly in Sean's warm neck.

"Why does something so wonderful make me feel horrible at the same time?" Brigitte asked.

"Because we both love Guy and society says a younger man and an older woman should not love one another. I know we both need to talk to God how we should handle this. In fact, it's time to go to Meeting and going to Meeting and in my state might be an embarrassment. Better get me a bucket of ice," joked Sean.

They giggled like children as Sean drove to Meeting where they met the Lafoussier gang, minus Guy. Sean and Brigitte sat at opposite ends of the Lafoussier bench. Meeting was difficult for Sean this time. He felt "the inner light" convicting him that he was going in the wrong direction with what had just happened. During the entire hour of Meeting, Sean continually slipped from reverence to thinking how Brigitte's body felt next to his. His thoughts went to Abington and how much he missed his friends and family. He prayed for all of them, but his guilt was consuming his soul.

The Discovery

Things were going along smoothly for Sean at Brebeuf, largely because Aubert continued to be Sean's guardian angel. It was early December when Sean devised a plan to avert any analysis about Brigitte and himself by the Lafoussier gang or the Brebeuf folks by dating Brebeuf girls. The options were slim—Martine or Claire.

When Sean asked Claire out, she burst out laughing. After composing herself, she said, "First of all, Sean, believe it or not, I've never been on a date. Second, the coolest boy in the school asking me is like—unreal. Third, my dad has to interview you, and if that doesn't discourage you, I'm thrilled! You know I love you to death, and if nothing else, I guess we would have had a good laugh, but why me, Sean?" she asked.

"Because you make me laugh more than anyone else I've met in Montreal."

"Good, then we can do what I want on a date—have sex, dance, have more sex…" They both got a good laugh out of that.

That Friday night, Henri drove Sean to Mont Royal to Claire's home. Sean rang the doorbell and a beautiful, petite woman answered the door.

"You must be Sean. Please come in. We've heard so much

about you. I'm Mrs. Harrison, Claire's mother." They entered a beautiful living room illuminated by the fireplace.

Mr. Harrison entered. Sean realized that this was no average man. He had to be 150-160 kilos and at least two meters tall.

"Sean, this is Claire's dad."

"*Bonsoir, monsieur,*" Sean said, offering his hand to shake.

"Please, have a seat," Mrs. Harrison motioned to the couch.

"*Bonsoir, Sean, bienvenu chez moi.* I have watched you play soccer at Brebeuf, and Notre Dame tells me you used to be one a heck of football player," Mr. Harrison said.

"Really?" Sean asked.

"Absolutement. Notre Dame gave a questionnaire to some recruits and when asked who the best football player was that they ever played with or against, their response was Sean Easley. Notre Dame called Abington and discovered you were now at Brebeuf, and then I got the call to check you out. Two of your buddies from Abington are among the hottest prospects in the country, by the way. What's the story with your not playing football?" Mr. Harrison asked.

"I got ill last summer...Wow! It sure is an honor to be considered by Notre Dame, but my football days are over...Is Claire almost ready?" Sean asked.

"No, she's not," Mr. Harrison answered as he arose.

"Why don't you step in here for a moment?" he said, leading Sean into his study. Mr. Harrison's demeanor suddenly changed.

"Young man, who do you think you are? If you think I'm going to let you take out my daughter, you're nuts. Getting a girl pregnant and not being man enough to fess up to it—no way! And if you ever touch Claire, I'll cut out your heart and then I will work down to the parts of your body you seem to care about most!"

"Mr. Harrison, if this is a test, I hope I passed," Sean said, smiling at this Goliath of a man.

"Big mistake, Sean," said Mr. Harrison. He was really pissed now and started going for Sean as Mrs. Harrison opened the door and announced, "Here she is."

Claire walked in, kissed her dad and said, "Don't you just love him, Daddy? He is my first real date and he happens to be the nicest boy in school and the most fun for sure." Like many fathers, Mr. Harrison's anger was defused when he saw his daughter so happy. "What time do you want me in, Dad?"

"Nine o'clock sharp," Mr. Harrison responded in a gnarly voice.

"Dream on, Dad. How about 11:30, if that's okay with you, Sean?"

"Perfect!" Sean responded, and they went out the door as soon as possible.

The Harrisons stood arm-in-arm as they watched their little girl begin a new phase of her life.

"Your dad's quite an interesting person," Sean commented as they got in the car.

"His bark is worse than his bite. Don't worry; he won't cut your heart out. My mother is yelling at him right now for not being nicer to you. Can we start making out now? It never made sense to me in the movies how they always make out at the end of the date," Claire said in jest but was serious as a heart attack.

With a big smile on her face, she scooted closer to him and started kissing him before Henri had a chance to pull away from the Harrison's home. Sean gave Henri instructions where to take them while she continued to kiss his neck and ears. To Sean's amazement, she was a great kisser and used her huge "ta-tas" in a very creative manner. Sean enjoyed being with her. She was proud that she could arouse Sean enough to get a "stiffy."

Looking at the mound in his pants, she said, "You know, the most important part of that is that I did that. You have no idea how important that is to me." She continued to surprise Sean with her frankness.

It was like an elementary school sexual exploration caper, but with two teenagers who just liked being with each other.

"Take us to the movies please," Sean instructed Henri.

Through most of the movie, Claire slept. She slept with her hand on Sean's mid section and her head on his shoulder. Her hair smelled great and she was extremely soft and cuddly. Occasionally, she would caress Sean or wake up, kiss Sean on the neck and fall back asleep. Turns out she hated movies and fell asleep in them all the time. Claire and Sean necked all the way back to the Harrisons.

"Sean, ask me out again. I had such a great time. I felt so proud to be seen with you—it was a neat, neat feeling. I'm sure you could be a gigolo; I'd certainly hire you!"

"I really love the free spirit that you are, Claire. I probably had a better time than you did, considering you slept all but ten minutes of the movie. We'll have to do it again after Christmas.

Swimming will be taking up most of my free time now."

"Swimming? Did you say swimming? That's my sport, or at least it was till I gained thirty kilos, and my boobs got humongous. Where are you swimming?"

"Pointe Claire."

"That's my old club, but you would be the only reason I would ever swim again. I'd do it just to feel you up and goose you underwater." They laughed as Claire continued, "I went 58.8 in the 100-meter freestyle when I was fourteen, and when I stopped competing, unfortunately, I got bigger—a lot bigger."

"Big is beautiful. Why don't you start again, and if nothing else, I'll have a bus mate for those long swimming trips," he said, raising his eyebrows up and down with a grin.

"You're unbelievable!" she said, giving him a little push. "Maybe, but for now, walk me to the door, give me a big kiss with a little grinding action, then run for the car, 'cause I know my dad will be watching," she grinned.

Sean delivered then ran to the car, giggling as he waved good-bye to her standing on the doorstep. Mr. Harrison, looking on with great displeasure, filled the upstairs bedroom window.

When he arrived back at the Lafoussiers, Martine was on the phone; he took the call in the living room.

"My mother saw you at the movie with Claire. She said that you are a *chaudhomme*. She was amazed at the energy you were giving off," Martine said.

"What the heck is a *chaudhomme?*" Sean asked.

"It means 'a hot man.' Haitian voodoo women idolize *chaudhommes*. They are men of real passion, hot-blooded and very rare. You're the first white *chaudhomme* my mother's come across. They can make women go crazy and can make a woman 'get off' by just being close to her. I told my mother about you when we first met, and she didn't believe me, but now she knows for sure," Martine exclaimed.

Sean heard a click. Someone was listening to the conversation.

"Are your folks at home?" asked Sean.

"No, I'm home alone. Why? Do you want to come over?"

"Sometime, but not tonight," Sean responded.

"You will think of me tonight, Sean, I promise. *Au revoir,*" Martine whispered and hung up. Sean heard two clicks.

Sean again wondered if something was wrong with the phones in the Lafoussier house. He sat in the living room thinking after Martine's phone call—his mind completely blown. Why was this stuff happening to him? He was never around voodoo. How could he possibly be a *chaudhomme*, if indeed he was? It was scary. The phone rang again. The rules of the house dictated that Sean was to never answer the phone.

"Sean, it's a Monsieur Goldman," said a man from Angola who had just moved into the house.

"Yo, Sean," said Sonny.

"Yo, Sonny!" Sean's face lit up.

"We're all at my house with our families. Your family's here too—Louie, Cassandra, a couple cheerleaders, and a bunch of other people. What a day! What a day! First, Louie scored forty-four points in hoops over Overbrooke. Can you believe it? But wait till you hear—all-state football was announced today." He lowered his voice to a whisper. "I was first team and MVP in Pennsylvania. Louie dropped down to second team, and he is pissed. But here's the kicker—I committed to go to West Point!"

"Wow! That's great news, Sonny!"

"Remember that guy, Coach Schroeder from West Point who saw us play on the beach in Wildwood? He's here as well. He recruited me all season, and it actually made me play better, knowing people like him were interested in me. My dad and your dad are sharing war stories with him—football, boxing, and track—wow! He says the Academy wants me for all three. What a deal, huh, Sean?"

Sonny was ecstatic. He was on a roll, talking faster than his normal cadence, "Sean, Sean, he wants you too! The first thing I asked him was if Louie, you, and I could be together again at the Academy. He said definitely! Can you believe it? How's that sound? Army-Navy game—together again in Philly at the classic, just like we always dreamed, Sean. Louie would not commit today, but I'm going to work on him. What do you say? Hey, here he is, Sean," Sonny said and passed the phone to Coach Schroeder.

"I know everything, Sean—no worries; we still want you, even though you played soccer this year. I knew when I saw you guys on the beach that you'd be a good recruit, but you're going to have to get in the Academy via a military prep school. Most Quakers quit the Academy shortly after arriving, but we can circumvent all that by having you go to a prep school to prove your military competency. How about it?" Coach asked.

"It sounds great, but I have to tell you, West Point's getting the best dang quarterback ever—congratulations!" Sean bragged on Sonny. "Can I talk to him again, please?" Sean asked.

"How are Louie and Cassandra?" Sean asked Sonny.

"Great. How come Brigitte never called Louie? Cassandra still won't have anything to do with him. Says she writes you every day. She told me she has sent over fifty letters and has yet to get a letter back from you. What's up, man? Wait…Sean, she's grabbing the phone."

"I miss you, Sean," she said and started to cry. "I thought you'd write me back or something. I need you…I want you…I'll always need you. When can I see you?" she sobbed.

"Cassandra, I've *never* gotten any letters from you. I thought your dad and mom were working you. I miss you all more than any of you will ever know."

As much as Sean missed her, he wanted to change the subject more and awkwardly asked, "Cassandra, this may seem weird, but where are your parents from?"

"Philadelphia—come on, Sean, what's up?"

"I mean originally," Sean responded.

"Try Africa, why? You think we are related or something?" Cassandra smirked.

Sean pressed on, "I mean, were there any intermediate stops before Philly?"

"Well, yeah, there were. Some of my father's kin came from New Orleans and Cuba, and of course, my grandmamma on my mother's side is from Haiti," Cassandra said.

There was a long pause from Sean. He started to get real scared about the probability of what might be a reality. "Cassandra, I have a feeling it will be tough to get together if your parents know I'm in town," Sean said, hearing another click on the line.

"You will never know how much I've missed you, Sean—any place, any time. Till then, I love you—really love you," she vowed, kissing good-bye into the phone.

Sean then talked to Louie for a long time. Louie apologized for trying to hit on Cassandra. They both agreed they had always been too competitive with each other, especially with women, starting with Brigitte. Louie realized how much he missed Sean and told him he would always love him—just not homo-like. Sean and Louie both chuckled. Louie thanked him, particularly for turning the Jacksons onto the Society of Friends and what it has meant to his mom.

"Please tell Brigitte I love her, and say hey to Guy for me," Louie requested.

Then Sean talked to his mom and dad. He told them all about Montreal Meeting, school, the Lafoussiers, soccer, and swimming. They were happy for Sean because he was in a new environment with unlimited potential, but he could tell they really missed him, and he really missed talking to his dad about things. His dad always had spiritual answers to difficult problems, so Sean dared to ask the question that was consuming him.

"Do you know anything about voodoo, Dad?"

"No, but Mrs. Johnson, your first nanny, sure believed in it. When your mom went back to work, she lived with us. She loved you. She was from New Orleans, out of the islands before she came to us," Big Sam said before Margaret interrupted.

"She was from Haiti and wanted to go back. She always had you playing with dolls, remember? And she made a special doll that you slept with till it fell apart. She claimed it stopped you from wetting the bed," Margaret said loudly, leaning toward the receiver.

All these things were adding up to really freak him out. After talking for almost 45 minutes with his dad and mom, Sonny came back on the line with Cassandra who squeezed in one final I love you. Sean hung up and saw it was nearly midnight. He climbed into bed and said his prayers, still feeling terrible about Brigitte and his lack of self-control with her. He was disturbed that someone was not delivering Cassandra's letters and was now convinced that someone was monitoring the phone system at Guy's house. But what really kept him awake was the *chaudhomme* stuff.

The next morning Guy announced that he was leaving again for Geneva for a week, after being home for only a few days. Sean went up and packed his bag and went to Brebeuf with Brigitte in the limo.

"Would you come in for a minute? Aubert wants to talk to you," Sean asked Brigitte.

"Absolument," she answered.

As they were walking through the administration building, Sean turned and said, "Aubert really doesn't want to talk to you, I do. Something weird is happening. I think all my calls are being monitored, and maybe your flat is bugged as well. I'm serious. We should be careful what we say in the car; I think everything could be bugged. I'm going to the Harrisons after swimming today. Can you take your car into the shop and get a loaner? Maybe pick me up at 7:00, okay? We need to talk about a lot of stuff, and by the way—till tonight." Brigitte broke a smile for the first time.

After swimming, Mrs. Harrison picked up Claire and Sean and headed for home.

"How are you doing, Claire?" Mrs. Harrison asked.

"Terrible. I tried to shoot Sean a moon underwater and some goofus by the name of Pierre got the wrong idea. It was not intended for him, and he is making a move on me now," Claire said.

"That's terrible, Claire. Why would you do such a thing, honey?" Mrs. Harrison asked.

"It makes me laugh, and it keeps us going in a hard workout. You're right, Mom. I shouldn't do stuff like that to anyone except Sean!" Claire said and they all laughed.

"Claire is really talented, Mrs. Harrison. She's improving quickly enough to enter the Papa Noel meet next week. I'm not going unless she goes. How about it Claire?" Sean asked.

"I'd go, but only to see you walk around in your Speedo, or what the girls call your banana hammock. I'm just not ready to race yet,"

"That's obscene, Claire," Mrs. Harrison said.

They arrived at the Harrisons, and Brigitte was waiting outside in a different car. Sean said good-bye and hopped in the car with her.

The Awakening

Sean soon discovered that one of the WPO workers had been intercepting his mail and possibly even listening in on his conversations. Some of the WPO workers scared Brigitte to begin with. She sent a telex to Guy requesting that he call her immediately. When he did, Sean answered. "Hello Sean, please put Brigitte on the phone," Guy said. He was obviously upset and gave her instructions to move home as soon as possible. He returned home that day and sent five of the Lafoussier gang back to their native countries.

After solving the phone incident and discovering that the same people were intercepting the mail from Cassandra, Sean wanted to get to the bottom of the chaudhomme thing. He was driving everywhere now because Guy had expelled most of the drivers due to mistrust. Sean pulled up to Martine's small house and rang the doorbell. Martine let him in. She was wearing the sexiest outfit he ever laid eyes on. It was a white dress that buttoned down the front the full length of the dress and had slits up the sides to show her leg. Sean could see she was wearing no undergarments at all and her body was perfect.

Haitian and African art, full of color and passion, filled the house. There was music playing in the background, with many different types of drums that he had heard before but could not remember where or when. Moving to the rhythm while pulling his arm, she led him into an exotically decorated den. He saw something he recognized.

"What's that?" he asked, pointing to a shelf lined with Haitian dolls. "That one I had as a child," Sean said, as Martine continued to move. "I called it Pere Giddy. I slept with it till it fell apart."

Martine corrected him, "No, Sean. That's Papa Ghede, the spirit of love-making and fun."

Frightened, Sean ran out of the house, fearing what it all that meant. He was no better than those people of the Bible who worshipped evil.

With tears streaming down his face, he drove to Brebeuf to find Brother Aubert. He told him everything and to his amazement Aubert said, "Remember first, that God loves you more than you could ever know. He is obviously getting your attention. Let's figure out what we can do. I do need to get some help on the Haitian thing. I'll call Father Claude, a Haitian priest I know, and Bernadette who you will remember is from Galway." Sean was able to muster a smile. "How about tomorrow after the last Mass and after dinner, let's say 1400?" Aubert suggested.

Sean drove to the Lafoussier house and went directly to his room. He broke down and began crying again. He had accomplished his mission of protecting his relationship with Brigitte, but in doing so and getting involved with Martine, he'd discovered some things about himself that really scared him.

Guy knocked and entered Sean's room and sat down on his bed, putting his hand on his shoulder. "Sean, life is not easy and is not meant to be. God understands us totally. Man just can't comprehend His love, and it's always confusing for man to understand the enormity and limitless nature of that love. Man always limits God. Your actions tell me that you know He wants you to change. Not everyone has the spirit of God in him. He is convicting you to lead a life more pleasing to Him. Remember, God is love. This old Frenchman thinks you're pretty special as well. One more thing, Sean, why don't you call your dad? He is a person of great depth and understanding in spiritual matters. I know when I need to talk things out I often call Big Sam. He has given me some great advice, and I know his wisdom is a gift from God. Call him. I love you, Sean, and I'm proud to have you in my home," and with that, Guy left the room.

Sean had slept for a couple hours when Claire called. "The only reason I went to a Saturday morning practice is because I thought you were going," she said.

"How was it?" Sean asked.

"The pits," Claire said. "The only reason I swim is because of you. I've lost ten kilos since I started, and my panties are starting to get baggy. I need to lose another twenty, and I know I will if you go to practice. My suit is getting looser also, so beaver shots and moons are very easy to perform. I'm sure that will really motivate you to get to practice." This got them to laughing.

"How is Pierre?" Sean asked.

"He's nuts! He won't let me alone. Hey, Sean! He asked me out tonight. Can you believe it? He wants to take me to his school dance. I told him I'd call him in fifteen minutes with a yes or no. What do you think?"

"You're a two-timing flirt!" Sean chuckled.

"I'll be forty by the next time you ask me out, so I guess I should practice dating, or at least that's what my dad says."

"Sean...Sean, are you okay? You sound kind of down. Why don't I come over and I'll expose myself—that would make you laugh for sure!"

"I'll pass, but give me a rain check. I have calls to make. Have a great time, and be sure to call me when you get back and give me a full report," Sean said.

Sean skirted the "down" comment completely. "Love ya, Wonder Woman," he said and hung up.

Sean called home to talk to his dad. Guy was right. His dad had sage advice, which would help Sean in his decision-making process. Big Sam approached things from a different perspective, telling Sean that anyone can run away in time of strife, but few love their fellow man enough to show God's love through patience, kindness, and asking forgiveness. "When your enemies hurt you, it deeply affects them by seeing God's love in your action of forgiveness. 'All men run, few fess up, and not enough look up.'" That was the saying that had helped Big Sam through troubled waters. He closed their conversation with a story that he had heard in Meeting.

"I cannot remember from whom or when I heard this story, but it always makes me cry when I think how wonderful God is and the miracles that happen everyday. An overseer of a downtown Meeting had the responsibility of visiting the oldest and the loneliest of Meeting. His obligation to service started to get him down, and several in the Meeting observed that he had lost his dedication to service. This overseer used to talk often in Meeting but his inner light was not as bright as it once was. Mrs. Dennison, a widow of twenty years, called the Meeting and asked to see this overseer, but he let weeks go by without calling on her. She called again and he finally visited her house. She met him at the door with the appropriate 'thees and thous,' and then offered tea and cookies, as they entered the living room. The overseer commented on the interesting paintings that hung in the foyer. She smiled and asked him to look at them more closely. So he did. He reported that he particularly liked the one of Daniel in the lion's den. She asked him to look at it again and tell her what he saw. He said that the lions were held at bay as Daniel, incarcerated in the pit, was left to die. She asked him to look once again at what Daniel was doing. Teary-eyed, he said Daniel was looking up at God who is the light in the picture, and not at the lions. She told him to stop reacting to other people and to keep his eyes fixed on God who loved him and would always protect him if he would only look to Him.

"When we hang up, I want you to pray about what your course of action should be to show God's love. I love you, Sean," and Big Sam hung up.

Sean drove to the Mertin's house and said a quick prayer before entering. It was nearly 1700 and just getting dark when he rang the doorbell. Mrs. Mertin, throwing off the most sensuous vibe, answered with a big smile and said, *"Bonsoir mon chaudhomme,* come in." She was wearing an outfit that one might see on a beach—a colorful halter top that exposed much of her chest and a white sarong that exposed almost all of one leg. Sean wanted to look at her body, but his attention stayed focused on her face.

"I'd like to talk to Martine," Sean said.

"Martine. Martine!" her mother called.

Martine entered the room in a bathrobe. The first thing Sean noticed was how beautiful she looked with her hair simply hanging down. She sat on the couch, took Sean's hand and smiled.

"I'm totally embarrassed about my mom and this voodoo stuff, and I want to apologize to you. I was trying to get up enough nerve to come see you at the Lafoussiers. I'm glad you're here," Martine said in a humble voice.

"My mom is forty percent Catholic and sixty percent vodoun. I want to be 100 percent Catholic. I thought the only way you would be interested in me was if I was a Haitian sexpot. I don't want to be that," Martine said, looking at Sean. "I hope you like me just because of me."

"God is good," Sean said to Martine, thinking about Guy's and his dad's advice.

Sean continued to ignore Mrs. Mertin who wanted to hear what they were discussing. "Tomorrow, I'm visiting Brother Aubert to try and understand what is going on with this Papa Giddy thing," Sean said. "Is that the way a *chaudhomme* would react?" he asked.

Sean suddenly felt like Joseph with Potifer's wife because of the constant vibes he was getting from Mrs. Mertin. "Let's get out of here. Get dressed and let's go for a ride," Sean prompted Martine.

On the way to her room she shut off the music and soon returned wearing a sweater dress with a wrap around her head. She put on a huge fur coat, took Sean's hand. "Let's go. I hate the cold," she mentioned, as they got into the car and drove off.

"I'm so embarrassed by my behavior and so exasperated with my mom. I do not want to be like her; I want to be me. I feel horrible and I never want to feel like this again. I'm so sorry about my mom taking a shot at you–that's disgusting," she confessed, as Sean parked the car in a spot overlooking the St. Laurence.

He told her that the reason she felt bad was the same reason he did—"the inner light" was correcting both of them, which was a positive sign. He also wanted her to notice that her mom felt just the opposite as they did. She felt no guilt at all due to her twisted priorities.

"What does your dad say about all this stuff?" Sean asked.

"He is all Catholic, 100 percent. Voodoo has always been a problem in their relationship. He went to Laval University and then went back to Haiti and married his high school sweetheart—my mom," Martine said.

"Does your mom cheat on your dad?" Sean asked.

"No, she doesn't because she doesn't consider sex cheating—she considers it a gift to her from Papa Ghede, and she is just practicing her religion."

"I want you to come with me to Brebeuf tomorrow to talk to Brother Aubert. I think it would help both of us," Sean insisted.

"I don't think so. I'm scared they will kick me out of school if they know I come from a voodoo family," said Martine.

"Just think how it would look for *me* to be kicked out of two schools in two months. I'm just as fearful as you are. But

I know that this is the right thing to do. Plus, I don't want to lose a friend," he said, as he squeezed her hand. "Good friends are too hard to find."

Sean continued, "It's funny but I always felt embarrassed about my family being different and not being accepted in our community. My best friends at home felt like outcasts. Part voodoo family—that's fine—that's who you are. I'm a Pennsylvania Quaker, and people continually try to make me feel bad about who I am. Brebeuf will not change where we are from—just help us know where we are going."

"1400 in Brother Aubert's office, okay?" he asked.

"Okay," she smiled.

The Right Way

Sean returned back to the house by 2130. His body felt like it had been through a war. Tired and weary, he went to bed, looking forward to his meeting the next day and fell asleep. At 2330, a phone call woke him.

"It is for you, mon cheri," Brigitte said. "It is Claire. She said it is important."

It took Sean a few moments to get oriented. He thanked Brigitte before he got out of bed. As she left she said, "Mon cheri, I miss you more than you will ever know," wanting him to know that her feelings hadn't changed.

"Sean, Martine called me and kind of told me what happened and that she needs to go to confession with you. She is freaking out because she feels terrible. Just remember, you can do anything to me you like. You could considerate it missionary work or something," Claire laughed. "But seriously, she is going with you tomorrow. Could you mention my name in confession? It would really impress Sister Bernadette if you told her you touch yourself thinking of me or something." Claire continued, "I was trying to call you when Martine called me, trying to decide whether to go or not. It was obvious today when I talked to you that you were in the absolute dumps—I've been worried. My dad thinks he knows how I feel about you, so he asked me to define my relationship. I told him I'm Sean's biggest fan, and there is not a kinder boy at Brebeuf. But I'm still worried. Are you okay?" she rattled on.

"Yep," he answered.

"Yep...yep," Claire said in a mocking tone. "Cut the shit, Sean, are you okay?

"Claire, I hope things will work out tomorrow. I have some questions about some spiritual stuff, and that's getting me down," he confessed. "I hope you won't give up on me. I like hearing your voice every day. I'll get over this, especially when I know people like you care. Heck, I almost forgot. Tell me about your big date!"

"Pierre, he's a total boob man. My breasts have totally consumed him—totally. Isn't life interesting? My biggest problem in swimming is my boobs creating too much drag, but it's what the boy's like; go figure. He tried to feel me up when we danced—how about that? Another notch in my belt," she laughed. "I had a great time. And by the way, I told him he'd better perform when he took me home. He had to hug me, kiss me and then give me a little grind at my doorstep and head for the car. My dad opened the door when we were grinding. Pierre was so shocked that he slipped on the ice and fell on his butt. It was seriously funny!" Claire roared.

"Would you date him again?" Sean asked.

"Absolutely, but I can see that might cause a problem on our away swimming trips for Pointe Claire. He'll want to sit next to me to on the bus to try and feel me up, but I'll be seated next to you!" she exclaimed.

"No problem. You can sit next to me by the window and he

can sit behind you. He can reach between the seats to get his jollies," he said and they both laughed hilariously.

"Oops, the ape is coming...my dad...got to go. Bonne chance tomorrow. Love you. Bye. She hung up.

As Sean climbed the winding staircase to the second floor, he saw an oriental woman he did not recognize on the third floor stairwell, in oriental clothing. They looked at each other and waved. He thought that she must be a new recruit for the WPO. He fell asleep, happily thinking about what a riot Claire was.

The next morning Sean met Dao, the Vietnamese woman that he saw on the stairs. He didn't get her relationship to the group. Dao and Sean instantly became friends. She was a Quaker who attended Penn then Harvard for her PhD in international relations and was about to start work for the United Nations. She had a Philly accent when she spoke English and a Vietnamese chop in French, but she had a beautiful voice. She told Sean more than he cared to know about what was going on in Vietnam, but he loved to hear her "talk Philly."

The Lafoussier gang, twelve strong, went to Meeting in three cars and then traveled to the Restaurant du Vieux Port Montreal, which was Guy's favorite. It had one room with a fireplace just large enough for the group, which was perfect for lunch and fellowship. Dao spoke a lot at the meal, always with great understanding and compassion. Sean discovered that Brigitte was a good friend of Dao's from their Philly days together.

Sean arrived at Brebeuf by 1400, and Martine was standing alone. They immediately held hands and entered the chapel. In an office adjacent to the chapel, he heard voices and found Father Nicholas, Brother Aubert, Sister Bernadette, and Father Jean-Louie, a Haitian priest. Sean could sense a new comfort level from Martine's body language, when she and Jean-Louie exchanged pleasantries in Creole.

Brother Aubert took the lead with his patented smile and warmth and said, "Sean came to me yesterday for some spiritual guidance, and I summoned you all here to see if we can help. Sean, why don't you tell everyone what is happening in your life and what is troubling you."

"Thank you, Brother Aubert. In the last couple days, I have discovered something about myself that is blowing my mind. I don't know why I've always had Haitian women in my life. My girlfriend back home—her family is originally from Haiti, and after spending time with Martine, I'm worried it might be some voodoo thing. Let me explain further. As a child, a Haitian woman whom I adored raised me. She taught me French and a lot of other things. She raised me from before I can remember until I was eight years old, and then Brigitte moved in and took over my care. Now people are telling me I'm a *chaudhomme,* but it didn't matter till I saw a doll in Martine's collection that she called Papa Ghede, the spirit of erotica from the voodoo tradition. The problem is that during my childhood I slept with this doll till it fell apart. I do not want anything to do with voodoo and neither does Martine. That's it—I'm scared," said Sean.

"Who told you that you were this "hot man?" asked Sister Bernadette.

"Martine thought something was very unusual about me; she told me that I was a *chaudhomme.*"

"Martine, what made you think this?" Sister Bernadette asked.

"I thought something was different because I'm not attracted to white boys at all. I was instantly attracted to him, particularly when I saw him dance. When I danced with him, he totally consumed me in a way I cannot describe. I became very aggressive and pursued him. When my mom and I were showing him around the house, he saw the doll, and we told him about the story of Papa Ghede. He got scared and ran out of the house. He came back several hours later and said we needed to get help and here we are," Martine stated. Brother Aubert smiled.

"Well then," Aubert began but was interrupted by Bernadette.

"Have you had relations with Sean?" the Sister asked, looking at Martine.

Father Nicholas stepped in before Sister Bernadette had a chance to pistol-whip the two. "I'm proud of both of you. You are doing the right thing by seeking spiritual help and guidance. Let's hear from Jean-Paul," Nicholas requested.

"In Haiti, the church has compromised its teachings and has allowed people to hold on to too much of their native religion and culture. It's not uncommon to see voodoo art and dolls in a Catholic home from Port au Prince to Cap-Haitien. As to a *chaudhomme* and the powers of Papa Ghede, they are real in the minds of many in Haiti, unfortunately."

Sister Bernadette had changed her demeanor on Father Nicholas' cue. "Are you Irish, Sean?" she asked in her thickest Irish brogue.

"Yes, and my ancestors are from the village of Cleggan. That's where my grandmother was born."

"You know, that does not surprise me," said Sister Bernadette.

"Yes, I remember that you said something about it when I helped you," Sean replied.

"I'm from Clifden, the town just south of Cleggan. The Irish have held on to several traditions in their own culture, which I found to be much like the people of Haiti. For example, in time of need someone with roots in Galway will be there to help—like you helped me, Sean. They believe that relatives continue to look after you when they pass on and that they're able to communicate with you from the other side. They believe in the wee little people too. Cleggan was famous for seers. What was your grandmother's name?" Sister asked.

"I think it was Megan O'Mungen," Sean answered.

Sister Bernadette was apprehensive by his response and turned to Father Nicholas and said in French, "It all makes sense to me now," becoming very pensive.

Father Nicholas intervened with his wisdom, "The world does not rejoice when God's people grow. In "Psalms 2" it says that kings and mighty rulers join forces against the Lord and his anointed. Powers and rulers want to break the unity and spoil the goodness that binds God's people, and they do not do this on their own. They use agents of the evil one sometimes. Voodoo is evil. It uses intermediate forces, which is an abomination unto the Lord. Just remember, we worship the one and only God who is in you and who is much greater than any other forces in the world. Let us rejoice in that and help these two beautiful young people rid themselves of whatever evil forces are confusing them," Nicholas offered.

Brother Aubert was smiling as he ushered Martine and Sean into the chapel. They got on their knees. The others gathered around them and prayed while laying hands on them, which was common among Franciscans. The prayers were long and heartfelt petitions for God to rid them of any evil spirits or demons and for them to be set free from their bondage of evil influences. Jean-Louie directed his petitions against Papa Ghede and voodoo. Sister Bernadette was still speechless since Sean told her his grandmother's name.

They all left with a sense of peace and joy, but Sister Bernadette was bothered. Martine stayed afterward with Sean to talk to Sister Bernadette who obviously wanted to talk.

"Did you ever know your grandmother," she asked Sean.

"No, Sister. She passed before I was born."

"I knew your grandmother," she said, her eyes moistening. "She was a famous seer from Cleggan. She was the first person to tell me when I was very young that I should go into the convent. I did not think anything of it at the time, as a wee child, but as time went on, I thought it was a possibility. If you're her grandchild, I understand what is happening to you. Your saving my life makes even more sense. In the heavenlies, things are linked in a way we mortals will never totally understand. I'm glad we are on God's side," she nodded with tears in her eyes and said good-bye.

Martine and Sean were relieved and happy as they walked arm-in-arm to the car. Sean drove her home and they hugged good-bye. He returned to the Lafoussiers.

In the study, Dao and Brigitte were sitting on the couch near the fireplace. Sean joined them and sat in Guy's favorite leather chair, facing them on the couch. They had been talking about the Easleys and Philly. "I just realized that I know your family, Sean," Dao said. "I've heard your father speak at several conferences, and now it's coming to me that it was you who spoke on one of the Martin Luther King discussion panels when you were a young boy. I think both you and Brigitte were on that panel. You were so cute," she said, "but you've turned out to be one handsome man," looking at Brigitte with a smile.

Sean wondered if Brigitte had been telling Dao stuff that she didn't need to know and made an excuse to leave the study, "Brigitte, I have to study for an exam tomorrow. See you both later." As he was leaving the room, the phone rang and it was Claire.

"Martine is one happy camper. Hey, did you tell Sister that you touch yourself at night thinking of me like I asked?" Claire and Sean laughed. "I'm glad things worked out. Got to run. The ape and my mom and I are going to the club—they're calling me," Claire said. "See you soon."

"Right," Sean said, after she hung up, looking at the vacant receiver.

Sean sat in his room and thought about the last two day's events—about how competitive women were with each other: Martine and her mom, Martine and Claire, and even Brigitte seemed competitive with Dao. As he thought about it, he realized that women were no different from men, like the competition between Sonny, Louie, and himself.

After a couple hours of reading, Guy called Sean to join him in the study. Brigitte and Dao were already there when he arrived. Guy beamed at Sean, saying, "We are going to Paris for

Christmas. The three of us have decided we would like to invite you to come along."

"That's great! Thanks. I just have to check with the folks. When would we go?"

Guy interrupted before Sean had his question out. "The trip will be from the 22[d] through the 29th. Dao and I have a meeting in Brussels on the 27th. Paris is a beautiful sight at Christmas. You will need a passport. Dao can you help on that end," Guy said with satisfaction and continued, "Call Big Sam and get his permission so we can arrange everything. Tell him we will stay at my family farm, pres de Beauvais. *Va! Va! Parle à tes* parents."

Sean was thrilled and grateful for the opportunity to see France, a country he had studied more than his own, but at the same time, how he missed his home! The thought of not getting home at all for break was unbearable. So, he set his mind to work and quickly figured out a way to get home from the 29th to the 4th and called his parents. Paris for Christmas, Philly for the New Year—what a combo!

Big Sam was excited for Sean. His mother cried the entire time on the phone, wailing in her unique dramatic manner about all the reasons why he shouldn't go, but Big Sam prevailed. Sean was going to Paris for Christmas.

He immediately called Sonny. It was the first day of Hanukkah, and Louie and Cassandra were there to break bread with the Goldmans. Sonny couldn't talk because they were about to start the festivities, but they called Sean afterward and expressed their excitement for Sean, all except for Cassandra.

"I can hardly breathe when I think of you, Sean. I miss you

so much!" Cassandra whimpered. "Don't go!" she pleaded.

"If I couldn't see you at all, I wouldn't think of going, but I'll be home for a whole week, and it will be great. If I had to choose between Paris and Cassandra, Cassandra wins every time! You know that, but to see Paris, wow!" Sean said in an attempt to change her heart.

"I think those Frenchies are up to something, but if you must go, be careful. And don't think those folks are looking out for your best interests. I just have a bad feeling. Hurry home!" Cassandra pleaded.

Paris

Dao worked a miracle to get all of Sean's necessary paper-work in time for him to make the trip to Paris. First class was a small, elite sitting area with only three rows: two seats *à droite* and two seats *à gauche*. Guy booked Sean and Dao sitting next to each other. The stewardesses knew Guy by his first name, since he took that flight often for WPO business.

The flight departed at 1700 from Montreal and was to arrive in Paris at 0800 the next morning. Dao talked a lot, as if she was a little nervous about flying, but Sean liked to hear her unusual accent—a combination of Philadelphian, Vietnamese, and French.

As Dao continued her chatter about world hunger, Sean drifted in and out of a dream with Jimmy Stewart starring in *The Spirit of St. Louis,* which re-enacted Lindbergh's historic solo flight crossing the Atlantic. He dreamt about how Lindbergh thought for sure he was a goner, being lost after twenty-seven hours in flight, until he saw Dingle Bay in Ireland. Lindbergh actually recovered his bearings when an Irishman he flew over pointed out the direction to Paris. Then he was off to Le Bourget Field in Paris to make aviation history. Sean wondered if that Irishman had roots in Galway, smiling to himself, drifting back into the dream.

"Sean," Dao said, nudging his arm, "I personally don't think world hunger is anything to smile about."

"I was just smiling at you, knowing that you will make a difference. Your passion and insight will make a difference to the world," Sean answered, trying to mask his drowsiness.

"You also say all the right things," she said.

Now what the heck does that mean, Sean thought. Was she trying to make him think that she knows about Brigitte and him? What was going on?

After they breezed through passport control and customs, an African woman met them. Guy told Sean that she was part of the WPO. They traveled north through Paris, toward Old Paris, taking in the sights from a Volkswagen van, which had windows in the roof. Paris was absolutely beautiful during Christmas, and they all enjoyed seeing the famous landmarks along the way. Once out of the historic district, they took the A16 towards Beauvais, exiting onto a beautiful country road before turning onto a narrow tree-lined dirt road with pasture-land on either side.

"How does it feel to be home, Guy?" Brigitte asked.

"Manifique! To be at the family farm...it's where I spent every Christmas as a boy," he beamed.

"I thought you grew up in Montreal, Guy," Sean said in an inquisitive tone.

"When you have a French mother and a Canadian father, you live in two worlds, but I liked it: Christmas and Bastille week in France, Easter and some holidays in Martinique in the Caribbean, and the rest of the year in Montreal."

"What kind of work did your father do?" asked Sean.

"He was an opportunist," Guy tittered. "He was in international trade. Whatever the world needed, he would find it and sell it to them. As a young boy I thought he was in shipping because he constantly engaged ships, but he used every transport possible. When he began shipping farm animals, he assembled them here then trucked them to Le Havre ou Marseille," he continued, not looking at Sean but fixing his eyes on the farm as the van pulled through a manned gate.

Everyone came out to greet Guy. It was obvious that these people loved him. Smiling, he looked each one in the eye, hugged them, and kissed them on both cheeks. It was natural for him to say something personal to each one. For the first time Sean realized Guy could speak many languages, as he spoke to each one in his native tongue. Guy led the entourage into the house then turning to Brigitte, Dao and Sean said, *"Bienvenue à la ferme de Lafoussier à Beauvais, France,"* with a gracious arm gesture.

It was a beautiful old farmhouse, built in the sixteenth century and formerly the country estate of the famous architect Andre Lucrat. Guy didn't hesitate to give them a complete history of the farm. Old Andre, Sean thought, did the farmhouse right with fireplaces in every room. The interior walls were stone, trimmed with fine cherry and exotic woods. The huge fireplace had a small fire burning to take the chill out of the room.

"Chantal, *s'il vous plait*, show Sean and Dao to their rooms, and please unpack Brigitte's and my bags in the master bedroom," Guy instructed the middle-aged Chinese-looking woman. "Sean, after you get settled, I'll meet you here as soon as you're ready," Guy continued.

The rooms were large, with a shared bathroom between Dao's and Sean's room. Sean showered first and locked Dao's door to prevent a surprise visitor, unpacked, and went downstairs to see Guy.

"Let's go for a walk. I'd like to show you around. Grab a pair of those rubber boots in the pantry. It's probably soggy in the low areas by the creek…and dress warmly," Guy instructed.

They sauntered down the tree-lined, stone-covered road towards a heavily wooded area about 1000 meters ahead of them. Guy concentrated on the pastureland on both sides of the road. "I think I'll always be a frustrated farmer; I'd much rather grow grapes and raise livestock than what I ended up doing. Let's go through here," Guy said as he opened a white painted fence to the pasture with some horses. "These are my favorites," he said as they walked towards a horse that was at least *quatorze mains* high.

"There he is, "Le Outrement Flash." He's won much money for me over the years," Guy said. The horse came over and was happy to see him. "I've always thought of the Flash as being somehow connected to my son. We've been good friends over the years," he said, patting the horse's shoulder firmly and stroking is neck. Flash nudged his owner's arm, wanting more attention. "Good boy, good boy, my beauty. He is one prolific breeder; many of his offspring have done extremely well," he said as they crossed the pasture towards a small cluster of trees on a bank.

"I'm taking you to my favorite place in the entire world. I spent much time here as a boy, dreaming and catching crawfish. Thank you for walking with me, Sean," Guy said as they arrived at the bank, gleaming with satisfaction that nothing had changed.

"Look at that huge willow tree. They normally don't get that large. The pond looks good, which means the creeks that feed it are all in good shape," Guy pointed out. They sat on a fallen maple limb. Off in the distance was a heavily wooded area and looking towards it Guy said, "That's where I discovered I was a Quaker—well, that is, as a result of an encounter in those woods, I made a consequent decision to join the Quaker faith. I went hunting with my grandpapa, and I shot a deer. I couldn't sleep for a week afterward because I had killed one of God's most beautiful creatures. The inner light was convicting me, and then a girl at school who belonged to La Rive Gauche Meeting in Paris introduced me to the Quakers. If we stayed in Beauvais for longer than just a short holiday, my father would place me in school till we went back to Montreal. She invited me to a Quaker Meeting and I really felt called to the Quakers. I was only twelve. My parents were very upset. Being avid Catholics they perceived the Society of Friends to be an English faith. Coming from a long line of Canadian French separatists, you could imagine how that was received—not well," he said with a chuckle.

"This is really a beautiful place. Your family must be very proud of it," Sean said.

"Unfortunately, I really have no family left, other than Brigitte, and now you. What I mean is that I certainly have enjoyed having you stay with us. In a way it has reminded me of how much I've lost—so many special times—lost with my son. I found myself feeling like a surrogate father to you during soccer season and trying to help when you were depressed. Life is a collection of special moments. I am thankful for all the wonderful memories I have of my son, Stephan, but I still miss him so much," Guy said, staring back in time and trying not to show emotion.

"You certainly have taught me a lot since I've known you; you're a lot different than I thought. You have a big heart that tries to help everybody. I'm sorry you lost your son," Sean said, interrupting the silence.

"One day I had a family the next day they were gone. I have always blamed their disappearance on myself because of my line of work. Someone had something against me and took it out on my family. Do you know what I do?" Guy asked Sean.

"You work for the World Peace Organization," Sean answered.

"Of course, but I sell the information that we collect to several other parties for profit. It all started after an international conflict broke out. The Friends could have saved many lives, if they could have persuaded the parties involved to resolve their differences peacefully before hostilities commenced. We were not only operating an underground railroad, but we started intercepting information and dispatching people to intervene. We were active with everyone during World War II, but once we got involved in the first pre Indo-Chinese war activity, the French and the Americans thought we were communist sympathizers befriending Ho Chi Minh rather than Boa Dai. Around that time, we started selling information, and my family disappeared," Guy said in a sorrowful voice.

"I can only imagine what you feel, but you're saving lives, aren't you, and doing what God wants you to do? I know it's the best feeling in the world when you save a life. I'm trying to figure out what God wants me to do to accomplish just that. I think He is calling me to the military. Isn't that weird?" Sean asked.

"Your dad and I have discussed the essence of war several times. You know he changed during the war and wanted to try to save lives. I called him before we left to tell him I felt guilty taking you to France during Noel. He laughed and said he will miss having you home during Christmas but went on to say that there comes a time in every man's life when his dad has little influence. I was flattered when he said that he could think of no more positive influence on his son than me."

"He's right," Sean agreed with a nod.

"Well, I'm starting to get cold," Guy confessed. "Let me give you the grand tour," he continued, as they walked back to the road and then to the well-kept stables, which held eight magnificent horses. Next they went on to what appeared to be a barn but was actually the offices for the WPO—telexes and radios of all types. Most of the personnel had headsets on, sitting around a large table, taking notes.

"This is where we process information. These people are listening to operatives communicate. This other room is a sort of command central where we analyze the communications and determine whether the information is pertinent and worthy of passing it to various interested parties. This hallway is the social services section where they work on giving assistance to the hungry, to street people, and for child abuse and prostitution. We also help with other tragedies like earthquakes, floods, avalanches, and so on. The information-gathering is what funds the entire operation," Guy reported.

Sean was amazed at the enormity of the operation, as they went into another building that appeared to be for storage. This was the living area for the entire WPO work group. There were both private and bunkhouse accommodations, with an extremely large table in the living room area that sat nearly fifty.

"This is where we will have Noel dinner with everyone, and where our world meetings are held twice a year," Guy announced proudly.

"How many of these operations are there, and do the Quakers know everything about how you do this?" Sean asked.

"The Quakers know all about the social services we provide, but few know how we fund, and they know very little about the information services. They contribute less than five million French francs per annum to a 150 million French francs operation. There is one on each continent with two in Africa, and some secret operations in a few potential hot spots," Guy divulged.

Guy and Sean stopped by the winery momentarily on the way back to the main house. Guy explained the operation of the winery and how it generated a modest income. He also mentioned that Andre Lucrat had designed the barn a good distance from the main house because he found the odors objectionable, but even more so because he believed animals could carry diseases harmful to children.

When they entered the main house, Sean's senses came alive with the savory aromas wafting from the kitchen. The fireplace warmed them, as they entered the living room. Brigitte and Dao were planning group activities for their stay while in France. After a delicious meal and conversation, Sean retired for the evening, having only slept for a couple of hours on the flight to Paris the night before.

For the next few evenings, Dao entertained a Vietnamese

fellow who also worked for the WPO. Hearing the high-pitched sounds that now and then sprang from her room, Sean smiled and thought she could have been an opera singer.

The Christmas season in Paris and Beauvais was truly magical. No shopping—the Lafoussier gang was not given over to the commercialization of Noel. Rather, evenings consisted of caroling and delivering food to the needy families of Beauvais. Twice the gang set up hot meals for the street people *pres de Notre Dame* in the *vieille ville de Paris*. Afterward, Guy showed Sean the sights of Paris. It was apparent to all that Guy was growing fonder of Sean, as their time together increased each day.

At midnight on Christmas Eve, the gang went to Mass at the Cathedral de Saint-Pierre in Beauvais. Sean was asked to sit between Brigitte and Guy during Mass. It was strange for him; he had come to admire and respect Guy but at the same time felt the electricity between himself and Brigitte. The Mass was a beautiful, candlelight service that set the group's spirits soaring. When they returned back to the farm, they had a short meeting and then everyone retired for the evening.

At the dinner table the evening following Christmas, Guy asked Brigitte if she wanted to go to Brussels with Dao and himself. She responded that she wanted to take Sean to the Palace at Versailles, since that would be their last sightseeing venture before their return to Canada. Brigitte was adamant on Versailles, and so it was arranged. Dao and Guy left at 0600 for their meeting in Brussels, and Sean and Brigitte departed at 0800 for la Gare de St. Denis to take the train to Versailles.

After settling into their seats on the train, Brigitte whispered, "Sean, I need you *now*." She embraced him passionately while the train was still in the station. This was the first public display of affection the two had ever exhibited, and Sean was looking around to see who was watching. Before he knew it the train had stopped at the Gare du Nord station. Brigitte took his hand and they exited the train. In just a few minutes, they were once again together in a hotel room. It was 1800 before they knew it, and they didn't get back to the station at St. Denis until 1830. They arrived at the farm at 1930 to an awaiting Guy. "How was Versailles?" he asked.

"Never got there," Sean quickly responded. Brigitte showed no emotion. "Stopped at an earlier station and got off," Sean continued. "When I found out that the opera and ballet were close to an earlier station, I asked Brigitte if we could check it out. What a place! They open in a few weeks and didn't seem to mind us watching them practice," Sean expounded as Brigitte went to the bathroom to collect herself after Sean's "story."

"How did the meeting go in Brussels?" Sean asked in hopes that the questioning would stop.

"I'm greatly encouraged by the reception of our efforts in the world community," Guy said as Dao entered the room. "Don't you think so, Dao?" Guy asked.

"I think the meeting went very well, especially in the world health arena. We are making real strides in polio. By the progress we are making, I think we can almost eradicate polio in the not so distant future," Dao responded as Brigitte re-entered the room.

"You look wonderful, Brigitte. You have some real color in your cheeks," Dao said.

"Mais oui; it's hard keeping up with Sean in high heels. It took quite an effort, and it's the first time in a long time that

I've gotten so much exercise," Brigitte's eyes smiled at Dao.

"Well, the exercise served you well," Dao smiled coyly.

That night Sean had great difficulty sleeping. His thoughts kept going to Brigitte then to Guy. Something was telling him he just had to stop. He couldn't escape the guilt and remorse he felt after seeing Guy when they returned. Guy wasn't the creep that he had originally thought. He was a man of real substance who loved Brigitte but knew that because of their age difference some of her needs would go unmet. Both Sean and Brigitte knew that what they were doing was wrong in God's eyes. Sean was again discovering that one little wrong has a way of snowballing into a bigger wrong. He vowed to himself to stop the Brigitte thing even though it was the fulfillment of every dream he had ever had. Sean started to think about his trip home to Philadelphia and how great it would be to see his friends. He started thinking of soft pretzels, Breyers ice cream, Philly cheese steaks, and dancing with Cassandra again. He sensed God was changing him and he was glad. He fell asleep, imagining Aubert on his toes, clapping for his newfound conviction.

The flight back was a duplicate of the flight to France but longer. Dao spoke about Vietnam constantly. You would think Ho Chi Minh and Boa Dai were very close, personal friends of hers by the way she name-dropped. Sean concluded that they very well may be, considering her vocal demonstrations of pleasure when her other Vietnamese friend visited her room at the farm. Listening to Dao, Ho was a good man, but Boa was just a horn dog who did not care about the people of Vietnam. Boa was using the United States to get his power and to fuel his habits, but the United States was afraid of Ho. Sean was surprised to learn that Ho was initially an ally of the United States to the downfall of the Japanese in Indochina during WWII, but was later declared an enemy of the USA because he was a communist. Sean knew there was much to learn from his new friends, but he had no idea where it was going to lead. It had to be fate.

Pointe Claire—a Saving Grace

Sean felt fortunate that he was able to squeeze out a few days in Philadelphia with his family and the Toujours Amis gang before returning to school in Montreal. "Good to have you back home, Sean," Guy greeted him at the airport.

"You know, I missed Montreal. I loved going home, but this is starting to feel like home now," Sean said.

"Everyone has been calling you. Brother Aubert called and Jean Claude from Point Claire Swim Club called about a swim meet in New York soon and one at Point Claire this weekend. Brigitte will have to fill you in. No one could reach you in Philadelphia. Brigitte also told me that you were on some new television show and that everyone was watching."

Someday they should invent a machine that takes messages when someone is not in—they would make a mint, Sean predicted to himself.

The trip to the Lafoussier estate was uneventful other than for Sean apprising Guy of the happenings of his friends from Abington. Sean went directly to his room to put on his school uniform because St. Jean's commenced school that morning. His first semester report card was on his desk. He opened it to find that he received all A's and an A+ in French. He started to cry and dropped to his knees to give thanks. Once again, he was convicted about Brigitte when he prayed. He knew if it weren't for Guy, he would not have had this opportunity in Montreal—he needed to do something.

Sean arrived at school by midday. On his way to the school office, a student passing in the hallway said, "Yo, Easy...saw you on TV. You made Brebeuf famous!" Another called out, "Yo, Easy Man." Sean wondered how the 'Easy Man' thing started. Later he found out that the Geator referred to him as 'Easy Man' on the "Dance Party" show.

"Happy New Year, Sean," a smiling Aubert said. "I'm so proud of your grades—and now you are a television star! Welcome back to Brebeuf. Here is your second semester schedule, and I'll take you to your classes," Aubert said, eager to accompany Sean to class.

"That's okay, Aubert. I'll find the classes; just please give me a note for being late," Sean requested.

School flew by that day. He met Claire in the parking lot after school to catch a ride to Point Claire. It was apparent that she had lost some weight since he had last seen her. "Wow, Claire, you look great!"

"Good enough for me to get a little before swimming practice?" Claire jokingly suggested.

"Sure, but I need my strength for practice," Sean responded, and they both laughed. "How's Pierre?" he asked.

"We dated a lot during the holidays, and by the way, we have a swim meet at Pointe Claire this weekend and I entered you. Next weekend we go to NYC. Would you please request me as your roommate?" Claire queried as she giggled.

"I'm not ready for a meet yet. I didn't swim while in France and swam only a few times back home. I'm not ready," Sean confessed.

"Tough shit! You talked me into starting to swim; you're going to New York and you're swimming this weekend," Claire said, giggling.

"You got me—I'd better get mentally prepared," Sean said with a grin.

Sean convinced the coaches to allow him to swim only one individual event and one relay each day. They were also aware that he did not want to miss attending Meeting on Sunday, so they scheduled him to swim only the 50-free trials on Sunday at 0900.

He was stunned when he saw Claire in her new bathing suit; she looked terrific. She did not wear a nylon suit; it was a black, girdled speed suit that compressed her body and showed off her shapely figure. She tucked her waist-length hair into her cap. He recognized that she was developing into quite a woman.

As Claire drove him home, she said he had become quite a "phenom" in Montreal because he had been seen on the "Dance Party" TV show when he was in Philly. "Ninety per-cent of teenagers in Montreal must have watched you. It was so hyped-up during Christmas break, and everyone was having "Dance Party" get-togethers in their homes."

"I went to Martine's house, and when you were on TV, Mrs. Mertin started convulsing and getting off over seeing you dance. Martine was embarrassed about her mom, but we still had a great time. All the girls were swooning when you were cha-cha-cha-ing with Cassandra."

When Sean didn't make much over being on TV, Claire took the opportunity to change the subject and continued, "By the way, Sean, I've never told you how much I appreciate your friendship and how you encourage me—not just in swimming but in everything. Your friendship has done a lot for me."

"I'm trying to stop thinking about women all the time because it screws me up pretty severely," confessed Sean. "Claire, I'm serious. I need to clean up my act. Please appreciate that."

"I'm serious too. I'm saving myself for you. What a dream—to be with your best friend forever. That's storybook stuff," Claire swooned.

Sean blew her a kiss from the steps of his house, and in return, she cupped her breast as sort of an offering. What a gal—smart, attractive, funny—she is going to end up with someone really special, he thought.

When Sean arrived at the Lafoussiers, the clan was at the dinner table. They all stood and greeted Sean, except for Guy. Sean took his seat next to Guy and across from Brigitte.

"I saw you on television last week on that teenage dance show with that African girl. What country is she from?" asked a Sudanese man who was relatively new to the house.

"She's an American that I grew up with in Philadelphia. I've been dancing with her since I was twelve. Her name is Cassandra," he said.

"She has a striking resemblance to that movie star Lena Horne," the East African replied.

"You know, she really does look like Lena Horne," said Brigitte.

Sean could tell that Guy purposely changed the subject when he said, "Well, Sean, it is really good to have you back. Congratulations on your performance *à l'ecole*. All A's are terrific. I, for one, missed having you around and really enjoyed having you with us in Beauvais."

"Thanks, Guy. Beauvais was like a dream come true for me, to be in France over Christmas. I certainly missed you all, though, when I was in Philly. I felt, somehow, like I had changed or that Philly was changing," Sean shrugged.

"We were just talking about that very subject—adapting to the changing times and being willing to adapt to what it means to our personal lives. Some people can't adjust and some can. The more pertinent question is will the Friends be able to keep their core values and change with the times? Will they react to the needs of the world? By the way, the Catholique Charities de Quebec honored our Brigitte for her work with street people and the homeless last Saturday. We were all there; it was a wonderful event," Guy said as he held Brigitte's hand in admiration.

"Wow, fantastique! Congratulations, Brigitte. You certainly deserve it, as hard as you work with the downtrodden. Congratulations!" Sean said and then changed the subject, "I learned today that I have a swim meet in two days, which I need to mentally prepare for."

"Is it at Point Claire?" Brigitte asked.

"Oui, it's at Point Claire," Sean answered.

"When will you swim—on *Samedi et Dimanchce*?" Guy asked.

"Probably 1200 on *Samedi* and 0900 on *Dimanche*, and if I make the finals each night, again at 1800," said Sean.

"We would all like to come and watch, if that is okay," Brigitte said.

"Of course, but I'm just not ready yet, and I don't want to disappoint you," Sean replied sheepishly.

"Stop it, Sean. You just need to have fun and race. That's what sport is all about. We won't enjoy ourselves if you don't. Sport is sport. It's supposed to be fun! That's why you are so much fun to watch in soccer; you had fun with no expectation of personal success. Don't change, keep things simple," Guy said.

Sean knew Guy was absolutely on the mark. Sean never thought like that before. He knew fear of failure stopped most great athletes from exploring their true potential. He needed to hear what Guy was saying.

"Thanks, Guy. You're right," he said with a big smile. "I promise I will keep it simple and just race."

The two days passed very quickly. Back at school Martine and Sean were spending almost no time together. She was now devoted to a Haitian beau who went to another school.

Sean knew that before he could break it off with Brigitte, he would need some time with her for her to understand the complexities of his emotions. He waited for the opportunity to make things right.

On Saturday morning, Claire picked up Sean, and they drove to Pointe Claire to the meet. Claire out swam everyone in the trials, doing all her best times, breaking a Pointe Claire record in the 100 backstroke and beating everyone in the 100-free trials. She was one happy camper. Mr. Harrison was there, beaming over Claire's metamorphosis. He was actually pleasant to Sean because the Ape's wrath had turned towards Pierre. Mr. Harrison's presence intimidated Pierre, so he swam horribly until finally Claire called him a pussy and told him no more ta-tas unless he got his ass in gear in the finals.

Sean swam well in the 100 free, qualifying 4th for the finals. Father Francois and Brother Aubert ran up and down the pool deck when he swam. He was so far ahead at the 50 that he let the others catch up a little to make them feel better.

The first event of the finals was the 100 free for women, then men. Claire swam her heart out but was touched out by 2/10 of a second by the supposedly fastest woman freestyler in Canada. She swam a 57.77 for the 100-meter short course, almost a full second better than her previous best time. Her dad was extremely proud of her feisty attitude exhibited during the race. Little did he know her true motivation.

In the men's 100, Sean was a body length ahead at the 50 but lost on the last stroke at 51.99. It was the 100 back that Claire showed just how good she was by breaking a Canadian record and receiving a standing ovation. Overjoyed, she beamed at Sean. After the meet, Sean was waiting with Brigitte and the Lafoussier gang. The press immediately hounded Claire when she came out of the locker room.

"How does it feel to be back in the pool? Did your dad teach you how to compete? Why such rapid improvement?" the reporters fired questions simultaneously.

"I'm just extremely motivated right now. I would like to say that it was my best friend who talked me into swimming again, and I'm very glad that he did!" she answered excitedly, looking at Sean.

"Who was it? What's his name?" asked a *Toronto Star* reporter.

"It's a friend from Brebeuf," Claire said. "Thanks for your interest, but I've got to go home now and rest for tomorrow. Bonsoir." Claire left with her family and the Lafoussier folks.

"Let's all go out to dinner!" Claire feigned, fully aware they already had plans.

"We can't, honey. You know that we have a dinner engagement," Mr. Harrison said.

"Unfortunately, Guy and I have a Red Cross dinner," Brigitte added. "Why don't you both have dinner on the way home and get ready for tomorrow? You were both terrific."

"Okay, I'll drop Sean off after we stop for a bite," Claire said coyly. "See you tomorrow," she said as they walked to Claire's car.

"Where're you going?" Pierre shouted, running towards them. "What's up, Claire? Where are you going? What's up?" he said again.

"You're a stone pussy, Pierre, the way you swam tonight," said Claire with more than a hint of disgust. "You're so intimidated by my dad that you can't get out of your own way."

"He told me before the meet if I ever touched you he'd kill me. A two-meter tall, 150-kilos of pissed off father is something to consider," Pierre admitted.

"Well consider this, Pierre. You are ranked 4th in the world in the 400 and you placed 4th in the 100 and 5th in the 400 at a provincial swim meet in Canada. If you don't get your shit together by tomorrow after trials, I'm telling my father that you feel me up all the time and that you're a pervert. See you,"

Claire threatened. Pierre knew she meant business by the look on her face. Sean and Claire drove off, as Pierre stood speechless in the parking lot.

"I hate guys that are pussies. Everyone at school thought you were a pussy because you wouldn't fight, but after you put those hockey bullies in their place without throwing a punch—that was the best!" Claire stated proudly.

"You certainly gave Pierre your own 1-2 combo," Sean responded.

"I know I wasn't being fair, but I only want to be with you, Sean."

"Let's go eat and talk some more."

Claire confessed that after watching Cassandra and him on "Dance Party," she would envision dancing with Sean herself as she swam, and it really helped her not to feel any pain at the end of a race.

After dinner they drove along the river and parked. Claire said that she just wanted him to hold her. Another car pulled up, interrupting the moment. They held each other a little longer and then returned home, knowing that there was something special happening between them. They didn't say much to each other during the rest of the ride home.

Early the next morning, Claire pulled up to the Lafoussiers and picked up Sean. "I dreamed that you swam real fast. I saw people standing up, clapping, with you in the water, facing the crowd," she said excitedly.

He didn't acknowledge what she said. "You know, the way you're going, you are going to make the Canadian Olympic Team," he assured her.

"I think I'd rather be with you than go to the Olympics," she kidded.

The next morning Sean swam the 50 trials and was by far the fastest qualifier. Brigitte picked him up afterwards to attend Meeting. "Guy is leaving town on Wednesday. I have missed you so. It's been a long time since we have been together," Brigitte said, running her hand along his thigh.

At Meeting, his guilt over Brigitte was flaring. He questioned whether he had the guts to break it off with his dream woman. What if he drove her into the arms of another man? Would it kill Guy emotionally? That would be worse than if Guy knew that Sean had been intimate with her. Finally, he realized that if he would let God do the leading, he would have the fortitude to do what was right.

The whole Lafoussier household went to Pointe Claire for the finals. Sean broke a Quebec record in the 50 in 23.97, and was a good 8/10 of a second ahead of second place; he was far ahead of the field at the 25.

"Not to fear, Wonder Woman. Tonight, you'll show the world how you can do it," Sean challenged Claire as she reciprocated with all smiles before her big race.

Claire's thoughts went to the heavenlies with a quick prayer.

Sean had triggered something in her. A peace and comfort came over her that she had never experienced before. It was like a clear message telling her to stop trying to compete for Sean like other girls and just be herself. The message was clear that if she were going to win Sean's heart, it would be spiritually, not physically. She now felt different in some inexplicable way, and knew that losing her virginity to Sean meant losing him forever. She was suddenly comfortable with taking the high road.

Everyone perked up when the announcer introduced Claire. She looked over at Sean and smiled. Brothers Aubert and Francois were really cranked up. Aubert was on his toes again, clapping his fingertips with assurance that a Brebeuf student was going to do something great. Claire was a great starter; she had her dad's jumping ability and clearly was three meters ahead when she broke the surface of the water. The announcer called the race like a horse race, referring to Claire as the daughter of a Montreal Allouette legend. With each lap Brother Aubert ran up and down the pool, cheering for her, which added to the already charged atmosphere. Finishing the race she looked at the scoreboard. She was truly surprised to see that she posted a Canadian record and the world's fastest time. Sean and Aubert celebrated with Claire at the finish line while the crowd gave her a standing ovation. "Thank you, Sean, I love you," Claire whispered as she hugged him.

Mr. Harrison bolted out of the stands and hurried to the pool deck and embraced his daughter, which brought the spectators to tears. The announcer was a huge Allouette fan who sparked a standing ovation for Claire's dad.

Reporters cornered Claire when she left the locker room. "Who was it that got you back into swimming, and how did they motivate you? How did you lose so much weight in just three months? Does your father coach you at home? Who was that Franciscan running up and down the pool when you swam?"

"That's Brother Aubert; he works at my school, and he got Sean Easley and I interested in swimming at Point Claire," Claire responded.

"How about the Pan-Ams and the Olympics?" the Montreal Match reporter asked.

"I'm starting to understand what it means to swim and race for fun. I had given up swimming, got fat, but now I'm back. Now, I feel more pressure to not get fat again than to swim fast. I'm just different than I was at thirteen. Let's just wait and see what happens." Claire spoke to the press with ease.

The press liked her story—pro footballer's daughter, from overweight to knockout, bubbly personality—not to mention the world's fastest time.

"There's your story," Claire said, nodding towards Sean who was near. "Athlete manifique who can swim too." The press did not react to her comment whatsoever.

When Sean got home, he went directly to bed, emotionally and physically exhausted from the weekend. During his prayers, Brigitte came to mind. He knew he wanted to be sensitive to her, yet knew he needed to be strong in order for her to understand what had to be done and why.

The High Road

The next day at Brebeuf was "Claire Harrison Day." Whenever someone did something special, Brother Aubert got on the intercom to brag to the entire school about his or her accomplishments. The *Montreal Match* featured her on the sports pages, and most of the school already knew that she had become the fastest swimmer in the world in the 200 backstroke.

When Claire saw Sean in the hallway, she asked if he had made his arrangements for New York. "No, superstar, I haven't," Sean said in an upbeat tone.

"Sean, I owe you *so* much. My fat butt wouldn't have gotten back in the pool, if it hadn't been for you. I just know something big is going to happen for you in New York. I dreamed it last night. See you after school."

Sean and Claire drove to Point Claire for practice after school. It consisted of a long meeting and an easy swim. Sean found out that he would have to fly to the meet because there was now no room left on the bus, but there still were rooms at the hotel. The meet was to be held at the Metcalfe Y, which was somewhere in North Jersey, so he planned to fly into Newark on Saturday and leave after the meet on Sunday.

Guy left on Wednesday morning for another ten-to-fourteen-day trip and Brigitte checked into her downtown flat prior to Sean's arrival from Brebeuf. A candlelight dinner for two was prepared, but from the moment he walked in the door, their minds were not on food until almost midnight.

"Mon cheri, I cannot go that long again without being with you, Brigitte murmured. I almost could not stand watching those mothers and their daughters look at you at the Pointe Claire swim meet last weekend. I heard women talking in the ladies room about you and found myself getting jealous."

Sean knew it would be extremely difficult to normalize his relationship with Brigitte, but after being with her, it seemed like it would be *impossible*. He really missed just holding her; everything else was a bonus. For her it was different; she harbored a vessel of emotions that exploded when they were together. He knew that she had helped mold him into a sensual man, and he was still in the glorious rut of being loved by Brigitte. Sean was spent when he arrived back at Brebeuf the next day. School went by quickly, and after the swim workout, his energy systems were exhausted.

When he left the flat the next morning to catch his flight to Newark, he was one emotionally drained young man. The first event was a disaster for Sean, swimming a 51.99 in the 100-yard freestyle with a 22.5 at the 50 mark; he died like a man who hadn't slept for several days. In the 400-freestyle relay, he was able to redeem himself by swimming the anchor leg in 48.88 but again showing obvious signs of total fatigue.

At the meet there was a team from Peekskill Military Academy in Peekskill, New York. They raced Point Claire stroke for stroke in the relay, until Sean finally pulled ahead to win. Sean was so tired after the meet that he asked permission to skip dinner and go directly to the hotel. Jean Claude said okay, so

Sean took a cab to the hotel while the others went out for a meal and a movie.

Sometime after he arrived back in his room, Claire's knock on the door woke him up from a deep sleep. Clad in a sheet, Sean quickly jumped back in bed after unlocking the door, making it difficult for Claire to balance the food while opening the door. She briefly caught a glimpse of his nakedness as she struggled to turn on the light with her elbow. Normally, this would have spiraled into a sexual fantasy for Claire, but she had clearly changed and was determined to take the high road.

"I was worried about you. Here's some supper and fruit. You looked absolutely like crap today. Your color is off—you look like Dracula's been sucking your blood. You need to eat."

"How'd you get here?" Sean asked.

"Taxi." I told Jean Claude that I wanted to put on a show in the 200 tomorrow and needed to get some extra rest. Now eat."

Afterward, Claire added, "I'll sit here till you finish eating, in case you need something else, sire?"

"You mean coffee, tea, or me, don't you?" Sean smiled warmly.

"No, Sean, not exactly, and besides, that's so corny. I would like you to invite me to Meeting. I think we should also go to services when Brother Aubert says Mass." Her strategy to win his heart by taking the high road was now in full swing. "He has become our greatest fan; I think we should reciprocate and support him. I know you're flying right back after the meet, so I wanted to talk to you about church. In fact, Aubert is saying Mass at 0600 on *Mardi,* when we return. I thought it would be a nice surprise for him," Claire appealed.

"Yes, let's do it," he said, after biting into his cheese steak. "By the way, you are so sweet to bring this," adding an affirming smile. She knew Sean liked Philly cheese steaks, especially when accompanied with a cream soda. Sean felt like he was back in Abington.

Claire hung around a while longer, listening to Sean's Wildwood Beach Patrol stories and just to be there for him. "Good night, Sean. Sleep well and kick ass tomorrow. I know you're going to do gr-r-r-eat!" she said, getting up and kissing him on the forehead. Taking the high road intrinsically made her feel great too.

Everyone witnessed a different Sean the next day. His skin color was as if he had a tan. In the 200-free relay he swam first, putting Point Claire clearly ahead of all the other teams and caught the attention of Dr. Parks, the Peekskill Military Academy coach. Just fifteen minutes after the relay, Sean swam the 50 free. He won in 21.88 seconds, new pool and meet records. The crowd gave him a standing ovation. As he walked down the deck to the victory stand, Dr Parks leaned over the balcony and asked Sean if he could talk with him after the awards ceremony.

Sean was finished for the day but his flight back to Montreal wasn't until 4:00 in the afternoon, so he had plenty of time to visit with Dr Parks. As he was leaving the locker room, he encountered two women. One was a swimmer's mother that he recognized from Philadelphia and the other a good-looking, middle-aged blonde woman.

"Are you Sean Easley?" asked the blond.

"Yes, I am," Sean said with his patented dimpled smile.

"I'm Mrs. Parks, and this is Mrs. McKay. My husband is Paul Parks, the coach at PMA. I believe you may know Mrs. McKay's son, Tommy–a new cadet."

"I didn't see him, Mrs. McKay. Is Tommy here?" Sean asked.

"No, but he is about to arrive. He's only swimming the mile at 4:00, and then it's back to school," Mrs. McKay clarified.

"How's he like PMA?" Sean asked.

"Loves it. Most of the people you grew up with in swimming from the tri-state area are going to PMA next year. You should consider it. Will you ever leave Montreal? I hear you're doing great in school and impressing a lot of people," Mrs. McKay continued.

"You certainly are a fine-looking young man, Sean, and a great swimmer. If you decide to go to Peekskill, I would be honored to be your mom away from home. Well, I just wanted to introduce myself and say hi," Mrs. Parks concluded.

Just after their meeting, Sean had another lengthy conversation with Coach Parks. He invited Sean to visit PMA as soon as possible in order to be eligible for financial assistance. Sean was excited about the possibility of using PMA as a way to get into West Point.

After returning to Montreal that night, he finally just told Brigitte, "I cannot do this anymore. I love you more than you will ever know, but God has been telling me to run away from this because it's wrong. I've felt it for a long time, but you're just so irresistible. We have to stop." They sat on opposite couches holding hands. "You know I love you, but something–no, God–

has been telling me we need to stop. But, I just don't know how," Sean confessed in a troubled yet compassionate tone.

"Mon Cheri, we have a loving and wonderful God. He has been telling me the same thing. I think that is why I have been so drawn to you the last few days. Somehow, I knew it was going to be over sooner than I would have liked; and neither did I have the courage to end it," Brigitte confessed. "I ask of you just one thing; just hold me tonight."

"Of course. I'll always want to be with you. It's just that Guy–well you know how close I've grown to him, and I don't want to hurt either of you. I still hope we can be more than best friends. I want always to have fun with you any time we are together. Just like old times. In fact, let's eat," he smiled.

"Where?"

"How about pizza?"

"Let's go!"

From that point on, Sean and Brigitte probably fell more in love. They read scripture, talked more than ever before and gave each other time to develop individually. Sean studied while Brigitte engrossed herself analyzing solutions to the social issues that were dear to her heart. A platonic week of sharing the same flat passed, and the tension had eased by the time Guy arrived back in Montreal.

Sean met Guy upon his arrived as usual. He immediately filled him in on the trip to New York and the opportunity at PMA and his desire to attend West Point. Because he was a Quaker, going to PMA would be the only way to prove he was not going to be a potential conscientious objector to the United States Military Academy (USMA) officials. Guy asked Sean if he and Brigitte had been intimate. Sean feigned that he had stopped trying and would just continue to act as her companion and sort of bodyguard in his absence. Sean thought Guy liked his response, and when they arrived home, Brigitte was all over Guy. This also appeared to be to Guy's liking, proving that maybe Sean was reporting the truth.

Claire and Sean started hanging out a lot together. They became regulars at Masses said by Brother Aubert, and Claire started attending Meeting with the Lafoussier gang. She was now less than sixty kilos and was truly a beautiful girl who was making all the right moves to win Sean's heart. She was steadfast in taking the road less traveled and continued to encourage Sean about his future.

The Door Opens to PMA

As soon as possible, Sean called home to explain the need to travel to Peekskill, New York, to visit PMA. At the Easley home, the prospect of prep school created some anxiety. The family's lack of finances would surely preclude such a luxury education, but Sean explained that financial aid was available, if they acted quickly. It was decided that Sean would again fly to Newark, where his mom would collect him and drive to Peekskill for the day.

The week before the trip was emotionally difficult for Sean. The fact that he and Brigitte no longer had a sexual relationship was difficult for him to come to terms with, but Claire was there to share his dreams and was always a source of encouragement for him.

Guy's curbside parting remarks at the airport encouraged Sean, "Have a great trip and remember, always be yourself. Do not be what you think PMA wants. Share your dreams with them to see if they are compatible. The school needs to evaluate you and you them."

"Thanks, Guy, for the ride and the advice."

"Bon voyage. mon ami."

Sean and his mother arrived late at PMA for their appointment with Dr. Parks. He was extremely charming and won Margaret over almost immediately. Sean took a two-hour aptitude test in math and English, which he easily finished in forty-five minutes. They analyzed the test right away, so that Dr. Parks, admissions, financial aid, and academics could discuss the possibility of Sean's attending PMA.

Dr. Parks and the Easleys walked to the dining hall as the Corps of Cadets assembled for lunch formation.

"Bat...tal...ion!...At...ten...hut!"

"A Company all present and accounted for, sir!"

The cadets heard "B Company...," and so on, before they led the march into the dining hall.

Dr. Parks explained that there were usually three formations a day, but athletes did not stand for supper formation. They did, however, have to be in their seats before the Corps blessing. The dining room was large with over fifty tables set for ten cadets each. A staff member or professor sat at the head of each table, along with their family. Sean felt a strong sense of family and found it appealing. This day the Easleys were to sit at the head table with the commandant and his wife, Dr. and Mrs. Parks, the headmaster Mr. Barringer, the superintendent and his wife, and a swimmer whom Sean knew from Philly. Standing behind their chairs, Sean again heard what would become routine for him.

"Bat...tal...ion...! At...ten...hut! At...ease!" came the commands from a cadet at the podium.

Another cadet officer went to the microphone, said a blessing, and gave the command to take seats.

Sean didn't have much time to talk to the swimmer who had pulled the duty of serving and bussing the table for each course. Food was distributed family style; it was a pleasant experience for Sean and Margaret.

Thrown for a loop when he saw that Sean had written his essay in French, the evaluator graciously interrupted Mr. Barringer, pulling him aside in a huddle of sorts, so as to be out of earshot of the rest of the table.

Returning, Mr. Barringer had a big smile on his face. "Well, Sean, you have the distinction of being the first cadet to get all the math and verbal correct but to flunk the written. You wrote your essay in French. Pourquoi?"

"Good question," Sean answered with a smile.

"Let me have you meet our French teacher, Mr. Begin," Mr. Barringer said, as he motioned for Mr. Begin to join the table.

Sean and Mr. Begin began speaking to one another in French. Mr. Begin was startled to discover Sean was a native Philadelphian and not from Paris as he had assumed.

"Your son speaks *le Francais parfaitement*, Mrs. Easley. How did that come about? Mr. Begin inquired.

Sean interceded and explained that his former nanny was from Paris. This led to a conversation about Quakerism. Sean could tell that the superintendent and commandant were extremely interested. Margaret explained that after playing football at Alabama, Big Sam joined the Navy, became a war hero and was still an officer in the Reserves. Sean added that *he* wanted to go West Point after prep school.

This seemed to appease any concerns about a Quaker in a military atmosphere. A student approached the table.

"Cadet Sole, How can we help you?" asked Superintendent Osborne.

"Sir, did I hear correctly that this is actually *the* Sean Easley from Abington High? General Osborne, Sean Easley is the best high school wide receiver in America," Cadet Sole practically shouted. "There were rumors he was playing pro ball in Canada; he is unbelievable. He's famous! I went to Cheltenham High School and saw him single handedly tear us up. He is also the fastest football player I've ever seen," an excited Cadet Sole continued as Sean unconsciously lowered his head slightly.

Sean humbly explained the situation regarding his damaged liver, and that his doctor thought his football playing days might be over. He made sure that everyone at the table knew he had played soccer in Montreal.

The lunch finished with small talk, but all knew that Sean would not be a typical cadet if he attended PMA. The headmaster accompanied them on the tour around campus. Sean instantly liked Mr. Barringer. He was a good-looking man who dressed as if he was straight from Madison Avenue. He also had a great sense of humor with a terrific smile. As they entered the Ford Building, he stopped at a beautiful crest imbedded in the floor.

"Sean, read the Crest," said Mr. Barringer, his eyes pointing to the site.

"Okay," said Sean as he walked around the crest. "It says Peekskill Military Academy, 1813, Quit You Like Men."

"What does it mean to you Sean?" Mr. Barringer continued, as Margaret marveled at the beauty of the wooded room.

"Well, for one thing it means PMA has been here a while," Sean answered with a smile.

"Yes, it's the oldest military academy in the United States, but what does 'quit you like men' mean to you?" Barringer pressed.

"Leave you like men, I guess," Sean replied.

"It means conduct yourself as a man. It's biblical and it's what Peekskill is all about. Preparing you for the challenges of life to be the best you can be. I know and trust you will develop into one of PMA's finest graduates. I personally want you to come here, and I will pursue everything on your behalf—finances, academics, and admission. I want you to promise me one thing: your priorities must be academics first, athletics second, military training third, and finally but certainly not last, no women. If you can live with that, I'll work hard for you," Barringer said.

"Our admissions office called Abington High School and got an earful. They were considering rejecting you at PMA before I took over your case. I called Brebeuf and got the most glowing reports I've ever received on any potential cadet. You see, if you have had problems in the past, you would not be eligible for financial aid at PMA, and I understand your financial situation requires much assistance. All right then, can you live the priorities I outlined?"

"Yes, I can Dr. Barringer," Sean said with a smile.

Dr Barringer extended his hand and said, "Welcome to Peekskill Military Academy." Giving Margaret a hug he said, "I'll work everything out for you. I have a feeling that this will work out superbly. Finish up at Brebeuf with all A's," he said, giving Sean a firm look.

They continued to walk around campus checking out everything: dorms, classrooms, and athletic facilities. Margaret was impressed with PMA's beauty even in winter. Sean commented on the lack of great athletic facilities only to be quickly corrected by Mr. Barringer.

"Sean, you're not coming here for athletics. You're already fine in that area. Remember your new priorities!" Barringer lectured as he turned to face the Easleys to make his point.

"You're right," Sean said. "You're right."

Mr. Barringer took them to Coach Sparks' office and then said good-bye. Sean walked with Mr. Barringer out of the athletic building.

"Thanks, Mr. Barringer, for this unbelievable opportunity. I want you to know how much I appreciate your helping me," Sean said while shaking his hand and looking him in the eye.

"You will do great here, Sean. Keep in touch."

Coach Sparks was happy to hear about Mr. Barringer's commitment to Sean. They visited for about fifteen minutes and then said good-bye. It was almost three thirty. They needed to get on the road for Sean to catch his flight and Margaret to skirt New York's rush-hour traffic.

The Easleys were impressed with the people at PMA and their dedication, particularly Mr. Barringer. Sean told his mom that whatever it took, he was going to PMA next year, and he would work three jobs during summer break to earn the necessary funds. Margaret dropped Sean off to catch his plane and returned to Philadelphia without a hitch.

Both Guy and Brigitte met Sean at baggage claim in Montreal. They were holding hands when Sean saw them, and he could tell for the first time that Brigitte had made the emotional transition to Guy. Oddly enough, Sean had feelings of jealousy and contentment at the same time, as he observed them together. They were excited to hear of Sean's new opportunity. Guy's reaction made Sean absolutely more convicted.

"Sean, you are more than a son to me. I enjoy your successes as if they are my own, and quite frankly, I'll miss you terribly when you leave Montreal. I'm sure Brigitte feels the same way," Guy said as they drove down the Boulevard de St. Joseph, along the St. Lawrence. Guy never liked the autoroutes of Montreal and often took smaller, more scenic highways.

Brigitte began crying and said, "Of course I'll miss Sean. He is like the younger brother I never had. But more importantly, I never have seen you so happy. Let's just make the most of the time we still have together."

"Bon, tres bien ma cherie," Guy said as he hugged Brigitte and gave her a kiss on the head.

When Sean got back to the house he called Sonny, "Yo, Sonny."

"Yo, Sean, where the hell have you been? It's been almost a month since we talked, but it's still good to hear your voice, you Quaker schmuck."

"Easy there, kosher boy. We might have to wrestle again, and I'm still prepared to pancake your butt. How have you been?"

"I'm so excited about the Academy, man! It's going to be everything I ever dreamed of—football, boxing, track. If they had swimming in the summer, it would be perfect. I told the boxing and football coaches that swimming helped me unwind and made me feel different muscularly during the season, and I didn't want to change that. The boxing coach completely understood. The football coach didn't get it, but he almost guaranteed I would start," Sonny explained. "I think the academics will be pretty easy compared to Abington, and my dad prepared me for the military part by kicking my rear end ever since I was born. Hey, I can't wait till you and I kick Navy's butt in the Army-Navy game in Philly. I still have dreams about it—I know it will happen. I can see you running under some passes that the Navy secondary gives up on. I see it. I can see it!"

"Sonny, I believe I have an entrée to the Academy. Peekskill Military Academy wants me. Believe it or not, it was swimming, not track, or ball that created the opportunity for me. Football is still out of the question—maybe for good because of my enlarged liver."

"You need to stop playing with your "schwantz," you dick, so your liver will get better. I don't care what you say; I know it's going to happen. It's us kickin' Navy. I know it," Sonny vowed.

"How's Louie doing, and how is Cassandra? Sean asked.

"Cassandra's been hanging out with me and my new squeeze. My new squeeze is a keeper. No humping but everything else. She always says if you want "it," you got to buy "it," and only with a giant-ass ring and a guaranteed life that goes with it. I've tried everything...not a chance. It's strange but I kind of like it. She is stronger willed than I am, but she still keeps a smile on my face. Guess what her name is—Sarah Goldman—and she is hot, hot, hot looking! She's going to Harvard next year. I met her at synagogue. Just went up to her, looked her in the eye and said, "I want you," in typical Easyman fashion. She smiled at me and said that I could do better than that. She told me that I'd been hanging around my famous friends too much. She's got my number. She knew who I was, all about my family, and about you and Louie. She's amazing. She said the girls at Cheltenham always talk about the three of us. We're legends at Cheltenham, dude, even though we're from Abington. Can you believe it?" Sonny rattled on.

"I'm happy for you Sonny. You were telling me about Cassandra," Sean pressed on.

"She says she is yours for life, man. She dates but the guys get real pissed off at you because she won't "be" with anyone else. One time another b-ball player was trying to move on her in my back seat while I was driving to a movie. She let him have it. He asked her what she saw in that honky Quaker, and she said you could just touch her or even look at her and she would be better off than being with him for a lifetime. He told me to stop the car and he got out!" Sonny howled.

"Guess I need to call her or something. Still can't call her house, and I know her parents have forbidden her to go to mine," Sean said and was interrupted by Sonny.

"Call me tomorrow after the b-ball game, and I'll get her on the phone. She has to cheer for the game, let's say around 10:00. Her parents have her on a short leash, and she has to be in by eleven, even on weekends till she denounces you. It's her mom. You have won over her dad, I hear. I'll even give her a private room in case the conversation gets hot. But I think I'd like to watch," he laughed. "I'll make sure she locks the door with me on the other side," Sonny said jokingly.

"You're starting to scare me, you horn dog. I'll do it. I'll call you tomorrow at ten. Thanks, man. Check with you tomorrow."

"Sean, my West Point dreams are so vivid. We will, someday, single handedly take Navy down. You'll see. I'm really happy about your PMA opportunity. Aren't you glad we started off together at the Abington Y? By the way, I won the 200 at districts in 1:49.5 and the 100 in 49.8. Eat your heart out, stud. You should feel lucky you're in Montreal because I'd be kicking your ass if you were back here," Sonny threatened.

"Till tomorrow. *Toujours Amis, mon ami*," Sean replied.

Sean hung up and called Dr. Barringer at PMA, confessing to him that he wanted to get occasional visits from Claire and Cassandra.

"Sean, you and I are going to become great friends. I appreciate the call and your frankness already. Quit yourself like a man. I'm not going to tell you it's good or bad or that it will complicate things at PMA for you, but I do not consider their visiting a violation of the priorities to which you agreed. I'm fighting to get you a full scholarship," Mr. Barringer reported.

"Thanks, Mr. Barringer. Thanks for everything," Sean added.

"You are going to do just great," said Mr. Barringer, signing off.

Tears welled up in Sean's eyes, as he starting thinking about all the terrific people who had come into his life recently: Brother Aubert, Mr. Barringer, and Claire–wow! Thank you God! Thank you.

Wildwood Revisited

The rest of the year flew by in Montreal. Sans sex, Brigitte and Sean grew to be great friends. Oddly enough, it was Claire who assisted with normalizing their relationship, of which became based on service to mankind. It all began during Meeting when Claire stood and spoke.

"I am not a Quaker but have been deeply touched by my experiences with some members of this Meeting. Sean Easley, Brigitte, and Guy Lafoussier have had a profound influence on my life. I don't know if I'm permitted to speak here, but I feel God wants me to share what's on my heart. Quakers are different in the most wonderful way. I know from being a member of the Holy Catholic Church that people sometimes institutionalize the pursuit of God to the point that the relationship with Him is lost. These wonderful members of your Meeting constantly remind me that the walk with the Lord is a relationship that requires time listening to Him and fellowshipping with other seekers and reading scripture. This is all new to me. Brigitte's service to the street people of Montreal has deeply touched me, as have other caring Quakers. They are more Christ-like and their service is much more important than any ceremony of any church. It's living the love of God. God is love, and thank you for allowing me to discover things that you Quakers already know so well."

It's odd but it was the reminder of things often taken for granted that allowed Sean and Brigitte to get back on the high road for the remainder of his time in Montreal. Claire and Brigitte became great friends. Claire began working with Brigitte on homeless issues through the Catholic charities and was able to rally a lot of Brebeuf students to man soup kitchens, clothing distribution centers, and shelters.

Saying good-bye to everyone in Montreal was difficult, but the hardest good-bye was to Guy. Sean and Guy had become not just like father and son but good friends. Aubert, Brigitte, and Claire would always hold a special place in Sean's heart.

Soon, Sean was in Wildwood. In early summer Brother Aubert had called to congratulate him on getting all A's. Sean immediately called PMA and reported to Mr. Barringer his accomplishment.

Mr. Barringer replied with, "You did your job, and I did mine. Tell your mom and dad that they will have to pay for uniforms only while at PMA. Congratulations, son."

Sean was indeed happy and mentally committed himself to preparing emotionally and physically during his summer in Wildwood.

The summer saw Sean taking on a lot more responsibility on the beach patrol. Dutch Hoffman had a heart attack that winter and had to retire from the patrol. John Caprice was promoted to captain. He was aware of Sean's athletic prowess, particularly in swimming and surfing, and needed him for a special assignment. During the winter, storms had washed much of the beach away. Now, at high tide the water would go under the boardwalk, leaving a hazardous area for bathers to swim. Getting caught in one of the piers protruding out into the sea was risky. Hunt's Pier was the most dangerous. The patrol forbade lifeguards to take rescue equipment with them on rescues under the pier because the waves could cause tragedy by trapping the lifeguard and victim around one of the pier's pilings, potentially causing them both to drown.

The captain, or "Cap," as he was usually called, asked Sean to sit on the dangerous side of the pier. He allowed Sean to handpick his stand partner and the two guards who would sit on the opposite side of the pier. These four had to have a great deal of confidence in each other's ability and work in a coordinated fashion. Most saves under Hunt's Pier were made purely by outstanding swimming ability and by understanding the waves, currents, and other pitfalls that could entrap a bather. Sean welcomed the challenge.

Sean's first recruit was his cousin Tommy. Margaret Easley had four brothers; the oldest of them was raising his family in Wildwood. Tommy, like Sean, knew the sea well. Growing up he had gone fishing and swimming with Sean and his other cousins and was taught about the sea by their grandfather. They had learned about rips, pulls and other sea phenomena. He was a good swimmer but wasn't like the other guards. He never had enough money growing up, always worked at least two jobs, was trying to finish at Seton Hall University, and just didn't have the luxury of partying. He was also a very funny guy. It's almost as if not having much growing up sharpened his wit so he could laugh about things that he didn't have. Tommy also took this assignment seriously, and was quick to get another local lifeguard to be his stand partner. He chose Billy Wiley, a Wildwood Catholic High product who was very straight and a lifetime friend of Tommy's and Sean's.

Sean was finding it difficult to get a stand partner and decided to talk to "Cap." "I've asked several guys that I trust to sit on Poplar with me, but they've all turned me down."

"That doesn't surprise me," Cap said. "First, who would want to sit with a stand partner who's always first to the victim, first to resuscitate—first, first, first. Sean, as a leader, you sometimes have to step back and let others be first. You have to train these guys and allow them to be proud of themselves. I know you can do it. Most of these guys are jealous of you, and the fact that you have a colored girlfriend scares some of the bigots off for sure. Why don't you pick one of the rookies? By the way, you need to recruit two more guards, not just one. Someone who has been trained has to fill in when the other guards rotate days off. I picked you because you're the fastest and the person who can do the best job. Just get it done," Cap said as Sean turned to leave. Slapping him on the back, Cap added, "By the way, you are administering the new guard test this year. It's Saturday morning. We have seventy-five signed up for thirty slots. Give'em a tough one. I'm giving a private test today at noon to a friend's relative. Call for the jeep at eleven thirty and come in the boat with me while we check him out."

During muster, Cap announced that all pier guards were to begin their workday with a planned workout before taking their stands by ten thirty each morning. The lieutenants or jeep drivers would have to patrol the pier while they were working out.

At muster, Cap sensed the displeasure and jealousy of the lieutenants and came down heavy on them by saying, "Knock off the bullshit and lead. Don't be just a bunch of jealous pansies. And if you don't like my decisions, then quit."

Unfortunately, Cap's little talk did not help the situation. Sean could sense the tension growing between him and the lieutenants, but it didn't matter. He was back on the beach and eager to save more lives this summer.

Sean and Cap launched a lifeboat around noon as a young, good-looking candidate entered the water for his test. The water temperature was a chilly sixty-three degrees Fahrenheit.

"This guy is the nephew of my old stand partner in '56," said Cap. "If the kid can swim, I am going to hire him." Cap proceeded to yell out to the candidate, "Swim out toward the boat till we tell you to stop."

He was a very good swimmer and stopped after about 200 meters then asked permission to swim backstroke for a little while. He passed the test easily, and Sean found his stand partner. All parties were in agreement—this rookie would begin by sitting the pier.

"Congratulations, you passed the test. Sean will be training you. When you're through here, come up to my office," Cap said as he jumped out of the boat and drove a jeep back to his office

"What's your name and where are you from?" Sean asked.

"John Eggert, but they call me Leeper. I live in Abington, well, actually, in a place called Hollywood. We just moved there from the D.C. area. What's your name?"

"Sean Easley, and I'm from Abington, actually, Hollywood," Sean replied with a grin.

"My dad is the new barkeep and manager of the Hollywood Tavern. I live on Pasadena," Eggert said. "Wait a minute; you're the legend of Abington who got kicked out of school for dating a colored chick and for punching out Dr. Hiram."

"Not quite accurate, but I'm the guy, and I live on San Gabriel," Sean said as he laughed at the coincidences.

"Looking forward to working with you, Sean. I'm cold as hell. I'm gonna hit a hot shower. See you tomorrow," Eggert said, as he dashed to the Beach Hospital.

That day only a few brave souls ventured onto the cold beach. Sean and Tommy used this free time effectively to discuss rescue methods to be used around the pier. Tommy came up with a very practical idea.

"All the pier guards should swim together under the pier during workout so we know every hole, every piling, every pipe, and every possible hazard. We should also talk to the Hunt's Pier folks to see if we can have a ladder on both sides of the Pier. If we can climb onto the pier, run the 300 meters to the end and then jump in when necessary, we'll reach the victims much faster that way."

Sean developed hand signals and a whistle code to communicate through the pier. Tommy knew the pier manager and persuaded him to allow the ladders during the day, if he promised to lock them in the "up" position at night.

Cap decided that he needed an additional guard each day stationed on the side of the pier most vulnerable to oncoming waves and currents. He selected an experienced guard who had worked a few years in North Wildwood as the last member of the pier team. His desire was to be as close to North Wildwood as possible, and he did not mind standing in chest-deep water all day catching people who were in danger of being swept under the pier. His name was Larry White, Laredo for short, because of his cowboy movie star-like looks and demeanor.

The five guards had trained together every day for about ten days when suddenly their training paid off. On a weekend when the beach was packed, some well-meaning parents placed their four-year-old son on the railing on Tommy's side of Hunt's Pier. He fell into the water at mid pier into about ten feet of water, and his father jumped in after him. The surf was almost head-high, and the water immediately sucked both father and son under the pier. The signals worked, and Tommy indicated to Sean that he was going in on rescue. Laredo was standing in waist-deep water and was the closest to the victims. Tommy took off while trying to keep visual contact as best as possible. Sean climbed to the top the pier from his side. John signaled down beach to inform the beach hospital and others of the emergency and then took off through the water to help find father and son.

Sean ran past mid pier and jumped off on Tommy's side. He made his way for about fifty meters towards shore and in the direction of the tidal waters. Laredo was some place under the pier. When Sean surfaced he saw Tommy with the father.

Exhausted, Tommy yelled, "Find the boy! His dad says he can swim a little. Laredo will help me get him in."

Tommy's legs were taut against one of the giant concrete pilings. He was holding up the father while trying to avoid the waves bashing him and slamming him into the piling.

"Get the kid!" Tommy yelled.

Sean had to quickly assess where the boy would be by this time. Calculating the surf and the pull, he guessed his location to be in chest-deep water at mid pier. He caught a wave and made his way to the determined site but saw nothing. His several underwater dives were fruitless.

Instinctively, Sean silently cried out to God for help.

Suddenly he thought he saw something pinned against a piling as the tide swept away from shore. It was the boy. Riding a wave, Sean found him hooked to the barnacles and to something sharp. The boy was lifeless and Sean needed to get to work on him as soon as possible. With the battered child in his arms, he used the power of the surf to push him into shore whereupon he struck the child with a few good blows in his back and started mouth-to-mouth and chest compressions. Sean then pushed on his stomach and hugged him from the rear because something seemed to be blocking his airway. The child eliminated both food and swallowed water and he went back to work. A huge crowd had congregated under the pier to see what was happening. Tommy, Billy, and John had gotten the father to safety and were now, along with the crowd, watching Sean work on the child. Tommy started to work with Sean. The boy slowly came back to life, and finally, he was breathing on his own. The crowd cheered when the child began screaming. The father and mother joined Sean and Tommy in the ambulance as it sped, siren blaring full blast, to the Beach Hospital.

The mother was holding the boy in her arms when they arrived at the hospital. He was still very dazed, and Sean was anxious for the doctors to examine him. He was worried about the length of time the boy was without oxygen and feared possible brain damage. He knew the water temperature in the low sixties probably helped him. His Korean War veteran physical instructor had taught him to check the eyes; they were the gateway to the brain. Sean urged the beach medic to check the boy.

"I think he is going to be okay," said Sean said to the parents. "Demand that they keep him overnight for monitoring. I think it's the safest way. No one knows enough about drowning or near drowning, medically speaking. They don't even teach mouth-to-mouth in medical school yet. I know just a little and am thankful I was able to put it to use today."

"How can we ever thank you?" said the mother, as they both looked at Sean.

"First off, thank Tommy. He saw it happen and immediately called us all into action. He developed the action plan for the pier. I just followed his instructions," Sean said as Captain John gave an approving smile, thinking that Sean had begun to understand the unselfishness of true leadership.

The news crews on the story were waiting outside Beach Hospital. Sean and the family were inside waiting for an ambulance to transport them to Burdett Tomlin Hospital. Tommy and Cap handled the press. It was a big story in Philly, NYC, and South Jersey. The headline in *The Philadelphia Inquirer* read, "Daring Cousins Save the Day in Wildwood." Pictures of Hunt's Pier, Sean carrying the child onto the beach, and Tommy in his lifeguard uniform took prominence.

The next day the mayor of Wildwood came to the beach to commend the pier guards for their heroism. Because the papers were all over the story, the mayor used it politically and made sure Tommy became the big story. Tommy did a terrific job with the media; they all loved him and his wit. He made sure to tell the press about their grandfather and how he taught all his grandchildren about the sea, waves, rips, and the surf when they were very young. Tommy also made sure that the media acknowledged what an exceptional athlete and waterman

Sean was. He told them that Sean was able to save many lives because of his exceptional swimming and land speed, coupled with this new mouth-to-mouth technique that he was sharing with others. There was a media follow-up for the next couple of days because of the stories that generated from Tommy's personality and wit. Two things happened because of it. Suddenly the public had a deeper appreciation for the South Jersey lifeguards, and the business on Hunt's Pier increased. From that point, the pier guards ate free of charge at their choice of restaurants on the pier.

The summer in Wildwood flew by for Sean, with frequent visits from Cassandra, Louie, and Sonny. The issue of race was becoming more of an obvious problem when Cassandra visited. In public, they endured stares and slurs. It didn't matter whether it was in the white or colored community of Wildwood; they were not well received.

Sean and Cassandra found they were spending more and more time alone with each other, deepening their relationship. They often went out in the Easely's boat or walked on the beach in the evening in order to be alone and escape the burden society placed on their union.

Sean, Louie, and Cassandra took time off from their summer jobs to drive Sonny to his first day at West Point. Beast Barracks was the start of his military career.

"I know I'll do just fine. I'm looking forward to these bozos trying to break me," Sonny said, as they exited the car to say their good-byes. "I love you guys. Thanks for spending my last few hours as a civilian with me."

Before walking to the processing center, he kissed Cassandra and bear hugged Louie and Sean.

"Come visit me before summer's end and write and all that good stuff."

"You got to be kidding me. Write you? No way," Sean said in jest. "We will be back soon."

"*Toujours Amis*," they said together.

As he entered the processing center, an upperclassman immediately disciplined Sonny for being so cavalier.

Sonny could sense that his friends were watching him get dressed down. After a few minutes he turned towards them, waved, and blew them a kiss as he smiled. Again, two more upperclassmen drilled him for his act of disrespect.

Leaving the area, Sean, Louie and Cassandra could hear the verbal berating that Sonny was receiving, "Smackhead, who do you think you are? Stop smiling. Give me fifty push-ups. Stop smiling."

As the gang left laughing, they knew that Sonny was having a better time than the upperclassmen. He was living his dream.

"West Point will never be the same," Louie said as he got in the car. "Thank God I'm going to Michigan. You guys will be able to see him a lot considering you'll both be in the New York area. Do you really want that Sean? It's hard to believe you would like the Academy."

Cassandra interrupted and putting her arm around Sean's neck said, "Oh come on, Sean can definitely take anything they could throw his way. I know one thing for sure though, if he does go to West Point after PMA, he will never be like those upperclassmen who were working on Sonny. My baby is too sweet."

"You two make me sick," Louie said in jest and they all laughed.

The rest of the summer was eventful. The pier guards made many rescues, and Sean won the Dutch Hoffman Iron Man Race in early August. The race consisted of a 400-meter swim, then a two-mile run, followed by a mile rowing competition against 100 of South Jersey's top lifeguards. Cassandra was on hand to cheer Sean on in front of thousands. She loved to watch Sean compete. No competitor was close to him after the run, and on the final leg he caught a wave in the surfboat about 300 meters from shore, dazzling the onlookers with his ability to row and tiller through the surf.

Other female friends of Wildwood Beach Patrol guards were downright nasty to Cassandra when she visited. They often tried to lure Sean away from Cassandra, but he had developed the ability to be nice to other females while communicating his faithfulness to Cassandra and never fell prey to the girls' advances.

Claire called at least once each week, always encouraging Sean. She also convinced him to attend Mass at St. Ann's a couple of times a week while he was in Wildwood. He felt God's influence on his life more that summer and liked the feeling.

Claire visited late in the summer after the Canadian swimming nationals. Margaret loved Claire and told Sean that she thought Claire was the marrying type. When Cassandra saw Claire for the first time, she was in shock. She had imagined her as an overweight jock type but in person found her to be a very wholesome, full-figured woman. Cassandra liked Claire, but much to her displeasure, understood that Claire wanted to win Sean's heart. Still, she found Claire extremely easy to talk with, and they became friends. It was difficult not to like her; she helped everyone with everything and always with a smile. She was so positive about life in general that consequently, during her brief time in Wildwood, she won the hearts of everyone.

Summer soon ended with Cassandra going to Columbia , Louie to Michigan, Sonny to West Point, Sean to PMA, and Claire back to St. Jean de Brebeuf.

New York

Peekskill Military Academy

Mr. Barringer called the Easleys and asked if Sean could arrive the day before soccer practice started to work on his academic schedule and to take care of general business such as getting uniforms. Margaret had returned to her teaching job the day after Labor Day, so she had to take the day off to deliver Sean to Peekskill.

Having made their first visit during one of the bleakest days of winter, both Margaret and Sean were taken by the beauty of the stately buildings set in amongst lush grounds of mature trees and colorful seasonal flowers. Beautiful annuals and perennials bordered the well-manicured sprawling lawns, and the ivy-covered buildings gave off a regal air. They parked and briskly walked to the administration building to be on time for their appointment with Mr. Barringer who was dressed in dungarees and a casual shirt and waved when he saw the Easleys coming down the hallway.

"Hello, there. It's really good to see you. Please come on into my office and have a seat. I have some good news for you. First, we have a complete set of uniforms for you donated by a cadet who is just about your size. He graduated last year. Of course, you may have to have them tailored a bit. I can recommend Romeo the Tailor on High Street. You'll have to get your own combat boots and service dress shoes," Barringer contin-ued as Margaret nodded her head.

"The best news, though, is that if you get all A's, West Point will take you next year. Evidently, the West Point swim coach heard about you and has already cleared it with admis-sions at the Academy for your appointment. Apparently, they knew all about you. I'm friends with the associate director of admissions, and he said if you improve your SATs to over 1400, you are a shoe-in, and of course, if you do well in all phases of development at PMA. He was really impressed with what you did at Brebeuf and with your 800 on the French Achievement Test. Plus, some Franciscan monk calls the Academy on your behalf constantly. He gave you such a glowing review that they thought you were too good to be true. All in all, do well here and you're at West Point next year."

"That's great, Mr. Barringer. Thanks so much," Sean said. Margaret was overwhelmed with the good news.

"Let's work out a schedule that will challenge you aca-demically but still allow you to make all A's," Mr. Barringer continued.

Margaret wanted Sean to take more history and social sci-ence courses. Sean wanted more math, so he would be ready for the heavy math orientation at the Academy. Barringer wanted heavy science to prepare him for next year. Sean's schedule in-cluded all the desired courses with a special French literature course arranged by Mr. Begin.

A very small man accompanied by a beautiful woman at least fifteen years his junior entered Dr. Barringer's office. Mo-tioning them to have a seat, Dr. Barringer said to Sean, "Meet Coach Bell and his wife."

She spoke to him in perfect French. Sean got a horrible feeling in the pit of his stomach. Why this complication, Sean thought to himself. She had a splendidly curvaceous figure with very large breasts, which she didn't mind showing off.

"Bonjour Sean, Bienvenue a Peekskill Military Academy," said Mrs. Bell in her snug-fitting sweater and tight red slacks, giving Sean the once over—standing there all tan with longer, sun-bleached hair.

The message she was sending alarmed both Sean and Margaret. The way she looked at Sean spoke volumes about her intentions, which were obvious, embarrassing, and made Sean and his mom most uncomfortable. Mr. Bell was either completely oblivious, in total denial, or a good pretender.

"It's great to have you here, Sean. I'm looking forward to your joining us. Your teammates will be arriving tonight; we start tomorrow morning at nine sharp. Just wanted to stop by and greet you. See you tomorrow. By the way, my wife is from Paris, if you couldn't tell, and she wanted meet you as well," Coach Bell said.

"Sean has to go to Romeo's with these uniforms and say good-bye to his mom," Mr. Barringer said in an effort to end the encounter, his eyes confirming his no-women policy to Sean.

"Great," said Mrs. Bell. "I'll take them to Romeo's, and then Mrs. Easley can drop Sean off to have lunch with Coach and me."

The meeting was over, and they soon found themselves at Romeo's. When Sean took off his shirt, Mrs. Bell continued to alarm both Sean and his mom.

Clearing her throat and gaining control of the situation,

Marge said, "Mrs. Bell, I'll take you home now. This is going to take a while, and I'd like to spend some time alone with my son before dropping him off at your house."

Fifteen minutes later, Margaret, troubled and concerned, returned to pick up Sean. "Mrs. Bell is real trouble for you, Sean. She is an unhappy woman who will gobble you up if you let her," Margaret said with fear in her voice and with hope that Sean would agree.

"Don't worry, Mom. My escape tactics are excellent, and I have taken Mr. Barringer's priorities seriously. I'll be just fine," Sean tried to say as convincingly as possible.

Marge drove by the dorm so Sean could drop off his bags, before heading to the Bells. They said their good-byes, and Sean waved to his mom as she drove away. As he rang the doorbell, he noticed that their house overlooked the parade grounds, and all the houses on the street were painted the same. They were handsome, two-story, Victorian homes with large porches and decorative railings. Mrs. Bell answered the door.

"*Bonjour Sean, entrez s'il vous plait mon cheri. Avez-vous faim,* Sean?" Mrs. Bell said as Sean stood at the door. Sensing that things were not quite right, Sean spoke English thinking it would somehow protect him from getting too friendly with his new coach's wife. She had changed into something even sexier and was wearing one of those island dresses that Martine's mother often wore, and it was noticeable that she was braless. The top half of her dress was unbuttoned to expose ample cleavage, and the bottom to mid thigh. Sean did not see Coach anywhere.

"Where's Coach?"

"I sent him to the store for a dessert. He'll be right back. Make yourself at home. Feel free to sit anywhere, and I'll get us something to drink."

Sean made one of his better decisions when he went out on the front porch and sat in a rocking chair.

"What are you doing out here, Sean?" she asked as she handed him a tall glass of lemonade.

"It's so beautiful today; I thought it would be nice to sit outside."

Smiling suspiciously, Mrs. Bell went back inside for a television tray to hold the drinks. Upon returning, she sat in the chair next to him, exposing most of her strikingly luscious leg. He was careful to make sure that his eyes never ventured where she wanted.

"Sean, Mr. Begin is the only French-speaking person on campus, and I was looking forward to conversing in the most beautiful language in the world with you," she said coyly.

"I'm sure we will sometime, but I almost didn't get into PMA because I wrote my entrance essay in French. I have to start thinking more in English—not French."

"Ever since your recruiting visit, the campus has not stopped talking. Rumors have it that you are a remarkable athlete who always gets in trouble because of your relationships with women. Personally, I look at that as an asset. It is what makes the world go around. I live for love, as I think most French women do. Coach is a very good man, but…," she stopped, seeing him approaching the front steps.

"Hi, darling. Our guest has arrived."

Sean and Coach talked soccer while Mrs. Bell went back to

the kitchen to finish preparations for their late lunch. They sat down at the dining table that could accommodate six. Coach sat at the head of the table. She was opposite Sean. Before lunch was over, Sean was sure that Mrs. Bell was bad news. Making up an excuse why he could not finish lunch, he thanked them and left quickly from a very uncomfortable situation. As Sean walked back to the dorm, he was thankful that he was changing. He now had the fiber to fight off womanly advances, and he realized that not too long ago Mrs. Bell would have consumed his thoughts. A cadet in full uniform stopped him.

"Who are *you*?" the cadet said in an obnoxious tone.

"I'm new at PMA. I'm...," Sean started to answer but was interrupted.

"Get off senior walk, dummy," he said in a belligerent voice. "You're on report mister. Report what you did to Colonel Doyle, and I'll deal with you later. His office is over there," he shouted, pointing to a sign that read Officer in Charge. "Now get over there and report yourself!"

Sean walked to Colonel Doyle's office and entered without knocking. He was immediately chastised for entering an officer's room incorrectly.

"Son, go out and try it again," Colonel Doyle said in an acerbic tone.

He was a full Colonel in his fifties with snow-white hair and a black, neatly trimmed mustache. Sean stepped outside and knocked on the door. Unsure, he delayed his entrance even after the colonel told him to enter.

"What's your name?" Colonel Doyle called from behind his desk as Sean slowly opened the door. "You're in for a rude awakening, *mister*."

"I find it amazing that the first two people I meet, you and some cadet by the name of Bard, think I should know everything to do around here by osmosis. My name is Sean Easley," he said, frustrated.

"You mean, Sean Easley, sir, don't you? I'm putting you on report, mister," Doyle said, getting angrier by the minute.

"Fine, what does that mean?" Sean said, still being too bold for the Colonel to calm down. Sean continued without letting him speak, "It's a terrible system when you start yelling at someone without first telling him what you expect."

"Stop," Colonel Doyle said. "You're right, I'm wrong. I didn't realize you were a new cadet. You look like a senior. I thought you were a returning cadet. Please accept my apology," the colonel said as he smiled and extended his hand to shake Sean's.

Sean thought how unusual it was that an officer would admit wrongdoing and apologize.

"Now, let's start all over," Doyle said with a smile. "Welcome to Peekskill Military Academy. Why are you here early? New cadets do not arrive for three more days."

"I'm here for preseason soccer. I had just left Coach's house when Cadet Bard jumped my bones for walking down the street that Coach lives on," said Sean.

"Cadet Bard was as wrong as I was; let me apologize for him as well. Where are you from and where did you go to school last year, Sean?" asked Doyle.

"I'm from Philadelphia but went to school in Montreal last year," Sean answered.

"Why?" Doyle asked.

"Well, I was kind of run out of my town for dating a girl of color. She came from a well-to-do family, and I'm a Quaker, so they thought it best for me to go to school in Montreal and live with family friends there," Sean said, sensing a positive reaction from Doyle.

"Do you know how many cadets lie to me about their background, Sean? You are certainly a refreshing change. I'm married to a gal from Puerto Rico. By American standards she's considered colored, so I understand firsthand what stupidity interracial relationships can fester in the hearts of men," Doyle continued.

"Sean, as part of the military system, you need to get used to using 'sir' when addressing an officer or cadet officer. For instance, cadets say, 'I am from Philadelphia, sir,' and then go on. 'May I come in, sir,' and so on," Doyle said as he was interrupted by an anxious Sean.

"Sir, it would be an honor to call you sir, but Cadet Bard, no way, sir!" Sean exclaimed.

"Britain Bard is the regimental commanding officer and captain of the soccer team as well as an all-league goalie. As a new cadet, you are required to call him sir, Sean," Doyle said.

"I think I just decided to become a goalie, and by the way, what do you do at PMA to settle disputes between cadets? He's just not a fair guy," said Sean.

"Sean, I like your feistiness, but you must follow military protocol. Saluting and addressing people formally is the military way. PMA settles personal disputes in the ring. We box or wrestle. Three rounds or periods and the Cadet Corps decide the winner," Doyle said proudly.

"Why did you come to PMA, Sean?" Doyle asked.

"Because I want to go to West Point, and this is my chance to prove I can excel in a military environment."

"Sean, we are going to be great friends, but you're going to have to play the game. You can't walk down "senior walk." When you leave faculty housing, you must go down the alley in back, get on High Street, and enter the Academy from the main entrance," Doyle instructed. "You will go through new cadet orientation for your first week, and hopefully, you will be taught everything by your squad leader. Let me see what company you're in—yes, B Company. You have a swimmer for company commander, a soccer player for platoon leader and a cadet by the name of Jerry Sole as your squad leader. I'm sure they will take care of you," Colonel Doyle said as he was shuffling papers at his desk. "My suggestion is to stay clear of Cadet Bard and the other upperclassmen as much as possible and get into your cadet uniform as soon as possible. Your hair has to go, now. Go down to the town barber or you will get a lot of grief until the West Point barbers come the second week of school. Believe me, they sheer, they don't cut hair. Meanwhile, give me fifty push-ups for how you first reported. I was wrong, I admitted that, but your reaction was wrong as well. Give me fifty push-ups."

Sean dropped and finished the fifty so quickly that Doyle was impressed.

"I have a feeling that Cadet Bard might have his hands full. Good meeting you, Sean," Doyle said as he extended his hand in fellowship with a smile that communicated true friendship.

"I do not want to see you here again for disciplinary reasons, but please stop by anytime to say hello—of course, with the right reporting procedures. Now, get out of here," Doyle finished, flashing a smile that spoke volumes about the man's true heart.

Sean was happy to meet the Commandant of Cadets who at first seemed like an ogre but was really a good guy. Sean found his bags and went to his room to unpack. The soccer and football teams were the only people invited to campus early for preseason. The football players were already in the dorms and getting ready for afternoon practice. They didn't look very impressive to Sean and weren't even as big as his former Huntington Junior High team but seemed like a nice group. Because of his size, some of them tried to get Sean to play football rather than soccer. At six feet, two inches and 190 pounds, he would be one of the largest players.

After a nap a bugle awakened Sean. Someone ran into his room to say that there were two minutes until formation and then dinner. He got dressed in a Carolina blue sweater, jeans, and sneakers and went outside and stood with everyone else by Old Oak—a huge tree that was supposedly planted in 1767 before the Academy was built. It was a remarkable tree, shading a large open area as well as two dormitories.

"At...ten...hut!" commanded Britain Bard.

Everyone stood erect. The football captain reported that the football team was present and accounted for as he saluted Bard.

"Soccer team—report!" Bard shouted.

Sean responded with, "I'm here."

Everyone chuckled with Sean. Britain Bard was not pleased.

"You're dismissed to the mess hall," Bard commanded.

Coach Bell's wife was waiting for Sean when he entered. She invited him to sit at her table and had reserved a seat right next to hers. Sean figured that he would be safe in the presence of over a hundred cadets and faculty members. The mess hall again conveyed a real family atmosphere for Sean and made him feel comfortable for the first time since his arrival. Coach Bell was excited to have students returning; his soccer players were all to arrive that evening. Many of the smaller football players chose to sit at Coach's table to make themselves feel larger next to his small, physical stature. But one player sat at the table to fantasize about Mrs. Bell. Most of the cadets couldn't take their eyes off her bosom, and Sean could tell she liked it.

None other than Britain Bard offered announcements and a blessing from the podium before the "take seats" order.

After supper, Sean retired to his room and got his gear out for the first day of practice. He knew the coach would test the first day and do skills followed by a little scrimmage. He already missed talking to Claire and Cassandra on the phone and decided to walk downtown to make a couple of calls. He went to the commandant's office to ask permission, and to Colonel Doyle's delight, he reported correctly this time.

"Sir, I would like to walk downtown to make a couple calls and maybe stop by Assumption to say prayers," Sean respectfully requested.

"You know new cadets are not to leave campus," Doyle responded with a smile.

"Yes, I know, sir, but technically I'm not a new cadet for a few days. Today, I'm just a mature soccer player here early," Sean asserted.

"Good one, Sean. Be back by 2130 hours and report directly to me upon your return."

"Thank you, sir," said Sean, starting for the door.

"Sean, say a prayer for me won't you," Doyle asked as Sean looked back at him.

He walked down the hill towards Assumption, reviewing his day. Assumption was on his way downtown, and fortunately, the doors were open. Sean blessed himself and knelt in the back row. He was saying his prayers when he felt a hand on his shoulder. He looked up. It was a Franciscan monk with a big smile.

"I need to lock up, my son," the brother said. "I do not mind if you want to stay longer, but you will have to leave through the rectory," he continued in a soft, warm voice.

"Father, I'll be finished in just a couple of seconds," Sean said quietly.

Momentarily, Sean finished, stood up, and thanked the Franciscan for waiting.

"Are you a member of the parish?" the Franciscan asked.

"No, Father, I'm not. I'm a new cadet at PMA," Sean answered.

"What's your name, son?" the brother asked.

"Sean Easley."

The bearded, red-haired monk smiled.

"Hi, Sean, I'm Brother Dominic. Irish dad, Italian mom. Do you know a Brother Aubert?" he smiled.

"Yes, I do; he is amazing," Sean smiled, waiting for more information.

"What just happened is what I like to call a divine appointment. We just received Brother Aubert's third letter here at Assumption, imploring us to minister to you. He obviously is very fond of you and fully explained your accomplishments at St. Jean de Brebeuf and your many talents. Welcome to Peekskill and PMA. Let's go into the rectory. I'd like you to meet Father Casey," said Brother Dominic as he led the way.

"Guess who this is, Father?" asked Dominic of Father Casey as he sat in his study reading *Sports Illustrated*.

"No guessing for me, but I'm sure I'm going to find out anyway," said Father Casey, a white-haired Irishman who spoke with a slight brogue, standing up to greet Sean.

"Great to meet you, Sean. I thought you would be wearing a cape by the way Aubert talks about you. Actually, you're more impressive looking than I imagined," he said, and they all laughed. "It's great to finally meet you. Anytime we can be of service, please ask," Father Casey said as he returned to his leather chair.

"It would be great if I could use your phone for long distance calls and pay for them by working at the rectory," Sean requested.

"Of course, that would be fine, and if you can't find time to work we will keep track, so you can settle your account. Don't feel that you're only welcome to make phone calls. Bring your friends and family to visit us. We promised Brother Aubert we would look after you. He'll be staying here when he comes to visit you. He tells us that you're an unbelievable athlete and thrilling to watch. Brother Dominic and I also promised we would attend every game so we can render a report back to Aubert after each one. He just wouldn't give up till we said Uncle," Casey reported.

"He's a terrific guy—a real saint—and definitely unusual. He sure has blessed my life," Sean said.

"Meanwhile, can we do anything more for you, Sean?" Casey asked.

"Could I use your phone now if it's okay?"

"Of course. Brother Dominic, please show Sean into my study and show him were the lights are," Casey graciously directed.

"Father Casey, where are you from in Ireland?" Sean asked as he began to walk with Dominic out of the rectory living room.

"Galway. Why do you ask?"

"Oh, no reason—just your slight accent," Sean smiled.

Dominic turned on a lamp in the large wooded room complete with fireplace and all the accoutrements of a study, including a huge old desk. Sean thanked Dominic and sat at the desk as he left the room. He stared out a window that overlooked an adjoining outdoor sitting area. Nightfall was near and dusk gave off a peaceful aura, but it wasn't the scenery that captivated his thoughts—it was how God connects people. Father Casey, Brother Dominic, Mother Superior, Brother Aubert, Galway, Cassandra, Louie, Claire, and Sonny weren't in his life without a reason, and neither was Coach Bell's wife or Brigitte.

Sean called Claire first. She was her wonderful uplifting self with whom Sean could have talked all night, but since he would be paying for the calls, he couldn't spend much time on the phone. He placed the next call to Sonny at the Academy. Some jerk answered the phone but promised to deliver Sean's message. His final call was to Cassandra at Columbia in her dormitory room. A guy answered.

"Is Cassandra in?" Sean asked.

"No, I'm in Cassandra," a male voice answered as Sean heard Cassandra's voice giggling in the background.

Sean's heart dropped to his stomach, and he began feeling sick.

"Tell her a friend named Sean called, won't you? Thanks," a shocked Sean said as he hung up.

He always knew this could happen, but she had been at school only a week and fell out of the tree a little too quickly. So quick, it really hurt. He immediately called Claire again, subconsciously needing to be wanted and wanting to reverse his feelings generated by the call to Columbia.

Claire put things in perspective for him and predicted that Cassandra would be in Peekskill in a few days to clarify what happened. She told him that, above all, he was not to worry.

"That just demonstrates our natural inclinations, Sean," Claire said. "God had his hand in the timing of the call—not pertaining to your relationship with Cassandra but to man in general. Put your trust in Him, not in man. It took me a long time to get there on that principal, but now, I totally grasp it," Claire finished.

She had become very spiritual and was spending much of

her time when she wasn't swimming with Sister Bernadette and Brigitte. She really wanted Sean more than ever but instinctively knew that by developing herself spiritually she would have a better chance of someday being together with Sean. She was quoting scripture, sharing dreams, and telling him to run away from sin, hoping that someday he would run into her arms. The only time she talked about herself was in connection with swimming, and even then, Sean had to draw it out of her. He liked to hear how much she was improving. She never spoke about any other guys, even though she was a hot commodity on the Montreal dating scene.

After the phone calls, Sean said good-bye to Father Casey and Brother Dominic and returned to PMA. He was still stunned over Cassandra and felt a kind of hurt that he had never felt before. He was thinking of her when he knocked on Colonel Doyle's door at 2158. He reported correctly on this occasion.

"Cadet Easley reporting back from town at 2158 hours, sir," Sean blurted out after knocking on Colonel Doyle's partially open door.

"Sean, a girl by the name of Cassandra called crying and wanted to find you," Doyle reported. "I told her you were the new cadet I had the pleasure of meeting today, and that you'd be back before 2200 hours. Do you want to wait for her call? You're welcome to take it here," Doyle finished just as the phone rang. He passed the phone to Sean and walked outside the office to give him some privacy.

"Cassandra, I'm too upset to talk right now," Sean said.

"Baby, it was an obnoxious football player who was visiting with two of his friends. I couldn't believe what he said to you. You have to believe me," Cassandra pleaded.

"That was devastating. I actually got sick to my stomach; I'm still going crazy. I can't talk to you now. When I get a grip, I'll call you. Good night," he said, hurt and confused.

Sean walked outside towards Old Oak and saw Doyle.

"Relationships aren't easy; concentrate on PMA for now, get a good night's sleep, and do well tomorrow at soccer," Doyle firmly encouraged.

"Yes, sir," Sean acknowledged.

Emotionally exhausted, Sean hit the sack, hoping a good night's sleep would be just the right therapy. However, sleep was elusive. He kept envisioning a large football player talking on the phone while on top of Cassandra. He knew all too well how stirred up some guys could get by being on the phone while in an intimate situation. He and Cassandra had talked about how some men got a bizarre sense of power from it.

Cassandra remained fearful and realized she needed to remedy the situation quickly.

Defense is Best

Waking to a new day, Sean's focus was completely on soccer. After a quick breakfast, and with no distractions from Mrs. Bell, he was mentally ready to put on a show, and that he did. Besides Sean, there was a good-looking Nigerian, an Iranian, and a couple of day students from the local Peekskill area who were required to do more of everything during warm up. Bard's snooty attitude, particularly to the new guys, and his being the center of attention during calisthenics fueled Sean's fire.

Coach, gathering the forty soccer hopefuls around, said, "I want to test you in a couple of things. The 50-yard dash, the 440, and an agility test. Then we'll scrimmage a little to see what we have."

He walked to an area marked off by flags and asked for Bard and another returning player to go first.

"I'd sure like to race Bard, Coach," Sean said hopefully.

"Sure, step up, Sean," Coach replied, knowing that Sean wanted to make a statement.

On go, Sean flew to a 5.5 over Bard's 6.4, with gratified onlookers who knew what was going on.

"Wow! That's pretty good," Coach said about Sean's speed, completely ignoring Bard.

As the testing continued, it became obvious that Sean was a physical specimen, the likes of which PMA had never seen. He ran close to 50 seconds in the 440, slipped during the agility test and was still faster than the rest. Word spread through the mess hall at lunch that Sean was not only the fastest but also that he had scored a goal and had two assists in a twenty-minute scrimmage. Unfortunately, so much talk about Sean put Mrs. Bell on a different level of commitment to get his attention. He sat on the far side of the mess hall with Colonel Doyle and his wife in an attempt to avoid Mrs. Bell. Thinking he was safe for the day, she surprised him after lunch, finding him near Old Oak, talking to Olu, a Nigerian soccer player.

"Sean, I understand you were a great performer today. Why don't you stop by in about an hour for dessert?" Mrs. Bell said provocatively in French.

"Thanks, I'm stuffed, Mrs. Bell. I can't."

She just turned away and went home. Her change in demeanor and abrupt departure concerned Sean, but he was glad she was gone.

Everyone was talking about Sean's phenomenal speed. The fact that he liked to assist rather than score made him very popular. Near the end of the next practice, Sean glanced at the sideline and was surprised to see Cassandra with another colored student from Columbia watching.

"Cassandra," Sean yelled to her as he ran toward the sideline.

"Oh Sean, I miss you so much! This is my roommate, Marie. Those bozos came over to visit her, and one of them decided to jerk you around. I couldn't sleep last night worrying about it. Oh, I love you, baby," Cassandra appealed. "Ask Marie, she'll tell you."

"Sean, I just couldn't understand how a beautiful colored woman like Cassandra could love a prep school honky. Yes, Sean, Cassandra is telling you the truth. I also have to tell you that I had hoped she'd like some of the brothers on the Columbia football team, but they repulsed her. I didn't get it till now. I'm sorry," Marie said in an apologetic tone.

"Introduce me, Sean," Olu interrupted as he ran over to check out the two beauties.

"Sure, Olu, meet the love of my life, Cassandra Washington, and her roommate at Columbia, Marie," Sean said as Cassandra breathed a sigh of relief.

"Pleased to meet you both," Olu said in a high Afro-British accent.

"Wow, Cassandra, I can see we are going to spend a lot of time at Peekskill. Olu, I'm very pleased to meet you," Marie said looking at him as if she were buying a new dress.

Cassandra took hold of Sean's hand.

"What are those marks on your face?" Marie asked Olu.

"They are tribal marks. I was born and raised in the bush. When you get to a certain stature in tribal life, you are marked. I left for school in Lagos shortly thereafter, and now, I am pleased to be here at PMA," Olu said as Marie was admiring his shiny, athletic physique.

"You're a fine hunk of manhood," Marie said, unable to contain herself.

"What's that mean, Sean?" Olu asked, his six-foot, four-inch, 180-pound frame dressing a young man with real depth and character.

Sean felt a tug on his arm from Cassandra pulling him aside. She whispered, "Is there somewhere we can be alone?"

"I think that can be arranged," Sean said, excusing them both and dropping Olu and Marie cold.

"Marie will tell you what that means, Olu."

Sean ran over to Coach who was leaving the field. He asked permission to miss formation, so he could take a quick walk with Cassandra and to invite his guests to dinner, considering they came to see him from New York City. He said Colonel Doyle would understand and requested that they sit at the Colonel's table.

"Is there anything else I can do for you?" Coach said with a smile, knowing he had a superstar on his hands. "Remember, you only have forty-five minutes to shower and get to the mess hall. Make sure you and your friends get to the tables before the prayer."

"Thanks Coach," Sean replied and made arrangements for Olu to escort Marie to the mess hall. He and Cassandra headed for the woods for a few minutes alone.

They arrived back just in time for Sean to have a quick shower and then join up with Marie and Olu as the bugle sounded and cadets fell into formation. Colonel Doyle and his wife were waiting outside to greet them. Still the topic of much conversation among the football and soccer players, Sean could hear his name among the din as they walked through the mess hall.

Marie was part Puerto Rican and spoke fluent Spanish and really hit it off with Mrs. Doyle but was anxious to talk with Olu more. He had a regal quality that was difficult to explain.

Marie was drawn to him and quickly learned that coming on too strong did not sit well with him.

"What brings you to Peekskill?" Doyle asked Olu.

"Sandhurst, sir. I want to be the first Nigerian bushman to graduate."

"You mean the West Point of England?" Doyle asked.

"Yes, sir. They have never accepted a Nigerian tribesman, and since my tribe is in power in Nigeria, I think I will have an opportunity if I do well at PMA. I'm a Yoruba from the bush; my father recently became the chief of all Yorubas. Ever since the end of the tribal wars and since England granted us independence, he has wanted me to go abroad to be educated," Olu said with authority.

"Were you in the tribal wars?" Colonel Doyle continued.

After a long hesitation, Olu answered, "Yes, sir," conveying that he did not want to talk about it.

"You mean, Olu, that you are royalty–African style?" Marie asked.

"I'll allow you to determine that," Olu answered with a smile.

Sensing Olu's desire to end the line of questioning, Sean interjected, "I think PMA will have a good soccer team this year, Colonel Doyle."

"You should. Everyone's returning from last year's team. And with the addition of you and Olu and the other new talent, this could be our dream team. Our football team is in a developmental stage, so most of the PMA family attends the soccer games. Football is still just too painful to watch," Doyle explained.

"The biggest surprise I've encountered in the USA is Sean," Olu said, relieved to be on to something different. "I've never seen a white man so fast. I was also told in Nigeria that whites do not like blacks in America, but I'm realizing this is not entirely accurate."

During the meal Cassandra could not take her eyes off Sean, and the cadets could not take their eyes off her and Marie. Marie was good looking, but Cassandra, an absolute knockout, was the ambition of most men and the object of many a cadet's fantasies.

Olu mesmerized Marie, much to her delight, while the experience in the woods with Sean left Cassandra speechless. Mrs. Doyle asked Sean and Olu to bring the girls to her home before they returned to New York. After a nice visit with the Doyle's and a casual walk around campus, the girls returned to Columbia different from when they arrived. The biggest difference was in Marie. Olu told her that unsophisticated women were a real turn-off, letting her know in his own way that she needed to step up her game around him. The trip also had a profound influence on Marie because she understood more fully the depth of Cassandra and Sean's relationship.

The school year got underway and was going great for Sean. He was out performing everyone both in the classroom and on the soccer field. The soccer team was dominating all the prep schools and college freshman teams in the eastern United States and Canada. Cassandra and Marie came to many weekend soccer games to watch their men play, and during this time, Mrs. Doyle grew close to the girls, even inviting them to stay in her home. Weekend soccer games were a big deal for Sean's fan club, found wildly cheering on the sidelines. They spent the rest of the weekend fellowshipping and enjoying the beauty of fall in the Hudson River Valley.

Guy was aging quickly. With each visit, the startling change in Guy's frail appearance saddened Sean. Watching Sean play soccer was one of Guy's true joys in life. Sean sensed this and always managed to put on a show for him.

Brother Aubert became a regular occurrence on weekends at PMA, making the four-hour trip from Montreal with the Lafoussier gang. Cadets loved his enthusiasm, and the spirits of his fellow men of the cloth soared when he was around. Brigitte and Sean were still in love but managed to keep their desire for one another under control. Claire was unique because she, like Aubert, served others rather than being concerned with her own needs. She was a remarkable encouragement to Sean whenever she was around, even when Cassandra was at Peekskill.

In late fall, PMA was slated to play West Point on a Friday night and then play their last regular season game at PMA Saturday morning at eleven. The entire PMA Cadet Corps was bussed to the USMA game, with the usual cheering section on hand. Sonny, who was having a great season in football, had received special permission as a plebe to attend the game and miss his football practice. He had convinced Coach Cahill to come and see the best wide receiver ever to play football go against the undefeated Army plebe soccer team. Coach had grown to respect Sonny's judgment and agreed to attend.

The West Point plebes were 15-0 for the season; PMA, 14-0. They played under the lights in front of 400 PMA cadets and 200 PMA well-wishers with half as many West Pointers and their supporters on the opposite side of the field. Sean ran to

Sonny and hugged him as soon as he arrived. They talked, did their Philly thing, and then Sonny introduced Sean to Coach Cahill.

"You're an impressive young man, Sean," Cahill said in surprise.

"Thanks Coach, hope you feel the same way after the game."

"Sonny tells me you're the best wide receiver in the history of football."

"Anybody would look great with Sonny throwing to them," Sean said and they chuckled. "Gotta go now. See you both after the game." Sean hugged Sonny and said, "T A," and ran onto the field to join the team.

Sonny continued to brag about Sean to Coach Cahill, "Watch, Coach, he'll dominate the game. And remember, he's a football player. He's been that way since we were kids. He is simply one of the most surprising athletes ever. It's as if he has to prove to himself that he can dominate everything. Watch."

When Sonny saw Cassandra on the sideline, he hugged her as he lifted her up and spun her around. They were excited to see each other. She introduced Coach Cahill and Sonny to the Lafoussier gang.

Twenty minutes into the first half the score was USMA-2, PMA-0, and it looked like the slaughter was on.

Sean, approaching the coach after West Point's second goal, said, "Put Olu and me as a two-man front. If we clear and just kick and run, Olu and I will outrun them and we'll get the lead quickly."

"Okay, let's do it," Coach said, and then shouted directions in code to the players on the field. At halftime the score was PMA-3, West Point-2. Sean had scored the first goal with ease, dazzling everyone with his speed. He threw a hip fake at the goalie and dribbled the ball untouched into the goal. West Point double-teamed Sean after that, but his speed outmatched both players again. He faked a shot and passed to an open Olu for two more easy scores. At halftime Sean asked Coach to put him in the goal and stack the defense, keeping Olu as a one-man attack on offense.

"Coach, they won't score on me if I play goal," Sean said softly out of the way of the other players.

"Go for it," Coach smiled.

One of the most amazing displays of quickness, courage, reaction, speed, and great hands took place in the second half. Sean stopped eleven shots on goal, intercepted every cross, and dove to catch with one hand a penalty kick headed for the upper right section of the goal. The fans were mesmerized. The West Point fans gave PMA a standing ovation as PMA beat USMA 3-2. When the gun sounded at the end of the game, Aubert was first on the field. Sonny was just as excited, following the skipping Aubert onto the field to celebrate Sean's performance. The Lafoussier gang, particularly Guy, was ecstatic.

"Coach Cahill, meet my Montreal family, Monsieur Guy Lafoussier and his wife Brigitte," Sean began. Guy took over and introduced the rest of the fan club from Montreal. When the introductions were complete, Coach Malone, the varsity soccer coach from West Point came to shake Sean's hand.

"Son, that was quite an unusual performance. I've heard about you from the swim coach. It would be hard to believe this if I hadn't actually seen it with my own eyes. I sure would like you to consider West Point in your plans for the future," he said in a sincere voice as the others listened.

"Coach, if I'm accepted I'll be here. My hero is Sonny Goldman who happens to be a plebe," Sean said and Sonny laughed.

"I'm also the boxing coach here at West Point. I helped recruit Sonny," Coach Malone said as Sonny said hi to him.

"I didn't know that you two were friends," Coach Malone said, acknowledging Sonny with a smile and a nod.

Rejoining the group, Coach Cahill told Guy, "This man is a football player not a soccer player. Sonny was telling me what an unbelievable receiver he is, and we need receivers."

"Get me in." Sean quickly said and changed his focus to Coach Bell to make arrangements to ride home with Guy and Brigitte instead taking the bus. Mrs. Bell was conversing in French with the Lafoussiers as Sean approached Guy and warmly hugged him.

"That's the best I've seen you play! In fact, that might be the best I've seen anyone play at any level. What a game! I'm so proud of you."

The next day brought soccer season to a close with a 7-0 wipe out in favor of PMA over a local prep school. Olu and Sean played only the first half, leaving the game with a 4-0 score.

Sean spent the weekend celebrating and balancing his relationships with Guy, Cassandra, and Brigitte. Saturday evening's festivities began with dinner followed by dancing. Cassandra and Sean's closeness on the dance floor prompted others to join in. Their dancing was an aphrodisiac for the others. Cassandra had an uncanny way of protecting Sean from the flirtations of others and keeping him under her spell. They often snuck away to unusual places for their special times together.

Brother Dominic, Aubert and Father Casey were always pleased when the Lafoussier gang attended noon Mass. After Mass, Guy would invite everyone, including the Peekskill clergy, for brunch before he and his group departed for Montreal.

When Sean was back in his dormitory, he thought about Claire and wanted to report on the games, so he walked downtown to the Assumption rectory to call her in Montreal.

"Hi, this is Sean Easley. Is Claire in?"

"No, the family is on their way to Brazil. Claire made the Pan-American team, and she swims this week," a housekeeper reported.

"Is there any way to get a message to her?"

"I do not know, but I expect a call from Mrs. Harrison shortly. If you call back later, I might know more."

"When you talk to her, please ask her to tell Claire that Sean is thinking about her and that I asked for her," Sean said with urgency in his voice.

"I will. *Au revoir, Monsieur.*"

"*Au revoir, Madame.*"

Peekskill Was Remarkable

Sean was thinking about Claire all that day and the next. He couldn't get her out of his mind. At mail call after lunch, he received a letter from her. She had sent it from Florida while training there prior to leaving for Brazil and the Pan-Am Games. As he read it, tears came to his eyes.

"Are you okay?" Olu asked as he put his hand on Sean's shoulder when he saw that something was wrong.

"I'm fine. Thanks, Olu," Sean replied as he continued reading Claire's four-page letter.

Claire wrote of how special Sean was and how much she appreciated him and missed him. She spent most of the letter lovingly challenging him to walk the high path of allowing God to use him and telling him how confident she was that he would do mighty things. She also thanked him for all he had done for her in her development as a person and a swimmer. She asked him to pray at the same time every morning during the Pan-Am Games. She would be praying simultaneously even though Brazil was in a different time zone. She also asked Sean to ask Brigitte, Guy, Brother Aubert, Sister Bernadette, and Big Sam to do the same. She knew it was a weird request, but somehow she needed to be more connected to the spiritual influences in her life while she was facing the challenges of the

Pan-American Games. She was very specific that Sean was to pray at Assumption on the front row closest to the middle isle, so she could envision him when she prayed.

Sean immediately called Father Casey so he could get into the church at 0455. He called the other requested prayer partners who were honored to take part. The prayer vigil began the next morning, and to Sean's surprise it was a deeply spiritual time for him. He never left the church each morning until after 0600. Brother Dominic and Father Casey had joined Sean after the first day, and the weekend was upon them before they knew it.

Claire was in the 400-medley relay on Friday evening during prime time television and in the 200-backstroke final on Saturday afternoon, followed by the 400-freestyle relay, which would be contested late Sunday night.

On Friday evening, Sean returned to Assumption's rectory and tuned in to watch Claire's race. Swimming the leadoff leg on the medley, she gave Canada the lead by nearly one meter. The next morning after prayer, room inspection, and a full Corps parade, Sean hurried down to the rectory and joined Dominic and Father Casey to watch Claire swim the 200 backstroke. She had qualified 2d behind an American girl, with two Americans seeded 3d and 4th, all under the existing Pan-American, U. S., and Canadian records. It was going to be a terrific race.

The media did an up-close and personal on the first qualifier from Santa Clara Swim Club in California. The announcers played up the fact that her dad was a professional football player, an all-American and former Notre Dame football great. Then the announcer introduced the Claire Harrison story by telling about her dad. This was followed by Brother Aubert on the screen in Montreal, interviewed live—on his toes. He talked about Claire losing nearly forty kilos and about what a wonderful person she was, spending every free moment working with street people in soup kitchens and shelters.

When the rest of the competitors jumped in the water for the start, Claire kneeled, prayed, blessed herself, looked up, and then entered the water. She had a tremendous start and came up almost two feet in front of the American girls, although she seemed to be off the mark as the race developed. She was 2d at the 50, 3d at the 100 and almost two meters back as she started her final lap. Suddenly she got high in the water and began closing the gap–3d, then 2d, and in the last fifteen meters she flew by them all to win in new Pan-American, World, and Canadian marks. Amazingly, all four girls had broken the existing world record.

The Assumption rectory was a site of great celebration as the television on-deck reporter interviewed Claire. With a smile and not out of breath she interviewed superbly and her humble demeanor prevailed.

"Any of those girls could have won. They are all very fast; we were all under the existing World record. I'm sure fortunate to have won and am very thankful for the opportunity to represent au Canada, the province de Quebec, family, friends, school, and my church in these wonderful games," Claire said as she stood with her arm around the second place finisher.

"Great race; you just came up a little short," the commentator said to the American girl.

"Yes, I did. Claire is a tough competitor, and I'm sure we'll have many more races, so I can have a chance to even the score. I also want you to know that Claire is probably the nicest person I've ever met, and for me, I race better when I don't particularly like my opponent," the American swimmer answered with a smile as Claire gave her a hug.

"Claire, where did you get that last length from? Unofficially it was 32.7, the fastest last length in history by a long shot," the announcer asked.

"I was fueled by the prayers of others. There are some special people with whom I'm connected. I know it may be difficult to understand, but it gives me strength beyond my understanding. Thank you all. Toujours mes amis," Claire said as she turned from the camera and hugged all the other girls.

"You can just sense her kindness. And the news here today is a new world record for Claire Harrison. Now back to you," the deck announcer said as the camera went back to the commentator in the studio.

The television network showed Mr. Harrison playing in the Grey Cup, playing at Notre Dame, and finally, showed Claire and Brigitte serving food at a shelter. She had become the darling of the American broadcasters.

Sean became teary-eyed. Father Casey asked everyone to kneel, and he said a short prayer of thanks. Sean went back to his room and studied. It was his first weekend alone in a long time, and he enjoyed the time of rest and the time he had to think about attending the United States Military Academy. He was overwhelmed over just how much he cared for certain people. He pondered his relationships with women, realizing that some of them were warped and complicated, and that his relationship with Claire was very different. He determined after several hours that West Point was absolutely the direction he should go.

In no time the year was almost over. After Sean's first semester of getting all A's and scoring the highest on the West Point physical fitness test, he was admitted to the Academy. His support group was excited for him and pleased that they would share in his West Point experience.

Just before spring break, Sean was required to attend several social functions at certain neighboring all-girl's boarding schools to ensure the development of his social graces. It was at these events that the cadets were escorts to dine and dance with the young ladies. They were evaluated on etiquette at the dinner table and on such protocols as making introductions, seating positions, posture, standing at required times, and dancing. It was a riot.

During the three-hour process, faculty members evaluated the cadets and the young ladies. The better the evaluation, the less one had to attend the functions. Usually fifty couples would go through this routine on a Thursday or a Friday evening. For Sean it was fulfilling a requirement, but for some of his fellow cadets, it was their only potential sexual encounter. The cadets knew that the worse they did the more they had a chance to "get some." If a cadet abandoned his assigned date, it was an automatic ticket to repeat the process. Some of them would ditch their girl, hoping to meet one of the other girls and get some nooky. They fully counted on a faculty member to reprimand them and tell them that they had to repeat the process. They would complain and then as a badge of manhood get on the bus and spill all, often exaggerating their encounters. Sean found it detestable to trash a girl's reputation for some perverse sense of accomplishment.

Surprisingly, they graded Sean, who was probably the best,

poorly for his dancing because it was too provocative. He was required to attend three of these affairs before faculty deemed him to have a gentleman's etiquette. His first assigned date ditched him to attend an hour-long interlude in the stairwell with her boyfriend. He began circulating to help cover for his escort and to get points toward graduating from etiquette school. Unbeknownst to the faculty, they were providing a sex education course as well as an etiquette course.

Turning the corner, a substantial, wholesome-looking young woman literally hit Sean in the chest and said, "I want to be with you!"

She was well dressed and good-looking with a funny accent.

"You didn't have to punch me in the chest to tell me that," Sean said as he held his chest and grinned at this unusual girl who was somehow elegant yet bold and built like a middle line-backer.

"Heck, it has always worked for me before. I'm Eleanor Donald from Sweet Grass County, Montana–otherwise known as Montana Molly here at St. Mary's. You're the only real man in this entire place. I like big guys. I like cowboys. That's why my daddy sent me to St. Mary's, so I'd stay away from men. He thinks I screw around. Hell, I'm still a virgin. Don't mind necking at all though," she boldly stated in a slight southern accent.

"Wow! You're certainly a breath of fresh air," Sean said. "I think we could become real buddies." So, they sat down and shared their life stories. Although Eleanor liked to talk a lot, she also liked to listen to him, and he found her fascinating. She rode, she worked cattle, and she lived the exciting life of the West. As a child Sean daydreamed about that life—living on a ranch and having horses.

"Sean, I'm a great kisser; at least that's what I've been told. I need to stay in practice, so if you can help me out here, it would be deeply appreciated," Molly smiled.

"Of course, I'm out of practice as well."

"That's not what I hear here at St. Mary's."

"What's that mean?"

"First things first," Molly said as she grabbed him and lead him down an empty hall to a closet. "You must not have been out of practice that long; you're even a better kisser than I am," Molly said after the first kiss. After a few minutes she abruptly stopped, fixed her hair, opened the door, and stood in the hall-way, analyzing their make-out session as if breaking down a football tape. "You are one hell of a kisser, Sean. Your lips are so soft and well, dang, you're the best kisser! and I like how you use your tongue, too," she continued before Sean cut her off.

"Hey, stop, please. Let's not analyze what we just did. Now tell me what you've heard about me at St. Mary's."

"Well, you're quite the topic. For that matter, you're al-most a legend for many here. Everyone knows you're on Jerry Blavitt's show, and you date a colored college girl, but rumor has it that you are screwing her roommate, a Peekskill coach's wife, and some lady from Quebec," she said bluntly.

Taken aback by her remarks, Sean was about to get upset when a St. Mary's school official came upon them standing in the hall talking.

"You know you're not allowed to be here, Eleanor," a wom-en in her forties said to Molly in a stern voice.

Sean turned to her and said, "It's my fault ma'am. I needed

to talk to someone and I sought out Molly for some female advice. I didn't want anyone else to hear," Sean said in an effort to protect Molly from any impending discipline. "Why.....let me ask you. What do you do when you're in love with a girl, but her girlfriend is constantly trying to pursue you?"

The woman totally took the bait, and after giving Sean a five-minute what-to-do lecture, she had forgotten her mission and escorted Molly and Sean into the function.

"Now why would you think I'm involved with the people you mentioned?" Sean said, getting back to where they had left off.

"Look, I know you are involved with most of them. I can tell a lot by the way you held me and by how you kiss. I know I'll relive our kisses until we can do it again. You're fun. I'll write," Molly concluded as she walked away, leaving Sean just as she had found him.

For the rest of the year Molly wrote to Sean, sometimes up to four times a week. Cassandra was starting to communicate less and less, and Sean sensed that she had probably found someone new.

During one of Sean's visits to St. Mary's, Molly introduced him to Marie Gavison, her best friend whose father just happened to be a big shot at West Point. Marie was dating a swimmer at PMA, so the foursome occasionally took in a movie or just hung out downtown.

Claire's swimming and Cassandra's track careers kept them so busy they were often unable to attend events at PMA with Sean. Molly was always very willing and excited to be Sean's date. He often reciprocated as her escort at St. Mary's functions.

Molly just plain liked Sean, and strangely, she seemed to be getting better and better looking to him. They attended several spring formals at Peekskill and on the New York City debutante scene. Sean always thought it uncanny how the rich socialized and interrelated. They seemed to possess an invisible radar screen that could calculate everyone's wealth. For sure, he was a middle-class guy but found that his looks, personality, and uniform opened many minds to his acceptance in the upper strata of New York's social circles. He wondered how they all knew that Eleanor Donald was a blueblood. Somehow they just knew.

Other cadets at these functions tried to win Eleanor's favor, but Sean didn't have one single pang of jealousy. When New York City's finest young men danced with Molly, he usually asked Marie to dance. Her escorts didn't mind because they didn't much like dancing with a six-foot-tall date.

The year ended with Sean winning most of the awards at graduation. His entire contingent, minus Cassandra, was present. Rumor had it that she had started to date a young New York City executive and was too embarrassed to ever talk to Sean about it.

It was a great time with the Goldmans, Easleys, Jacksons, Lafoussiers, and the Brebeuf gang all in attendance to celebrate Sean's graduation. Because St. Mary's was still in school for two weeks after PMA's graduation, Molly became part of Sean's support group. Amazingly, there were no rivalries between any of the women in his life. Brigitte had always invited Mrs. Bell to all of their gatherings, and after graduation she made sure to invite the Bells for dinner and dancing at the

Peekskill Inn.

Sean had a memorable time and the chemistry of the group was spectacular. Everyone loved each other in a natural, uninhibited way, which they demonstrated on the dance floor. Most importantly, Sean's high school graduation celebration was a great time for Louie, Sonny, and Sean to share their dreams and further solidify their unique bond.

Duty, Honor, Country

As Sean and his mom entered Hotel Thayer, Margaret read the history of West Point's founder, Colonel Thayer, which was on a plaque posted on the wall in a foyer.

She turned to Sean and said, "You are now officially one of our country's finest young men. I'm so proud of you. You're going to do great. Someone is here to surprise you."

As they walked into the lobby, he saw that bubbly Franciscan with another priest, both laughing, of course. When Brother Aubert saw Sean, he skipped over in excitement while clapping his hands in his usual way, smiling broadly, and gave him a Friar Tuck-like hug.

"Sean you look fantastique!" he said in his thick French accent. Let me introduce you to Father Casey. "He is the Catholic chaplain and the highest ranking Catholic here at West Point who is not in the U.S. Army. We went to graduate school together at Boston College."

"Aubert is one of those people in life you never forget," Father Casey said with a big smile on his face as he turned to Sean. "And you are the fortunate one who Brother Aubert calls his greatest project. He has selected me to assist you in any way I can during your stay at USMA. Father Casey extended a hand and introduced himself to Margaret.

The four visited for about an hour over coffee, and Margaret learned of the parade of new cadets to Trophy Point at 1400. General Merryfield would give a sort of duty-honor-and-country speech to the new cadets after they were officially sworn into the Army. Brother Aubert tried to persuade Margaret to stay for the swearing-in ceremony, but she had to leave to beat the traffic in the New York City area. After farewell hugs and kisses with Margaret, Sean got in Father Casey's car with Aubert for a ride to the processing center for new cadets.

Knowing what was about to happen, Sean entered Beast Barracks at 1055, just five minutes before the deadline. There was a reason why the first sixty days at the Academy were called Beast Barracks. The Academy designed it to be pure Hell. The Academy allowed hazing, and the days went from 0545 to taps at 2200 with no stopping. It was more than basic training. The purpose was to get rid of poor investments for the Army by running certain cadets out, change the personalities of the new cadets to be subservient, and then to take the next four years to build them up to be leaders. Cadets endured screaming by a cadre of third-year students who trained them in marching, manual of arms, care of equipment, correct wearing of the eight different cadet uniforms, basic weapons instruction, physical training, memorization, hand-to-hand combat. All this, of course, was done in an atmosphere of abusive hazing and purposeful belligerence.

After the first week, five percent of the class washed out because it wasn't for them. Another five percent would depart USMA before Beast was over. Sean had many distinct advantages compared to the other new cadets. Peekskill Military Academy taught him everything and more to expect from Beast and he made it all look too easy. He excelled in everything physical, including hazing. It frustrated the upperclassmen because they could not get the smile off his face. He approached the whole thing as a game and was determined to win.

Bracing was one of the most distinguishing requirements for plebes while in public or when addressing an upperclassman. Protocol required that they squared corners as they traversed the cadet area and that they braced and squared off in the mess hall. Cadets never made eye contact with an upperclassman. Bracing necessitated retracting the chin as far into the neck as possible, and squaring off required raising and returning eating utensils at ninety degrees angles. Hands went immediately to attention while chewing. The entire eating process took place in the bracing position while staring at the plate. Food rarely made it into the plebes' mouths at first and many lost over thirty pounds during the first sixty days.

After a week at the Academy, a large football-type character passed a note to Sean in the mess hall. The message was from Marie Gavison, his friend from St. Mary's whose home was only fifty meters from his barracks. She was asking to meet at Trophy Point after Taps on Saturday night to say hello. The rendezvous site meant Sean had to sneak out after his roommates fell asleep and get past the guards unnoticed. It would also involve crossing major roads around West Point and hiding until he met Marie, then returning to the barracks undetected. Sean was up to the challenge.

Coming from behind a row of bushes to hug Marie, Sean called in a loud whisper, "Marie, you crazy woman. How are you doing?"

"Oh, I'm just fine. I can't believe it's you! Molly called me to see how you're doing, so I had to check you out. What's it like being a plebe, you superstar?" Marie asked as she rubbed his "buzzed" head. "Wow! That feels great!"

After they talked for about thirty minutes, he hugged Marie good-bye and returned to the barracks. Marie had pledged to help him by way of a few upperclassmen that she knew well and to keep Molly abreast of his successes. It was apparent that she got a thrill from sneaking out just to talk to Sean and from the possibility of his getting into trouble.

Soon after their first meeting, there were rumors circulating around the Academy that a certain plebe had been sneaking out to see the commandant's daughter at night. Fortunately, no one thought it was Sean, but now it would be a bit more difficult to go undetected. For the rest of Beast Barracks they decided to meet far from Trophy Point. Eventually, after dealing with the ongoing rumors, Commandant Gavison beached Marie just in case the rumors were true.

They had been meeting weekly just to talk. In defiance of their respective worlds, they reveled in how they pulled off their secret rendezvous. Marie did it in rebellion to an overly controlling, military father. For Sean, it was a test of his ability to pull off the impossible in a closely watched environment.

Marie made good on her promise, and always made sure Sean ate a full meal by having upperclassmen invite him to eat at the regimental commander's table, where he represented his new cadet company. He could always count on a "fall-out" meal, no bracing, just by reciting some extraneous material they knew Sean had memorized.

It also became obvious that Sonny had put the word out to the football team's receiving corps when a tall first classman sought out Sean during an inspection.

Approaching Sean's new cadet company commander during the first new cadet formal dress inspection, the first classman said, "Do you have smackhead Easley in your company, sir? Have him fall out yonder to visit with me."

"Cadet Easley, C69225, reporting, sir!" Sean shouted as he had squared all corners and snapped to attention in front of the firstie.

"Smackhead, you dooley," he said loud enough for the others to hear. Then in a quick whisper he told Sean, "I'm here for Sonny." He shouted again so the others would think he was disciplining Sean. "Do you understand that, mister?"

Sean caught on quickly. "Yes sir! I do, sir!"

"Tuck that chin in, you waste of humanity," he continued loudly before quietly getting to the meat of the matter. "Are you okay? Sonny wanted me to check on you. Said he'd overthrow me all football season if I didn't." Then loudly he said, "Now, recite 'How's the Cow,' mister."

As the cadet filled him in on Sonny, Sean began, "Sir, the cow—she walks, she talks, she's full of chalk. The lacteal fluid extracted from the female of the bovine species is highly prolific to the nth degree, sir."

Walking around, pretending to check out Sean's uniform, he whispered, "Are you getting enough to eat?" Then quickly yelled, "That's not good enough mister, do you understand me?"

The other new cadets, unaware that Sean was being cared for in the West Point way, were beginning to feel sorry for him. He represented what they could expect.

"No, sir," Sean replied in code about the lack of food.

"What? You smackhead! Why don't you understand?"

"No excuse, sir," Sean replied.

"Fall back in your squad," the first classman commanded.

"Yes, sir!"

The first classman went to the company commander and said, "Sir, if all the new cadets are coming along like Cadet Easley, you and your detail are doing a great job with this band of idiots. They're almost ready to join the Corps. Congratulations to you all. Keep up the good work."

The company commander snapped off a salute with his sword, which was quickly reciprocated by the firstie.

Turning to the new cadets, the company commander said, "That was the Corps' highest ranking cadet, the brigade commander and the best wide receiver on the football team, Cadet Bobby Joe Barr. By tomorrow all of you will have memorized his poop sheet, his hometown, number of receptions last year, his high school and more. Do you understand that, New Cadet Company Seven?"

"Yes sir," they responded in unison.

As a result of both Sonny and Marie's intervention, Sean was gaining weight and getting in great shape while most of his classmates were losing weight. His connection with Sonny and Marie also paid dividends in the daily shower formations during Beast barracks. At 2000, new cadets reported to the basement of the barracks for hazing in the most bizarre fashion. Standing at attention in their bathrobes, they were required to recite extraneous information for the pleasure of their superiors and then brace hard in an effort to sweat through their cotton robes as a prerequisite for dismissal to the showers. Sonny and Marie both had contacts who could ensure Sean's early dismissal, but his forethought ensured his own early dismissal when he spent a few minutes running in place in a closet before heading for the basement—just enough time to begin to work up a sweat.

Sean's reputation got around West Point when they tested all new cadets for physical combat potential. They timed each cadet in a mile run while wearing fatigues and combat boots. Sean ran his in 4 minutes 47 seconds without any difficulty; however, it was not a record. A current West Point varsity track runner held the record of 4 minutes, 44 seconds. He was reportedly 144 pounds compared to Sean's 200 plus pounds.

It was in the pool where he broke a long-standing record for West Point in the combat swim test. They placed cadets in learn-to-swim classes if they could not swim. The ones who could swim were tested in full combat fatigues, including helmets, boots, and M-1 rifles. Fully adorned, they were required to jump off of a thirty-foot platform into the water and then swim 200 yards for time. During the pre-test, instructions were to first sling their weapons, take off their boots, place them around their necks, and swim breaststroke for 200 yards.

"Do we have to use the recommended technique, sir, or can we adapt to our skill level in the interest of saving time, sir?" Sean asked.

The instructor had already stated that time was of the essence, and speed could someday save your life in combat. He didn't think Sean capable of developing a better technique on the spot.

Flippantly, Captain Reynolds answered as the other cadets laughed with him at Sean's request, "If you think you're an expert and can do it a better way, you're welcome to it, but if you fail, you will do forty extra hours of duty before Beast is over."

The record was 5 minutes, 37 seconds, and the average cadet took over 10 minutes to finish the 200 yards. Sean noticed that some cadets would use minutes just taking off their boots in deep water and slinging their M-1s before they would start swimming. Sean ran full speed off the platform, landing almost twenty yards farther down the pool than any other cadet. While in mid-air, he slung his M-1 over his shoulder. He kept his boots on, filled his pants with air by pushing water down and creating bubbles, so that the air caught in his fly gave him some extra floatation, and finished the first 25 yards in less than 20 seconds. He swam mostly crawl stroke and occasionally backstroke with only slight hesitation to re-inflate his fatigues and completed the course in three minutes, forty-nine seconds.

Captain Reynolds was dumbfounded when Sean exited the pool to the applause of the other forty new cadets. Another officer, Colonel Mannon, had entered the pool and caught the last part of Sean's record-breaking performance.

"Why didn't you do it the way everyone else did, cadet?" the bird colonel asked in an unusual southern accent.

"I want to be in the Special Forces, sir, and I figure there will be many times I will have to use every asset I possess in order to accomplish my mission, sir. I can swim with a lot of weight faster than most. I used to dive for large clams in water over thirty feet deep and bring up over ten pounds each time when I worked as a clammer, sir," Sean responded.

"But why did you use that technique?" Colonel Mannon continued.

"It makes sense. Time is lost taking the boots off, and in combat my life would be in jeopardy. Keeping my boots on in a river would allow me to exit quickly. In the ocean I would use breaststroke and take my boots off. But with all due respect, sir, I joined the Army, not the Navy."

"That was an amazing display of talent, and that's what makes the U.S. Army the best. Congratulations, Cadet Easley, on the new record," Colonel Mannon said as he shook Sean's hand. "Congratulations, Captain Reynolds, on a job well done. Carry on while I watch the others," he continued as he sat down to observe.

Shortly after the start of another testing sequence, the colonel's aide asked Sean to join the colonel.

"Where are you from, Cadet Easley?" Mannon asked.

"From Philadelphia and Wildwood, New Jersey, sir."

"Where in Wildwood?" a surprised Mannon asked.

"West Wildwood, sir. On the bay overlooking Grassy Sound. Do you know the Wildwoods, sir?"

"I'm originally from West Virginia, and when I was a kid we would go to Wildwood Crest. I think we used to rent a boat from a place called Dot's, so we could fish and crab on Grassy Sound," Mannon said as he saw Sean light up.

"Yes, sir. Dot's is at the bridge just before you get to West Wildwood. You must have gone right past my house on the point that looks over Grassy Sound when you were in the boat on the way to fish," Sean added, thinking what a small world it was.

"We mostly crabbed and it was great fun. You said you were a clammer; where did you clam?" the colonel continued.

"Mostly by the Bunker Factory near Rio Grande Boulevard

for cherry stones and little necks, but for the really big ones, I had to dive in the Grassy Sound channel.

"I remember it well, but I thought the channel was very deep. Even at low tide when it was too low to crab we would fish for flounder in the channel, and it had to be over thirty-feet deep."

"I don't know for sure how deep it was, but I had to equalize pressure both going down and coming up. Sometimes, I had a tough time getting back up to my mom's boat with a big haul. She started putting a clothesline on me and would only let me stay on the bottom for two minutes before she would start pulling me up." Sean continued as Colonel Mannon's interest in him increased.

"Why West Point, Sean?"

"Several reasons, sir. I didn't do well in public school, but I loved going to a private Catholic school in Montreal and Peekskill Military Academy. My brother, Nicky, is my hero. He's a captain in the Army who has already served as an advisor to the French in Vietnam and wants to go back. I'm a Quaker who believes that without Quakers in the military, more lives will be lost in conflict. And Sonny Goldman, West Point's quarterback, is my best friend and old teammate. That's just about it, sir."

"Do you play football, Sean?"

"I used to, but I've got injured, so now soccer is my fall sport."

"Does Coach Malone, our soccer coach, know about you, and for that matter, do any of the coaches know that you're at the Academy?"

"Yes, sir. During Beast, I've made the football, soccer, swim, track, and water polo teams. The swim coach and soccer coach both saw me in competition and recruited me to the Academy. I don't think I'll ever be able to play football again because of my injury, but I tried out because they only play two-hand touch during the tryouts. I was able to play soccer here last year when PMA upset the plebe team."

"I was there, what a great game. Are you the guy who scored or set up PMA's goals and then played goalie, and blocked a penalty shot? Yes, you are that same person. That was a great game, Cadet Easley."

Cautiously interrupting, the Colonel's aid said, "Colonel, you are expected to observe drill, sir, at 1600 hours."

"Cadet Easley, you have made my day. To watch a twenty-year-old USMA record go by the wayside by one of my troops is outstanding. But to find out that the record breaker and I have some common roots in Grassy Sound makes it truly special," said Colonel Mannon as he stood and again shook Sean's hand.

"Thank you, sir. Anyone who can fight off the greenheads of Grassy Sound can handle almost anything," Sean concluded and they both laughed.

At the end of Beast the plebe class took part in a forced march, donning full combat gear for twenty-two miles to an area lake. After a day marked by plenty of running, they set up camp with perimeter patrols all night and broke down the encampment the next morning for another forced march, returning to the barracks by 1800. It was extremely hot both days with highs in the 90s and night lows only dropping about ten degrees. Physically, the maneuver was a cakewalk for Sean. He ended up carrying the equipment of at least three other new cadets so they could make it through the march and the encampment process.

Sean didn't like sleeping in the two-man tents, particularly with the high humidity, so he volunteered for two patrol duties during the night. Between patrols, he opted to catch some shut-eye on the bank of the lake near the encampment control tent. While he was trying to sleep, a strange noise began that sounded like a hose was running into the lake. Checking it out, Sean discovered it was a fellow cadet relieving himself in the lake.

"That might be the loudest piss in history," Sean said, about twenty feet down the bank.

"I like to hear the percussion of a great piss versus pissing against a tree or the dull sound of it hitting porcelain. Pissing for me is an art form," the cadet said as he finished his business and walked toward Sean.

"Steve Lakeman is the name, partying is my game, and in football I'll render you lame, as they say in northern Kentucky. I'd shake your hand but I might still have some on me." The cadet was at least six-and-a-half-feet tall and 250 pounds and was now identifiable in the night light.

"I'm Sean Easley. No surf too rough for the Easy Man, so they say in Philly." They laughed at each other's quips.

"How come you're not slumbering in your U.S. Army accommodations? Most of my body is outside the tent, even though I'm in it. Hey, Easley," said Lakeman when Sean's name registered. "You're the guy who broke the combat swim record. Way to go. How'd you do it? By the way, back home they call me Big Tree. You can just call me Tree," Lakeman said in his southern accent.

"Thanks, I just used a different technique. I guess I just lucked out."

"Running under five minutes and then breaking the swim record, you've made quite a name with our class already. Most impressive to me is that you had the balls to do it your way. Sounds like the Frank Sinatra tune, *I Did It My Way*," Lakeman crooned in a good voice. "You didn't luck out, you be a S-T-U-D—stud, my man. What do you think of the United States Military Academy, Cadet Easley?"

"I like it. To me it's a big game, but I sure do miss the women, a bunch."

"Amen to that," Tree emphasized. "Caught both roommates relieving themselves by mid-Beast. I understand their need, but whacking it mid-day in their bunks—pretty sick, huh? Do you know any women in this area of the country?"

The two bonded as they talked for an hour about sports, their backgrounds, and their dreams.

Approached by an officer and an accompanying enlisted man, they rose to salute and together said, "Good evening, sir."

It was Colonel Mannon.

"What are you troops doing up, Cadet Easley and Lakeman?"

"About to do my second tour on watch, sir. Just trying to keep alert, sir, and struck up an acquaintance with Cadet Lakeman, sir. Plus, I thought I'd become the aggressor on the mosquito attacks rather than surrender, sir," Sean said and they smiled and nodded.

"Hi, Steve," Colonel Mannon said, extending his hand. "Are you going to Todd's party this weekend?"

"Yes, sir, if I'm allowed," responded Lakeman.

"Cadet Lakeman's cousin is my next door neighbor here at West Point, Cadet Easley. The entire Beast Brigade will have a thirty-six-hour reservation leave, once you complete the graduation ceremony, that is, if you successfully negotiate your return march. Cadet Lakeman is probably the best defensive lineman to ever come to the Academy and a Parade all-American out of high school. I helped recruit him to West Point. The Class of 69 looks exceptional. Just finish up with a bang, and by the way, Cadet Easley, report to my office right after you return to the Academy," Colonel Mannon finished as he left them and entered the command tent.

"Yes sir!" Sean popped off and then turned to Tree and said, "You be the stud, you Parade all-American."

"Let's get together this weekend after the parade. I'll meet you at Trophy Point about fifteen minutes after it's over," Tree suggested. "Later," he said as he swaggered into the darkness singing "Down in the Boondocks."

The Sound Heard from Afar

Beast Brigade wasted no time returning to their barracks. Running at what seemed like full speed, they were motivated by the impending thirty-six-hour reservation leave. Furthermore, if they broke the Beast record for returning the twenty-two miles, they would receive a full "fall-out" leave, enjoying life as they had known it. They wouldn't have to brace or square off their meals and could entertain guests after the parade. The parade would serve as graduation, a culmination of their first summer in the Army, and the leave would be the reward for doing well. Everyone was still required to keep all military decorum, hours, and dress during the leave.

The record for the return was seven hours and fifty-five minutes. The Class of '69 smashed the record and returned in under six hours. Others assisted weaker cadets by carrying their equipment or giving them an arm-up during the run, and they literally carried some cadets part of the way. The first thing Sean did upon returning was report to Colonel Mannon's office.

"Cadet Easley reporting to Colonel Mannon as ordered, sir!" he said as he snapped to attention and saluted in the Colonel's office.

"At ease. Please take a seat, Mr. Easley. I'm pleased to inform you that we have selected you as one of the "Best of Beast." I've called your folks and they're excited to share this honor with you; they're even bringing some of your friends. We'll assemble at Hotel Thayer after the Beast graduation parade. You'll need to report to Cadet Bobby Joe Barr's room two hours prior, and he'll advise you of all protocol for the parade and the ceremony. I couldn't be happier for a fellow Grassy Sounder," Colonel Mannon said, saluting Sean. "You're dismissed."

"Thank you, sir."

The next morning after breakfast Sean knocked on Cadet Barr's door.

"Come in," Sean heard from the inside of the firstie's room. Sean responded to the command. Cadet Barr then ordered, "Sit down, Easley. Take off your dress jacket and cross belts and let's talk football. By the way, call me Bobby Joe unless someone else comes then you're going to have to play the game. Till then, let's talk football. Sonny wanted you to explain how you used to run patterns and how you were always there for him. I'm a jealous person by nature and practice starts in a few days; it's my last year, and I thought I might tap into your head a little."

Sean and Bobby Joe talked football for almost an hour with Bobby Joe interrupting many times with questions or comments like, 'who taught you this stuff?' or 'that's very good.' Sean explained a new way to think about running pass patterns, so that for every play, he could adjust to the defense and give Sonny a greater advantage to get the ball to him.

Sean noticed that Bobby Joe's room was bigger and nicer with all the extras that could make life at the Academy more pleasurable. He had a single room with a sitting and study area on one side and his bed, a radio and hi-fi on the other. They were in the sitting area when someone knocked. Bobby Joe asked Sean to stand at attention, so as to hide the casual nature of their relationship. Two other cadets entered the room, and Sean was back to plebe status and prepped on protocol for the parade.

"We need to talk more, cadet. Have a great day." He positioned himself and whispered, "I'll be joining you and Sonny at lunch with all the brass later on."

The three plebes being honored were not to march in the parade but were to stand off to the side of the reviewing stand and, on cue, march to the front of reviewing stand. The parade was better than most during Beast Barracks. The official Army 100-piece band led the procession, and the graduating class looked like they were a precision drill team, demonstrating their marching expertise.

For the first time, the magnitude of what was about to happen hit Sean. In less than one summer he had become the "best of the best" and was about to be officially honored as such. Welling up with tears before receiving the award, he thought about the miracles that had happened to get him to this place—people like Aubert, Claire, Sonny, Brigitte and Guy, his parents, and places like Brebeuf and PMA, and the miracle that he no longer stuttered. He thought of how exceptional all his classmates were, and said a prayer of thanks to an awesome God.

The announcer told the few thousand spectators about the rigors of Beast Barracks and how this class had fared so well. He told them that the United States Military Academy wanted to recognize three exceptional new cadets who represented the excellence of the entire class and their excellent performance during the class's first summer in the Army. He spoke of William Stone of Fort Campbell, Kentucky, who was already a veteran as an enlisted man and decided to become an officer by gaining entry into USMA. He received special recognition for saving and treating an enlisted man he had found unconscious in a burning car. Colonel Mannon pinned a medal to his chest.

The announcer introduced Lionel Addison from Arcata, California, who risked his life covering flaming live rounds with two mortar plates and then extinguished the fire. His quick thinking and courage saved countless lives of fellow servicemen. Colonel Mannon pinned a medal to his chest.

The announcer then turned his attention to Sean Easley of Philadelphia, Pennsylvania, and stated, "Sean has written himself into Academy history by setting a new combat readiness standard for the combat fitness test and breaking a twenty-year combat swim fitness record by over three minutes. Sean was an all-state football and track athlete in high school. He is an example of the tremendous fitness level that this year's class has achieved during their basic training in the United States Army. Joining us today are his parents, Navy Commander and Mrs. Samuel Easley, to pin the Army Service Medal on Sean."

With the band playing in the background, Sean's mother smiled as tears ran down her face. Trying to contain sobs of joy, she pinned his medal on, while his father, clad in civilian attire, stood behind her.

The three cadets saluted Bobby Joe Barr and returned to the side of the viewing area to watch the rest of the parade. Afterwards, Sean hurried back to change into his dress whites to meet Tree at Trophy Point. Tree looked much bigger than he remembered.

"Tree, my folks are in town and we're having dinner. I want you to come to the Hotel Thayer with me."

"That was some honor, those medals, parade, and stuff, Easy Man. Yep, that parade was quite a deal. Sure, I'd love to meet your parents, but I need to hunt down a woman after…if you don't mind." Tree sounded desperate.

The two made the twenty-minute walk to the hotel. A bond had developed between them that they did not yet understand. They didn't really like to talk about sports, but mostly about the women in their lives and what they wanted from the Academy. One thing for sure, they both liked to laugh.

When they entered the lobby of the hotel, Sean knew it was going to be a complicated time. His mom and dad, Sonny, Abe, Brigitte, Aubert, and Father Casey were in the lobby to meet him.

"Who the hell is that, Easy Man?" Tree asked, referring to the red-silk-bloused Brigitte, looking her all-time best.

"That was my nanny," Sean grinned, making eye contact with Big Tree.

"You have lived a charmed life, my man. I'm cool now as long as I can "whack it" under the dinner table, fantasizing about rocking her. Yes indeed."

Sean greeted everyone warmly with hugs and kisses and introduced Big Tree. Brigitte sensed Sean was emotionally and physically vulnerable, and when they embraced, they confirmed they wanted to be together.

"Take her in the closet and do her now," Tree whispered to Sean.

"No, you have the wrong idea, Tree," Sean responded.

"Bullshit, that lady is on fire, and you be the only person in the room that can extinguish that flame."

Although Brigitte was now talking to others, she could sense that Tree knew what was up between her and Sean. Fortunately, Sonny entered the room precisely in time to change the chemistry. He greeted everyone and invited them to follow him to the veranda overlooking the Hudson River. It was a gorgeous setting with ample space for sixteen at one gigantic round table. The table was set exquisitely with flowers, special linen, crystal, and silver. When everyone had arrived on the veranda, Sonny took over.

"Ladies and Gentleman, please allow me introduce everyone, so the West Point folks can meet the Easley group. But before I make the introductions, I would like to say a few things about my best friend, Sean Easley. Sean and I grew up together in Philadelphia and have been very best friends from almost the first day we met. Sean, I'm very proud of your accomplishments, and I'm not one bit surprised by them. You have a gift for doing exceptional things—things that have brought honor to yourself and now things that will bring honor to your country and the Academy." Giving Sean a big hug, Sonny said, "Congratulations, Sean," as everyone clapped.

Introducing each person, Sonny told how he or she was related to Sean. Bobby Joe Barr, Colonel and Mrs. Mannon, and General and Mrs. Gavison represented the Academy folks, along with Sonny and Big Tree. As Sonny introduced each family member, Sean hugged them to show his gratitude and broke protocol to hug Mrs. Gavison and Mrs. Mannon.

Sonny began the meal with a champagne toast, "To Sean Easley. We raise our glasses to honor your accomplishments and to the greatest institution in the world, The United States Military Academy."

Sonny announced the seating arrangements, making sure he balanced the table. General Gavison asked Margaret to tell him about Sam's military career, citing that men don't like to talk about themselves. Sean learned a lot of things about his dad of which Sam never spoke. Everyone at the table was enthralled with her recounting of his military life. Sam had been on ships sunk by the enemy in both the Atlantic and Pacific. He was the recipient of the Navy Cross and a Purple Heart. Margaret also spoke of Abe's background in World War II and the Israeli Wars and asked General Gavison and Colonel Mannon's wife to do the same. Their stories were interesting and demonstrated the depth of military experience at the table.

Colonel Mannon asked Margaret more about Sean's clam diving in the Grassy Sound channel. He went on to give General Gavison details about Sean's record-breaking performances. After that, table chatter began between people sitting close to each other. It was obvious that Big Tree and Mrs. Easley were enjoying their conversation, and Sean was trying to dodge the bullet in a conversation with the Gavisons about their daughter. They asked if he had met her at Peekskill. Sensing that they might be putting two and two together about Marie and Sean's meetings during the summer, Sean concentrated on her boyfriend from Peekskill and on being the escort for Eleanor Donald at most of the New York City debutante affairs. Fortunately, Mrs. Gavison remembered Eleanor and Sean from one of those parties and redirected the conversation in that direction.

Everyone was having a grand time when the Easley inevitable happened. Big Sam was sitting next to Mrs. Mannon when it started. At first everyone tried to ignore it, but it kept coming and was getting louder and louder, and longer and longer. Long enough for Sonny, Tree, and Sean to look at each other and start giggling. Aubert fell off his chair laughing, and Father Casey could not regain his breath, he was laughing so hard. It continued to the point where all conversation stopped to witness in amazement the world's longest fart. Colonel Mannon placed his napkin over his eyes to disguise his laughter.

After what seemed like the most strident thirty-second opus, the most comfort-producing flatus in history, Big Sam leaned away from Mrs. Mannon in a manner so as to release any lingering gases in his trousers and then leaned back to ask Mrs. Mannon, who by now was laughing, "Did I get any on you?" With this, everyone lost it, everyone except for General Gavison. Colonel Mannon was under the table, Brother Aubert was clapping, the cadets were laughing hysterically, and the waiters were frozen in disbelief.

Abe summed it up with," That's my Sam!"

Witnesses to this Guinness world-record feat were either embarrassed, entertained, or strangely enthused. General Gavison, although, was not a happy camper. Mrs. Gavison discreetly and gently placed her hand on his as if to say, do not react, and just let it go. He was the only one who was not in tears laughing. Brother Aubert and Father Casey had the most difficulty regaining their composure.

Sensing a need to do something, Sonny, who had been talking football to General Gavison, stood up and proposed a toast, "Here's to Sean for breaking West Point's longstanding record for the combat swim test and to Mr. Easley for setting an all-time wind-breaking record at West Point." The table cracked up again.

Fortunately, a three-piece musical combo came to the rescue. Abe and Sam sprang to their feet for their wartime jitterbug. Father Casey and Brother Aubert made an attempt at dancing with Brigitte as others joined in. It was spontaneous and fun. Abe and Sam jitterbugging to the war-era song prodded General Gavison into his World War II mentality.

"By the looks of it, you've done that before," Gavison said to Abe.

"Anytime "Boogie-Woogie Bugle Boy of Company B" is playing, I just have to dance. When I was in the 101st, it was automatic when we heard that song," Abe told Gavison.

"I was in the 101st," Gavison said as he made a connection with Abe.

As they continued to talk, they realized just how much they had in common. Meanwhile, the combo, sensing they had a live group, switched to a slow song. The cadets asked the wives to dance and Brigitte asked Bobby Joe.

While Sean was dancing with Mrs. Gavison, she said, "I know Marie was sneaking out to meet with you this summer. But now that I've met you, I understand why. She is a wonderful young lady, and her dad would go crazy if he knew."

Dipping her in a surprise dance move, Sean responded with, "I would not like to confirm that ma'am, but I do agree that Marie is a wonderful person."

As the song ended, the dancers headed back to their seats and noticed that Abe and General Gavison were hugging and possibly crying.

When General Gavison saw everyone watching, he switched

back to his General mode and said, "Abe and I ate some of the same dirt together."

The combo played a few more tunes. The cadets danced with the ladies while the men talked about World War II and current events in Vietnam. The men had bonded and the ladies had a great time.

After dessert, General Gavison rose for a final toast and said smiling, "To a luncheon I shall never forget."

The group gathered in the lobby to say their good-byes to Abe, Susan, Sam, and Margaret who were off to Philadelphia. Brother Aubert and Father Casey invited Sonny, Sean, Big Tree, Bobby Joe, and Brigitte to ten o'clock Mass, which Brother Aubert would officiate.

"I'm very excited and appreciative that Father Casey has allowed me to say Mass. Please come," Brother Aubert said as he left with Father Casey.

Brigitte told Sean she was returning to Montreal after Mass with Brother Aubert and said, "Sean, I'm so proud of you." Then, hugging Sean she whispered, "*J'ai besoin de toi,* Sean. *Un, un, deux Hotel Cliffe, à neuf heures.*"

"Merci, Brigitte, au revoir," Sean responded to disguise what just went on.

Tree, Sonny, and Sean left for Tree's cousin's party. They had a great time. The Mannons were there and Tree met Marie Gavison, over whom he went absolutely "ga-ga." After a good while Marie snuck away to talk to Sean. He shared with her his conversation with her mom about sneaking out. They decided it might be a good idea for her to start dating Tree. Marie liked the idea; she knew Tree was obviously a misplaced, free spirit who was also one huge good-looking guy. Mid party Sean excused himself to return to his barracks.

"If you think I don't know where you're going, you're nuts. You stud you," Tree said.

"You have it all wrong, Tree, all wrong," Sean said as he walked out the door.

Back in his room Sean dressed in all black and went into the West Point woods to change, so he could sneak out of the reservation undetected, visit Brigitte, and get back in his room by lights out. He had no idea where Hotel Cliffe was other than it was south of the main gate. It ended up taking over an hour to travel less than four miles in order to go undetected by the military police.

That night, Brigitte and Sean just held each other. Before they realized, it was 0040 and Sean was going to need a ride back to make curfew. Sean needed to get into the woods undetected, change clothes and get into his room prior to 0100. Fortunately, he made it back just in time.

As he lay in bed, he felt wonderful yet horrible at the same time. How could he fall back into wanting to be with Brigitte? How come he couldn't resist her touch? How could he go to church when he promised God and himself that he wouldn't do that again? His thoughts went into prayer and then to Claire. He realized he hadn't heard from her in weeks and eventually fell asleep thinking of her.

As he marched to Catholic chapel, Brigitte was waiting for him. Wow! She knocked him out the way she looked. She was unbelievable, like a beautiful flower that just had its petals shined. Tree, Bobby Joe, the Mannons, and Sonny had arrived there before him and were all talking. He knew she was waiting patiently for him. Bobby Joe had to be in the march-in with Brother Aubert and then escort Brigitte to a seat in the first row. The 700 other cadets were spellbound by Brigitte's beauty. Meanwhile, Mrs. Mannon had captured Sean and Tree to escort her and sit with her on the other side of the chapel on the first row. The music started and the processional began. As the congregation arose, Brigitte and Sean, on opposite sides of the church, locked eyes in a loving stare. Brigitte looked away, sensing that Big Tree was checking them out. Sure enough he was.

As Brother Aubert marched down the aisle with Father Casey, he acknowledged all of his friends with a nod and a smile. Father Casey introduced Aubert as one of the most alive, fun men of "the cloth" that he had ever met. The topic of Brother Aubert's homily was, of all things, repetitive sin. His words convicted Sean. Aubert spoke with certainty yet retained his patented happy spirit.

"Fear not. We are all tempted and sometimes lose the battle to sin, but our Father in Heaven loves us in spite of our weaknesses. When we understand His love more completely and put on the armor of His word, we will not give in to temptation so readily."

He was unwittingly throwing daggers at Sean's heart as he spoke. Despite Aubert's sermon and his horrible feelings of guilt, Sean could not stop thinking about Brigitte and wanting to be with her.

"What's up gang?" Tree said. "What are we doing?" He asked again to everyone who was standing in front of the church congratulating Aubert.

Tree and Sean walked back to the cadet area as Sonny and

the Mannons took off in their car. Brigitte said a lengthy and emotional good-bye.

"Appreciate you including me in your weekend activities—well, almost all your activities. By the way, 'the fart' is all over campus. And everyone has figured out that you were the guy who was seeing Marie Gavison during Beast," Tree added.

"Marie is way too innocent for that, and she would never allow anyone to get close to her. Make sure people realize that. Just so you know, Tree, I will never talk about being with any woman," Sean interrupted. "I learned a long time ago that what people think is happening is not always accurate and can be very hurtful. I don't know about you, but I want my life to be positive."

"All right. I got it. Put me in, Coach. I can play," Tree said and then started singing "Down in the Boondocks" with a giant smile on his face as he swaggered along the walk overlooking the Hudson, all knowing.

An About-Face

Plebe year continued to be a challenge for Sean, trying to beat the system while excelling in sports and getting by in school. For Sonny, fall was the best time. Football season was when he got to do his thing. Bobby Joe was becoming a heck of a receiver and West Point was winning. Big Tree was in a league of his own, which *Sports Illustrated* depicted with a photograph of Tree picking up a Notre Dame back over his head and throwing him like a toy. Varsity football allowed freshmen to play for the first time, and Lakeman was making quite a name for himself.

After Claire qualified for the Canadian Olympic Team in four events, she took off from training a week to visit Sean and Sonny at the Academy. It would be her first visit to West Point. She had discerned from her phone conversations with Sean that he was changing. Sean had been elected the class cadet activities officer, responsible for all social events for his class. Whenever there was a dance, he booked the bands, determined the motif, and invited certain women's colleges, and wild NYC women to party with his classmates. He also had to stand in the receiving line with his date and introduce each cadet and visitor to the officers and their wives. Such was the case when Claire visited. Claire had only a few minutes to change after her arrival from Montreal and drive to the dance at Cullum Hall.

"You look gorgeous, Claire," Sean said as she entered the hall.

"So do you, Sean," she said with a smile.

Sean took her to meet Colonel Mannon, his wife, and the officer chaperones in a sitting room adjacent to the great hall.

"Claire, I need to run around and prepare for this affair. I'll be back to start the receiving line soon," he said and left her to visit with the others. When he re-entered some fifteen minutes later, Claire had bonded with everyone, as always.

"Claire is my kind of people. She is quite a catch, Sean," Mrs. Mannon said genuinely as they exited the waiting room to hundreds of cadets and their dates waiting to enter the dance.

Sean introduced Claire first, and she, in turn, introduced Mrs. Mannon, and Mrs. Mannon introduced the Colonel, etc. The receiving line took an extraordinarily long time because Claire visited with every cadet and his date. Several cadets commented that they were not used to Sean being with someone as nice as Claire.

The last group to enter the dance were stag cadets and the literally hundreds of young ladies who were all invited by Sean's efforts.

After the receiving line finished, the music started playing.

"You have quite an assortment of girls for your classmates to choose from. All different types and experiences it seems," Claire said as they walked to the table. One girl from Columbia University made a special effort to ensure I knew that she was friends with Cassandra," she continued as Sean seated her.

Sean turned to Mrs. Mannon and said, "Let's dance," and started to twist.

The Colonel reciprocated and asked Claire. About thirty minutes went by with Claire dancing with both officers and cadets alike. She noticed that Sean had disappeared. Claire sat and wondered whether she should look for him but instead struck up a conversation with Mrs. Mannon.

"I'm glad you're here, Claire. I want you to talk to Sean. Rumor has it that he is sneaking out every night and going to NYC. Something is happening to him. It's almost like he doesn't care anymore and the girls say he has become the consummate party animal."

Both Mrs. Mannon and Claire saw Sean leaving a nonfunctional cloakroom adjacent to the dance floor with two young ladies who looked like they had just given Sean a heck of a workout.

"I'm so sorry, Claire," Mrs. Mannon said, holding her hand in support.

Claire reacted swiftly, realizing that Sean was indeed slipping backwards, and she would not be part of his downward spiral.

"I just wanted to say good-bye before I left. Have a great night," Claire said to Sean and then raced down the grand steps of Cullum Hall to her car. This was a wake-up call for Sean. He adored her and realized that he had become a rude, inconsiderate schmuck. He tried to convince her not to leave, but to no avail. He then left the dance to contemplate his behavior, pondering whether his attitude was due to the realization that the military might not be the right career for him. Was he reacting to Vietnam or to the fact that the previous year's Army football captain lasted only fourteen minutes in Vietnam combat. Furthermore, word was getting around that an infantry second lieutenant stood a slim chance to make it back from Nam. He sat and thought what a waste of life. The rumors of innocent Vietnamese losing their lives began playing on his Quaker mind as well.

Soon after Claire's wake-up call, Sean, now an upperclassman, headed for Camp Buckner for summer training. Camp Buckner, dedicated to training yearling cadets in different branches of the service, was on the West Point reservation. It was located on a recreational lake, and it was the first time that cadets were free to party openly on weekends. Weekdays lasted from 0545 to 2030 every day with some very challenging physical tests. Sean excelled in the physical, tactical, and mock scenario training. The brass made a big mistake by allowing Tree and Sean in the same Buckner Company; they were constantly pulling pranks on others and making hard drills look easy and fun.

It was during his ranger training that something happened to Sean that would truly change the direction of his life. The cadets were equipped with a map, compass, knife, and canteen. They were partnered-up, blindfolded, and dropped from a helicopter. The challenge was to get to home base undetected within seventy-two hours after their drop off. The enemy army, dressed in blue fatigues, was trying to capture them and put them in a makeshift, holding area. The maneuver did not come with food, so they had to live off the land. As fate would have it, Tree and Sean were partners for ranger training.

When they removed their blindfolds, they realized the chopper dropped them in a hot LZ training site, which meant the enemy had their eyes on them immediately. Sean began running for the thickest brush with Tree following.

"Run that direction—towards that mountain! I'll stay here and see how many are after us. Go!" Sean directed Tree.

"Yes, my dear," Tree whispered and hauled ass.

Within thirty seconds, seven blue-fatigued enemies made their way out of the other side of the landing area, and Sean started running at top speed towards the mountain. Within a few minutes he caught up to Tree. They were at a sheer wall at the base of the mountain.

"What now, superstar?" whispered Tree.

"It's either rock climbing or tree climbing, my man," Sean beamed at Tree.

"It looks like I better make like a tree because those branches are too high for my big butt," Tree whispered. Sean used hand signals to relay that at best they had less than three minutes until they would be captured. He motioned for Tree to follow him.

Sean put Tree on his shoulders and pushed him to the lowest branch. Big Tree climbed to the top and held onto the trunk as the enemy approached. Sean used his belt to put around the trunk of another tree and went up the tree faster than the best lumberjack. Sean could hear the "blues" coming; he got Tree's attention and put his finger to his mouth. Tree reciprocated by elevating his middle finger. Undetected, they both started to giggle.

The enemy surrounded them from below. "One of those guys was Big Tree Lakeman; I always wanted to meet him," a "blue" said.

"We only have one more group coming in tonight. These were the only guys who got away in our LZ. We're okay. The other LZs are averaging about a fifty percent capture rate," another said.

They heard an incoming helicopter overhead. "Let's get back and nail those guys as they take their blindfolds off," the leader said.

A few minutes later Big Tree saw Sean at the base of the tree, waving him down. "Where to now, honey?" Tree asked demurely in a high-pitched voice.

"Back to the LZ. Those "blues" will lead us to their base camp after they capture the next team. We just need to haul ass and get on the other side of LZ before the chopper lands," Sean said in a hushed voice.

They moved quickly and sure enough in a few minutes they were following the "blues" to their base camp. Sean thought that the enlisted men probably went back to their regular barracks at night, leaving only a skeleton detail to oversee their captives. By midnight, Sean and Tree freed some seventy classmates, by capturing and tying up the "blues." Tree took pleasure in saying to those he and Sean had captured, "Pleased to meet you. My name is Stephen "Big Tree" Lakeman. I play football. Come on the field after a game and say hi." He sang his theme song, "Down in the Boondocks," as he continued tying up the "blues."

The rest of the cadets went in one direction while Tree and Sean returned to the mountain and scaled to the top.

"Thought we would rest up here tonight and then start moving at daybreak. But first, I have a present for us," Sean said as he busted out some stolen "blue" chow.

"You are my man!" Tree exclaimed.

Sometime near dawn Sean went to be alone on the mountain to talk to Him. As he petitioned for guidance, he felt God impressing on him that he needed to get out of the Army because there was something else he was to do with his life. Sean was certain of that now, but He had not told him what that something else was. Sean was happy inside because he knew what it felt like to be in fellowship and he loved the feeling.

Big Tree awoke and caught sight of Sean. "Where you been, man? You look different; you almost glow. It's a nice look; how do I get it?" Tree asked.

"I know now I've got to get out of West Point. God touched me during prayers this morning, and now I know for sure that's what I'm supposed to do. I'm at peace for the first time in years."

"You're a natural-born leader, man. To see first-hand what you did yesterday—West Point will not let you go, and for sure, the U.S. Army won't let you go," Tree said passionately.

Sean and Tree got to a road and hopped a ride to NYC. There Sean introduced Tree to some of his debutante friends. Forty hours later they got a ride back to home base. They finished ranger training in seventy hours. In their written reports, Tree said Sean was the greatest natural military tactician ever, and Sean said he partied the whole time. Sean was best in class in ranger training, but he was still resolved to leave the Academy as soon as possible. He was definitely different after ranger training.

Tree didn't cotton to Sean's decision to have a "no-women" summer, but that didn't stop them from having a good time at social functions that Sean arranged as Cadet Activities Officer. One of the last events of Camp Buckner was that each of the eight companies put on a skit, depicting any phase of their summer's training. Tree and Sean developed a two-act play about prisoner-of-war training that featured Sean as a gay German prison camp commander who loved *all* his prisoners. It was the last official weekend at Buckner, with a show on Thursday for all military personnel of the region. The Friday night show was for parents and dates. After the show there was a dance followed by an all-day beach party, cookouts, and no curfew until 0600 on Sunday.

Their two-act skit was so funny that most of the 800 present gave the cast a curtain call with two encores. The brass went back stage to discourage a repeat for the next night's review, labeling their skit inappropriate. That was all they needed to repeat the same thing the next night, bringing down the house with three curtain calls. Sean took the hit for demerits for disobeying an order, so Tree would not be compromised during his upcoming football season. Sean was going to leave when he returned to the Academy anyway, so the demerits were superfluous. It was a great summer, but Sean would never be the same.

His Destiny Is Set

As soon as Sean returned, he talked to Coach Malone about leaving. Coach Malone was a great guy and always did what was best for the individual. "Sean, you should do what your heart tells you. I was kind of hoping you were here for the season, but if you're not happy, you will not play your best, and it will not be a satisfying experience," Coach Malone advised.

After an extended visit with Coach Malone, Sean agreed to remain at the Academy for another year or at least until after soccer season. The season went great, and Sean was the reason for the team's success. He and Guy spent a lot of time talking on the weekends.

Sean told the Army brass that he would be leaving West Point after the semester, but it didn't sit well with his tactical officer in charge of his company. Retention of cadets was part of the evaluation of the tactical officer, as well as the rest of the brass, and considering Sean's visibility as an athlete and combat fitness superstar, it was not going down well.

"I apologize for making the mistake of attending West Point. It's a great place, but I know God wants me to do something other than kill people," Sean told his tactical officer.

"That's very nice, but you do not have an option. Either you stay or I will see to it that your ticket is stamped *Vietnam*.

If you don't think I will do that, just test me. The United States Army does not revere cowardice, so stay or start packing and getting ready for Vietnam—you pick. You're dismissed," the tactical officer responded.

Sean always discussed his options exclusively with Guy. On the weekends after Guy analyzed Sean's soccer plays, they would separate from the rest of the gang and discuss Sean's leaving the States to seek asylum in Canada from the Vietnam conflict. Canada's government was anti war and accepted draft dodgers and those who were AWOL, fleeing from mandatory participation in Vietnam.

Sean gave up at mid semester; academics became a joke, amplifying his desire to leave USMA by going AWOL. Even though he attended all of his classes, fluid dynamics, electricity, and physics were of no interest to him. He filled his evenings by talking to friends on the telephone and secretly preparing to vanish after the soccer season.

Sean took pleasure in watching Big Tree and Sonny enjoy the finest year in recent West Point football history. It looked like they had a particularly good chance at a bowl bid if they had a good showing against Navy. Sean felt obligated to tell only one person other than Guy about his leaving, and that was Sonny.

Sean waited at the West Point field house to catch Sonny after football practice. "Sonny, we need to talk," Sean said with a serious face.

"Is everything all right?"

"Not really."

"Come to my room after dinner," Sonny said. "See you tonight, mon ami," Sonny smiled. "By the way, you really helped Bobby Joe become a good receiver. When I get in trouble, I look to him, thanks to you. Later," he said as he walked into the varsity football locker room.

That night Sean told Sonny that he was leaving West Point immediately after the last soccer game and not finishing the semester. He did not tell him he was going AWOL. Sonny told him not to do it—that things would get better in Nam and that by the time he graduated, America would have kicked ass and had the Viet Cong well under control.

The next weekend the Army soccer team defeated Hartwick College in the regional NCAA Championships and qualified for the national championships held at Southern Illinois in ten days. That weekend Guy and Sean finalized the plans for Sean's leaving the Academy, and Sean returned for his final days as a cadet.

The same weekend, Bobby Joe Barr was injured in the football game against Rutgers and would be out for at least a month, which meant no Classic for Bobby Joe. At 8-1 with losses only to Notre Dame, Army had a legitimate shot at a bowl if they beat Navy or played a good game. Rafe Steele was quarterback for Navy. People were comparing Sonny to Steele.

Sonny ran excitedly into Sean's room on that Sunday eve during study time.

"Sean, you know everything happens for a reason. I know if you start playing football again, you will not want to leave the Academy. I had a dream again recently that we were playing together. I saw it—you *are* going to play in the Army-Navy game. I actually ran the idea by Coach already, and he said if it was okay with Coach Malone, he would give it a try. Bobby Joe also tried to convince coach to give you a shot and told him that you taught him things that made him much, much better this year. What do you think?"

"You're nuts. I'm leaving West Point. Football is history for me," Sean said with half a laugh.

"Sean, my dream was real—just ask Coach Malone. Come on, you douche bag, do it, Sean. I'm not kidding—I just know this will happen!" Sonny exclaimed. "I also know we will get invited to a bowl because of you. I saw it—it was real!"

Sonny left Sean's room and went directly to Coach Malone's house. Malone was also Sonny's boxing coach. Sonny convinced him to call the football coach and make arrangements for Sean to play.

At the next soccer practice, Coach Malone asked Sean to get a physical to see if the doctor would allow him to play football. Coach thought it would be a great boost for Army soccer if, during the Army-Navy football classic, everyone knew that a USMA soccer player was good enough to play in the Classic. To Sean's surprise he no longer had an enlarged liver and the doctor cleared him to play football. They took him from the doctor's office to the football equipment manager who knew him well from soccer. Sean asked the manager for quarterback shoulder pads and the smallest facemask, but not for knee or thigh pads.

Coach Cahill didn't seem interested in giving Sean a try until punt return practice. Sean returned his first punt—eighty-five yards going untouched, which caused quite a stir among the coaches. The only reason he got that chance was because Big Tree's cousin was the special teams' coach. When practice was nearly over, Bobby Joe hobbled over on crutches and said something to the head coach, and he then called for Sean.

"Easley, show me what you have, but only two plays," Cahill said sternly. Sean entered the huddle. Sonny told the boys to block and for the receivers to run "outs." He didn't tell Sean anything—he didn't have to. Sean threw two fakes, ran long past everyone over the middle, and caught a sixty-yard pass. After one play, the coach replaced Sean. Sonny was excited, but Sean could sense some hostility from the coaches and players. He knew the annual football classic would never allow a soccer player to participate, but by going though this exercise, there would be a chance to see his family once more before going AWOL. Guy had made arrangements for Sean's disappearance from Philadelphia. It was a federal offense to aid or abet a soldier going AWOL, so Guy needed to be very secretive.

The plan was for Sean to visit with his family before the game and afterwards at the Deli-Land party. He was to excuse himself from the party and appear to be joining the team downtown, but instead go to the North Philadelphia Airport, where a private jet to Quebec City would be waiting. Guy would catch up with him during a business trip some days later at a safe place.

At Sean's second practice with the football team, he burnt the defense, but again the coach only used him sparingly. He never broke a sweat. Sonny wasn't worried about the big game because he knew with Sean they had an ace-in-the-hole, and Coach Cahill would have to use him if the team fell behind.

The Army soccer team was soon off to the NCAAs and lost the opener in a shootout. Sean played great. Guy was emotional, knowing this was the last of Sean's soccer games. Army won the consolation game against St. Louis University to finish 3d in the U.S.

Returning back to school, Sean asked the football trainer if he could take off Monday and Tuesday because of an injury to his right leg that he received during the soccer tournament. It was expected that football players show up for practice, injured or not. Soccer wasn't like that; when a player had an injury, he rested. When Sean returned to the football practice field, Coach Cahill gave him a thorough chewing out in front of the whole team, but at the end of his emotional outburst, he congratulated him on Army's soccer season.

"Gentleman, we might not have a great football player here," Coach said, pointing to Sean, "but he's a hell of a soccer player!" Everyone laughed. For the rest of the week he was not in one play during practice, but it didn't matter to him. He only cared about going home to say good-bye.

As soon as the team arrived in Philadelphia, the coaches invited the Army players' parents from that area to the team meal. The Easleys, Lafoussiers, and Goldmans were there. The Philadelphia papers were making a big deal about Sonny being a tough Jewish kid who distinguished himself in the ring, in the pool, on the track, and on the football field. They lauded him as a true leader of the best Army team in recent history. Still, Philly had always been a Navy town, and the papers predicted a Navy victory. The dinner conversation was largely about the game until, to everyone's surprise, Cassandra showed up. The room became still. She looked great and she knew it. Sean and Sonny each received a big hug while someone added a seat for her next to Sean.

Numb to the others, Cassandra's full attention was on Sean as she caressed him and expressed her excitement that he was playing football again. She couldn't keep her hands off him.

That night, the eve of the big game, Sonny gave two television interviews and predicted it would be a great game and told them Army had a secret weapon that would not be unleashed until the following day. The 80,000-seat game was a sellout. Bowl officials from the Sugar, Orange, Cotton, Peach, Gator, and Liberty Bowls were there to make their final selections. The game had national television coverage and much media interest.

That night alone in the room that he and Sonny shared, Sean started thinking about the next day and how it was going to be the last time he would have any contact with his family and friends. He needed to start making phone calls. First he called Louie in Michigan, then Aubert in Montreal, and most importantly, Claire. Little did they know those calls were good-bye calls. His conversation with Claire lasted over an hour. She had become Sean's most trusted ally and friend, even though Sean had abused his friendship with her at times. She always could make him laugh at himself for becoming such a "horn toad" and was always concerned about his welfare. In the middle of a conversation she might stop and say, "Let's pray together." He asked her to pray during the game and asked her to watch. She promised to lift him up in prayer all during the game and would continue to pray for him daily. She could sense that she was winning his heart the right way—not the way she had started at Brebeuf.

Sonny and Sean never talked football before a game. They liked to talk about their growing up, the stupid things they did together, different teachers, and characters that made their life at Abington enjoyable. The next morning they left for JFK stadium three hours before game time. A soccer ball signed by the entire football team that read, "Good to have you with us," was on top of Sean's locker. He got a good chuckle out of it. Sean's game jersey was number seven, which put a smile on his face. Getting to wear number seven was important to him. It meant Sonny had to have pulled some strings because it was Sean's old number in high school. Sean asked one of the coaches if he could wear his soccer shoes because they were lighter. The coach replied in a way that communicated to Sean that he didn't matter.

When Sean took the field for pre-game warm up, there were already thousands in the stadium to watch the midshipmen march in and then the cadets. It was always a spectacle—one which Sonny and Sean had watched many times from the stands with their fathers. Sam would cheer for Navy and Abe for Army but today they would both cheer for Army. For Sonny and Sean, one of their childhood dreams was about to come true. The roar of the crowd was deafening. Although he was pumped by the roar of the crowd and knew that something big was about to go down, the game itself was no big thing to him emotionally. He was loose and fast when he ran onto the field. His destiny was set.

The entire Army Cadet Corps went into a frenzy. The noise was extreme. During the national anthem, Sonny and Sean had tears rolling off their cheeks but for different reasons. Right from the kickoff, Army was in trouble. Navy ran the kickoff eighty yards and scored on their first play from scrimmage. Then they recovered a fumble in Army territory, after Sonny had only run two plays. They blitzed Sonny on every play. Navy scored again—15-0.

Sean shared an idea with Sonny while they were watching

Steele leading the Navy team and looking like the Heisman winner he was. "You need to do some 800 quickies to freeze their linebackers. Then I'll go deep and we will get on the scoreboard," Sean said to the stressed out Sonny as they stood on the sidelines.

"He'll never let us do it," said a confident Sonny.

"Nothing he has done has worked in the first three series. He has nothing to lose. Go get him to do it," Sean pleaded.

Sean could see Sonny and Coach going at it. Army got the ball back with ten minutes to go in the second quarter. On the first play of the series, Army lost two yards. Sean had a burst of adrenalin, which he had not experienced in a while, and uncharacteristically, put himself into the game. He knew he was toast in less than three hours anyway, and his impudence would not matter. He ran into the huddle and replaced the right end.

"P-P-Pro," Sean said in the huddle, pretending to have his stutter back. Sean's humor loosened Sonny up and they both laughed. Sonny told the others, "Long story."

"Pro set, sweep left, 800 quickie!" Sean told Sonny.

"On two, ready break!" Sonny gave the snap count.

Normally, Sean would line up eight to ten yards outside the tackle, but this time he almost lined up as a tight end. The ball was hiked to Sonny who jumped in the air and pushed the ball over the middle to Sean. Sean was behind the linebackers when he caught it and cut to the outside. He was simply too fast and elusive for the Navy defense. It looked like he was playing a game of tag with the Navy players, ending the play when he stepped out of bounds for a forty-four-yard gain virtually untouched. The play took almost 15 seconds, with Sean running well over 100 yards in a serpentine pattern to advance the ball the forty-four yards. It was Army's first, first down of the game. Coach took Sean out of the game immediately. The coach was ripped about Sean going into the game, but at the same time conflicted because it was the most offense Army had exhibited thus far. Expecting their wrath, Sean moved down the sideline as far away from the coaching staff as possible. Meanwhile the stadium announcer did not even know his name nor did any other media, and after Sean's first play, everyone was scrambling to identify number seven. The stadium announcer deviated from protocol calling number seven the Army's secret weapon.

For the next two series, Army gained nothing. Now in the third series, at third down and sixteen to go, Sean put himself back in without the coach's permission.

"T-formation, Sean wide right, post, on one, break," Sean said as Sonny beamed. It felt just like old times. Sonny knew Sean was in deep doo-doo, but it loosened him up nonetheless.

They then did what they had practiced thousands of times as young kids. Sean would throw some head fakes and then streak towards the goalpost. Sonny would throw it while Sean would run under it. It worked just as it had all their lives. Sean ran under a forty-yard pass and scored Army's first touchdown. In the end zone he simply put the ball down and ran to the sideline. For the extra point, Army faked a pass and Sonny did a quarterback draw for two points: Navy-15, Army-8. The Stadium announcer was having a ball with no one knowing who Sean was, continuing to call Sean "Army's secret weapon" to the crowd's pleasure.

"Army's secret weapon has now gained over 100 yards. If anyone knows who number seven is, please contact the press box immediately," the announcer implored the crowd.

Army interrupted Navy's momentum, and they fumbled on the eighteen-yard line after driving sixty yards down the field. Fueled by Sean's success, Big Tree Lakeman was making Rafe Steele's life miserable as halftime approached. He knocked the ball out of Steele's hand as he was about to pass to a wide-open receiver in the end zone. Tree recovered the ball on the twenty-two-yard line.

"It's our time, Sean. Let's do it, Easy Man," Sonny said as they jogged on the field together.

"Strike now, Sonny!—long, long. Long! Throw the ball on a streak and I'll run under it," Sean said, bumped by Tree running to the sideline.

"Showtime, Sean. This time you and I will party in the end zone. Do it Easy Man," Tree smiled, having to yell over the stadium noise.

"Pro set, pull left, bootleg roll right, Sean streak on two, break!" Sonny commanded in the huddle. The coach saw Sean in the game and let it just happen.

Everyone appeared to be running left. Sonny hid the ball on his hip and ran right by the defensive end, planted and chucked the ball to a streaking Sean. Sean was twenty yards down the field when a defender almost knocked him off his feet. They called interference and threw the flag down, but Sean continued. The pass appeared to be way overthrown to the television announcers, but Sonny had thrown a floater by design and Sean knew he had a chance if he kicked in the afterburners. Sean got to it in time and tapped the ball up in the air once to get further control of it and scored a spectacular touchdown.

The television announcers went crazy. The stadium erupted.

He uncharacteristically blessed himself and he pointed to the sky. Sonny and Tree ran to congratulate him in the end zone and wanted to party, but he cut the celebration short.

At the Harrison home in Montreal, Claire, Aubert, and the Harrisons were celebrating Sean's heroics. "Wow, Sean, wow!" Claire screamed. Aubert started dancing with her, while her parents clapped, and then he dropped to the floor and began doing the Gator. Mr. Harrison finally acknowledged to Claire, who was beaming, that Sean was indeed special.

"He *is* special, Daddy; I always told you that!" Claire directed her comments to her parents who were sitting on the couch.

"He just might be pro material," Mr. Harrison speculated.

Meanwhile, for the extra point, Sonny bootlegged the ball around the right end to bring the half-time score to Army-16, Navy-15. The press box was still scurrying around, trying to find out who number seven was. When Army's sports' information department released the news that number seven was Sean Easley, the Philadelphia press hurried to see if they had any information on him.

Before the bands marched onto the field at halftime, the stadium announcer said, "Army football has identified their secret weapon. Number seven is Sean Easley of Philadelphia. Sean hails from Abington and ran the anchor leg in the Mile Relay Championship of America at the Penn Relays." The Philly crowd roared their approval.

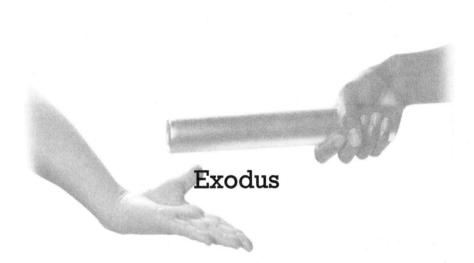

Exodus

The Get Away

Entering the locker room at halftime, Coach Cahill exclaimed, "Sean, you're a football player!—a natural receiver. You should be playing all the time!"

"Thanks, Coach; I'm having fun," Sean said. Big Tree began singing his anthem, "Down in the Boondocks," sitting next to him with a big smile.

"I've got to go to a defense meeting, superstar; you rest! We're going to need two more touchdowns to win this game!" Tree said, slapping him on the back.

Sonny motioned to Sean to come to a meeting with the backfield coach and players. "Sean, I'm going to run you out of the backfield on some pass plays," said Coach Thomas. "I went to college with the defensive coordinator, and I know he's going to start double- and triple-teaming you on the line. He knows how to screw up our timing. We'll run flares and screens to you from the backfield and then trick them with the sideline play. Do you know the sideline play?" Coach Thomas asked.

"Yes, sir, if it's the same one we used in high school. That's when you pretend to come out of the game, but you're really not off the field, then you run a streak," Sean said.

"That's it, except all the Army players on the sideline have their helmets off and are holding them over their heads. You keep your helmet on and go out for a pass," Thomas said.

"Sounds good to me," Sean grinned.

"What's he doing here?" Sonny asked, as he saw General Merryfield's aide enter the locker room. The aide talked to Coach Cahill briefly then left. Sonny went over to find out what was up and quickly reported back to Sean.

"I can't believe it. Merryfield wants you benched. What a dick!" Sonny said.

"I know why," Sean said.

"Probably too much celebrating after you scored. Just get ready and hopefully, you'll get another chance," Sonny said, leaving to appeal to Cahill on Sean's behalf.

The second half started slowly for Army with no first downs in the first three series. Navy went to an uncharacteristic ground game and Steele scrambled twenty yards for the first score of the second half. Midway through the fourth quarter, the score was Navy-22, Army-16, then Navy added a 40-yard field goal: Navy-25, Army-16.

"Easley! Easley!" Sean heard Coach Cahill calling him. "Run back this kickoff," Cahill said with a devilish grin, as if he were saying, "To hell with Merryfield!"

Sean hadn't returned a kickoff in years, but he *could* do something few returners knew how to do and that was to run fast right up the middle of the field. When he got the ball, he hesitated for a couple of seconds to get some blocking in front of him, then he cut right up the center of the field, did an amazing spin move and was pushed out of bounds after a 60-yard return. Cahill took him out immediately. The Army team kicked a field goal: Navy-25, Army-19.

After three and out, Navy had Army pinned back to their own 20-yard line, needing over 80 yards to score. Sean entered the game this time by design to set up "the sideline play" with less than a minute left. Army ran a sweep out of bounds to stop the clock. The coach sent in two substitutes; Sean was one of the three Army players who appeared to run off the field. Sean appeared to be part of the rallying cry, but stayed two yards inside the field of play. The play worked like a charm, and Sonny hit Sean perfectly in stride for a touchdown to dumbfound the Navy team. He pointed to the sky and ran back to a very jubilant sideline. Army-25, Navy-25, with 20 seconds on the clock. Navy miraculously blocked the extra point to end the game: Army-25, Navy-25. The classic was over. The Army faithful stormed out of the stands as though Army had won. Television reporters were creating a Sonny/Sean sensation by telling their *Toujours Amis* story.

When they walked into the locker room, the media was all over them and swept them off to a media center. They told them they were co-MVPs. Sean and Sonny hugged for a long time. Only they knew how many countless hours of play, work, sacrifice, and dedication to each other it took to be able to do what they did. They looked at each other, shook their heads, and grinned.

"I have dreamt about this moment all my life, Sean. We did it!" Sonny exclaimed, jumping with his arms held up and fists clenched.

"Yes w-we d-did," making fun of his former malady.

Sonny cracked up and they hugged again as reporters crowded around. They wanted to know how Sean got to play. How Sonny, a Jew, and Sean, a Quaker, become best friends, growing up in Philadelphia. Their story fascinated the press. Sonny told everything—how they met, the meaning and significance of *Toujours Amis*, Brigitte's role in their youth, Louie, Cassandra, the Penn Relays, swimming, dancing, their parents, their fathers' relationship and then he started bragging about how fast Sean was.

"How fast are you, Sean?" one journalist asked.

"I guess we'll never know," Sonny jumped in to the laughter of the other media people in the room. "Sean is faster than anyone knows, but he only runs as fast as he needs to," Sonny added, and more laughter broke out.

One of the Philly reporters asked, "Which was more exciting or rewarding: anchoring Abington High to win the Mile Relay Championship at the Penn Relays or being MVP of the Classic?"

"Both because both were done in Philly," Sean quietly answered with the acumen of one much older.

"How does it feel to be co-MVPs of the Army-Navy Classic?" a television commentator asked them.

Sonny choked up, cleared his throat, and said, "As kids we always played like we were in the Army-Navy game. We have thrown those passes you saw today thousands of times before to each other. Believe it or not, two weeks ago I dreamt all of this. That's why I had to make sure Sean played, particularly with the loss of Bobby Joe in our last game. He's out for the rest of the season."

"You guys are definitely going to Bowl. I know America will be tuned in to see you both together in action again," a CBS commentator said. "The phones won't stop ringing—the country wants to know more about you two, Louie Jackson, Cassandra and this Toujours Amis thing!"

"We'd like to celebrate with our families now. We have to go," Sonny told the press. They both got up, thanked the reporters, and Sean left. A couple reporters cornered Sonny to get more answers.

Before Sonny got back in the locker room, Sean had quickly changed and, without any fanfare, hailed a cab waiting at JFK stadium. About thirty minutes later, the cab arrived at a serene, quiet, empty Abington Meeting House. After leaving the cab, he took off his cadet jacket and entered his boyhood place of worship, sitting alone in the darkness. Time flew by. Thankfully, the cabbie was still waiting when Sean left the Meeting House—happy. He needed to come to peace again with what he was about to do.

Many media members followed Sonny from JFK, ending up at Deli-Land. Typically, Abe invited all the media to join in the celebration. The Lafoussiers, Easleys and Goldmans, as well as anyone else who wanted to party, were included in the celebration. The local ten o'clock news aired live from Deli-Land, talking about Sonny and Sean and showing their now famous gathering place.

About thirty minutes into the party, Sean announced he had to go downtown to meet Big Tree and asked Cassandra to give him a ride to the Fern Rock subway station, where they said good-bye, agreeing to see each other at Quaker Meeting the next morning. They hugged, being old friends but no longer being an item, and Cassandra drove off.

There was a car waiting for Sean on the other side of the subway station that took him to a private plane, which flew him to Quebec City, Canada. One of Guy's operatives met him and took him to a safe house. Sean's life had now changed forever. Despite the anguish this decision was causing him, somehow he knew it was what he needed to do.

The next day most of the major newspapers carried the story of Louie, Cassandra, Sonny, and Sean with pictures of the game, Deli-Land, school photos, and the Penn Relays' picture from *Sports Illustrated.* The headline of *The New York Times* read, "Army's Secret Weapon Pays Dividends." Sean was oblivious to the media coverage and the fascination with their story.

No one, other than Guy, knew what Sean had done, and Guy played his role to the hilt, appearing shocked when Sean didn't show up for Meeting. The Easleys contacted West Point officials and were told that he would not technically be absent until the bus left at 1600 for the return to West Point. His absence was not an immediate concern to anyone but Cassandra who sensed that something was wrong. When he didn't show up for the bus, Sonny was concerned because he knew that Sean truly wanted out of the Academy. Big Tree sat on the bus smiling to himself, knowing that only Sean would have the *cojones* to "skate."

The team learned upon their arrival back at West Point, that both the Cotton and Sugar Bowls had invited them. They would either play Texas in the Cotton Bowl or do a reenactment of the Classic with an Army-Navy battle in New Orleans at the Sugar Bowl. The Bowl officials told the Army brass that the boys' story and the show they put on during the Army-Navy game was an important factor in Army's bowl selection. The country truly wanted to see these boys in action again. Army had seventy-two hours to respond. Meanwhile, Sean was AWOL.

It took less than forty-eight hours for Merryfield to respond. He knew Sean was AWOL and didn't want the boys' story perpetuated any longer. Not wanting to disclose that an Army football player went AWOL, he released a statement to the press saying, "The Army football team is honored and privileged to be invited to the Sugar Bowl and the Cotton Bowl. Because of the escalating hostilities and involvement of the United States Army in Vietnam, West Point regretfully must decline both invitations this year."

Reporters continued to follow the story. The Army brass covertly started an all out manhunt for Sean, without disclosing to the media that Sean was AWOL. Federal officials interviewed the Easleys, Lafoussiers, and Sean's friends, and searched all his old haunts, including those in Montreal—no Sean.

Guy and Sean were the only ones who knew that Sean was sitting in a farmhouse near a little town north of Quebec City. Sean began to think that he would rather go to jail than live without his family and friends. He was miserable. Absence amplifies the desire for what is longed for, and he was desperately struggling with his decision to leave the United States. He missed his family terribly.

He read many articles in the *Quebec City Press* about the escalation of the United States in Vietnam. One was about the new U.S. draft system that was going to be a numbered lottery. The selective service would probably draft the first fifty percent that were eligible from ages eighteen to twenty-four. More than likely they would see action in Vietnam. Another article claimed that five percent of those drafted to go to Vietnam would escape to Canada. Yet another article told of the Vietcong's commitment to take over Vietnam. In a forth article, General Merryfield was going to be appointed the supreme commander of all American forces in Vietnam. The articles comforted him in his decision to go AWOL.

Guy called soon after Sean arrived in Quebec City. "Sean, we think our phone lines are bugged in Upper Outrement. I'm calling from a phone booth. I also think I'm being followed. U.S. officials have interviewed Brigitte and me, and have searched the house. They are committed to find you. Are you okay?"

"I'm okay—just having some misgivings about the way I left West Point and the Army. Maybe it would have been better for me to just quit the Academy and take what was coming to me. I miss my friends and my family."

"Sean, just pray. God will show you the way," Guy said. "There is a suspicious person around the booth. I'll call you tomorrow, and by the way, do not shave. Au revoir."

The next morning Guy called again to confirm that Sean was sure he wanted to go. "Now is the time to move you; otherwise, you may get caught."

Overnight the different options weighed heavily on Sean's mind, but it came down to a simple choice of dead or alive. He knew he had to be alive to fulfill his purpose in life and was still determined to pursue his calling.

"Guy, fighting for the U.S. Army in Vietnam is not the answer," Sean responded.

"Okay, your hair needs to be darkened and remember, don't shave. I'll fly you to Marseille soon and will contact you there within ten days. On the flight, study the history of the person you are to officially become, according to your documents," Guy hurriedly said, calling from a public phone.

Within a week, Sean and Guy were in a beautiful villa in Marseille, where Guy had arranged for Sean to stay. They had a long talk about how Sean could best serve mankind. Guy told Sean about the Underground Railroad that the WPO was organizing in Vietnam. Listening to both sides transmitting on the radio, they attempted to save lives by picking up troop movements. If either side got themselves in a troubled spot, the Underground Railroad would guide them out of harm's way. It was dangerous work. Both sides could kill you. Death traps, like mines and pungi pits aimed at the enemy were just as dangerous for underground volunteer peace workers.

"Sean, you have had more military experience than anyone who is currently serving in the Underground Railroad, and I would like to offer it to you, that is, if you so desire," Guy said after a lengthy discussion.

"I would like to think this one through. It's ironic that I left West Point so I wouldn't go to war, yet I'll end up in Vietnam sooner this way." Sean was prepared to use his talents in a meaningful way.

Guy made arrangements for Dao to help orient Sean to the Vietnamese language and culture. He said, "When it's time, Dao will get you to Vietnam for further orientation and when you are ready you'll go into the field. She is a communist used by both sides and has inroads to everyone of authority in Vietnam. You will be safest under her wing."

Meanwhile, Guy felt relatively secure being with Sean in public in southern France, and they really enjoyed dining, soccer games, and being together for a few days in Marseille. Guy left and returned to Montreal, and Sean waited for Dao's arrival, working out vigorously twice a day.

Dao arrived within a few days, and they finally settled down to commence Sean's education about Vietnam. He was a quick learner of the Vietnamese language with its French sounding accent. After a month, Dao decided that Sean was ready to go Hanoi and Saigon for further training, and she decided that he would stay at her apartment.

His travel documents and passport were for Monte Guillet from Nice who had jet-black hair and a full beard. Sean had no difficulty getting into Vietnam with Dao. He noticed that most of the police and high-ranking military knew her. There was a car waiting with a PRV flag on it as they exited baggage. Sean could understand bits and pieces of Dao's conversation with the driver who was fascinated by Sean's size and curious as to their relationship. Sean thought she told him that he was her Parisian plaything to which the driver laughed.

The car stopped in front an exclusive apartment compound on a tree-lined street in Hanoi. They entered a well-decorated flat, which exhibited Dao's class and interest in the arts. It was a two-bedroom apartment. She directed him toward the bathroom and the extra bedroom and instructed him to put his clothes in the closet. As she went to the kitchen, Sean opened the walk-in closet to find a wardrobe of military uniforms for men. By the amount of gold on the shoulders, Sean knew Dao was well connected.

"What's up with the men in your life, Dao? They have a lot of gold on their shoulders, and it looks like they're both Peoples Republic and Vietnamese uniforms."

"Those men are men of convenience, which means when they visit you must not be here," answered Dao as she walked by.

"What if they knew I was here?" Sean asked.

"They already do, believe me—they know everyone who is in this country. You're a Quaker, it's okay. They know you will help both sides. Those men know about each other and it appears to be okay, mainly because they are both married. I'll tell you more about them later," Dao explained.

"Is there anybody in Vietnam that would recognize you if they saw you with long, black hair and a beard?" asked Dao.

"Maybe my brother, Nicky. I don't think he's started his second tour, but if he had, he would probably be around Saigon. The only others would be former academy teammates," answered Sean.

"You will be more effective if no one knows you're here. The passport control officer knew you weren't Monte Guillet. That passport you have has been too doctored-up, so I'm going to call you Stephan, which is Guy's lost son's name. You are safer being Stephan Lafoussier because his name carries weight in the intelligence world. You know, Guy runs the most valuable and trusted intelligence service in the world. He gives most of the money to charities. Plus, he has become fabulously wealthy himself. I know he loves you like a son. I will get your passport changed to reflect that you were born in Beauvais, France, with his son's birth date.

Sean's Vietnamese orientation was going well, but Dao thought it best that he go to Saigon to test his language skills. This would require his being shipped off every two weeks for a weekend alone there, until she felt confident about his skills. Even though the language was the same, there were subtle cultural and language differences between North and South Vietnam that Sean had to master. He assimilated into the culture,

and his first engagement with troops was in Laos and Cambodia where he became aware that unapproved U.S. military
activity was taking place. There Sean became familiar with the
elaborate tunnel system that the North Vietnamese developed.
The tunnels were less than five-feet high, so his maneuvering
ability was limited. His claustrophobia also compromised his
expertise in these subterranean passages.

"I think you're ready to do your work, Sean. So far, the
Underground Railroad has saved hundreds of North and South
Vietnamese lives. As the war escalates, we will save many more
lives, including Americans," Dao said.

"I'm not afraid of anything in the bush except snakes, and
I don't think I'll master that one," Sean answered.

Sean joined forces with four conscientious objectors who
were practicing Quakers (formerly Buddhists) and a London-
er in his forties. They listened to radio transmissions from
their jungle compound and used the information to attempt to
steer troops away from danger. They often administered first
aid to wounded troops after a gunfight and helped get them
back to their respective lines. Soon the Vietnamese called
Sean, Hu'ang—angel in Vietnamese. The American troops
thought they were South Vietnamese sympathizers, thus pro
America. Sean alternated between three weeks in action and
one week in Saigon with Dao.

After a few months, Guy visited Sean in Saigon and gave
him a complete briefing about the conflicts worldwide and noticed that for the first time Sean seemed to have a real passion for the WPO. Dao bragged to Guy about Sean's heroics
on the battlefield. She told him that he saved several hundred
wounded Americans, dragging them out under fire. Dao also

reported to Guy that she thought he was becoming less reluctant to help the Cong and most recently he had saved many of their injured troops.

Sean did not want to talk about the battlefield. He only wanted to hear about his family, Brigitte, Claire, Sonny, Louie, Aubert, Cassandra, and the Goldmans. Guy was proud of Sean's development as a determined peacemaker and was encouraged by his exploits and spirit of peace. Guy updated Sean about Big Sam and Margaret. Both were fine but very anxious to know of Sean's whereabouts.

"Sam feels you just could not agree with the Vietnam War and are in a foreign country. I told Brigitte you were alive and in hiding; I had to because she had become so despondent. None of your loved ones have any idea where you are, which keeps them safe. The authorities are still looking for you, as you well know. Aubert thinks you're dead, probably killed by a Philadelphia bookie that lost a bundle on the Army-Navy game. Claire always tells me you're alive because she says she can feel you. I've not talked to Sonny or Louie lately," Guy reported.

Guy and Sean had a wonderful time visiting and catching up with each other. One night while dining at one of Saigon's finer restaurants, Guy told Sean that he really liked the fact that he took his son's name on his passport ID and that he was known in Vietnam as Guy Lafoussier's son.

"You have done a great job here. Both sides have referred to you as my son. I have to say I am very proud. I missed out on so much. I'll never know the joy that my son would have brought to my life, but no one has given me as much joy as you have in the last four years. I'm looking for someone to take my place as head of the WPO when I pass. I've given it much thought, and

I want you to take over. If you are interested in continuing with the WPO, I'm going to ask you to accompany me to meet with the necessary parties. We will go to South Africa first. Apartheid is deplorable there. We are funding the African National Congress and a gentleman by the name of Nelson Mandela."

"When?" asked Sean.

"Maybe this week, if I get the telex that I'm waiting for. Meanwhile, I need to explain how we work, where our money is located, cash flow, the services we supply, and how we support the causes of harmony and peace. It will take a few trips to understand it all and meet everyone, but it is time to get started."

Guy and Sean worked tirelessly together for a week. Guy was impressed at how quickly Sean caught on to everything. He intrinsically knew that Sean had the ability and moxie to carry on the WPO.

During breaks in Sean's orientation, he and Sean walked to various parks in Saigon. While watching some children play, Guy said, "I got the telex today that the meeting is on in Johannesburg. We may travel to Cape Town as well. It is soccer season in South Africa, so I am most fortunate."

"I think you travel just so you get to watch more soccer," Sean said with a smile.

"Well, it is one of the benefits, but South Africa is a little bit rugby crazy as well, you know. You will like South Africa. It is a beautiful country. We will fly to Singapore, and then visit Madras, then through Nairobi, and on to Johannesburg. I have extended meetings in Johannesburg, and finally, we will visit Cape Town. After we finish, I will return to Montreal and you will go back to Saigon. But Sean, maybe I'm being presumptive about everything. Do you want to travel with me? Do you want to take over the WPO? What do you want?" Guy asked as they sat on a bench watching some boys play three-on-three soccer.

"Do you remember when I had that trouble with Martine? You gave me the best advice I have ever received—Face your problems, head on. Tell people you're sorry and sort things out. I did exactly that and felt like a man of God trying to make things right. It felt good to face Martine and her mother. I feel terrible for running from this problem. Quakers do not run; they face their problems. On the battlefield, I did some pretty stupid things just to prove that I didn't run from war and that I wasn't a coward. I want to go back home and face the problem. Besides, I miss my family and friends terribly. I miss Claire; for some reason she is dominating my thoughts. After I face my problem, yes, I will be honored to be with the WPO and will be particularly fond of traveling with you and continuing to learn from you," Sean said compassionately.

Guy said nothing and started walking back to the flat. He liked Sean's response and was proud that he had helped to develop such a fine young man.

Enlightenment

Guy and Sean began their journey to South Africa, with an intermediate stop in Madras, India. Flying first class on the flights was quite a treat for Sean. Guy brought selected reading material for Sean to increase his understanding of various movements and people he was about to meet from the WPO perspective.

Guy introduced Sean to the material by saying, "Some of the people you will meet on this trip are personal friends of mine or have started movements that the WPO is particularly interested in funding. You know those reports you file from the bush everyday on troop movements and what you hear from your listening post, well, those reports and hundreds of others from around the world are sold to governments and agencies, so that the WPO can fund movements that can literally change the world. Such is the case with movements in India and South Africa that are spearheaded by great leaders who the WPO have helped. The reason I travel personally is to see first-hand what is happening so I can offer assistance through WPO. If you take over for me, you must know certain key players and movements. Before we talk, read this material."

Sean started reading a file labeled Mohandas Hiramchand Gandhi. Sean was familiar with some of Gandhi's work because Abington Meeting had prayed for his nonviolence pact to take hold throughout the world. Sean soon realized that he really knew very little about this great leader, after reading the reports.

"This man that you're reading about, I'm proud to say, was a dear friend who certainly had a great influence on my life and the WPO. I wish he were still alive," Guy said, looking out the window to hide the tears.

Sean hadn't known that Gandhi, who was born in India, had been educated in London. Schooled in law, he attempted to make a go of it by establishing a practice in Bombay, but with little or no success. After a few long years of frustration, he joined an Indian law firm in Durban, South Africa. Treated as a member of an inferior race, his views on racial injustice and human rights began to take shape.

Sean learned that after being beaten, attacked, and often imprisoned, Gandhi began to teach passive resistance and non-cooperation strategies to evoke change. The writings of Tolstoy, Thoreau and the teachings of Christ influenced Gandhi. He labeled his peaceful method of change *Satyagraha,* meaning truth and firmness. Gandhi became the leader of the home-rule movement in India's attempt to claim back from the British her native right for self-rule. Thousands of non-resistant Indians regularly confronted the English who often beat them unmercifully. Gandhi's pacifist actions changed world sentiment toward India's self-rule and eventually won independence for India. Gandhi became the international symbol for a free India and the greatest advocate for the abolition of the caste system. During evening prayer, he was assassinated in 1948, by a radical seeking Hindu dominance in Indian society. However,

Gandhi's peaceful resistance methods still became the most effective way to evoke social change. The report that Sean was reading went into detail describing Gandhi's influence on Martin Luther King's efforts in America and Nelson Mandela's efforts in South Africa.

"Who wrote this stuff?" Sean asked Guy.

"WPO personnel study world leaders, research their backgrounds, and also sell that information to many groups. Nations are watching each other constantly and each then corroborates and processes the information to feel secure. Examine how much of the world is closed to Westerners and vice versa. We help countries know what other countries are doing. The Iron Curtain and China comprise most of two continents and have given the WPO access allowed by few others," Guy lectured.

"I would think that the English would be perturbed if they knew that the WPO funded Gandhi's movements, and, if they knew that for sure, that would put you in danger," Sean inferred.

"You are correct, Sean, but the home office in Britain is dependent on intelligence from us regarding other hot spots of interest, and so they tolerate us at best. I was beaten by the British when Gandhi was alive, and I soon discovered that the closer I was to Gandhi, the safer I would be. The media was there in the heat of the struggle, photographing every incident. The British knew they could get to Gandhi by hurting others. He was such a compassionate man to all mankind. To address your observation, yes, they were very upset, but they informed their upper echelon commanders to not interfere with the WPO folks. Finish reading the reports, so you'll understand the Hindu, Buddhist, and Muslim conflict within India and how factions within each religion continue fighting within Indian society. We will be in Madras shortly," Guy said.

A multicultural entourage met them and whisked them away to an office in downtown Madras. There they had meetings with several different constituencies of the Indian culture. Guy introduced Sean as Stephan and asked him to speak in French rather than English, but he mainly listened. Sean was happy to speak French but preferred to mostly listen.

"Why do you think you can change these matters, and how would these things change with funding?" Sean asked in French to a well-spoken Indian Muslim, petitioning for support.

"We do not need much—just start-up money for a construction company. If we can provide education, teach families how to build their own homes, how to create revenue while living in smaller towns, we can change the overcrowding that exists in many cities," the Indian said and continued with a well thought out plan to relocate families from big cities to the country.

The meetings took place for over three hours before an official car dressed with bumper flags arrived. An Army officer came inside and escorted them to a caravan of limousines where a large crowd was gathering. Sean and Guy got into the middle car, which transported them to their next destination.

"What's this all about? Where are we going?" Sean asked.

"We are going to see Indira Gandhi, the prime minister. Settle back—it will take a while. As you can see, Madras traffic is legendary for a mish-mash of cows, cars, and people."

"You mean we are going to see Gandhi's daughter?" asked Sean expectantly.

"Yes, we are going to dine and stay at Indira Gandhi's residence, but she is not Gandhi's daughter, she is Nehru's daughter," Guy explained.

"I was friends with both Gandhi and Nehru, and the WPO funded both Muslim and Hindu efforts in India and will continue doing so. Indira is a mixture of her father and Gandhi. If you noticed, most of the requests we heard pertained to a return to rustic life. In order to undercut British industrial superiority, Gandhi encouraged a return to rural life, but Nehru's vision had India modernizing. You will find her interested in both," he continued as their caravan went through the crowded streets of Madras.

Sean was appalled at the poverty, the street scenes, and the dichotomy of the culture. The pungent odors particularly overwhelmed him, as his eyes filled with incredulity. He had witnessed revolting scenes in Vietnam—even to some extent in Philly and New York, but what he was seeing now was over the top.

"How can these people ever overcome their problems?" asked Sean, consumed by the poverty and confusion.

"They can't do what God can do. That's why we need to lift them up in prayer. The little assistance the WPO gives keeps their hopes alive," Guy said.

They discussed the different groups with whom they had just met as they arrived at what Sean called the Taj Mahal. "No Sean, the Taj Mahal is in Agra in one of the northwest provinces of India. Many of the provinces built Muslim-type structures like the Taj Mahal, and this is where Indira stays when she is Madras. Notice the military presence. Her life, like her father's and Gandhi's, is always in jeopardy by warring zealots from the different factions of Indian life," Guy said as they drove through beautiful gardens that lined the entrance of the compound.

Once the staff greeted them, they escorted them to her living area. Indira embraced Guy and they exchanged warm greetings. Guy then introduced Stephan to Indira.

Sean was okay with his new name and was responding naturally as if he were Stephan. It was obvious to him that Indira esteemed Guy highly. He also noticed that she was occasionally checking *him* out. As she left the room to ready herself for dinner, Guy said to Sean, "I think she likes you, Sean, or should I say Stephan," nodding approvingly.

"Why was she looking at me like that?" he asked.

"She is very perceptive and probably has already determined that you're the next me. She was just sizing you up," Guy replied with a smile.

After being shown their rooms, they had time to refresh themselves and then conversed over dinner for hours. During that time, Sean relayed some interesting observations about what he saw in India and how amazed he was by the complexities of the Indian society. As Indira showed Sean the rest of the mini Taj Mahal, she said to Guy, "I really like him. I'd like him to meet my sons Sanjay and Rajiv tomorrow morning before you leave. You know, he reminds me of a young man I met while at Oxford," she said, her eyes drifting off in thought.

The next morning before breakfast, Sean was running around the grounds in an attempt to workout. He found a soccer ball lying on a beautiful lawn and began volleying the ball from head to foot to chest as he jogged around. A young man dressed to workout approached Sean.

"Do you mind?" asked the young man, wanting to join in. The two ran back and forth passing, heading, and volleying for several minutes. Two others who were off-duty guards asked to join in. Before long, Sean and the young man were playing two on two against the guards. Sean was a skilled player compared to the rest, but he, in typical manner, let his teammate score most of the goals, as they proceeded to trounce their opponents seven to one.

Guy and Indira were sitting at a table on the veranda overlooking the game, being thoroughly entertained. When the boys finished, they approached Guy and Indira. "Stephan, I want you to meet your teammate, my oldest son, Sanjay," Indira said. The boys looked at each other then laughed.

"You're faster than most tigers in India!" Sanjay said.

There was an immediate bond between all of them as they started making fun of Guy's compulsion with soccer. "We know Guy is a soccer-holic. He is absolutely obsessed with the game. He used to make my granddad stop at every park in New Delhi just to watch children play. It has been a family joke for a long time. How could such a beautiful man be a soccer junkie?" Indira asked with a smile.

"How long have you known my family, Guy?" Indira asked.

"A long time. It has been my pleasure to watch the prime minister grow into the woman you are today," Guy responded.

"You can tell a lot about a person and the society they're from by watching them play soccer," Guy said, attempting to rationalize his love of the game.

"In that case, I officially declare that Stephan is going to be an asset to me the rest of my life because he certainly made me appear better than I am in our little game," Sanjay confessed.

After some levity, they were served Banger's and eggs—a full British breakfast. Guy remarked on the irony of their breakfast choice, considering that Indira had largely dedicated her adult life to running the British out of India. It was a gorgeous morning and the four of them enjoyed each other's company immensely throughout the meal.

Sean and Guy were off to the airport after breakfast. Once airborne, Guy gave Sean a plethora of material and dossiers to read on apartheid, the African National Congress, Nelson Mandela, tribes of South Africa, Afrikaner culture, the Dutch of South Africa, and British roles in South Africa.

"The reading material should keep you busy until we reach Nairobi. There we will get a few hours of rest then board a flight to Johannesburg. So, read on," Guy instructed. "I will prepare you for South Africa on the flight from Nairobi," Guy said.

"Can I ask some questions before you doze off?" Sean asked. "Those people who petitioned you back in Madras, will the WPO fund them? How? How do you keep in touch...analyze their projects...? I'd like to know the logistical part for implementation purposes."

"All of them will be funded," answered Guy.

"Even that weirdo street guy who said he needed money to disperse food to the poor on the street? That was an Indian con artist. You certainly wouldn't fund him, would you?" Sean asked.

Guy smiled, waited, and then responded, "If a man came to you and said, 'give me four fishes and two loaves of bread and

I'll feed thousands,' would you give them to him?"

"It would depend. My decision would be based on the individual, their purposes, and the probability of success," Sean responded, trying to be cerebral but falling into Guy's trap.

"Then you probably wouldn't have helped Christ perform some of his great miracles," Guy said.

"I surrender. You got me, Guy. I got it," Sean said in French to emphasize that he totally understood Guy's point.

"The WPO has a lot of money; I mean a lot of money. By funding those people, we will give them hope and it will not make a dent in the WPO's assets. I have their bank account numbers, and in about a month, I will send them funds from our accounts in Switzerland. And then we lift them up in prayer. The reason the prime minister of India sees us is because she knows that the WPO funds Muslim and Hindu interests. She has good feelings about what the WPO has meant to India and knows we have made a difference. We will continue to help her and the Indian society in any way we can," Guy continued.

"How much money do we have?" asked Sean.

"A lot—hundreds of millions in English pounds and over a billion Swiss francs."

"How did the WPO fund grow to be that much?"

"The need for intelligence is at an all-time high and we have some great investment strategies, mostly in real estate," Guy answered. "I take a relatively humble salary, just over a $100,000 Canadian. It's getting harder and harder to keep up with the finances. I have basically done everything myself except in the intelligence area. That's Dao's charge. Never trust her by the way. She is terrific at what she does, but when money is at risk, it gets interesting how people can rationalize using it for their own purposes. I will inform Dao that I've told you about her position, but never share any financial dealings with her. For your information, Sean, Aaron, Burkhart, and McCloskey, barristers in Montreal, handle all the legal and financial concerns for the WPO. Only Aaron, their senior partner and I, and now you, are aware of the WPO's financial status. More than twenty years ago while on a trip with me to India, Aaron met Gandhi. Since then, he has not charged the WPO anything for all the work that he does. I will also inform him that you are at liberty to execute anything on behalf of the WPO. Anyway, I need your help, Sean. Traveling all these years has taken its toll on my body. I'm ready to pass the baton to you, as soon as we can get you up to speed."

The money tied up in the WPO and Guy's long-term commitment to peace blew Sean away. He thanked Guy for the confidence and trust he placed in him. Sean had several hours of study under his belt when the plane landed in Nairobi. The airport was not modern and the airport hotel was humble, but they caught a much-needed six hours of sleep.

With an hour and fifteen minutes until departure, Guy asked for all the paperwork on South Africa. He walked outside the hotel and asked the taxi driver to take him to a place where he could burn some things. Ten minutes later, with the taxi waiting, Sean and Guy disposed of all their paperwork, except for the notes that Guy had taken in India.

"If they stop us in South Africa, Sean, and you have these materials, they could hold you as an enemy of the State—it's better just to destroy them," Guy said as they stood by a smoldering barrel. Sean and Guy arrived at the airport just in time for the flight to Johannesburg.

Again, sitting in first class, Guy turned to Sean and said, "I really need you, Sean. I am getting very weary of travel; I just can't do this anymore."

Sean looked at Guy, "I want you to know that you can count on me, but I'd like to ask you a few questions about South Africa."

"It's the most complex society I know. It has to be one of the most beautiful countries in the world, yet with the greatest problems," continued Guy.

"What's up with the African National Congress? They have got to be communists! We certainly don't fund them, do we, Guy?"

"What does it matter if they implement programs that help save the innocent?" Guy responded as Sean interrupted him abruptly.

"But communism is anti-God, anti-Christian, anti-everything except state!"

"Guy looked at him sympathetically and said, "Sean, giving—and giving money in the spirit of love—means just that, not being judgmental. We certainly wouldn't fund missiles or arms, but if they ask for money to feed their people, clothe their people, provide medical services for their people, we gladly would fund that. You see, if you give people a gift and you tell them you love them, God creates a special bond, and hopefully, they will see through the Friends how man can treat man. Sean, you need to keep your Quaker thinking cap on and take off your military cap. I've seen you do just that on occasion. It is a discipline you must develop for this job. I know you can do it."

"Well, okay. You're probably right, but in your opinion, is the African National Congress a communist organization?"

"Probably...leaning in that direction if they aren't already," said Guy.

After a four-hour discussion on South Africa, they touched down in Johannesburg, and an entourage of five African National Congress members escorted them to the African National Congress headquarters in downtown Johannesburg. There they talked for several hours, and Guy said yes to every request they made.

Before heading back to the airport, Guy asked a congress member to take them to Soweto, an all-Black township. Sean was flabbergasted to witness the harsh treatment inflicted by the whites on the people of the Soweto. He sat in the car in disbelief and shock. Police were hitting people indiscriminately, like animals. As they drove on, Guy asked the driver to stop, so he could watch the boys playing soccer in the street. After a few minutes, Sean saw a tear rolling down Guy's cheek. He started to understand, more fully, Guy's concern for this country and was deeply moved as he thought of man's atrocities to his fellow man.

On the way to the airport, Guy said, "The U.S. dollar goes a long way against the Rand. It may appear that we gave away a lot, but it really wasn't a substantive amount."

Upon arriving at the airport, a young police officer, incensed that Guy was with a group of coloreds, immediately challenged him. He pushed Guy with his police baton until he was against a wall and then shoved it against his neck. Sean stepped between the police officer and Guy, his fists clenched. Before the incident escalated further, Guy blurted something out in a language that Sean did not recognize. The confrontation attracted the attention of a superior officer who asked Sean and Guy for identification. Holding his throat, he reached into his coat pocket for his and Sean's passports and handed them to the older officer.

"Oh! Mr. Lafoussier! We were expecting you and your son this morning in Cape Town. We are very sorry for the misunderstanding. It is just a case of mistaken identity, you realize." The older officer took control of the situation. Guy nodded his head and again responded in the unfamiliar language.

Boarding the flight to Cape Town, Guy held his neck, still quite shaken. Sean said, "They just didn't like us being with the ANC, did they."

"You're right. It's incredible. It's really the same all over the world, Sean. You probably experienced it even at Abington or Brebeuf. If you are different, whether by color, race, gender, religion, or in any other way, the dominant part of society tends to treat the other or the minority unfairly. It's fear, Sean, the fear of the unknown and unwillingness to celebrate one's commonality," Guy said, continuing to rub his throat.

"Are you sure you're okay?" Sean asked.

"His baton hit my Adam's apple; I think it's feeling better, thank you."

"What was that language you spoke to him?" Sean asked.

"Pig Dutch—Dutch Antilles Dutch. He speaks Afrikaans, very similar to Dutch. I learned it as a child, traveling from Martinique to the Dutch Antilles with my father. He did a lot of business there. I just said to the young officer 'you're mistaken, you're mistaken.' Your assistance diffused the situation as well.

Thank you."

Guy advised Sean, "Language is very important in this business; smiles and hugs are also just as important. Sean, I would like you to learn some Cantonese, Arabic, Spanish, and also German and Russian. Because you're already multi-lingual, you will be surprised how quickly you will master other languages."

After getting a drink of water, Guy appeared to be somewhat better. Sean admired Guy's lack of wrath for the young officer, as they talked about the Soweto situation. Sean discovered that blacks were jailed at an alarming rate and were often killed for no reason in many of the townships. It was insane. They talked incessantly about the ruling party, and Guy told Sean that he would soon meet the South African president J.J. Fouche. They fell asleep talking to each other.

Upon arrival in Cape Town, an emissary took them to an old Victorian hotel near the waterfront where Sean watched the gulls and took in the smell the sea as they dined. It reminded him of the Jersey shore. Fatigued, they turned in early.

Sean rose at first light and went for a run. The beauty of this magnificent city captivated him. He looked out over the sea from the Mt. Nelson Inn and saw where the waters of the Indian and Atlantic Oceans collide. It appeared that there was a mountain directly in the middle of the city. It was the famous Table Mountain. He went for a fifteen-minute jog, did some calisthenics, and walked in the lobby of this traditional British landmark. The concierge and bellman looked at him as if he were wacko for exercising and breaking a sweat, as though exercise was for hired laborers only—not for those staying at this hotel. He had felt those same judgmental looks growing up in Abington. It made him laugh.

Sean caught up with Guy at breakfast. Both were dressed in suits. The dining room was exquisite: beautiful lace and silver, art, high-back chairs, and coffee served in a formal fashion by colored men in white gloves.

"This is a nice place, but not my style—way too stuffy," Sean said to Guy.

"We're going to be here for a couple days. You will find Cape Town one of the most beautiful cities of the world. This morning, we have a meeting with President Fouche. He's fairly ineffective, but will ask the WPO for lots of financial help. Of course, we will say yes. I think you are going to find today very interesting," Guy said.

During breakfast, a government official, dressed in black, came to their table and informed them that a car was waiting to take them to their appointment with President Fouche. As they drove through Cape Town to the President's home, Sean liked the feel of this great city.

"It's almost a different country compared to Johannesburg. How can this be?" Sean asked rhetorically.

"You know the answer, Sean. The British and Dutch are saving Western Province for themselves and want no Native African interference. The Zulu's are native to the Durban area and the native African population is minimal in Western Province. Other tribes are near, but not as powerful and plentiful as the Zulus."

Sean and Guy entered the president's house, which was more like a palace. A butler wearing a wig came to the door and escorted them to President Fouche's study. They sat on a beautiful leather couch, facing a crackling fire. Mounted on the dark wooden walls of the study were many game trophies. President Fouche entered and asked his assistant to wait outside.

"Great to see you, Guy. I am so terribly sorry that you were hassled in Johannesburg. I received a full report, and the young officer is going to be disciplined," Fouche said as he shook hands with Guy.

"J.J., do me a favor and don't have the boy disciplined. Just tell him that God is love and that we are Quakers trying to help both sides of the apartheid issue."

"And who is this?" President Fouche asked, ignoring Guy's last request and looking at Sean.

"This is my son Stephan. He is going to be working with us."

"I never knew you had a son," Fouche answered.

"We've been estranged for years, and I am glad to finally have him onboard. He's a God-fearing Quaker who has a heart of gold. You will enjoy working with him," Guy said proudly.

"It's very nice meeting you, President Fouche. You certainly have an absolutely gorgeous city. I am very impressed and like it very much," Sean remarked.

"Sit down please," the president offered as he sat in a beautiful high-back leather chair.

They talked about the latest in current events: apartheid, education, women in the workplace, feeding the poor, protecting the whites, township problems, the ANC, and communism. After a couple of hours, the president flat out asked, making it sounded more like a demand, "RSA needs two million U.S. dollars to make a difference with these problems in the short-term and, of course, more at a later date."

"It will not be a problem, but I would like you to do something for me. I want you to allow Stephan and me to travel to Robben Island to speak to Nelson Mandela," Guy said expectantly.

"That's impossible!" Fouche responded quickly.

"Someday impossibilities might cause one to forget to make the necessary arrangements for those financial transfers. I wouldn't ever want to forget RSA. It appears that you really need this financial assistance now," Guy said, smiling at the president.

"I'll see what I can do," President Fouche said with a slight smirk.

"Some Portuguese vintners have asked that you visit them in Stellanbauche, and then hopefully, you will be able to return for our evening dinner with members of the cabinet," Fouche requested.

Sean and Guy were then off to wine country. There they met with some people who needed a new start. Interestingly enough, the Portuguese thought that the key to success in South Africa was to have native African partners so they could benefit more financially. Sean was amazed at the beauty of the whole area. After an excellent dinner, they met with the president and his cabinet privately. Sean then went for a long walk, following his sense of smell to Victoria Wharf. There he found ships from various countries that were rounding the Cape on their way to and from India. He was fascinated with the international nature of Cape Town.

Sean and Guy continued on to a meeting with the Quakers of Cape Town regarding their efforts. While there, a government official entered and indicated that the arrangements Guy had requested were made and it was necessary for them to leave right away. A limo took them to Victoria Wharf to take a chopper to Robben Island. Sean was in shock when he looked onto the prison yard and saw all blacks working at breaking stone. Guy and Sean were ushered into a room overlooking the main yard. A large black prisoner entered the room, and upon seeing Guy, he lit up like a Christmas tree.

"Guy, so good to see you. How did you arrange this? I have so much to visit with you about." He turned and looked at Sean and said, "Thanks for coming." The three sat and talked about world events, Africa, South Africa, WPO, Willie, Martin Luther King and his beloved ANC. Guy was obviously a long-time, trusted colleague, and they made the most of their time together.

A tall guard entered the room after the meeting and politely stated, "Nelson, I need to get them to the helicopter in five minutes. Please finish quickly."

Guy and Nelson hugged for a long time and then Nelson shook Sean's hand with a great smile and just said, "Thanks. Good-bye my friends," and was led back into his ward by another guard. The tall guard offered, "You're only the second visitor he has had in almost seven years."

Guy and Sean climbed into the chopper and returned to the Mt. Nelson Inn where Guy asked Sean to sit with him in the lobby for tea.

"Sean, I'll be leaving you after tomorrow morning. I'm off to Paris and you're backtracking to Saigon. You've done a great job on this trip. I think you are a natural leader who can rightfully undertake the leadership of the WPO. It should only take only a few months for me to prepare my friends in the state department for your return. I am proud of you for wanting to face up to your problem back home. Hopefully, resolving it will only take a short time and then you can start traveling for the WPO. While in Saigon and in the bush, I would like you to do something—study Cantonese," Guy said as he sipped on his tea.

"I will do that; it has been a wonderful trip for me, Guy. I have learned much, seen much, and know that what the WPO does is extremely important in serving mankind. It also has helped me focus on what I have to do in facing my AWOL problem. To think how much Mandela and Gandhi endured to hold to their principles is extremely convicting. I have to take care of this," Sean said in reflection.

"Remember this after I pass, and use it to guide your life and *your* life *will* make a difference: Make the decisions in your life, however painful they may be personally, based on serving God and His work with all your heart and soul. That's what men and women who have made a difference in the world have done. You just met one man who is a perfect example of it," Guy said very seriously.

"I think I'm looking at a man who is a perfect example of it. Thanks, Guy," Sean said. He got up and hugged him and said good night.

A Change of Face

Sean reviewed how much he had learned from Guy, but his mind often wondered back to Montreal and Philly—thinking about his friends and family. His friends weighed heavy on his mind, and he looked forward to having them back in his life, once he made things right.

Back in his shared flat with Dao, he thought about how you can think you know someone but never really do. Here he was a roommate to one of the most important intelligence network leaders in the world, and Dao never gave a hint that she knew about anything outside the Vietnam theater.

"Lanh and An, two of your best, were injured last week in the field, so you will be dealing with rookies. The Hoe Chi Min Trail is getting really hot. Troop movements from the north are heating up to the south. The Cong appear to be getting ready for some major offensive. Why don't you chill here with me for a while until things are safer in the field?" Dao suggested as they shared an evening meal.

Sean knew that his system in the field would have to change but was not willing to chill in Saigon. He wanted to do his time in the bush and get back home and take care of business. He postulated that most of the action was going to be on or near access points to the Ho Chi Min Trail. Upon returning to the field, he found his colleagues agreed that the Trail was the location of most of the recent activity.

Total mobility for the Underground Railroad presented many complexities, and the dangers were increased exponentially. Without comprehensive knowledge of the territory in which both sides had tunnels, booby traps, and mines, their operations and escapes became extremely dangerous. Several additional listening posts to intercept and interpret messages were needed in order to enact the new mobile system and in order to more fully understand troop movements. Dao recruited the necessary people, and Sean implemented the new system, which proved extremely successful.

Their efforts led several small groups from both sides to safety. Sean was at the central listening post as two major forces were about to collide. A U.S. Army ranger company was waiting for anticipated troop movement down the Ho Chi Min Trail. They had men in position waiting to take out the Cong as they traveled south. To their surprise the Cong knew where they were located. The Cong had outflanked them and were ready to strike.

"Echo 1, this is Star Mover, report. Echo 1, this is Star Mover," Sean heard as he was relaxing, trying to figure out what the WPO needed to do next. The voice had a twang and sounded strikingly familiar.

"Star Mover, this is Echo 1," the other responded.

"Echo 1, move two clicks south and secure at HCMT, coordinates 12.9er and 183.4, copy?"

Sean couldn't mistake the voice of Colonel Mannon. He wondered what a "bird" colonel was doing with a ranger expeditionary force. He kept listening as one of his assistants got a map so Sean could see where Echo 1 and Star Mover, aka Colonel Mannon, were located. On the map he could see how the Cong had completely encircled the Trail and were about to annihilate Colonel Mannon's troops. Sean jumped up and grabbed the radio. "Star Mover, Star Mover, this is the Grassy Sound Kid, over."

Sean was over a mile away from Mannon. He had never used English on the radio in the field before but could not help himself. He knew Mannon's troops were about to get wiped out. Mannon's radio operator looked strangely at his receiver and quickly reported to Mannon that someone called the Grassy Sound Kid was shouting for him.

Grabbing the radio, Mannon responded to the one person in the world he knew it was—the one and only Sean Easley. "Grassy Sound Kid, this is Star Mover, over?"

Using the West Wildwood code, "Swarm of green heads two clicks northeast of current anchoring spot. Pull up anchor, follow channel and head immediately to West Wildwood railroad trestle. I repeat, pull up anchor, and head out now. More green heads than you've ever seen!"

Colonel Mannon pulled out his map as he recalled telling Sean where he had spent his time in Grassy Sound. He quickly drew a map and pinpointed a line south-southwest—the direction of the West Wildwood railroad trestle from his childhood crabbing spot. Knowing his troops were about to be overtaken, he got back on the horn to move Echo 1 south to the other side of the Ho Chi Min Trail and moved his troops out south-southwest. He called in fire from air support on the Viet Cong. Mannon was able to escape, losing only a few troops while causing great damage to the Cong offensive that had hoped to surprise Mannon's large ranger force.

Mannon returned to Saigon to personally report to Merryfield. "Great job, Terry! From our report you wiped out about 500 of those little bastards. What tipped you off to those gooks trying to surprise you?"

"Bill, it was Sean Easley. Do you remember him from West Point? He came on the radio and gave me directions to safety. He used terms only I would recognize from visiting with him during his Academy days. He saved hundreds of our troops," Mannon continued with uncertainty as he regarded Merryfield's acceptance of this news.

"You have to be mistaken. You mean that AWOL Quaker commie saved your life? Are you sure of this?" Merryfield shot back.

"Yes, sir, I'm sure it was Sean Easley."

"Well, thank you, Terry. You did a great job. You're dismissed."

Mannon could tell that his revelation about Sean did not go over well with Merryfield. After Mannon left the office, Merryfield asked his aide to have Captain Roberts, head of his Special Operation's unit, report to his office immediately.

"Captain Roberts, we've recently had reports of the WPO groups assisting the enemy. Mannon just reported that a Quaker commie bastard by the name of Sean Easley is one of them. Send your best snipers to take him out. His info is in the file. He was last located within radio distance of Colonel Mannon's last enemy engagement. Take him out and do it quickly," Merryfield said with utmost zeal.

Within a week, Dao informed Sean of Merryfield's plans. It was obvious that she was extremely unhappy about Sean's bias for one man and the Americans during his last major engagement which resulted in the deaths of hundreds of North Vietnamese.

"Sean, you have to move. According to reports, they are sending snipers and looking in the area where you are now operating. Stay north of Binh Duong and stay off the Trail," Dao commanded. "Most importantly, don't ever use English on the radio again."

Sean went north but remained much of the time in Phuoc Vinh Province. Most of his work was with downed pilots in Cambodia or near the border supplying the needs of Vietnamese villagers ravaged by war. He stationed his listening posts to surround some Vietnamese strongholds that were waiting for unsuspecting ranger airborne troops to drop into a landing zone. The zone would instantly become as hot as hell when they landed.

A couple of months passed with little or no incidences aside from removing the wounded from both sides out of harm's way. He was always conscious to lace his Celtic cross into his boots each morn, not knowing how many Galway ancestors would be handy if he got in tight spot and needed them.

Sean was stunned when he again recognized an American voice emanating from a chopper's radio that was about to land. It was Sonny and he was directly over Sean's camouflaged outpost. "Eagle 4, Eagle 4, stay up and provide cover," Sonny commanded, in his Philly accent, to one of his choppers instructing them to delay landing and provide cover for the others choppers.

Dao had made it clear that what he had done for Mannon was way out of line and that a sniper hit had been put out on him. Sean knew that his unauthorized actions would jeopardize the entire WPO's Underground Railroad. His heart was racing as he kicked into action knowing Sonny's troops were about to land in the hottest LZ in Vietnam. Sean broke radio silence, he had to—it was Sonny.

In his best French accent he said, "Toujours Amis, Toujours Amis, tres chaud, tres chaud, tres chaud," speaking louder with each word. "Nine hundred sweep, immediatement," breaking into English football jargon then back to French.

Sonny heard the voice, knew it was Sean, and couldn't help himself. "Easy Man, Easy Man," Sonny cried out over his radio as his company began taking fire from a superior force while landing. The command chopper and two other choppers were taking on much ground fire, but the men appeared to be okay as they poured out on a frying pan of an LZ.

Sean was visibly shaken thinking Sonny was about to be taken out. He sent his best WPO operative, wearing a white bandana, to the ravine that could lead Sonny's company out of danger.

He began speaking in English because every second counted, "Follow the white bandana. He's friendly."

"Got it, Easy Man." Meanwhile the Cong started scrambling Sean's transmission with static. The Cong's intentions were obvious to him, and he left the safety of his bunker to assist in directing Sonny's troops to safety. He knew they needed to use the nearby ravine in order to escape. Sean knelt to tie his boots and was troubled to find that his grandmother's Celtic cross was gone.

One of Sonny's squad leaders found the man with the white bandana, and Sonny commanded everyone to follow. The rescuer led them into a ravine laden with heavy foliage while Sonny remained near the edge long enough to call in an air support strike that would toast the area. Traversing the ravine, a few of his company returned enemy fire. Before proceeding down the ravine, Sonny saw, out of the corner of his eye, the longhaired Quaker running from the area of the ravine to draw fire away from Sonny and his troops. Last going into the safety of the ravine, Sonny noticed that a marine sniper was observing the situation from outside the ravine. At once, he signaled him into the ravine because of the imminent strike.

The evening sky was soon aflame as hundreds of munitions fell from Sonny's requested airstrike. One landed on a trail in front of Sean. The blast knocked him unconscious. Coming to, he became aware of a Vietnamese major standing over him, looking down, while a Cong regular was about to thrust a bayonet into Sean's torn body. The major's hand pulled the regular back.

"That is Hu'ang. Carry him back. He was on the wrong side this time," said the major. "He has saved many of our lives, including mine."

Semiconscious, they transported Sean through the jungle to a North Vietnamese field hospital where Dao met him. His face and hands were completely bound with rag-tag excuses for bandages. Sean was in great pain as he slowly regained consciousness and felt his entire body ravaged.

"You really did it this time," Dao said. "You're lucky the major recognized you and kept you alive. You helped him about six months ago when he was wounded. I'd call it a miracle that he recognized you. I made a deal with him. You're going to leave Vietnam, but quite frankly, after looking at your face, you may come to wish you had stayed. Guy has sent a plane and he'll be meeting you in Paris."

"Au revoir, my dear," Dao said in stone-cold voice, standing there in a North Vietnamese officer's uniform. "Of course, you'll be traveling as Stephan Lafoussier with all the necessary identification. I'm having it brought here from Saigon," Dao continued in a matter-of-fact voice, void of any emotion.

Guy hired a Lear jet to expedite the trip. Heavily sedated, Sean found himself in a Paris hospital with little or no memory of the trip. Guy and two doctors woke him. He was still dazed from the trauma. "They think they can repair the damages and you'll be as good as new. Dr. Strasbourg believes it will take several surgeries over a span of up to two years to get it right," Guy said summarizing what he'd learned by conferring with the doctors for the previous hour. "You'll have to make some decisions," Guy said, trying to get through to Sean.

Dr. Strasbourg interrupted, "We'll have to do bone reconstruction after your burns heal, then work on your facial tissue. We'll take grafts from several areas of your buttocks for use on your face. I'm good at it. You will be beautiful again. The human body is an incredible organism, as you well know," Strasbourg said slowly. "You need to rest now and make some decisions in pretty short order here. Tell Guy your decisions and we will start preparing everything as soon as possible. For now, just rest, mon ami." The doctor and his assistant left Sean's bedside.

It hurt for Sean to talk, so Guy instructed him on how to move his finger for yes and no. He painfully managed to say,

"Thanks, Guy," through his bandages.

"That's okay, Sean. I know things will work out fine. It's my pleasure to do everything I can to get you right and back to WPO work," Guy said. "You still want to take over, don't you?" Guy asked. Sean shook his finger yes.

"This will take some interpreting, but I need to determine your wishes. First, I want you to know the extent of your injuries. You have first-degree burns on thirty percent of your back, second-degree burns on ten percent of your arms and on twenty percent of your neck, and about ten percent damage to your facial tissue. The most serious problem is on your left side; you have crushed zygomatic and orbital arches. The bones shattered and some are really close to your optic nerve. All in all it will just take time," Guy said to Sean bluntly. "That leads me to a series of questions that will help me make arrangements on your behalf. Do you want to go home for the surgeries?" Sean answered no.

"It appears we have two options then, after you've recovered. Number one, you return to the United States to face the AWOL charge and when your situation is handled, you'll take over the WPO. The second option is complicated. Very complicated." Guy became emotional. Sean made a gesture by moving his hand for Guy to continue.

We would bury Sean Easley. You'd become Stephan Lafoussier for good and take over the WPO as soon as you're healed." Guy tried to hold back his tears.

"Which is best for you?" Guy asked as Sean raised his hand, turning it back and forth to indicate he didn't know.

"The advantages of the first option are that you'll be able

to stand up for what you believe in publicly, and see your family and friends again. The disadvantage, from my perspective, would be the delay in your taking over the WPO for an indefinite period of time while setting things right on the AWOL charge. Selfishly, I'd prefer option two. You could take over much sooner. I would, of course, bequeath all my worldly possessions to you and Brigitte. The disadvantages of this option would be that we would have to declare Sean Easley dead. You would assume your new identity and pledge never to make contact with your friends or family ever again. A most difficult decision, Sean."

Sean lay there with no response for several seconds then raised his hand palm up again; signaling he didn't know what to do. A nurse entered and inserted medication into the intravenous tubes hanging near his bedside then whispered to Guy, "He'll be in la-la land for the next couple hours."

"*Bon nuit*, Sean," she said, leaving his room.

Guy left Sean's bedside emotionally torn. He was hoping Sean would choose the second option. At the same time, he loved Sean and knew what he would sacrifice with that option. . . and the pain it would cause him for years to come. Guy was very tired and worried about the transfer of power in the WPO. He had waited much too long to prepare someone for this and rationalized that he had never found anyone before Sean whom he trusted enough.

Sean drifted in and out of sleep. As the sedatives wore off, Sean determined to try to remain lucid. There was so much to consider. He felt the great ache in his heart for home, family, and friends. Scenes of former times flashed in and out of his mind. A serene and secure feeling enveloped him. He wasn't sure if it was the medicine or the remembrance of fonder days. Surely he could work through the desertion charge, especially in light of saving Sonny and Colonel Mannon and hundreds of their troops. There was no disgrace in going back and cowardice wasn't even an issue anymore. It would take some time, but the outcome would finally bring him peace and the entire situation could be put behind him.

On the other hand, Sean wondered if his need for peace was more important than the need to help the hopeless and helpless. Guy was getting old and weary. Sean wondered why he was in this situation. Surely there was a reason—one much loftier than his own self-interests and desire to be back with family and friends. Would home be the same or had everyone gone on with their lives? Then again, he knew he had changed. Guy had exposed him to so much—so much hope for what seemed to be so hopeless. His military training was no coincidence. Perhaps he just wasn't meant to use it in the conventional way. His gift with foreign languages, his love of history and travel, and of course, his current state of being a man without a face; these thoughts were racing through his mind. It was all too much to comprehend.

Sean's mind waivered back and forth between the options Guy had outlined. The premise of what Guy had talked about back in South Africa kept dominating his thoughts. 'When making a decision, no matter how difficult, if it serves God and mankind, then it can't be wrong.' This was the answer for which he was searching. Content with his choice, Sean drifted into a deep, deep sleep.

Relieved of the burden he had been carrying, he had no difficulty sleeping, even after the sedation wore off. Sean found he was able to manage his pain by thinking about Claire. He wished he could just talk, pray, and be with her. He missed that spiritual bond he had with her. Somehow thinking about her love for Christ released his agony.

Guy was at his bedside shortly after first light. "Good morning, Sean, or is it Stephan?" Guy smiled.

Sean raised two fingers. Guy smiled and nodded, knowing what that meant. He prayed silently over Sean for more than a few minutes. He opened his eyes and smiled again at Sean.

"I want to make sure of my understanding of this, Sean. Does this mean you want to become Stephan Lafoussier?" Guy asked slowly.

Sean moved his fingers up and down then uttered a painful yes that Guy could hear through the bandages.

"Does it also mean you are willing to change your identity through surgery? That you will never contact friends or family ever again? That you will become, when healed, my successor of the WPO? and finally, that you agree to bury Sean Easley forever?" Guy was serious and precise.

Sean shook his finger yes and audibly said yes again.

"I will tell the doctors about your decision and publish a WPO release about Sean Easley's death." Sean reached for his hand, pulling Guy close to say something.

Guy had to get really close to hear. "A great man once told me that when you make a decision based on how to best serve God, however painful it is personally, you always make the right decision," Sean struggled with the words, as he looked Guy right in the eye then added, "Thanks." Exhausted, he went limp in his bed.

The nurse chased Guy out of the room this time. Seeing that the new Stephan had his head elevated too high, she adjusted his bed and again administered medicine and sedatives intravenously. Sean fell into a deep sleep. While sleeping, they moved him to a more private hospital. He awoke thinking of his friends.

Meanwhile, Guy went to work. He called Aaron H. Aaron in Montreal and had him begin the process to amend all legal documents relating to WPO matters, his estate, and other holdings in regard to Stephan. He issued a press release through the WPO offices in Beauvais, France, about Sean Easley's death in a Parisian hospital after sustaining wounds while working for the Underground Railroad in Vietnam. He called some of the elders of Abington Meeting and Abe Goldman to make sure they'd be at Sam and Margaret's side. He was about to break the news to them.

The phone rang in the Easley home. "Good morning," he heard Sam say.

"Sam?" Guy responded.

"Hey, Guy, how are you, my friend?"

"Not well, Sam. Not well at all. I'm afraid I have some very bad news. Is Margaret there with you?

"Well, yes, Guy...oh no...no!" Big Sam knew what was coming.

Sam, I am so sorry to have to tell you this. Sean just passed away in a Parisian hospital," Guy said with compassion. There was a long pause.

"I'll be in Paris tomorrow to bring him home," Sam said, his voice cracking.

"I'll wait for you here, and then I'll return to Abington with you," Guy assured him.

"You mean you are there?" Sam said in surprise.

"Yes, Sam. Sean was operating the Underground Railroad in Vietnam and was critically injured. I am so sorry to tell you that Sean passed only a few hours after being brought to the hospital," Guy said slowly.

"Would you mind bringing him home?

"Of course not, Sam, but you will need to make a decision on how to handle his body. His remains will have to be embalmed here before we can fly him home, or cremated, and I could bring his ashes home. Please allow me to be of service in any way I can. Speak with Margaret and let me know your wishes," Guy gently paced through the options.

"Bring home the ashes. We'll lay him to rest in the Abington Meeting Cemetery." He started choking up again.

"Sam, can you telex me your authorization to carry out your wishes concerning Sean?" Guy asked. "I'll give you the number."

"Yes," Sam said, crying as he reached for a pencil.

"I've already called Abe and some members of Meeting to come and help." Guy said hearing Margaret in the background asking what was wrong.

"Good-bye, Sam."

Sam prepared Margaret as best he could, but she knew by the look on his face that it was Sean. She became hysterical and then collapsed. After getting her to bed, he told the rest of the family. In no time, Abe and Susan Goldman were at the door. They made arrangements for the funeral at Abington Meeting on Saturday morning and for the interment of Sean's ashes at the Meeting Cemetery immediately following.

The announcement of his death was on the wire services and became an international news story. The anti-war-movement press, the student radicals, and the hippie movement used Sean's death as a battle cry. Meanwhile, the sports world ran the story throughout the United States. His death was the topic on all the major networks.

Claire heard of Sean's death on the television while in her dining room having breakfast. She was so devastated that she broke down and could not talk for hours. When she regained her composure, she called Brigitte who Guy had already called. Claire then called Aubert, and it was determined that many would accompany Brigitte to the funeral.

His Abington, Peekskill, and West Point friends attended as did Sonny and Colonel Mannon. Louie and Cassandra were at the Easley's the next day to assist the family. The Army brass, excluding Merryfield, decided that it was their best option to ignore his AWOL charge and let his friends honor him. Meanwhile, Merryfield fed the press negative comments about Sean.

The funeral was to be a simple good-bye and prayer time for family and friends. However, over 4000 people showed up at the Meeting House including media from all over the world. The seating capacity was only 300. Polite and gentle Quakers stood at the doors and said, "The Easley family welcomes you to celebrate Sean's life, but they respectfully request only family and friends in the Meeting House. You are welcome to join them in the cemetery for the interment."

Most of the anti-war people stayed outside, but all the doors were opened to allow more participation. The service consisted of elders sitting at the facing benches. They announced that Sean was a member of Abington Meeting and briefly described the Quaker traditions of worship. Those attending were asked to pray and told that when they felt moved by God, they could stand and share it with the Meeting. Many shared during a very emotional hour.

There was only one visual remembrance of Sean—the *Sports Illustrated* front-page cover was blown up and placed on an easel in the front of the Meeting House. The Easley family thought that photo, with his *Toujours Amis* friends, best depicted Sean's life.

Déjà Vu

April…Philadelphia…Pennsylvania. Many years had passed since Sean's funeral. For Abe Goldman and Sam Easley, it was going to be a special day of memories. The Penn Relays' Organizing Committee was celebrating the amazing Abington High School win of the 60s in the High School Mile Relay Championship of America, which was the reason for this reunion and party. There had been other great high school relay teams since the Abington win, but none from Pennsylvania. It didn't matter to Sam and Abe that it wasn't solely because of the 60's Relay that the committee wanted the three to return. It was also because of what the relay members had become. The Penn Relays' committee knew it would draw much additional media attention. Either way, it was going to be a great reunion.

When Sam and Abe heard about the ceremony, they contacted all the families and encouraged them to be sure to come. Of course, the day would begin at Deli-Land for breakfast, then off to attend the ceremony at the Penn Relays, and end with a dinner at Bookbinder's Restaurant, a longtime Philadelphia tradition.

Time had taken its toll on the Relays' families. Sam was a slow mover now and used a cane. Marge didn't look her eighty years young and had a full-time job just keeping up with Sam.

Abe, however, faired very well as an octogenarian. He looked sixty, still worked out daily, and was without a stitch of gray hair. Susan, on the other hand, had become rather girthy on one too many Deli-Land pastries and had a difficult time even walking. Louise Jackson, although in her seventies, was still vivacious. The parents of Leander Davis had passed away while he was in college.

Leander had made quite a name for himself as the Philadelphia city commissioner. He had moved from Abington Township into the city, where he had entered the Philadelphia political scene to become the longest-standing commissioner in Philadelphia history. He had married his Temple University sweetheart and they were raising two children. Life was good for Leander. He remained active in the Penn Relays' committee and it was due to his prodding that the reunion and the ceremony became a reality.

Louie Jackson was the assistant head coach of the Detroit Pistons and had coached the USA Olympic Basketball Team to gold. Louie was very visible on the national sporting scene and was, as always, a good-looking, well-dressed, and in-shape kind of guy. He had remained a practicing Quaker throughout the years. Louie's wife, Mary Booth, was a sensational actress whom he had married during his playing days with the Philadelphia 76'ers. They had two boys in medical school; both of whom would also attend the reunion.

Sonny became a Congressional Medal of Honor recipient for his heroism when he landed in the hot LZ, and went into Pennsylvania politics after getting his master's degree. He spent a term as governor, and then went on to become the senior senator from Pennsylvania. His work on the Senate Intelligence

Committee and his post-9/11 support of Presidents Bush and Obama for their position on the war in Iraq and Afghanistan put his popularity at an all-time high. He was one of the few democrats who was undaunted by criticism over his support for the U.S. military. He met his wife, the former Betsy Abbott, at the University of Pennsylvania while completing his masters in political science. Betsy was not Jewish. Susan Goldman had refused to speak to Betsy for the first ten years of their marriage; however, she finally normalized relations with Betsy after becoming the grandmother of two fine-looking grandsons. Then, and only then, did Betsy and Susan become great friends.

Of course, Cassandra Washington Turnquist was invited to the reunion and was excited to be there. She graduated from Columbia and became a famous designer, first in New York and then internationally with her own fashion line. Still an absolute knockout, she looked a good twenty years younger than her age. Her appearance correlated to her success in the world of fashion. She was now living in Nassau with her husband, Gaylord Turnquist, IV, a Bahamian financial guru and fellow Columbia graduate. Gaylord was an avid track and field junkie. He had watched the Bahamian high school boys' team win the mile championship several times at the Penn's, and this year he a financial sponsor of the Haverhill College of Nassau's foursome.

Abe was worried about the Easleys during the reunion weekend. Sean's burial had been more than four decades ago, but the wounds of losing Sean had never really healed. Margie and Nicky had blessed them with several grandchildren and great grandchildren, but the hole in their hearts over Sean's loss remained open.

Deli-Land was crowded on Penn Relays' day. Abe had told

everyone about the reunion, so many of the Abington township and neighborhood folks wanted to catch a glimpse and give their best wishes to the fabulous Abington foursome—minus one. For the occasion, Abe had reserved his backroom, which held about thirty. When Sonny, Betsy and their two children entered, the entire restaurant gave them a standing ovation. It took a good fifteen minutes for Sonny and his family to make their way to the backroom. Many of the Beth Shalom Synagogue members, Huntington Valley neighbors and old high school friends and families were there to greet him. Once in the backroom, he introduced his family and a hug fest followed.

Pandemonium abounded upon Louie's arrival. He didn't spend much time in the restaurant; he quickly introduced his family and proceeded to the backroom, where Sonny met him with an embrace.

"You look wonderful, Sonny," smiled Louie, squeezing and firmly patting his arms.

"That's Washington, D.C., for you. You look a helluva lot better than I do, and I see you still have that silky, sartorial splendor. In fact, you look fine, mighty fine—good enough to kiss!" jabbed Sonny. They laughed and kissed each other on the cheek and hugged again.

Turning to Louie's boys, Sonny said, "Look at these guys. Thank goodness they look like their mother!"

"Hey, Mary," Louie said, as he hugged Sonny's wife.

When Leander and his family entered the restaurant, there was little to no reaction, but he still worked the room, epitomizing the consummate politician. Entering the backroom, he introduced his family.

Abe had prepared a five-course brunch, followed by a sweet kosher wine, and timed it so everyone could get to Franklin Field by three o'clock to watch some of the events prior to the ceremony and the championship series races. The actual ceremony was to take place around four o'clock. The high-school mile relay was the first event.

Standing with his glass in hand, Sonny said, "I would like to raise my glass in honor of the person who brought home the victory for our Abington Relay team. He's not here physically, but he will always be in our hearts and minds. The leg that he ran was typical of Sean—the fastest white boy I've ever seen." Sonny still had to hold tears back when he talked about Sean.

Standing, everyone said in unison, "mazel tov!"

"I would also like to toast two people we all sorely miss— Brigitte and Guy. May they rest in peace."

"Here! Here! the gang shouted.

Sonny remained standing while the rest took seats and continued, "Not only am I here to celebrate the great win he secured for us, I am alive because of him. I know it was Sean's voice and his words that led my company to safety in Vietnam. I'll never know if he lost his life giving me life, but I have paid tribute to him by working on things that meant a lot to him, like brotherhood, equality, fairness and providing for the needy. Being a fiscally conservative democrat and Jewish social liberal at the same time may seem to some to be impossible, but it's not. Sean was the most dominant force in forming my views towards my fellowman. More than words can describe, I still miss him." His eyes began to water again.

Sonny sat down and Cassandra stood without wine for a

toast and said, "I want to say something about my Sean, the love of my life. Sorry, Gaylord," she continued as her husband smiled. "Sean was the first boy to tell me I was beautiful. He held my hand in the hallway at Huntington Junior High School and said, 'Has anyone told you how beautiful you are?' and then he just smiled and walked away. Eventually, as you all know, we became an item. Now-a-days, black and white is common, but not then. Sean did not care what people thought; he never saw skin color as an asset or obstacle but always looked at the internal beauty of a person. And let me tell you something else, he also knew how to make a woman feel wonderful. Sorry, Gaylord. Sorry, Margaret."

Laughter erupted as Cassandra sat down and Louie stood to say, "Everybody knows how I feel about Sean, but right now I wouldn't feel like I was at home unless I saw Mr. Goldman and Mr. Easley dance together." He traveled to the jukebox and played "The Boogie-Woogie Bugle Boy of Company B." Cassandra, Sonny, and Leander joined in Louie's enthusiasm. This song automatically initiated dancing the jitterbug for the two patriarchs. With the added years, Sam just stood leaning on his cane and wiggled a finger to the music as the youthful Abe danced around him to everyone's enjoyment.

After Sam and Abe's dance, a great meal, and fellowship, they piled into the limos and headed for Franklin Field. The traffic was light until they got close to the field. Sonny's security detail was waiting as they arrived at the drop-off point. Since 9/11, Sonny had received several death threats for his anti Bin Laden and Al-Qaeda position, and also for his vehement stance on the sovereign integrity of Israel. He did not release news of these threats to the media, thinking it would not only frighten his family unnecessarily but would also encourage more threats. He was very cautious, though, and petitioned the Secret Service, FBI and the president for personal security when threats became an everyday occurrence. Security agencies made special arrangements to keep him safe. Large stadiums presented major problems and the extra security was quite noticeable when the limo arrived.

Agent Larkin, his security chief, pulled him aside as he got out of the car.

"Senator Goldman, *The New York Times* ran a picture of you and Sean Easley as MVPs of the Army-Navy game. The article announced the tribute that the Penn Relays was making. We believe Al-Qaeda operatives have been moving into Philadelphia since this morning. *The Philadelphia Inquirer* got a call saying, "We're getting that Kike bastard." They surmised the phone call was an announcement that they were planning to get you. I recommend you get right back in the limo and head to the airport for D.C.," Larkin said professionally.

"Thanks, Steve, for your staying on top of the situation, but I will not run from terrorism. As soon as we do, we're licked. Do whatever you have to, but Al-Qaeda is not taking today away from my family and friends. If I'm taken, so be it. Please report to your superiors my decision, so if anything does happen, you and your men will be exonerated. Meanwhile, I'm going to enjoy this very special day. Yo, it's the Penn Relays! Know what I mean?" Sonny said in a thick Philly accent, exchanging grins with Agent Larkin.

Larkin informed the rest of the security detail and of Sonny's decision and why. Although they admired him for his bravado, it was always precipitating more and dangerous demands on them.

Soon, spectators encircled the entourage as it entered the packed 60,000-seat stadium. Many fans recognized them and stepped through security to shake hands as they worked their way to their box on the finish line. Knowing that Sonny wanted to be assessable at all times, the officers would only step in if they perceived danger.

After they settled into the box, the stadium announcer called out in that amazing all-encompassing voice, "Good afternoon, ladies and gentlemen." With great pauses in between words to stop the echo, he continued, "Welcome to Franklin Field, to one of the most famous relays of all time. Let's welcome Senator Sonny Goldman, Detroit Piston's Basketball Coach Louis Jackson, and Philadelphia City Commissioner Leander Davis and their families to the Penn Relays. They are sitting at the finish line on the north side of the field. Let's give them a big Penn Relays' welcome!" His voice echoed throughout the stadium.

The crowd responded with a standing ovation in honor of these three men.

Sonny caught the eye of Agent Larkin, nonverbally expressing his concern that the announcement had made him a potential target. Sonny had steps placed in front of his box, giving them easier access to cross the track and to get to the microphone on the infield. A gentleman from the Penn Relays' committee escorted them to midfield and lined them up approaching the microphone. As they stood silently by the microphone, the stadium announcer's voice resonated throughout the stadium, "Welcome back to one of the greatest relays of all time. This relay gave our country hope that both whites and blacks alike could accomplish great things by working together.

Their picture and story in *The Inquirer* and *Sports Illustrated* touched the hearts of the nation. The Abington High mile team ran five seconds faster than their previous best time to pull off the miraculous upset win." The crowd applauded loudly.

He continued, "Let's give a welcome to Mr. Leander Davis who ran the leadoff leg for Abington, and who is now a Philadelphia city commissioner." Leander approached the microphone to applause.

"This relay changed my life. It helped me believe in miracles and to depend on men of different color and nationalities. I continue to pursue that trust by continuing to make Philadelphia a better place. Thank you, Penn Relays, and by the way, I passed the baton to our U.S. Senator, Sonny Goldman, in 5th place." He stepped back from the microphone and Sonny stepped forward.

"I was the slow guy on the relay and was passed by at least five runners by the 220," he quipped to a chuckling crowd. "Somehow I managed to recover and kept us in 5th place when I passed the baton to the coach of the Detroit Pistons, Mr. Louie Jackson." The crowd applauded.

"I'd like to share what our team prayed just before we left that paddock over forty years ago, 'Dear God, we are different colors, different religions. Allow us to be used by You to teach others Your love.' Now, it's my pleasure to introduce you to the greatest basketball coach ever, Mr. Louie Jackson!" The crowd went from utter silence to a fever pitch in seconds to welcome Louie.

"By the way, Senator, I got the baton in 6th place, not 5th." He turned to smile at Sonny. The stadium laughed at the discrepancy in their reports. Louie continued slowly so all could hear in the echoing stadium.

"Sonny and Sean Easley have always been my best friends. They were friends when to hang with blacks brought them much criticism, disapproval, and condemnation. Sonny and Sean always loved their fellow man and literally changed a racially divided community by showing that love through sport. I passed the baton to the fastest white boy I've ever seen, Sean Easley." The stadium was silent.

Sonny stepped up to talk on Sean's behalf. "This stadium is the home of the Quakers of the University of Pennsylvania." Pausing for the applause to die down, Sonny continued, "Sean Easley was a Quaker. He died in Vietnam, not fighting, but saving others from the perils of war. He was one of the finest athletes and the best person I've ever known."

Agent Larkin ran in to the infield, placing himself just a few feet from Sonny, ready to pull him from the microphone while scanning the south upper deck. Sonny simply acknowledged Larkin with a hand gesture, conveying that he was going to finish this no matter what, and then proceeded without hesitation.

"That anchor leg was anointed! I'm sure he ran *not* for himself, but to prove that by working together, we can change the world. If he were here, he would ask only one thing of us—love each other. His favorite saying was "God is Love." Good luck to all the teams in this year's race." The stadium rose to their feet applauding. The three raised their hands, communicating unity and spirit just as they had on the cover of *Sports Illustrated*. Simultaneously, the cover picture appeared on the giant scoreboard, in full color. Photographers for the press were snapping away as the three hugged.

The crowd continued to applaud and cheer as attendants escorted the entourage off the field and back to their seats, surrounded by Secret Service personnel. Larkin led, making his way toward the entourage on the opposite side of the field. Meanwhile, the introduction of the High School Mile Relay Championship leadoff-leg runners began.

"This year's finals are the fastest ever assembled in the history of track and field," the stadium announcer echoed to a frenzied stadium.

"In lane one, St. Regis from Puerto Rico; in lane two, Abbotstown from Kingston, Jamaica; in lane three, St. Thomas Moore from New York; in lane four, Haverhill Prep from Nassau, Bahamas; in lane five, Meadville High from Western Pennsylvania ..." He continued introducing the twelve finalist by lane.

"No high schools from Philly—that's a shame, and they're all black it appears, no mixed relays," Abe remarked to Big Sam.

"Most of those island runners look old enough to have graduated from college," Louie offered as they exchanged knowing nods and glanced at Gaylord.

"The green team with the large H is this year's winner. My Nassau team is the winner," Gaylord started bragging, ignoring their joke.

"Put a lid on it, Gaylord," Cassandra ordered, reminding everyone how much they always enjoyed her frankness.

The race was about to begin when Agent Larkin, speaking into his radio, crossed the track by the starting line and entered the stands to talk to Sonny. This delayed the start of the Mile Relay Championships; however, most were unaware of what was happening.

"Relax boys," said the stadium announcer. "We're going to have a few minutes delay." The leadoff legs stepped back from the line to stay loose.

Agent Larkin spoke to Sonny while the announcer covered the delay with more announcements.

"We had an incident during the ceremony," Larkin announced as Cassandra squeezed Sonny's and Louie's hand.

"A potential sniper was neutralized by an unknown man. He stripped him of his weapon, and removing all the munitions he disappeared into the crowd. We've got the sniper, but we can't find the man who saved your life. This is not an option, Senator. You and your friends must leave immediately! We need to move you over to the tennis center until we get the 'all clear.'"

The entourage departed immediately to the adjacent building. All were not completely aware of what was happening, but Cassandra was stunned and pensive. She left without Gaylord because he was just not going to miss his team's race.

Sonny wanted the facts from Agent Larkin as soon as they were secure in the tennis center.

"How many were there, Steve?

"It appears now to be one; that's why the Relays are continuing. You're either very lucky Senator or *someone* up there wants you alive. Your mysterious angel was well trained and knew what he was doing. We will find him," Larkin stated with confidence.

"Thanks, Steve, for standing in the line of fire," Sonny replied in appreciation, shaking his hand.

Feeling safer, they sat in the VIP area watching the final of the Mile Relay via closed circuit television. To date, they were the only Pennsylvania team to win the coveted race, so all were naturally rooting for the Western Pennsylvania team. The telecast was interspersed with the stadium announcer's play by play. Within minutes, the excitement of the Relay had overshadowed the emergency.

"Meadville is moving up, St. Jago, Haverhill, Cal Poly-Long Beach, then Meadville," the announcer proclaimed. The gang could hear the frenzied spectators prior to the last exchange. Suddenly a white runner wearing the Meadville "M" appeared on the television screen. He wore his hair long and resembled a runner they knew well. He started moving up on the leaders. Cassandra ran out the door wanting to catch the finish in the stadium and get a better look at the young lad. Sonny and Louie followed, flanked by two security men. As she reached the track the announcer was saying, "Running the anchor leg for Meadville is Beaux Lafoussier, one the fastest prep 400-meter runners in the United States and wide receiver for the Meadville High championship football team." Cassandra had an immediate confirmation in her heart.

"Senator, do not do this!" Agent Larkin shouted, attempting to hold him back.

"I have to!" Sonny demanded. "Stay with me." They reached Cassandra at the railing with a clear view of the finish line, and Louie quickly joined them.

"It's Meadville...St. Jago...It's Meadville...It's St. Jago... Yes! It's Meadville at the tape!" the announcer echoed. His teammates swarmed the Meadville runner as the crowd came to their feet and cheered their stellar performance. Cassandra knew it was Sean's son.

"Sonny, Sean is here! I feel it. I know he's still alive. I always have. I can't explain how I know. Sean was your angel!" Cassandra cried out, almost hysterically. "It's no coincidence that boy's name is Lafoussier. Don't you get it? Sean's here!"

Cassandra now pleaded to the rest. "Sean *is* alive! It *was* Sean!" She stood, looking at them all, as they began considering if it could be.

Frozen in time, the three stood, hugging each other in love and with hope, holding onto that sweet, unspoken possibility that the *Toujours Amis* gang would be complete once again.

FINIS